Cody C. Engdahl

To Tom,
I hope you
like this one
I Think It's my
Best I Love You
Cody C. Engdahl
3/4/23

Cover art: The Battle of Chapultepec, by Carl Nebel 1851

Contents

Preface 5
Acknowledgments 8
Glossary 9
Dedication 15
Epithet 16

Prolog 17

Part I: The Old World
Chapter One: The Prophecy 20
Chapter Two: Graduation Day 25
Chapter Three: The Beautiful Man 32
Chapter Four: Prisons and Freedom 40
Chapter Five: Night Work 50
Chapter Six: The Work of Nations 57
Chapter Seven: Little Birds 67
Chapter Eight: Hunters and Prey 78
Chapter Nine: The Shadow 85
Chapter Ten: The Angel of Death 94
Chapter Eleven: The Date 99
Chapter Twelve: The Ruin 107
Chapter Thirteen: The Reckoning 115
Chapter Fourteen: The Difference 121
Chapter Fifteen: The Help You Need 129
Chapter Sixteen: Brides and Bandits 136

Part II: The Crossing
Chapter Seventeen: The Best Day 145
Chapter Eighteen: Abd al-Qādir 155
Chapter Nineteen: The Hat Dance 162
Chapter Twenty: The War with France 170
Chapter Twenty-One: The Evil that Men Do 178
Chapter Twenty-Two: The Unexpected Visitor 187
Chapter Twenty-Three: The Cargo of Sorrow 195
Chapter Twenty-Four: Black James 205

Part III: The New World
Chapter Twenty-Five: *El Caudillo* 214
Chapter Twenty-Six: A Hero's Welcome 224
Chapter Twenty-Seven: Fathers and Sons 235
Chapter Twenty-Eight: The Siege of Los Angeles 245
Chapter Twenty-Nine: The Old Woman's Gun 255
Chapter Thirty: The Fall of California 263
Chapter Thirty-One: *Los San Patricios* 273
Chapter Thirty-Two: The *Céilí* 282
Chapter Thirty-Three: The Truce 291
Chapter Thirty-Four: Punishment 298
Chapter Thirty-Five: Friendship 304
Chapter Thirty-Six: The Commencement of Hostilities 313
Chapter Thirty-Seven: The Feast of the Gods 323
Chapter Thirty-Eight: The Gates of Belén 334
Chapter Thirty-Nine: "So Far from God" 339
Le Dénouement 343

Historical Note 348
Sources 359
Works by Cody C. Engdahl 362

Preface

Hello, and thank you for joining me on another grand adventure. I want you to know that this book has always been in the plan since I wrote the first chapter of Rampage on the River: The Battle for Island No. 10. This is a prequel to my American Civil War trilogy entitled The 2nd Michigan Cavalry Chronicles. Before we go any further, I want to say: YOU DON'T HAVE TO READ MY PREVIOUS NOVELS TO ENJOY THIS ONE. But if you like this, I invite you to read my others for sure!

I'm a big fan of K. M. Ashman, who writes medieval historical fiction. I noticed once that one of his new releases didn't have a book number in the series I was following. Like the foolish fanboy that I am, I sent him a Facebook message telling him that the book was missing a series number. He told me that numbered books don't sell as well because people think they have to read the whole series just to enjoy the latest installment. I took that lesson to heart. I've written each of my novels to stand on its own even though they all exist in the same world and create an overall timeline together. So please, by all means, if this is the first of my books you've picked up, go ahead and read it. I'd be curious to hear your opinion, especially if you haven't read any of my others.

This book also covers another very controversial war for the United States. I should tell you that I am an American and love my country, warts and all. I love it enough to be critical of our past and to try to learn from our mistakes. I want to say that, in any war, the people caught up in it, on either side, are just that: people, neither inherently good nor evil. They're just people.

Most modern scholars agree that the Mexican-American War was pretty much a thinly disguised land grab by the much more powerful United States of America over the hardly prepared United Mexican States. The result was that Mexico "agreed" to sell the US California, Nevada, Utah, and what they controlled of what is now New Mexico, Arizona, Colorado, Texas, Oklahoma, Kansas, and Wyoming for a mere $15 million, which was about half of what the US had offered before the war. I think it's important to remember when you travel through these areas that many of the people who speak Spanish are from families that lived there when these areas were part of Mexico, and before that, Spain, and perhaps even before the arrival of the conquistadors.

In a way, this book is a love letter to Mexican culture and the things I loved as a child and still do today. I've always loved the swashbuckler genre with its swords, muskets, pirates, and battles. There are a lot of references and homages to some of my favorite works and authors including Alexandre Dumas, who will make a few appearances in this book. There are other references that I make that are a little more subtle. It was a fun game for me to work them in. I hope you'll catch them as you read.

Historical Setting

Mexico won its independence from Spain in 1821. At the time, its territory extended far north and included what is now California, Nevada, Arizona, Utah, New Mexico, Colorado, and Texas, as well as parts of other states.

The Spaniards had opened Texas to Anglo settlers from the US to populate its vast unsettled regions. The Mexican government continued this practice until those settlers revolted and declared independence. The Anglo-Texans defeated and captured President and General Santa Anna at the battle of Jacinto. Santa Anna was forced to sign a treaty under the pain of death giving Texas its independence. Because this treaty was signed under duress, the Mexican government refused to officially acknowledge this newly won independence but made little effort to reconquer the territory.

The Anglo-Texans then lobbied the US government to annex them into the union. The Mexican government stated that annexing the contested region would be an act of war. As the US pondered this, another international conflict was brewing over the contested Oregon Territory. It was co-occupied by US and British settlers. The two countries squabbled over control and where the boundary should be drawn if they split it. Both nations were contemplating war to settle the matter.

Two philosophies were driving the US into possibly fighting a dual war with its neighbors. One was Manifest Destiny which aspired to create a continuous nation that would span from the Atlantic to the Pacific Coast. Wresting the Oregon territory from the UK and Alta California from Mexico would achieve this goal. The other was the Monroe Doctrine which sought to quell European colonialism in the Western Hemisphere.

Mexico was increasingly weak and unstable in its early years of independence suffering from multiple coups and insurrections. European powers watched this instability closely, looking for opportunities.

Once again, thanks for reading my work. I'll catch up with you again at the end of the story in the Historical Note section with more details about some of the real history depicted in this novel.

Your friend,

Cody C. Engdahl,
Nashville, Tennessee, 2022

Acknowledgments

As always, I must first thank the two women who have lifted me up and carried me through my toughest times: my mom, Nancy Thompson, and my girlfriend, Laura Reinert. Not only are they my editors, but also my confidants and counselors as I plot these books and dream of the overall universe I'm creating. I'd like to thank my dad and stepmom, Larry and Mary Engdahl for reading everything I write, for their love and support, and for not being afraid to tell me the things I don't want to hear but need to hear. I'd like to thank all of my wonderful family: the Engdahls, the Beenblossoms, the Thompsons, the Trevers, and all the other names I am bound to by blood, marriage, and friendship. It's your love that gives me the confidence to chase this crazy dream.

I want to thank all of my friends, too many to list. However, I'd like to say thank you to my old army and Nashville punk rock scene veteran friend, Mike Ward, and to my fellow Trevecca Symphony Orchestra veteran, Anne Smith Nee Royster for always being the first to want an autographed copy of my books.

And most of all, thank you, dear reader, for joining me on this grand adventure!

Glossary

Abatis: an obstacle such as a felled tree and sharpened sticks used as a field fortification

Abuelo/Abuela: grandfather/grandmother in Spanish

Afwan: you're welcome in Arabic

Aguardiente: a Spanish distilled spirit much like brandy or schnapps

Artillery: the branch of arms dealing with cannons, mortars, and other large projectiles

Asesino: Spanish word for "killer" or "assassin"

l'Asile des Aliénés de Marseille: the Marseille Asylum for the Insane

À votre santé: a French toast like "cheers" Literally, "to your health"

Ayuda: Spanish word for "help"

Bastion: an extended corner of a fort designed to allow defenders to fire at troops climbing the wall

Battery: a unit of artillery typically made up of four to six guns

Bayonet: a long knife or spike-like weapon that can be attached to the end of a rifle, turning it into a spear

Belaying pin: a device used to secure lines on a sailing vessel and also used as a weapon similar to a short club

Bear Flag volunteers: Anglo-American settlers in California who revolted against the Mexican government

Blue Death: Cholera

Boarding pike: a spear-like weapon used by a sailor

Brevet: a rank like "brevet captain," for example, is a promotion for outstanding performance without the raise in pay that would normally come with that rank until it is confirmed and made official

Breech: the rear of a gun barrel

Brown Bess: a smoothbore flintlock musket used by British military from 1722 to 1851

Caballero: in the Mexican sense at that time, it would mean a gentleman and aristocrat

Caisson: a two-wheeled wagon used to carry ammunition boxes as well as a spare wagon wheel and limber pole for a cannon

Canister: a cannon shell filled with smaller balls meant to disperse upon firing

Cartridge: a prepackaged bullet and gunpowder unit wrapped in paper or metal casing, as opposed to loose powder and projectiles used in earlier muskets

Caudillo: Spanish for a military or political "strongman" leader or warlord

Centime: a French penny

Carbine: a shorter version of a rifle designed to be fired from horseback

Castilian: the dialect of standard Spanish spoken in Spain

Cavalry: the branch of arms made up of horse-mounted troops

Chiromancy: fortune reading from examining the lines of one's palm

Criollo: a person of full Spanish blood but born in the New World

Cutlass: a short, curved, single-bladed sword favored by sailors for close-quarters fighting

Dragoon: a kind of cavalryman who typically dismounts to fight. They are also known as mounted infantry

Earthwork: a tall mound of dirt piled up as a defensive wall

Embrasure: an opening in a defensive structure from where cannons can fire

Enfilading fire: shooting into the flank of a line of men where the maximum potential targets are exposed

Exchequer: British government accounting agency

Feint: a false attack meant to distract the enemy from the real attack

Felucca: a small sailboat with a lateen-rigged sail mounted at an angle to the mast instead of flush

Flintlock: a style of musket or pistol that uses a flint striking steel to cause a spark for firing

Flying artillery: light cannons designed to be quickly moved by horses during battle

Frizzen: part of a flintlock firing mechanism in which the flint strikes, causing a spark to fire the weapon

Gadje: plural of gadjo masculine, gadji feminine; a non-Romani or non-Gypsy person

Grapeshot: an artillery round, like canister, but with larger projectiles resembling grapes

Gendarme: French police

Habibti: Arabic for "my love" used for females. *Habibi* is the term for males

Howitzer: a low-velocity cannon that uses elevation to lob shells. They can also fire directly at near targets

Infantry: the branch of arms made up of foot soldiers

Lance: a spear-like weapon typically used on horseback

Lanyard: a cord used to fire a cannon

Laudanum: an opioid in liquid form

Launch: a rowboat used to ferry men and supplies from a larger ship to the shore

Le fils: French for "the son" or "Junior"

Limber: a horse-drawn two-wheeled cart used to tow cannons, caissons, traveling forges, or battery wagons. It also carries an ammunition chest

Limber pole: a long pole used to attach a limber to a team of horses

Linstock: a pole with a burning wick used to fire cannons

Malinche: an indigenous woman who acted as a translator, and allegedly, concubine to Hernán Cortés during his conquest of Mexico, she's traditionally considered a traitor to her people, her name carries meaning in Latin-American culture much like the names "Judas" and "Benedict Arnold" do in Anglo-American culture

Martinet: an overtly strict and disciplinarian military leader

Mazel tov: a Jewish toast meaning "Good fortune!"

Mestizo: a person of mixed Spanish and indigenous American descent

Mezcal: a Mexican distilled spirit made from agave plants. Tequila is a form of mezcal

Mortar: a large cauldron-shaped artillery piece that lobs its shells instead of shooting directly

Mon ami: French for "my friend"

Moukahla: an Arabic musket popular in northern Africa

Mountain howitzer: A lightweight cannon designed for mobility (see Howitzer)

Musket: a muzzleloading black powder long gun

Muzzle: the open end of a gun barrel

Ojalá: a Spanish phrase taken from Arabic meaning "God willing" or "hopefully"

Orderly: an aide assigned to do menial tasks for officers

Percussion cap: a small pre-manufactured primer used to fire muskets

Penisulares: Spanish-born aristocrats living in Latin America before independence from Spain, they were considered the top of the class system and often were involved in running the colonies

Picket: a small group of men set out from the main group as a lookout or a guard

Pince-nez: eyeglasses without earpieces that sit on the nose, literally "pinch-nose" in French

Por los santos: "by the saints," a common exclamation in Spanish

Por supuesto: "of course" in Spanish

Quadrille: a popular ballroom dance involving two couples

Reveille: a bugle call meant to wake troops in the morning

Redoubt: a small fort

Rifle: a long gun with grooves in the barrel that causes the bullet to spin Rifles can still be muzzle-loading muskets Rifles eventually replaced smooth-bore muskets. Cannons can also have rifled barrels and also be called rifles

Rosbif: a slur the French use for British people, referring to their consumption of roast beef

Saber: a single-bladed, curved sword designed for slashing from horseback

Scimitar: a Middle-Eastern saber typically having a pronounced curved blade

Shako: a tall cylinder-shaped military hat with a short visor

Sharpshooter: a sniper, marksman, or soldier trained to shoot targets from a distance as opposed to a regular rifleman who provides volley fire

Shukran: Arabic for "thank you"

Siento: Spanish for "sorry"

Smala: a traveling community

Su Alteza: "Your Highness"

Sub-lieutenant: or "subteniente" in Spanish, comparable to a 2nd lieutenant in the American Army, it's the lowest rank in the officer corps

Sutler: a merchant who follows an army to sell goods

Tiller: a pole attached directly to a rudder used to steer small boats

12-pounder: a cannon that shoots a 12-pound ball, cannons are often called by the weight of their shot

Vanguard: the foremost part of an advancing force

Vaquero: Spanish for a cattle driver or "cowboy"
Vedette: like a picket but on horseback
Volley: multiple muskets or cannons firing in line at the same time
Works: short for "defensive works" such as trenches and fortifications
Worm: an artillery tool consisting of an iron corkscrew mounted on a staff used to clean debris out of a cannon barrel

Army Ranks (simplified)
-Enlisted
Private
Corporal
Sergeant
Sergeant Major
-Officers
2nd Lieutenant or Sub-lieutenant
1st Lieutenant
Captain
Major
Lieutenant Colonel
Colonel
Brigadier General
Major General
Lieutenant General
General

Second and 1st lieutenants are typically called "lieutenant." Same with colonels and lieutenant colonels who are typically referred to as "colonel." All officers with the rank of brigadier general or higher are typically referred to simply as "general."

Navel captains are equal in rank with army colonels. Army and marine captains are much lower in rank and would be equal to a navy lieutenant.

Typical Military Units:
Company or a troop: about a hundred men, but varies greatly. Typically commanded by a captain.

Battalion: an unofficial subdivision of a regiment made up of several companies. In modern times the battalion has replaced the regiment in the US military.

Regiment: made up of several companies, typically ten to twelve, commanded by a colonel.

Brigade: made up of several regiments, typically three, commanded by a brigadier general.

Division: made up of more than one brigade, commanded by a brigadier or major general.

Corps: made up of more than one division, commanded by a brigadier, major, or lieutenant general

Army: the largest field command made up of more than one corps, commanded by a major general or higher.

Dedication

This book is dedicated to Nancy Thompson, who complained that I never put enough romance in my books. Well, Mom, here you go.

Epithet

"Es un pedazo del alma que se arranca sin piedad"
María Teresa Vera, "Viente Años"

Translation
"It's a part of my soul that was torn away without mercy"

Prolog

Autumn 1864: Detroit

Claudette sighed as she gave the old home one last look before making the journey. For sixteen years she had haunted this place, living as the ghost of the girl she once was: a girl that was happy, excited about life, willing to risk everything for love and adventure. *The folly of my youth*, she thought, looking at the furniture covered in dust sheets.

She pulled the sheet from the full-length mirror and looked herself over once more. What she saw was a wraith of broken dreams. She was slender in her form-fitting black dress. Her hair was black and wild with streaks of grey, hardly containable under the hat and veil she used to hide herself in public. Her dark eyes burned with an intensity that masked the sorrow buried below.

"I am being foolish," she mumbled, then covered the mirror once more.

She had raised a child alone in this home, a child who was too much like his father: reckless and in love with adventure. That child was gone now too. He had run off to fight in a useless war, just like his father. Now she was caring for the young wife he left behind and their child to come.

"I'm not having a child alone in Detroit," her daughter-in-law Anna had told her. Claudette could hardly blame her. Fortunes were quickly changing for Anna's family, and perhaps for the united Germany Anna's family had been dreaming of for generations.

No, Anna shouldn't have her child in cold and lonely Detroit, she decided. They would make the crossing together, back to the Old World where life could be new again. Claudette's grandchild may be missing a father, just like her son Carl who grew up missing his, but this child would have a family, a family like she was never able to give her own baby boy.

Her son Carl hadn't written in months. The last letter had come from Memphis. For all she knew, he was dead now, lost forever like his father. There was nowhere to write to him, even if he were still alive. Still, Carl should know where they were if he should ever come home. Now that he was going to be a father too, he should know the truth about his own.

She uncovered the table, sat down, and began writing.

My Dear Sweet Carl,

It is my dearest wish that you should live and find this letter in good health, with a sound mind, and a full heart. It's time I told you the truth about your father, how much I loved him, and how much my heart aches every time I see him in you. It haunts me still. It's hard for me to recall these memories, but if you still live, you deserve to know the truth. I shall endure to tell you.

Even when I was a young girl, I knew my love would be great and tragic…

Part I: The Old World

Chapter One: The Prophecy

Summer 1838: Provence-Alpes-Côte d'Azur, France

The open window didn't help. Claudette threw off her bedsheets in frustration. It was impossible to sleep in the stifling heat. She fanned herself in the darkness, wondering if it was worth lighting a candle to try to read herself back to sleep. Moonlight spilled into her room which was nestled at the very top of her family's countryside home. Perhaps, she thought, if she pulled the chair from her writing desk to the window, she could use the moonlight to read.

She was careful not to bump her head against the steeply vaulted ceiling as she slipped out of bed and softly shuffled across the floor, careful not to cause any creaks that could wake everyone below. She placed her hands on the sill and leaned out into the night air. Below, the moonlight fell on the neatly lined rows of grapevines giving them an eerie glow. The vineyard rolled out before her then disappeared over the hills. Somewhere on the other side was Marseille with its cafés, bookshops, and life.

She sighed softly. A light breeze rolled in through the window rustling her simple white shift. It brought a welcomed cooling to her body. It smelled of the sea and the world outside full of adventure just outside the harbor. There was life out there, but she was stuck here in this endless maze of grapevines and boredom with only a handful of books that she had already read over and over again. She was hidden away from the rest of the world.

Her family had been hiding for centuries now. They had once been noble, but her line came from a long succession of second and third sons who married into wealthy merchant families instead of seeking titles and peerage. They hid their wealth as they found themselves on the wrong side of politics time and time again. They had backed the Huguenots against Cardinal Richelieu and lost. They had resisted the summons of the Sun King to live in his pampered prison of Versailles, then fell into obscurity in his shadow.

They finally found victory in the revolution and rode high on the Bonapartist wave. Her grandfather and great-uncles fought in *La Grande Armée,* bringing liberty and republicanism to the rest of

Europe. But the Emperor was gone now. He died a prisoner on a lonely island, far from France. Those who prospered with him retreated back into the shadows under the return of the monarchy.

So the Moreaus hid, sold their wine, and stashed their money. But most annoyingly, they hid their daughter.

"You are too pretty for the eyes of men," her mother warned her. "They will be driven mad with temptation and try to drag you down in their sin." Her mother insisted Claudette be kept away from the eyes of the world until they could marry her into a family that could lift the Moreaus from hiding and into the restoration of nobility under the king.

She sighed again, gazing at the dark hills and imagining the grand life hidden beyond them. Then she heard it. It was thin and bright, too rhythmic to be natural, too melodic. It was dark and lively…it was music!

"Where is that coming from…?" she mumbled. She leaned out farther, cocking her head to the side to hear better. It seemed to ride on the sea breeze that swirled around her ears. It was a violin and it couldn't be far! "Who in the world…?" she wondered out loud.

She looked at her bedroom door. Walking across the floor and turning the knob would surely wake the entire house. She looked back into the nightscape outside. There was no way she could sleep now. There was a mystery out there and she was going to get to the bottom of it. She grabbed onto the ivy and swung her body out of the window, clutching the vines with her bare toes.

"Huh…!" she gasped as she slid down the wall dragging her nails through the vine as she tried to grab onto something to stop her fall. Needles of pain sparkled through her bare feet as they smacked against the ground. She fell flat on her butt, hissing in pain as she shook her hands in agony. Her fingernails felt like they'd been nearly ripped out. She sucked in her breath and listened carefully. Surely all of France had heard her fall. She waited until she was sure that all she could hear were crickets and the lonely violin.

The sound got louder as she crept around the house. The window in the detached kitchen flickered and glowed. She approached carefully. There were stories of wraiths and souls that haunted these hills. They played tricks on the living, enticing them into sharing their damnation.

Claudette clutched the sill, propped herself onto her toes, and peered inside. A dark form was playing a fiddle. It sat at the table next to a candle. Its hair was long with wild brown curls. Claudette found herself mesmerized by the music. *The phantom has captured me!* she thought, trying to will herself to turn away before it was too late, but she was unable to break the spell.

The creature stopped abruptly. "Huh...!" Claudette drew in a breath. She could see a single green eye appear over the top of the instrument. It was looking at her. Icy chills ran down her back. The creature set the fiddle down and waved her in. Claudette wanted to run, but she was trapped in the ghoul's spell.

"You should be in bed, mademoiselle." The creature spoke French with an accent spiced with Eastern European flavors as Claudette entered the room. She sighed with relief. It was merely a woman, a kitchen servant.

"It is too hot for sleeping," Claudette said, "and I had to know where the music was coming from."

"My apologies, mademoiselle," the woman said fearfully, "I did not mean to disturb anyone."

"No, not at all," Claudette was quick to assure her. "It was wonderful!" Claudette looked her over with fascination. The woman had olive skin, wild hair, and striking green eyes that reflected the flickering candlelight. "Are you a Gypsy?" she asked.

"I am merely a woman who needs this job, child. My breeding has no bearing on the quality of my work."

Claudette gazed at the woman for a moment, "I think you're beautiful, whatever you are. Please, put yourself at ease."

The woman stared at her for a moment. The fear slipped away and turned into a broad smile that enthralled Claudette with wild mystery. "Thank you, my child. Yes, my people are Romani, but I must be careful. We are not always welcomed in the houses of the French."

Claudette sparkled with happiness. "Well, you are welcome here. I am Claudette," she said offering her hand. "I don't have any friends. It's nice to have someone to talk to."

The woman looked around nervously for a moment, then took her hand, "You're going to get me fired, child. It's not permitted to talk to the masters of the house."

"No, I won't," Claudette protested. "We're friends!"

The woman closed her eyes and sighed with a laugh. She opened and focused them intensely on the girl in front of .her. "Okay, my little friend. You can call me Lavinia."

Claudette beamed with excitement. "Is it true that the Gypsies can talk to the spirit world? Can you tell fortunes?"

"That is a myth, child."

"Please, tell me my fortune. Will I ever know love?" Claudette leaned forward in her chair, grasping her hands together in pleading anticipation.

"You are going to get me burned at the stake," Lavinia leaned back in her chair, putting space between her and the girl.

"Oh, pooh! They don't do that anymore!" Claudette scoffed.

"You'd be surprised at man's capacity for cruelty and violence when he fears," she said flatly. Claudette fell silent, blinking her dark eyes at the woman in disappointment. Lavinia blinked back then let out a sigh, "Alright, child, give me your hand."

"I knew it!" Claudette bubbled over with excitement as she thrust her hand forward.

"Careful, my passionate little friend," Lavinia warned as she took the little girl's hand. "There are some things in one's fortune that are best left unknown. Things that only become true because you're expecting them. Be careful not to force the hand of destiny. The spirits are always swirling around our decisions. They're constantly writing and rewriting our destinies." With that, she began to examine Claudette's palm. A wave of concern washed over her face but was quickly replaced by a smile. "Just as I suspected!"

"What?!"

Lavinia looked up from the open palm to the little girl's eyes with a sly grin. "You have a very strong head line, perhaps too strong for your own good!"

"Mamá always says I'm stubborn," Claudette admitted.

"Perhaps you should listen to her."

Claudette rolled her eyes and then returned them to Lavinia with renewed excitement. "What else?"

"Let's see…" Lavinia mumbled, looking over the child's palm. "I see a strong life line. You can expect good health and a long life, child."

"I see…" Claudette answered, then with mischief in her eyes asked, "What about love? Will I know great love in my life?"

"Yes, it looks fine," Lavinia said quickly then looked away.

Claudette eyed her for a moment suspiciously. "You're not being honest with me."

Lavinia returned her eyes to the girl, "Chiromancy is not a science, child. It's a game we play to fool the *gadje* out of their money."

"Tell me!" Claudette protested impatiently.

Lavinia stared at her for a moment then sighed. "You have great passion and a capacity to love deeply. Look at how strong this line is as it swoops down from your index finger."

"Huh!" Claudette gasped with excitement. "But then it stops here," she said.

"It does, child, right where it intersects with this vertical line that descends from between your middle and ring finger. That line is fate."

"What does it mean?" Claudette asked with fear creeping into her voice.

"It only means what you make it mean, child. Like I said, chiromancy is a mere game to play on fools."

"Will I have my heart broken?" she asked.

"Child, you must not close your heart, no matter your loss. Let me look again. Ah!" she said. "This line here! It seems your heart line starts again, but later, and it is strong!"

"So there's hope?" Claudette asked feebly.

"So long as you live and you keep your heart young, there is always hope, my sweet little friend."

Claudette looked at her palm in wonderment, looking at the line interrupted by a gap on her palm. "How long must I suffer?"

"It is unclear. Time in the spirit world expands and contracts like the accordion. Remember, you are still in charge of your destiny. The spirit world can only give you hints along the way."

Claudette blinked at her for a moment, her mind running wild with enchantment. "Teach me!" she said at last. "Teach me how to find the spirit world and to read its hints!"

"The spirit world is all around you. You just have to learn how to open your eyes and see it in front of you."

Chapter Two: The Graduation Day

Spring 1844: La Unversidad de Barcelona, Spain

WHAAP!

"Hng!" Diego grunted, clenching his eyes shut as he bit into a leather thong to keep from crying out. He opened his eyes again to see the shadow of the aging clergyman holding a switch flicker against the damp stone wall of the ancient monastery.

Fray Alfonso sighed and shook his head as he watched the boy try to recover from the blow in the dim candlelight. He rolled his eyes, drew his arm back once more, then swung the switch around again. It whistled through the air, then gave a hard crack as it struck the insolent young man's bare rear end. Diego grunted from the blow, clutching the arms of the chair he was leaning over as his knees buckled from the pain. He seized up over the back of the chair before straightening his legs again, just in time to receive the next blow.

WHAAP!

That one caused him to lift his leg as he recoiled in agony. Fray Alfonso sighed again as he watched the boy slowly uncoil from the last shock of pain. "Your father doesn't pay us enough for the effort it takes to whip the wild Indian out of you," he said, lisping hard and leaning into the harsh arabesque sounds of his academic Castilian Spanish. With that, he brought another blow across the young man's backside. Diego let out another grunt. "Honestly, I don't know why the *criollos* of the New World still send their sons to Spain for education. They don't even consider themselves Spaniards anymore! Here's for your damned Mexican Independence!" The clergyman drove his outrage at the ungrateful colonials into the swing with new ferocity.

WHAAP!

"Ayee!" Diego let out, ejecting the leather thong from his mouth. "Señor..." he gasped, panting, his softer tongue giving away his New World dialect, "the De la Vegas have been educated in Spain for generations. Our estates may be in California, but our noble blood still pulses from the heart of Spain."

WHAAP!

"Your bastard blood is tainted with that of mongrel Indian servants and has little to do with nobility or Spain! Now shut your mouth and take your beating quietly, you insolent New World mule!"

WHAAP!

"Gaaaa!" Diego gasped. "Señor, I'll have you know my mother carries noble Nahua blood from a long line of Aztec warriors."

"Your mother was nothing more than a *Malinche* succubus whore who enchanted your fool of a father into damnation and a bastard son!" Fray Alfonso bellowed as he brought his switch around with a WHOOSH. His angry face broke into a startled gasp as the young man spun around and caught the switch in his hand.

"Ayee!" Diego hissed and cringed from taking the blow to the palm. He clutched the switch and focused his big green eyes at the stunned friar before him. "Señor," he said in a flat low voice through his teeth, "due to your age and position, I will allow you the opportunity to apologize and take that back before I extract satisfaction for the insult you have laid most foully and unjustly upon my mother and my family name." He glared at the friar as he pulled up his trousers and buttoned them with his free hand.

"Have you gone mad?!" the clergyman gasped. "I'll do nothing of the sort! Now let go of my rod and submit to your punishment before I have you arrested and properly flogged as a man, you fool!" he said as he tugged back on his switch.

"I will submit no more, you dog! This is your last chance. Apologize or pay the consequences!" Diego said, stepping forward menacingly.

The old man blinked at him for a moment in stunned bewilderment then shouted, "*¡Ayuda...! ¡Ayuda...!*"

Diego roared in defiance as he lurched forward, causing the old man to stumble backward and step onto the back of his robe with his heels. He crumbled to the cold stone floor. Diego was quickly upon him, clutching the collar of his robe in his left hand while drawing his right hand back to strike. The old man's blue eyes widened with fear. "No, please..." he gasped softly.

Diego grimaced with frustration and rage, then roared in anger as he swung his hand toward the old man's face, pulling back just in time to deliver a light tap to his cheek. Fray Alfonso flinched and let out a gasp, clenching his eyes shut as he braced for a harder blow. It didn't come. He popped open an eye and saw the devilish *mestizo* leering over him with a grin. "There!" Diego said with satisfaction, "That will teach you to speak dishonorably about another man's mother."

Fray Alfonso regarded him for a moment in blinking bewilderment. Just then, he could hear the sound of sandals slapping against the stone steps outside his chamber. His eyes darted toward the door, then back at his assailant. He opened his mouth wide and screamed, "*¡Asesino! ¡Asesino! ¡Ayuda me!*"

"Damn you, you liar!" Diego grabbed the switch and sprung to his feet. The footsteps were getting closer. He scanned the room for anything useful. He snatched a bag of coins from the table. "You say my father doesn't pay you enough, Señor? I say he has paid you far too much for the insult you have committed against my family!"

"Put that down, you thief!" the friar propped himself on his elbows. Two hefty friars burst through the door at that moment, panting from their run up the stairs. "Seize him! He tried to kill me and now he's taking our Lord's money!"

"Now, Diego," one of the younger friars called out, "put the whip and money down before you get in any more trouble!"

"I'm afraid it's too late for that now, Fray Rodrigues," Diego said placing the table between himself and the two men.

"Enough talk!" Fray Alfonso screeched. "Grab him and hold him still so I can give him a proper thrashing!" The two men lurched forward with their arms stretched out to grab him. Diego kicked the table over at them, knocking the candle to the ground. The light died as the tumbling table trounced the flame. Diego bounded over the upended furniture and thrashed wildly with the switch, feeling it hit soft targets as yelps of pain cried out in the darkness.

More sandals were slapping against the stone stairway outside the door. Diego leaped to the narrow window. The moonlight revealed his silhouette crouching on the sill. "Diego, please!" Fray Rodrigues called to him. "Think of your education!"

"I just graduated," he declared, then crossed himself and looked up to the inky darkness pooled in the ceiling. "Please forgive me for my sins," he mumbled then kissed his crucifix. He tossed the switch out the window, hearing it clatter on the cobblestones below. He squeezed his body through the window. The rough stone wall outside gave him enough purchase to find a toehold. His fingers found small crevices in the mortar. He scurried down the wall, mostly falling as he clung to what he could to slow his descent.

"Oof!" he let out as he landed on his back.

"Stop, thief!" Fray Alfonso called out from the window.

"Damn him..." Diego muttered, getting back to his feet and retrieving the switch.

"You there! Stop!" Down the street, he saw two soldiers with blue jackets, white cross belts, and white pants. Diego turned and ran. The soldiers clutched their tall shako caps and gave chase. He stole a glance at them as they slowed to a trot and fumbled with their muskets, lifting them to their shoulders.

"*¡Por Los Santos!*" he exclaimed, rounding the corner. The old M1752 flintlocks fired, splitting the night with jets of smoke and fire. The balls sent shards of stone and puffs of stucco dust into the air as they struck the wall behind him. Dogs began to bark. He heard the metallic click of bayonets snapping into place. Then the men called out again.

"Stop!"

"To hell with that!" he mumbled. He darted down the street, quickly turning corners as he ran, hoping to lose the soldiers in the maze of narrow winding streets and alleys.

Nassar lifted his face off his prayer rug, sat back on his knees, and mumbled, "*La ilaha il Lal Lahu. Allahumma salli ala Muhammadin wa Ali Muhammad,*" then looked at his brother kneeling next to him. "Let's go," he said, switching to his North African dialect of Arabic. They quickly rolled their rugs, tied them, and slung them over their backs. Nassar knew it was dangerous to rush the morning prayer, especially before setting sail, but he had a whole vat of fresh sardines that needed salt and the tide would be coming in soon. If he didn't get out now he'd have to wait another twelve hours and Spain was no place for Arabs to loiter.

They picked up their buckets of salt and made their way to the docks. It was still dark. "We said our prayer too soon, brother," his brother noted, looking up at the starlit sky.

"We will make up for it at noon, Akbar. God is merciful," he assured him.

Akbar mumbled something of an assent, then spoke more clearly with surprise, "What is happening at the docks?"

Nassar looked up to see soldiers walking among the boats with torches. "I don't know but smile and be friendly. The infidels can be quite suspicious of us when aroused."

The two brothers kept their heads down as they waddled under the weight of the salt buckets they were carrying toward the little felucca they used to ferry goods from port to port.

"Hey, you!" a soldier barked as he grabbed Akbar's arm. Akbar let out of frightened screech.

"Smile, you fool!" Nassar said in Arabic. His brother offered his captor a weak shuddering grin. Nassar then addressed the man in broken Spanish, "I'm sorry, sir, my brother doesn't speak Castilian."

"Then what the hell are you doing in my country?" the soldier demanded.

"We're simple traders, sir. No trouble to anyone," Nassar offered. "We are leaving now, I assure you."

"Where were you last night?" the man glowered at them.

Nassar was wondering how to explain in Spanish that they had traded the cotton they got in Morocco for fish and then bought salt to preserve them for their trip to Marseille when another soldier interrupted. "Those are Arabs, you fool! We're looking for a mestizo from Mexico!"

"Huh…they all look the same to me," the soldier scoffed, shoving Akbar away. Akbar smiled nervously, giving the soldier a short bow.

"*Shukran…*" he mumbled, backing away.

"Fuck off, heretic," the soldier mumbled, turning away.

"Come, brother, before they change their minds," Nassar hissed at him in Arabic. Their boat rocked as they stepped aboard. The tarp covering the vat moved slightly. *There are still some live ones under there,* he thought. It was a good sign that their load was still fresh. He whipped off the tarp and hefted a bucket of salt to his shoulder to pour on the fish.

"Huh?!" he gasped at the sight of a young man lying in the vat among them. Sharp fear flashed through the stranger's eyes. The man put a finger to his lips, then moved his other hand to show he had armed himself with the fillet knife they kept aboard their vessel. Nassar frowned, pushing his lips to one side and cocking his head at the stranger's ridiculously implied threat. The stranger's eyes widened with fear even more. He quickly dropped the knife and showed that he had money.

Nassar looked back at the soldiers searching boats with their torches. The last thing he needed was this fool to draw their suspicion and delay them further with whatever trouble he was in. Nassar shrugged and dumped the salt on the man and the fish, then hefted the next bucket, and the next. Then he began to spread the salt around, coating the fish and burying the man with the sardines.

"You, there!" a soldier called. "What's in that vat?"

"Fresh sardines, señor, just salted. Would you like some?" Nassar smiled at the man, holding up a dying sardine that wiggled weakly from his grasp. The soldier briefly peered into the vat full of squirming salt-encrusted fish with a frown.

"No, they stink!" he said and walked on.

Nassar watched the soldier walk away, dropped his smile, and tossed the fish back into the vat. He pulled the canvas over it once again then turned to his brother. "Quickly, let's go." Akbar didn't need any encouragement.

They shoved off and worked the oars to put some distance between them and the dock. Nassar could feel the breeze coming from across the bow. "Try the sail," he told his brother. Akbar stowed his oar and hoisted the triangular sail up the mast. It began to fill with air and balloon to the side. The boat began to lean as Nassar put away his oar and took hold of the tiller. He set the felucca on its path to the opening in the break wall and out to sea. Akbar tied down the large sail and then hoisted a smaller headsail.

They turned to the east and into the wind once they were clear of the harbor. Akbar brought the sails in tighter. The boat was now leaning hard to its side. The brothers moved their bodies to the windward side of the boat to help keep it balanced. The sun was rising in the east. This is my prayer, oh, Merciful One, Nassar thought as he looked at the brilliant orange sky.

Akbar let out a screech as some slime-covered thing crawled out of the fish vat. "Peace, brother," Nassar chuckled, "he is harmless."

Diego flopped onto the deck and gasped. "Water…please," he groaned in Spanish.

"Give him some water, Akbar," Nassar told his brother in Arabic. Akbar brought the stranger a skin full of water. Diego took it and drank greedily. Then reached into his purse and produced two gold coins. Akbar's eyes flashed with surprise and excitement.

"This is for saving me," Diego said.

Nassar regarded the stranger and his money for a moment and frowned. Then spoke in broken Spanish. "God is great and merciful. He commands me to be so too, especially when a man is in need. Keep your money, Spaniard, but remember the mercy."

"Thank you," Diego said, "but I'm Mexican."

Nassar blinked at him in confusion.

"Oof...!" Claudette gasped as Lavinia tugged on the drawstrings of her corset. *"Mon Dieu!* How am I supposed to breathe in this thing?" she complained. Lavinia tugged at the strings once more before tying them.

She put her hands on Claudette's shoulders and peered over them to admire her mistress's figure in the mirror. "You will breathe easier, child, once you are wed and fat with babies!" she said in her Eastern European accented French.

"Oh, pooh! I'd rather be free like you!" she said as she unconsciously admired how the uncomfortable garment turned her already slender figure into a more pronounced hourglass shape while pushing what little she had developed so far as breasts into ripe bountiful spheres, seemingly on the verge of bursting.

"Trust me, darling, you want no freedom such as mine," Lavinia said, admiring the beautiful young lady that had blossomed from the rambunctious little girl she had been seemingly just yesterday. She wondered if her own daughter would have grown to be such a beauty, a child long in the grave, along with her father. Lavinia had lost them both to the Blue Death that swept through her village. She had laid on their graves, weeping for days, waiting for death to take her too. When it didn't, she realized she was hungry and that if she had to live, she would have to eat.

She eventually found work in the Moreau kitchen. It was a good job and the food was plentiful. Then the curious little girl appeared, like an angel in the night's gloom, and gave her a life worth living. Their secret friendship brought her favor in the Moreau house. Claudette eventually insisted that she be her personal attendant. Of course, this all had been Claudette's mischievous ploy to force Lavinia into teaching her the science of divination. It was more of a science of swindling fools than magic. It had more to do with reading people's faces than the wills of the spirits. But the girl's dark eyes beamed with devilish delight every time they delved into the forbidden arts.

"Well, freedom such as yours is far more agreeable than marriage to some brute of a man," Claudette quipped as Lavinia pulled the first in a series of petticoats over her head and shimmied it down to her waist.

"Ah, but Monsieur Pierre Godfrey is said to be tall and handsome from an ancient Norman family that has the King's favor. Their restoration to nobility is said to be imminent!" Lavinia countered.

"So that's it, isn't it?" Claudette dropped her arms to her side. "This ball is nothing more than a pretense to an agreement that's been already arranged between our families. I'm to be paraded around like a show horse before the purchase can be finalized."

"Clearly, there are other reasons for the ball than finding you a mate, child."

"No, I am quite sure that all affairs in Marseille revolve around me," Claudette said, putting her hands on her hips and smirking at herself in the mirror.

"The only affair you should concern yourself with is getting dressed in time, young lady. Quickly now!" Lavinia pulled the silk garment over the young girl's head, threading Claudette's slender arms through the short sleeves. She fastened the ties, tightening the garment to her waist, then rustled out the billowing skirts below. Claudette sighed dreamily, looking at herself in the mirror. The low-cut neckline wrapped around her arms below her shoulders, barely covering the top of her breasts. The rich blue fabric contrasted with her fair skin. Lavinia began to pin up her raven black hair and adorn it with pearls.

"Do you think he'll like me?" she asked, smiling at her image in the mirror, clearly knowing what the answer would be.

Lavinia scoffed and shook her head. "I already feel sorry for his poor heart."

Claudette sat quietly across from her parents as the carriage clattered through town. Her mother had looked her over before they left, giving her a nod of approval before dismissing Lavinia for the night. Now the older woman looked out the window at the passing street scenes as her husband grunted and mumbled at the evening paper. Claudette wondered if the two ever spoke when she was not around, or if it was always this awkward silence. She looked out the window as well, trying to catch the faces of the common people who walked the street. *Why can't love be fun?* she wondered. *Is it always so dreary, or does it become this way?*

The carriage came to a stop. Her mother drew her eyes back to her daughter. "On your best behavior now, our futures depend on it," she said.

"Of course, mamá," Claudette mumbled, looking down at her feet. The footman opened the door and helped the ladies down the little steps of the carriage to the carpet. There they waited for Monsieur Moreau to take his wife's arm. Claudette followed her parents, holding her skirts as they climbed the veranda steps to the grand house. Her nerves mixed with excitement as the doormen opened the glass-paned doors. Music, the glow of candles, and the damp heat of people dancing washed over them as they entered. The smell of flowers, perfume, and sweat mingled with the aromas of sweet pastries and savory roasted meats that passed around the ballroom on trays carried by servants who were still wearing powder wigs from an age gone by.

"The Monsieur and Madame Moreau and their daughter Mademoiselle Moreau!" a servant called as they entered. Monsieur Moreau grunted and nodded to those who weren't dancing. They raised their glasses or lightly applauded in return. Claudette blushed and hid her smile behind her fan. They made their way through the welcomers, the ladies receiving light hugs or kisses on the back of their hands as Monsieur Moreau exchanged handshakes with the men and kissed the hands of the women there to greet them.

Claudette spotted a gaggle of girls collected on the edge of the ballroom floor. "Oh, mamá," she pleaded, "my friends!"

Madame Moreau looked toward the collection of teenage girls and scoffed. "On your best behavior, and don't fill up your dance card with rogues. Remember, Monsieur Godfrey will be here."

"Yes, mamá..." she said, sheepishly.

"Go on and go, child, and not too much wine!" she added as Claudette peeled away and scurried down the steps to the dance floor. She collected herself at the landing, trying not to appear too excited. She had to remember to carry herself with the same sense of aloof disinterest the ladies of society walked with. Still, she couldn't help but grin as she clutched her skirts and shuffled her way to her friends. A tall blonde girl turned to her as she approached.

The girl was intimidatingly beautiful as she smirked at Claudette's arrival.

"Oh look, it's the little country goat, escaped from the barn again and is now wandering through the dance floor," she said with a sneer. The other girls gasped and blinked wide-eyed at her.

"Oh, I see they've hung up the doormat used by sailors to try to air out the smell of fish," Claudette retorted, putting her hands on her hips. The girls gasped in wide-mouthed astonishment before breaking into peals of giggles.

"Come here, you little bitch!" the blonde girl laughed, throwing her arms around Claudette and hugging her. "I should rather like to be a doormat for some beefy sailors than suffer these arrogant popinjays," she said, looking at the elegantly dressed young men around her. "I can only imagine what they'd do to me with their rough hands and scarred backs," she groaned in feigned ecstasy.

"Veronica, you are terrible!" Claudette slapped her arm lightly with her fan. The girls giggled wildly, covering their embarrassment with their fans and lace-gloved hands. Veronica halted a servant carrying a tray of high-stemmed glasses filled with amber bubbly liquid, "Hand them over, sweetheart!"

"Mademoiselle," the man replied nervously, "I'm not supposed to serve young…"

"Shhhhhh," Veronica put her finger to her lips then blew him a kiss as she snatched up drinks and handed them to her friends. The man blushed wildly. He looked around to see who was witnessing this indiscretion, then tucked the empty tray under his arm and darted away before he got himself in trouble.

The girls laughed at his embarrassed flight. "To getting what we want, girls!" Veronica held up her glass. The other girls were quick to clink their glasses to it. Claudette beamed with delight as she sipped, feeling the tiny bubbles tickle the inside of her mouth. She watched her tall friend command this corner of the dance floor like a queen.

Veronica let out a feline-like growl as she spied a man coming through the door. "Now there's a lion I'd like to tame."

A servant made the announcement, "The Monsieur Alexandre Dumas de la Pailleterie!" A gasp went out around the room. Some of the dancers even stopped to catch a glimpse of the man.

"Is that the famous playwright?!" one of the girls asked.

"The same," Veronica answered, watching the man work his way through the throngs of greeters and well-wishers eager to shake his hand.

"He is too old for you, Veronica! And he is recently married to Ida Ferrier, the famous actress!" the girl protested laughingly.

"I hear Monsieur Dumas doesn't let such trivial things get in the way," Veronica quipped, not taking her eyes off the man. The girls blushed and giggled in delight.

"I hear he's the grandson of an African slave! You wouldn't dare!" another girl challenged.

"I hear they make better lovers. They have much bigger… shall we say…spears?" Veronica answered slyly. The girls almost fell over with laughter, eliciting hisses from the older women nearby and tantalized grins from the young men who wondered what had the young ladies so riotous.

Claudette stood on her tiptoes, trying to get a glimpse of the famous man that had so many guests enraptured with his arrival. She first caught a glimpse of the puff of light-brown hair that rose above the crowd like a flame raging on the top of his head. Then she saw the large round eyes that bulged with delight and betrayed a smile that was still hidden by the crowd. As he emerged she could see his full lips drawn into a mischievous grin. His light-brown face beamed with friendly energy as he nodded and spoke with those he passed. The crowd swooned around him, completely taken by the larger-than-life man.

My God, he's coming this way, she thought.

He had spotted the girls as he took a glass of champagne. He tossed it down and replaced the empty glass on the tray before the servant could even stop to offer him one. He smiled devilishly as he adjusted his trousers and marched toward them. Startled and suddenly nervous, Claudette cleared her throat and wondered what to do with her hands.

"My God, there's a hole in the firmament and the most beautiful of the angels have escaped to our humble earth!" he said with a bow, catching Claudette's eye with a wink as he lowered himself before the giggling and blushing girls.

"Oh, Monsieur Dumas," one of the girls swooned, "whatever are you doing in our modest little town?"

"Research, my dear!" he said, delighted at the prompt. "I must visit *le Château d'If* in person!"

"Oh, dear," she said, "the old prison in the harbor? How dreadful! Whatever for?"

"It is where my next work begins. The hero is a prisoner!"

"A prisoner? Sounds awful!" another girl piped in.

"Ah, yes, it is, my dove. But in order to triumph, we must know defeat. We cannot enjoy the beauty of life without tasting its sorrows," he said turning his eyes to Claudette. The sudden attention rattled her. She swallowed hard, her mind racing for something to say.

"What's it like living in París?" she asked, then immediately felt stupid for asking such a dumb question.

"It's tricky," he smiled at her kindly. "Everyone knows who I am. I can't even walk down the street anymore without being hawked by people asking me to recite from my plays or even to make up a rhyme."

"Is it really so dreadful?" she asked.

"Yes, so much so that I've decided to move away. I'm building a chateau in the country."

"But surely you prefer to live in the *City of Light* than the county, monsieur!" Veronica stepped in, much to Claudette's relief.

"It's pity," Dumas shrugged his shoulders. "In the city, I just can't hide," he said shaking his head.

"But Surely you can ride in your carriage and darken the windows," another girl stated.

"Ah, yes," he said, holding up a finger, "but tinted windows mean nothing, my dear, they know who's inside."

"Well, I think you've been entirely rude, monsieur," Veronica said sternly.

Dumas's eyes bulged as he placed his open hand on his chest as if to ask if she were truly talking to him.

"You've been standing here for five minutes and you haven't even asked me to dance," she explained.

His look of feigned shock broke into a smile as he held out an arm for her. He smiled grandly as she took it, then led her to the dance floor.

"Oh, I like you!" he said devilishly as they moved into the swirl of dancers.

Claudette sighed as she watched them disappear into the crowd. *What it must be like to have such confidence!* she wondered.

More people were streaming into the already crowded ballroom. She could hear the servant calling out their names and titles as they came. She fanned herself. The air was stuffy regardless of the opened windows. The heat and champagne made her feel lightheaded.

Then she heard his name called out, barely over the music, chatter, and clinking of glasses. *My God, he's here!* she thought, fanning herself frantically as her eyes widened. She looked around for the easiest path to a window. She suddenly needed fresh air as she fought the instinct to flee altogether.

"Excuse me," she said meekly to her friends as she moved away. She could see the route laid before her. There were just a few people to maneuver around and she'd be there. She walked briskly, keeping her eyes locked on the sanctuary of the darkness outside of the window.

"Claudette!"

Her mother's voice stopped her in her tracks. Her shoulders seized at the sound. "There you are, child! Come here! I have someone I want you to meet!" Claudette closed her eyes for a moment, then opened them, drew in a breath, and turned around with a smile.

"I want you to meet Monsieur Pierre Godfrey. His family was Norman nobility before the revolution. Their return to peerage is imminent!" her mother said. Claudette's smile dropped. She flinched at the sight of him. His appearance completely took her by surprise. Pierre's delicate lips curled downward in what should have appeared to be a frown, but was clearly an amused smile.

"It's a pleasure to finally meet you, mademoiselle," he said softly. He took her hand and bowed to kiss it. His large sapphire-blue eyes locked onto hers until they disappeared as he bowed and were now hidden under his full head of long blond hair. His thin lips touching the back of her hand sent a cold shiver up her arm, causing the fine hairs to stand on end. Her skin rippled with goosebumps as he lifted himself out of the bow, catching her eyes again with his own and smiling with his curious upside-down grin.

"The pleasure is all mine, monsieur..." she said vacantly, blinking at the image before her. He looked to her like an angel from a painting who had stepped off the canvas and traded in his white robes for a dashing military uniform that perfectly fit his tall lean build.

"You are in the army, monsieur?" she asked.

"Only when my country calls," he laughed, looking down at his extravagant costume. "Mostly, I'm a dressing doll for my father's obsession with our family's martial heritage."

"I see..." Claudette said, returning the man's infectious smile.

"He'll be leading our nation's troops soon enough!" the older man next to him boasted, slapping his son on the shoulder. His father appeared to be a more masculine and older version of the pretty young man. His grey and balding hair was cut short. Thick sideburns and a wide flamboyant mustache adorned his face.

"Let us hope France will soon be done with wars," Claudette's mother said. "Such a waste of young men."

"Ah, but war is the cleansing fire that clears away the deadwood so the strong trees may grow!" Pierre's father said, beaming as he slapped his son's arm with pride. Pierre stood silent, smiling at Claudette. Claudette smiled back, then suddenly felt awkward as she held her smile and eye contact during the pause in conversation. "Well...?" Pierre's father said at last, giving his son a gentle shove. "Do I have to do everything for you?"

Pierre chuckled lightly with embarrassment. "Of course not, father," then turning his eyes back to Claudette, "Would you dance with me, mademoiselle?" he asked extending his arm.

"Of course," she said, taking it. They stepped into the stream of dancers. He took her hand and set his other on her waist. They started to take their first steps and then the music stopped.

"Hmmm...it seems our timing is all off," he said lightly.

"It appears so," she said. She looked up at him, watching him scan the room. The chatter and clinking of plates and glasses helped mask the strained silence between them. Someone was speaking, giving instructions to the dancers. Soon, the couples were arranging themselves in groups of four.

"Ah, a quadrille!" he said, with some relief that the awkward moment had passed.

She was relieved too. Veronica and Monsieur Dumas joined their quartet. The two swept away the awkwardness she had felt with their bounds of charismatic energy and wit. The dance began, and soon she was twirling around into the arms of the other dancers who laughed and smiled warmly at her. Pierre seemed to look away every time their eyes met. Instead, his eyes always seemed to find Veronica as she whooped and laughed, constantly drawing attention to herself. The tall blue-eyed blonde was like the sun in the gloomy candlelit room, blinding men to everything else around her.

"So she was beautiful, you say," Thomas asked, sipping his brandy in Pierre's bed chambers in the quiet hours after the dance.

"Yes, and I, the fool...I couldn't even look at her! I kept catching myself looking at other women just to avoid her gaze. She must think I'm a cad!" Pierre said dropping his head to stare into his snifter. His jacket and waistcoat were thrown haphazardly on the bed and floor. The two friends sat in their shirtsleeves, trousers, and boots at the small table in his room. Their dress swords hung lazily at their sides.

"I'm sure it can't be that bad," Thomas tried to console. "You just lost your nerve. I'm sure she didn't even notice. What you need to do is make a grand gesture. Show her how interested you are in her!"

Pierre sighed, "I never have problems with women. I couldn't keep them off me during my studies in Spain. But her...that raven black hair, those dark eyes, that delicate fair skin...I couldn't bear to look at her without my knees buckling beneath me."

"Ah, sounds like the sweet suffering of love, my friend," Thomas sighed grandly. As if on cue the breeze blew in through the open doors of the balcony. It brought the salty air from the sea. "You see? The angels are listening!" he said, then furrowed his brow, turning his head to listen more closely.

Pierre's eyes widened as he heard it too. Something was moving out there on the balcony. "Or perhaps the Devil!" he gasped. They both stood and unsheathed their swords. They stood frozen as they heard the now distinct sound of footsteps outside the doors. A dark form appeared before them. The two friends took a step back in fear.

The figure stepped into the light revealing his face causing Pierre to gasp in surprise.

"Pierre Godfrey, it's been a long time since we crossed swords," the dark form said in Spanish with a low menacing voice.

"Diego! I did not expect to see you again!" Pierre said in French-accented Spanish.

"Yet, here I am..." Diego said gravely.

"You know this man?!" Thomas asked in French, bewildered at the unfolding scene.

"Yes," Pierre said in French out of the corner of his mouth, not taking his eyes off the intruder, "from my days in Barcelona," then in Spanish, "Why are you here?"

"To collect a debt," Diego stepped farther into the room. Thomas raised his sword, took a step back, then looked to his friend worriedly.

Pierre let the tip of his sword drop, straightened himself, and scrunched his nose in disgust. "You smell like fish."

"I..." Diego paused to think, "...was making love to the sea."

"You what...?" Pierre asked, drawing his face back with even more revulsion.

"I was...you know...the sea...I was making love to it," Diego paused, then raised an eyebrow, "like a mad seal!"

Pierre blinked at him for a moment, then broke into laughter. "A mad seal?! What are you talking about?!"

"I don't know," Diego shrugged, "I was trying to think of something clever."

"What is going on?" Thomas asked in French.

"It's alright. Diego is a good friend," Pierre replied in French, then in Spanish, "Let's draw you a bath and get you some fresh clothes, then you can delight us with the story of how you've come to be on my balcony smelling like fish in the middle of the night."

"Well, I certainly couldn't've knocked at your front door like this," Diego said, pointing to himself with exaggerated incredulity.

Now clean and in fresh clothes, Diego relayed his adventures while Pierre translated them into French for Thomas.

"You struck Fray Alfonso?!" Pierre said in astonishment.

"Well, only lightly so he'd know that I could. I could not let an insult to my mother go unanswered," he said, shaking his head as if the mere thought was beyond reason.

Pierre shook his head too and chuckled softly, "Diego, Diego, Diego... and you say he was beating you for fighting in the first place..."

"As you know, Pierre," Diego said gravely, "it is not easy being a foreigner in Spain, especially for a Mexican. I have to constantly defend myself and my honor."

"That is true," Pierre nodded, remembering his own experience. He turned to Thomas and spoke to him in French, "Diego was my first true friend in Barcelona. The Spaniards still resent us for Napoleon's occupation. One night a group of thugs cornered me in the street. They taunted me for being French. I was sure they'd kill me once they started to attack, but then this wild and crazy Aztec warrior here came out of nowhere, like the curse of *Quetzalcoatl.*" Pierre gestured to Diego who was trying to follow the story in French as much as its similarities to Spanish allowed.

"Ket-sul-ko-wa-tul," Thomas attempted the name slowly with wonderment.

"*El Serpiente de las Plumas,*" Diego nodded with mystical reverence. The Frenchman understood the Spanish immediately.

"The Serpent of the Plumes..." he said in French.

"A vengeful god of an ancient warrior race," Pierre nodded, sharing the eerie mood that had set upon his friends. He then broke into his infectious upside-down smile, brightening the room once more. "Anyway, this flying dragon here most surely saved my life that night."

"It was a good fight," Diego said in Spanish, "and you fought well, my friend."

"Only once you beat the wild pack of dogs off me," Pierre patted him on the shoulder. "I meant it then and I mean it now, I am in your debt, my friend. How can I help you with your current predicament?"

"Well, I'm a wanted man in Spain," Diego said, "so, I'm returning home to Mexico. I must write to my father in Alta California to arrange passage." Then he slumped his shoulders as some of his bravado slipped away. "I don't know if he'll welcome me home after what's happened."

"Sure he will! He can't have any love for the Spaniards! Didn't he fight against them in your war for independence?" Pierre tried to assure him.

"That was my grandfather," Diego said gloomily.

"Ah, yes, the *Fox*!" Pierre said, remembering Diego's stories about his grandfather's adventures.

"I'm afraid my father is a bit more practical. He'd rather trade with the Spaniards than fight them. That's why he sent me there to be educated. That and to keep the ghost of my grandfather from putting a sword in my hand and wild ideas in my heart."

"Well, I may be able to help you get home," Pierre said, clutching Diego's shoulder affectionately. "In the meantime, you may stay here as my guest."

"I would hate to be a burden," Diego said sheepishly.

"Nonsense!" Pierre insisted. "Perhaps you could be of some use to me while you're here. I could use a good *fox* like your grandfather to help me with some business. That business may lead to your ticket back to Mexico sooner than you think, but I might have to put a sword in your hand."

"Put a sword in my hand and I will wield it happily for you, my friend," Diego said with serious resolve.

Pierre's lips curled downward into a smile, "Excellent, but before the sword, I must ask, do you still play guitar?"

Diego blinked at him for a moment, weighing the question, then spoke. "Of course, I am a *caballero*, after all."

Claudette tried to concentrate on her book but realized she had been merely scanning the words for the last two pages without taking in any meaning. She sighed and flipped back to where she must have lost focus. It was hard to read with so many thoughts dancing in her head.

She had been up late with Lavinia, trying to divine whether Pierre was the great love she had been expecting. Lavinia did her best to assure her that he was. She read Claudette's tarot cards and peered into her crystal ball as they sat cross-legged on the floor, late into the night. But Claudette could tell she wasn't being sincere. It was clear that she was seeing something different from what she was saying. She could tell that Lavinia thought Pierre was a good catch and didn't want to convince Claudette otherwise. But Claudette could see there was concern beneath the woman's assurances.

He was beautiful for sure, and charming as well, but something just didn't feel right. Perhaps it was only her nerves although he did seem to be more interested in the women around her than her. How could she blame him? Every man seemed to fall for Veronica. She was blonde, beautiful, and could match them in confidence and wit.

Oh, but then there was Monsieur Dumas. She tried to shake him from her thoughts. He was old enough to be her father, married, mixed-race, and known for being a romantic adventurer. Still, these reasons to stay away made the forbidden fruit all the more alluring. She found his cheerful wit and inquisitive eyes magnetic. *Oh, what would I do if he were here in my room with me now?* She shook her head, trying to banish the thought.

The clatter of an approaching carriage took her from these wild fantasies. "*Oh, mon Dieu...*" she muttered as she looked out the window, "he's here!"

"Yoo-hoo!" Veronica shouted from the open carriage, waving her arms wildly. "We are going to prison! Won't you come?!" Monsieur Dumas sat next to her, grinning broadly. A little old lady dressed in black sat opposite them.

"Are you mad?!" Claudette laughed.

"Of course we're mad, but in the name of research!" Veronica answered. "Monsieur Dumas has invited us to tour le Chateau d'If with him. It's for his next work. Don't you want to come?!"

"Without a chaperone?!"

"I brought my grandmamá. She's nearly deaf and blind, so we have nothing to worry about!"

Claudette laughed and shook her head at her friend's audacity. "Okay, one moment! I must leave a note for my parents." She was quite happy that her parents weren't there to stop her. Only Lavinia was there to disapprove.

"Do not allow yourself to be alone with Monsieur Dumas," she said, giving up on trying to stop her. "He is up to no good, bringing you girls."

"Of course," Claudette assured her, squeezing her forearm.

"You don't want your reputation damaged on the eve of your betrothal to Monsieur Godfrey," Lavinia warned.

"Never," Claudette insisted, *but wouldn't that be grand?!* the thought jumped into her mind. Lavinia's eyes narrowed as if she heard the thought out loud. "What...?" Claudette asked, suddenly self-conscious.

Claudette could barely look at him as she climbed into the carriage, but his friendly countenance and warm inviting voice put her quickly at ease.

"Monsieur Dumas insisted that we bring you along," Veronica said with a little bit of a playful pout. Claudette's heart fluttered at the thought.

"It's true," Dumas responded. "I'm afraid to be left alone with her!" He gave Veronica a sideways wink.

"Oh, you impossible man!" Veronica protested, slapping his shoulder with her fan.

The three laughed and bantered as the carriage clattered through the streets on the way to the quay. Veronica's grandmother smiled and nodded, pretending to hear the conversation the young people were having. Claudette reveled at the street scenes, wishing to run freely among the people who walked casually in and out of the shops and cafes. *Oh, what it must be like!* The salt in the air and the fresh smell of the sea filled her with excitement as the masts and smokestacks of boats and ships came into view.

"I'll be just a moment," Dumas told the women as he hoisted himself out of the carriage and walked to the water's edge. He spoke to several boatmen standing in their small crafts until he finally found satisfaction. "Come!" he said, helping the three ladies out of the carriage. Claudette's eyes widened at the sight of the two Arabs in the small felucca as they boarded. The stories of Barbary pirates snatching white women from ships and selling them as slaves into harems popped into her mind.

Dumas caught the panic that flashed across her face. He laughed, "Don't worry, my dear. I am an excellent judge of men. When you are a minority like me, you learn that the other minorities aren't nearly as bad as people tell you. Plus, Mohammedans are typically cheaper!"

Claudette smiled nervously, putting her hand to her chest to steady her heart. One of the Arabs smiled warmly, beckoning her aboard.

"Not to mention, it's three against two. If they attack, Veronica can fight them while we watch and enjoy the wine," Dumas said, holding up a demijohn in one hand and a picnic basket in the other. His eyes twinkled with devilish delight as Veronica hit him with her fan. Claudette joined in the laughter. She wondered nervously whether the Arabs and the old lady understood the humor.

The two Arab sailors rowed a bit, then set their sails, which tugged the little boat into motion. Soon they were making their way out of the harbor and into the Mediterranean. Claudette watched in wonderment as the big steamships chugged past them, belching out black smoke into the air.

"A little lunch!" Dumas said grandly, lifting the basket once again. He uncorked the demijohn and poured cups for the girls. He offered some to the Arabs, who swiftly refused, but happily shared their smoked fish which the little party enjoyed with bread and cheese.

Ah, this is life! Claudette thought, letting the breeze rustle her hair.

"There it is!" Dumas called out, pointing to the rocky island that sat sentinel to the harbor, "Le Cháteau D'If!"

The sight of it filled her with dread. Its high walls sat on steep rocky cliffs, which the sea lashed with white foamy tentacle-like waves. Inside the walls sat a lonesome castle with few windows adorning its three towers. "What an awful prison!" she gasped.

"Ah, but it is only a prison because we call it a prison," Dumas noted. "It was once a fortress, built to defend our shores from Charles V and his imperial armies. But who could imagine anyone invading our mighty France now in these modern times? It is much more useful as a prison. The sea itself makes it nearly impossible to escape!"

"*Nearly*, Monsieur Dumas...?" Veronica asked, raising an eyebrow.

"That is what I'm here to see," Dumas smiled slyly.

Claudette felt the knot in her throat tighten as they approached the landing. Everything about the place told her to flee. She was fighting the urge to refuse to go ashore when uniformed men on the docks shouted and waved to them in with friendly excitement.

"Monsieur Dumas and guests, welcome to our humble little island!" a man greeted them as he helped the ladies out of the boat. "We are honored to have you! The governor is away but says I am to guide you wherever your needs may take you. I am Sergeant Babin, at your service!"

"Thank you, Sergeant!" Dumas smiled grandly as the man helped him out of the boat.

Claudette found the scene inside the walls surprising. Prisoners walked freely on the grounds, some in rags, others in new and fashionable clothing. Some of the men sat with their backs against the walls, staring at the ground in despair. Others were quite cheerful, taking in the fresh sea air as they got their daily exercise. Soon a small group of well-heeled prisoners, as well as some of the guards, were crowded around Veronica as she bantered and caught them up on the latest news and gossip from the mainland.

"You seem perplexed, my dear," Dumas came up next to Claudette. He watched her take in the scenes around her.

"This just isn't what I thought a prison would be," she said, watching the men happily chatting with her friend.

"Ah, well, like I said, it's only a prison because we call it one. And who are the prisoners, would you say? The men in rags? The wealthy political dissidents? Or perhaps the guards assigned to stay here and watch them? Prison, my dear, is more a state of mind than it is a place where you stand."

"Probably having money helps one's state of mind," Claudette quipped.

"True. The wealthy men confined here can live quite comfortably. Many of the poor are held in the dungeons below." Claudette shivered at the thought of the poor souls locked away from the sun for years. Dumas smiled softly at her, knowing it was time to change the subject. "You are a very beautiful woman, Claudette. You should visit me sometime in *Paris*."

Claudette pushed her lips to one side and looked at him with a bit of humorous scorn. "Are you not satisfied with the attention you get from my friend Veronica, monsieur?"

Dumas laughed and turned his eyes back to the tall blonde beauty. "Shiny objects will always catch a man's eye, but it is the dark depth of a kindred soul that will satisfy him in the end."

"Does your wife's soul not satisfy you then, monsieur?" she said, then immediately felt nervous that she had pushed too far.

Dumas paused for a moment, frowning as he thought, then laughed. "Okay, mademoiselle, you have beaten me. But please remember this: marriage, family, race, sex, age, religion, nationality…these are all prisons in which we imagine ourselves. Please believe in my true friendship and sincerity when I say, I hope someday you will set yourself free."

Chapter Five: Night Work

Diego pulled the new black leather boots over his black trousers. He rotated his ankles, trying to loosen the stiff leather.

"It's okay, Diego," Pierre said with mirth, "we won't be walking much."

Diego shrugged and slid the black sleeves of his blouse into the black waistcoat. "All black, eh? Will I be working in the theater tonight?" he asked, fastening the buttons.

"Well, it'll certainly be theatrical," Pierre smiled.

Diego unsheathed the sword Pierre had given him. It was a light and elegant thing, more for a gentleman fighting a duel than the heavy cavalry sabers used to cleave heads in two from horseback. It had a long straight blade made from hard but flexible Toledo steel. It was sharpened on both sides which came to a needle point. A small dull silver cup and crossguard protected the hilt. The lower end of the crossguard looped downward toward the pommel to protect the knuckles. The silver pommel gave just enough weight to balance the weapon so that the hilt could lay loosely on his open palm without the weapon tilting one way or the other.

"Theatrical, you say," Diego smirked as he hefted the weight of the sword in his hand with satisfaction before re-sheathing it and slinging it loosely on his hip.

"Well, we still have to keep the appearance of gentlemen and not reveal the grim barbarians that we actually are," Pierre said, donning his own waistcoat, which was a rich blue silk against his white shirt and trousers.

"I see…" Diego said, sliding the long thin dagger into his right boot. He watched with interest as his friend slid a small, two-barreled pistol into his own boot.

Pierre then picked up a larger single-barrel flintlock pistol and handed it to him. "It's already loaded."

"Ah, the Devil's weapon," Diego said, tucking it into his sash.

"Well, let's hope we don't need the Devil's help tonight," Pierre said, donning his luxuriant blue cape.

"Ojalá," Diego replied, sweeping his own black cape around his shoulders and tying it around his neck.

"Don't forget this," Pierre said, handing him a guitar.

Diego raised an eyebrow with irony, "Of course not," he said as he slung it over his back.

"And now, the little *green fairy* for courage, my friend," Pierre said.

He brought out a tray with two small glasses, two slotted spoons, a bowl of sugar cubes, a bottle of chilled water, and a decanter of green liquid. Diego's eyes widened with wonderment as he watched his friend perform a well-practiced ritual. Pierre poured the green liquid into the glasses, then laid the slotted spoons across them. He placed a sugar cube on each one and then slowly drizzled them with cold water until the cubes dissolved into the green liquid below. He handed Diego a glass and said, "Careful, this might make you see things that aren't really there."

"Ah, much like our mezcal back home, except we use a worm and a lime to drink it instead of sugar and water," Diego said.

"Sounds great," Pierre said ironically, "perhaps we'll drink some together in Mexico one day!"

"*Ojalá,*" Diego grinned, raising his glass.

"Yeah, whatever that means. *À votre santé!*"

They tossed down their drinks. Diego grimaced and shuddered at the burning green liquid sliding down his throat. It left a heavy black licorice taste in his mouth.

"Ah!" Pierre said with satisfaction. "Let's have another!" They drank a few more rounds until Pierre seemed satisfied with the effect. "Let's ride!" he said, slamming his glass down on the table.

They clattered down the street at twilight. Pierre led on his immaculate white horse. Diego rode alongside on the all-black horse Pierre insisted he ride. "Best not to draw attention," he told him.

A light breeze blew into Claudette's room reminding her of the vast world that existed outside her window. She set her book down and sighed. Lavinia looked up from her own book and gave a knowing smile. "You are restless, child," she said.

"It is hard to focus my mind while my heart wanders," Claudette answered, blinking at the darkness outside.

"Tell me, where does your heart wander? Perhaps your mind can come too!" Lavinia set her book down.

Claudette sighed again as she collapsed into the back of her chair. She looked over to her friend, "It's like I'm homesick for a place I've never been...like I miss someone I've never met."

"Ah, you are tormented by the blue devils!" Lavinia narrowed her eyes.

"Monsieur Dumas says I live in a prison of my own construct," she said, looking around the ceiling of her room. "Well, I certainly didn't build this house, nor did I pick my suitor."

Lavinia smiled with her lips pushed to one side of her mouth. She looked at the young woman with sympathy. "Monsieur Dumas just wants you to live in his prison, even if it's only for one night."

Claudette laughed, "You're terrible!"

Lavinia laughed lightly and sighed. "You really should give Monsieur Godfrey a chance, child. I know it seems your path has been laid out for you without your consent, but love is something that has to be nurtured. It's a seed that you plant in the ground and water. It takes time to harvest the benefit."

Claudette sighed, "I know...I will, it's just...I want it to be more romantic. I want to experience love at first sight!"

"Hmmph...!" Lavinia scoffed. "Love at first sight is something that happens in cheap romance novels meant to infect young girls with melancholy."

The breeze blew in the distinct sound of a guitar strum. The two women's eyes widened as they looked at each other in amazement. The strum turned into a rhythm and a man's voice began to sing.

Quanto è bella, quanto è cara!
Più la vedo, e più mi piace...

"What in the world...?" Lavinia gasped. The two leaped to their feet and dashed to the window.

ma in quel cor non son capace
lieve affetto ad inspirar.

Claudette let out a gasp at the sight below, then covered her mouth with her hand as she giggled with embarrassment.

Essa legge, studia, impara...

non vi ha cosa ad essa ignota...
Io son sempre un idiota,

Pierre stood boldly below her window, gesturing with his free hand as he sang. The lantern in his other hand bathed him in amber light that bounced off his white trousers and gave his blond hair a halo-like glow. His lips curled downward in a delightful self-ironic grin as he belted out the Italian love song.

io non so che sospirar.
Chi la mente mi rischiara?
Chi m'insegna a farmi amar?

A dark form was standing next to him. Only the guitar in its hands reflected any of the flickering light. A wide-brimmed hat covered most of its face revealing only a grim-set mouth. The shadowy figure continued to pluck the strings with its fingers as Pierre took a large dramatic bow. Claudette blushed and gave a light applause, then drew her hands back to cover her mouth once more in embarrassment. "*Mon Dieu*, are you crazy?!" she said in a loud whisper, suddenly panicking over the commotion. "My parents...!"

"I've thought of everything, my dear," Pierre smiled warmly. "Your father gave me permission to express my undying admiration for you, as poorly performed as it was, and perhaps to court you if, of course, you'd be kind enough to offer a simple fool like me some of your time."

Claudette froze for a moment, realizing that this was a question. It was a question she was not prepared for, a question that could very well set her on the path everyone expected her to take. The answer could very well determine the rest of her life. Pierre's blue eyes blinked in the lantern light, waiting for a response. The seconds that followed seemed to be an agonizing eternity. Then, the sound of a violin drifted up over her shoulder. Pierre blinked again, then furrowed his brow at the unexpected addition to the music.

Lavinia stepped to the window, her long brown curls draped over her shoulder as she played the melody of the Italian song. The guitar player began to accompany her. Pierre dropped his eyes from Claudette and turned toward the shadow beside him. Claudette followed his eyes to the dark form which now stepped forward into the light, locking its rhythm with Lavinia's violin. Its grim lips drew to the side in the beginning of a smile. The brim of its hat tilted upward. Flickering light hit the large green eyes below, igniting them with fire. Claudette gasped at the sight. Suddenly there seemed not to be enough air to breathe. She set her hands on the window sill to steady herself, embarrassed at her sudden lightheadedness.

No one seemed to notice as Lavinia slowly introduced darker minor notes into the melody giving it a more Semitic flair. The guitarist followed. Soon the music became a rhapsodic Arabesque romp which ended in a flourish as Lavinia ripped the bow from strings and Diego pulled his strumming hand from the guitar with a flash.

Pierre widened his eyes and pursed his lips in a surprised expression of approval. "Well done, bravo!" he said, clapping his hands. Then threw his arm around Diego's shoulders and drew him in for a hug. Diego smiled and shrugged sheepishly.

"You play excellently, my friend!" Lavinia called down to him. Diego looked at her and smiled dumbly, not understanding the French.

"My friend Diego is full of surprises!" Pierre laughed. The woman spoke again to Pierre in French. Diego heard Pierre say the words *"Espanol"* and *"Mexicain"* in the same language. He watched the woman nod understandingly. His eyes moved to the young woman next to her. He flinched. She was staring at him. Her dark eyes seemed to bore straight through him, reading all of the weaknesses and insecurities he thought he had hidden from the world.

"Diego…" Pierre nudged him, snapping him out of his trance. "The rose, do you still have it?" Pierre asked him in Spanish.

"Of course!" Diego said, reaching quickly into his cape. "Aiyee!" he hissed, pulling his hand away quickly and shaking it in pain. The rose tumbled to the ground. He sucked on the blood from the thorn prick to his finger for a second, then mumbled, "Siento." He lowered himself to retrieve the rose.

The other three blinked and watched in various stages of humor as the dramatically dressed guitarist fumbled with his instrument while performing the seemingly simple task of picking up the rose.

The bottom of his scabbard stuck into the ground as he squatted, causing him to stumble forward. The stumbling was made more awkward as he stepped high to avoid crushing the rose with his boot. The stiff leather ankles made this even more difficult to manage. He finally caught his balance, gave a brief nervous laugh, then bent over and picked it up, trying to delicately brush away the dust with his other hand.

"Here," he handed it to Pierre.

Pierre regarded him with incredulous mirth as he took it. "Thank you, my friend," he said in Spanish, then looked up at the ladies above him in the window and spoke in French. "He's good at other things, I assure you." Lavinia let out a giggle. Claudette stood silent, watching the black-clad guitar player slip back into the darkness as he dusted himself off. Pierre drew her attention back. "Claudette, will you accept this…dusty, and um…blood-splattered rose as a token of my affection for you? It's, uh…been through quite a lot to get to you," he said with humor. Lavinia giggled again.

Claudette blinked, still in a state of bewilderment, "Um…yes. Yes, of course."

Pierre extended it to her as she reached down. Lavinia held onto her to keep her from falling from the window. The distance was still too far.

"Let me help," Diego said in Spanish, recovering from his embarrassment. He set his guitar down and pressed his back against the wall. He laced his fingers together, then held his cupped hands low. He looked up at Pierre, "*Ándale, arriba.*"

Pierre put his foot into his hands, then stepped up as Diego hoisted him. The women watched as the pretty blue-eyed man seemed to levitate into the light from their room like an angel floating upward from the Earth. Claudette took the rose and looked at it as if it were something suddenly alien. There was still blood on the thorns. Pierre leaped back to the ground.

"May I call upon you then, perhaps tomorrow afternoon?" he said, smiling at the ladies above.

"Yes," Claudette said flatly, still trying to process the swirl of emotions dancing in her heart.

"Then you have made me a very happy man this evening, mademoiselle," he said grandly, taking a deep bow. Claudette used the opportunity to steal a glimpse at the strange companion with him. Diego was already looking at her with an intensity that she found both startling and alluring. Her eyes snapped back to Pierre as he rose just in time for him not to see that she had looked away to his friend. "Until tomorrow then, my dear!" he said, then turned to his companion, "Come on, my friend," he said in Spanish, "we have more work to attend to."

Claudette watched the two slip into the darkness once Pierre doused the lantern and beckoned his companion to follow. She heard them mounting horses, then saw the silhouettes move down the lane towards the hills and out of sight. She turned to find Lavinia watching her with concern on her face.

"What is it?" Claudette asked at last.

Lavinia remained silent for a moment, scanning her eyes, looking for something and not liking what she found, "Be careful with your heart, girl."

Chapter Six: The Work of Nations

Pierre insisted on no lights and as little sound as possible as they rode. Diego was happy for the silence and darkness. His mind was racing as things suddenly seemed unearthly. The strange liquor was playing with his senses. His vision became compressed as if he were viewing the world from inside a tunnel. Vibrant colors seemed to weave in and out of the fabric of the darkness. Objects appeared as if they were made of soft clay in the gloom. Even the sounds of the horse hooves seemed like he was hearing them underwater.

He shook his head, trying to clear the strange feeling. Panic began to creep into his stomach. How was he going to perform his duties during this evening's mission like this? He tried to focus on something positive to clear his mind: home, beautiful women, her eyes. He shook his head. The vision had crept in unexpectedly: The dark-eyed girl in the window, Pierre's girl.

He exhaled grimly through his nose. He had let her creep into his mind and now he couldn't shake the thought of her and those dark eyes. What was she looking at? What was it that she was seeing in him that he couldn't hide?

"There they are," Pierre whispered. Diego was happy to be pulled out of his mind and back into the world around him. He had lost track of where they were going in the darkness. He only knew they had not ridden back into town.

The dark forms became clearer as they approached. Pierre gave out a short rapid series of whistles, mimicking a night bird. The call was answered by one of the dark forms that began to take the shape of a man on horseback as they approached. There were three of them. Behind them were four carts, each with a team of mules. A small party of silhouettes lingered near the carts.

"Good evening, Thomas, Levi, Atilla," Pierre greeted the horsemen.

"Good evening, Pierre," Thomas smiled. "I see you brought your wild Mexican," he said, motioning with his head toward Pierre's companion. Diego focused his eyes on Thomas, having heard the French word for his nationality spoken.

"Yes, he's turning out to be a very useful man, especially since he doesn't speak French," Pierre said with a light laugh. Then he turned to Diego and spoke Spanish, "These are my friends: Levi, Atilla, and you've met Thomas," then in French, "this is Diego de la Vega, my friend from school. You can trust him. He's good with a sword and is virtually unknown in these parts."

The three horsemen nodded to him muttering, "*Bonjour*."

"*Buenos noches*," Diego tipped his hat to them.

"What about the laborers?" Pierre, motioning to the collection of men and carts. "Can we trust them?"

"They are the finest villainous scum money can buy," Atilla piped in, grinning slyly "and not one of them can speak a lick of English."

"Good!" Pierre replied in the fore-mentioned language. "The less they know what we're doing, the better."

"I agree," Levi said in English as well.

Diego's eyes widened. He had become so accustomed to not understanding conversations in French that hearing them suddenly speak the language of the *Yanquis* was stunning. Anglo invaders had been slowly filtering into Alta California for years. Many thought them and their heretical religion a nuisance. But Diego's father saw them as a business opportunity and a way to open up trade with their distant country on the other side of the continent. He insisted his son learn their language, hiring tutors, and even insisting on continuing his English studies at the university in Spain. Now, the boring lessons and beatings from his tutors seemed to be paying off.

Pierre smiled to his friends. "Let's go start a war, gentlemen," he said, nudging his horse forward. The carts and laborers rolled in behind. The remaining horsemen took their positions, guarding the flanks and rear of the small procession.

Diego rode alongside Pierre, constantly looking behind him for followers, then turned his eyes to the rocky crags that lined the trail that could hide an ambush. Soon the smell of the sea rolled in with the breeze. He could hear waves crashing on the beach ahead. There, he could make out silhouettes of men gathered and the outline of a launch that had been pulled ashore.

"I don't like the look of this," Pierre mumbled in French, then whistled his signal. The signal was repeated from the group of men on the beach. Pierre's party dismounted once they reached the sand

and walked forward. Diego and the other friends spread out into a protective ring around their leader. The workers stayed back with the carts and the horses, waiting for the business to be done before the work could begin.

"Ahoy there!" one of the figures on the beach called out to them in English.

"Hello!" Pierre called back. "I've brought my friends. Their names are not necessary here," Pierre replied in the same language.

"Of course," the man said, "we're all using false names anyway. No sense in boring ourselves with pretenses. Tonight, we do the work of our nations, gentlemen, not ourselves."

"Where are they?" Pierre said suspiciously.

"So direct for a Frenchman," the man chuckled. "It's quite refreshing, really," he said, then turned to some of his men and nodded. Two of them shuffled toward the launch. Diego scanned the others the best he could in the darkness. None of them were wearing uniforms, but their military demeanor was undeniable. He could make out the dark forms of muskets some of them held. Others, like the man who seemed to be in charge, carried short curved cutlasses on their hips and pistols in their sashes.

The two men returned with a long crate and dropped it at Pierre's feet. Then one of them knelt and opened it for him to inspect the contents. Diego furrowed his brow, trying to make out what those contents were. The kneeling man handed Pierre a musket from the crate.

"The Brown Bess, my friend, carried by Her Majesty's forces for over a hundred years," the leader of the other group chimed as Pierre inspected the long firearm. "Still a perfectly good weapon. No need to supply them with the pesky percussion caps of the newer guns. Each one's fitted with a new flint that will last far longer than any American force can endure, I can tell you that."

Pierre put the musket to his shoulder, sighted it, then pulled the trigger. The hammer fell forward, causing the flint to strike the steel frizzen, briefly giving off sparks that twinkled in the darkness with a loud click. "So then, you didn't have to change flints during their revolution."

The Englishman gave a light chuckle. "They certainly performed well enough against your *empereur* at Waterloo, if I recall."

Pierre conceded the point with a shrug. "Where are the rest?" he asked flatly.

"Safely aboard our ship," the man replied. "Where's the money?"

"You'll have it once we receive full shipment, sir, not a centime before."

The Englishman straightened himself, "My frugal friend, we are practically giving you these muskets. I'm sure the price will make the exchequer think I'm pocketing the difference."

"Bring all the muskets ashore and you'll be paid," Pierre said stiffly.

"We did not come here to play games, sir," the British man said, matching his tone.

"Yet you are engaged in a deadly one," Pierre replied.

The men blinked at each other for a moment. Only the waves filled the silence that ensued. Diego's senses heightened. The threat of violence emanated from the two parties. He watched the men around him intently, waiting for someone to make a move. The man nearest him went for his gun. In a flash, Diego pulled his sword and ran it through the man's hand, pinning it to his hip near his pistol.

"Bloody fucking hell!" the man screamed. "He stabbed me!"

Swords and pistols flared out of their sheaths and holsters. The wounded man sank to his knees, causing Diego's sword to slide out of his wound. The man clutched his bleeding hand and bellowed in agony. Diego darted forward and snatched the man's pistol. He cocked and pointed it at the nearest enemy he could find.

"Whoa! Whoa! Whoa!" the English leader threw his hands in the air. "No one fire a fucking shot or we'll have the gendarmes all over us and then no one will get any guns or money!"

The two parties stared at each other, their extended arms shaking from the weight of their weapons held at the ready. At last, Pierre put up his hands, straightening himself from his defensive crouch. "It's alright, my friends. Put your weapons away," he said in French. Diego saw the others sheathing their swords and holstering their pistols. With a shrug, he wiped his blade on the injured man's jacket and sheathed it.

"I'm sorry, my friend," Pierre said to the man in English. "We are a little on edge tonight."

"I see," the Englishman said, dropping his hands. "Perhaps we are too." Then to his party, "Put away your weapons, boys. We're all friends here." His men started sheathing and holstering their arms.

Diego uncocked the captured pistol, flipped it around, and offered the handle to the groaning man on his knees. The man glared at him, not letting go of his injured hand. Not sure what to do, Diego delicately laid it next to him, then patted him on the shoulder. "Siento," he said sheepishly. The man merely growled.

"Signal the ship," their leader said. "Let them know they can bring the rest. Take Toby back in the launch. We need to get him to the ship's surgeon. Come back with a bottle of brandy and a barrel of beer." His men started moving to carry out his orders. "…And some damn glasses and mugs so we don't have to drink like bloody pirates!" Diego watched as one of the men held up a shielded lantern. He opened and closed the door facing the sea. A couple of flashes of light responded from the darkness out on the water. Two of the men were shoving the launch back into the water with the injured man aboard.

"Honestly, the money's not even important," the Englishman sighed, then smiled at Pierre. "Our purpose is the same. The enemy of our enemy is our friend, as they say. Plus, we'd much rather see these weapons be put to good use than rot away in storage."

"Nonetheless, we'll happily pay you as agreed. I am a man of my word," Pierre said. Then to his friend, "Atilla, let them count it." Atilla came forward with a small chest and presented it to the Englishman, who in turn, nodded to one of his men to take it. The man sat and began to count the contents.

Soon, more launches were coming ashore laden with crates. Pierre's work party came forward and began transferring the load to their carts. "I brought beer for your workers," the Englishman told Pierre, "but first let us gentlemen share a glass of brandy to toast our common cause." Once the glasses were shared amongst them, the Englishman raised his and pronounced, "To our Mexican friends, may they give our expansionist American cousins a good what for!"

"Hear, hear!" some of his men let out, raising their glasses before tossing the amber liquid down their throats. Diego raised an eyebrow at the mention of his countrymen, then followed the examples of the others, trying his best to hide his shuddering from the liquor.

Pierre smiled, watching the confusion on his friend's face. "We brought our very own esteemed Mexican here tonight," he said, gesturing grandly toward Diego with his hand. "May I present our dashing swordsmen: Señor Don Diego de la Vega!"

The Englishman examined Diego with a sly grin, "My word, if they all fight like that, I rather feel sorry for our foolhardy American friends. Another round, boys! To our Aztec warrior, Señor de la Vega, and to Toby's quick recovery!"

"Hear, hear!" the men cheered. Diego scanned the happy faces with a raised eyebrow, then slowly raised his glass to them in return, and drank.

The work went quickly once the crates arrived. Pierre was adamant about not giving the workers the beer until they were completely done. "Hopefully, they'll get drunk and stab each other to death tonight so there'll be no witnesses" he humored darkly. His friends chuckled grimly. Diego narrowed his eyes watching the men work, wondering if his friend would ask him to kill them afterward.

Pierre thanked the British leader before the man stepped into his launch. "It's our pleasure, and this is just the first shipment!" the man told him. "There'll be plenty more, my friend. I must ask, however, that you keep a gentleman's discretion. If word gets out of our involvement, we will deny everything, of course. We must keep up our friendly appearance with the colonials, even as we threaten them with our own war." He laughed with his last sentence, then sighed, "Oh, politics! It makes for such strange bedfellows. I never thought I'd be working with the French to arm the Mexicans to fight the Americans, all while doing a robust trade with all three!"

"These are strange times indeed, *mon ami*," Pierre patted the man on the shoulder, then helped him climb into the launch.

Diego's mind wandered as they rode away, flanking the loaded carts. The Americans, the British, guns for Mexico; what was this game he was caught up in? What part was he playing?

The men unloaded the crates into an underground cache hidden beneath an old barn of a small farm. Pierre paid the men and gave them the barrel of beer to share.

"There'll be more work for you soon," he told them in French, "so long as you can keep your mouths shut. Let me be clear: if any word gets out about this, or if I find any of my cargo missing, we will know who's responsible and you'll never see the shadow that comes for you, nor you will live to see another day." He indicated with his head toward Diego with the last bit. The workers followed his motion with doe-eyed fear to the grim-looking man in black sitting on a black horse. Diego narrowed his eyes at the attention he was getting, not understanding what was being said in French.

"He'll probably eat your children, too," Pierre added, enjoying the reaction from the workers.

"To our Mexican!" Atilla raised his glass in celebration back at Pierre's home. The friends did the same, then tossed back the contents. Diego smiled and drank as well.

"By God, I think I was more startled than the *Rosbifs* when he ran that man through!" Thomas added.

"You did well," Levi said in broken Spanish, patting Diego on the shoulder.

"*Gracias, amigo,*" Diego smiled at the man, appreciating the attempt at his language.

"I told you he'd be useful to our cause," Pierre told them.

The friends enjoyed a small after-party, sipping brandy and sharing stories, recounting their own nervousness at the exciting events of the evening. At last, Pierre begged off, claiming exhaustion. He invited his friends to stay and finish the bottle, but he was off to bed. He could hear them still sharing stories as he climbed the steps to the dark hall that led to his bed chambers. With a sigh of relief, he closed the door behind him, finally alone and at peace.

"Huh!" he gasped at the shadowy figure waiting for him in the darkness. "Good God, Diego! I think you just took two years off my life!"

"I wanted to talk to you alone," Diego told him.

"Why do you always have to be so damn dramatic?" Pierre said, taking his hand off his racing heart. He lit a lamp and then collapsed into one of the chairs. He looked up to see the light flickering in Diego's wide emerald eyes. "Well, let's talk," Pierre shrugged.

"What is this business you have with the English and my country?" Diego asked.

"Please sit," Pierre gestured to the other chair. Diego paused for a moment, then slid into it silently like a cat, still keeping his eyes on his friend. "Please relax," Pierre said, feeling Diego's heightened sense of alertness. "I'm sorry I didn't explain before. This is a very secretive affair and the fewer people who know, the better." Pierre then sighed. "But of all people, I trust you the most, my friend. I should have told you what we were doing first."

"I am listening now."

"The Americans are talking about annexing Texas. Your country is threatening war if they do. There's fear that the Americans want more than Texas. They want to expand all the way to the Pacific."

"The Pacific!" Diego let out. "They wouldn't dare try to take part of Alta California!"

"I dare say they would take all of it if they're able."

"We should have never let those heretics into Texas in the first place." Diego sat back in his chair, shaking his head as he pondered the swirling events. He then turned his eyes back to his friend, "Why are the British involved?"

"They have their own impending war with the *Yanquis*. They're arguing over the Oregon Territory. Both sides are threatening war, but if the Americans are too busy fighting with Mexico, they may not be so interested in also dueling with the Brits."

"Why you? Why don't the British sell the guns directly?"

"Diplomacy, my friend," Pierre smiled. "England can't appear to be negotiating in good faith if they're simultaneously arming America's enemies."

"I see," Diego said, rubbing his chin, contemplating the moving pieces. "Why France, what's in it for you? I thought France was our enemy. Did we not just fight a war over pastries?"

"Ah, the *Pastry War*," Pierre chuckled. "That was five years ago... a misunderstanding amongst friends. Trust me, France has nothing to do with this. As a private citizen, I can simply get the guns past the inevitable blockade sailing under a neutral flag. I'd probably be arrested if my own government knew what I'm up to."

"So why do you do it?" Diego asked.

Pierre looked at him for a moment, then spoke, "I won't insult you with a lie about lofty ideas of an independent Mexico, free of imperial meddling of any of these nations. It's simply money, and perhaps a love for mischief and adventure."

"I see...*Brown Besses*?" The English nickname for the muskets felt strange in Diego's mouth.

"Great weapons. The British used them for over a century. They've switched to percussion cap rifles, and now there's an enormous surplus of the old smooth-bore flintlocks. They may not be as accurate as the new rifles, but we can arm thousands of Mexican patriots to stand against an American invasion. These are the weapons that defeated Napoleon at Waterloo and destroyed his beloved Imperial Guard forever. Imagine the cost they'll inflict on the expansionist Americans if they dare step onto Mexican soil."

"I see..." Diego pondered. He thought of the ragged, heavily bearded Anglos who seeped into California almost daily. Their families were half-starved from the journey. The missions often fed and cared for them regardless of their heretical denial of the true faith. Now it seemed these vagabonds wanted it all. From his experience, he could hardly imagine them being a threat. But somewhere, across the desert, over the mountains, and past a sea of grass, there was a growing nation that was consuming everything around it.

"They must be stopped..." Diego muttered, shuddering at the thought of California falling to the Protestant interlopers.

"Exactly!" Pierre's eyes lit up, knowing he had him. "It's providence that you came to me at this time. You're exactly the man I need. I will send you home with a boatful of guns, Diego. You'll be my man in Mexico. We will push the American imperialists out of Texas, California, and more."

Diego lay exhausted in bed, staring at the ceiling. His mind was racing, keeping him from the sweet sanctuary of sleep. He wondered which letter would get to his father first: the one he wrote saying he needed money to come home, or the one from the university saying he attacked a clergyman and stole from the church. He couldn't bear to think of the disappointment. What would his father say to him once he came home a disgrace and a failure?

What was this intrigue with Pierre? Was this truly his ticket home? Maybe even as a hero? It all seemed wonderfully enticing, yet he couldn't help but feel apprehensive. Was he being used? Was Mexico merely a chess piece in a larger game?

He blinked hard, trying to clear his mind, hoping to find peace before the roosters started crowing. He saw her eyes in the gloom that swirled around the ceiling of his room, the eyes of Pierre's woman, dark and beautiful, seeing everything inside him. He wanted to reach out and touch that angelic face, that delicate white skin. What would it be like to kiss those lips? He groaned, lying awake thinking of her.

Chapter Seven: Little Birds

Pierre's eyes popped open at the sound of someone knocking on the front door below. He blinked at the daylight pouring through the balcony doors. He listened as his servant, Bernard, spoke to this visitor. He couldn't make out the words, but Bernard's voice seemed worried. The other voice was cheerful, bold, and masculine. He could hear the man's boots clatter on the marble floor as the man entered. *Jesus, what time is it?!* he thought, groping for his pocket watch on the nightstand. It was a little past ten. He sat up, putting his feet on the floor, smacking his lips to try to find some saliva in his mouth.

"I'll let him know you're here, monsieur," he could hear Bernard say. "Please allow me a moment to alert him,"

"Fuck..." Pierre gasped. He poured a small glass of brandy and tossed it back, swishing it around to lubricate the pastiness in his mouth before swallowing. He could hear the patter of Bernard's soft shoes coming up the stairs, then a small rap on the door. "Come in, Bernard."

The balding, middle-aged man stuck his head through the small opening he made between the door and the frame. His pronounced nose gave him the impression of a frightened hen that made Pierre smirk, despite his alarm. "Monsieur, there's a man here from the gendarmerie. He asked for you directly."

Pierre let out a sigh, thought for a moment, then spoke, "Tell him I'll be down in a few moments."

"Yes, monsieur," Bernard began to withdraw his head from the door. Pierre caught him before his nose had completely disappeared.

"...and, Bernard..."

"Yes, monsieur," Bernard's frightened eyes peered back through the door.

"Bring me some water and a washing bowl, please."

"Of course, monsieur."

Pierre sat on his bed with his mind racing. *What on earth...?* he pondered. He suddenly felt a chill of panic. *Have I been discovered so quickly?* "Those damned drunken peasants..." he mumbled out loud. Bernard returned with a light knock. "Come in!" Pierre called to him, then hoisted himself off the bed. "Thank you," he said as the man slipped back out of the room. Bernard had set a tray on the dresser with an ewer of water, a towel, a bowl, and some soap. There was also a glass, which Pierre filled with water and drank down in one go. He picked up his bone-handled, pig-haired brush and started scrubbing the film off his teeth.

He splashed his face, then used his wet hands to smooth back his long blond hair. Once in his trousers, shirt, and waistcoat, he poured another brandy and drank it in one gulp.

"Ah, Monsieur Godfrey *le fils*," the man in the blue uniform turned from the painting he had been admiring to address him as Pierre came down the grand steps into the parlor. The man held his bicorne hat under his arm. "Are your parents not here today?"

"No, they've returned to our estates in Normandy. I am here alone with just my servant, Bernard. How can I help you?"

"Ah, so direct for such a young man, it's refreshing," the man said, stroking his heavy mustache. "I am Lieutenant Saint Cloud. I hope I am not disturbing you."

"Not at all, Lieutenant. How can I be of assistance?"

"Oh, it is but a trifling matter," the man smiled. "We have reports of a mysterious ship unloading on the beach. You know how smugglers are constantly trying to avoid our tariffs at the quays. A party was seen carrying this load on several carts to an unknown location."

"What does this have to do with me?" Pierre interrupted, allowing too much anger to seep into his tone.

The gendarme paused to regard him for a moment, then smiled slowly, "Nothing, of course, monsieur. I just had it from one of my little birds that you were out and about late last night. I'm just wondering if you saw anything suspicious, like the movement of several laden carts in the middle of the night." He then let out a light chuckle, "Please have mercy on a poor lawman. I'm just following any lead I can find."

"Who is this *little bird*?"

"You must forgive me, monsieur. But I must protect my informants. I assure you, there was no malice meant."

"I see. Well, if you must know, I was engaged in wooing a young lady last night. I was nowhere near the beach nor did I see any carts full of contraband," he said stiffly.

"How romantic! May I ask whom?" the lieutenant beamed.

"As a gentleman, I beg that I don't have to bring her name into this. But if you must know exactly where I was last night, I can have her father, with whom I had permission, vouch for me," Pierre said, losing his patience.

"Monsieur, you entirely misunderstand me. I was merely being nosey and perhaps overstepped a line of decency. I beg your forgiveness," he said with a slight bow.

"Of course, lieutenant, no offense taken. I appreciate you protecting our harbor from smugglers and what other mischief comes from the sea. Unfortunately, I cannot help you. Last night my eyes were only for a beautiful young lady. I assure you, though, if I find any information about such clandestine trade happening in the moonlight, I will contact you, Lieutenant…?"

"Saint Cloud, monsieur. I am ever thankful and humbled by your helpfulness."

"Yes, of course," Pierre offered him a slight smile. The man smiled back. They looked at each other for a moment in silence. Pierre's lips started twitching from holding the expression under the gendarme's gaze.

The lieutenant's eyes narrowed at the slight tremor. He then expanded his own smile. "Good day, monsieur." He bowed, then made his way to the door, setting his bicorne on his head as he stepped outside.

Pierre waited for the door to shut before closing his eyes and sighing. He dropped his face into his hands and held it there for a moment before drawing his fingers through his hair and clutching the back of his neck. He drew in a sibilant breath through his teeth. He stood there for a moment, wondering if he was revealing too much of a reaction in front of Bernard. Then he felt a shadow hanging over him. A new presence had come into this space.

He recovered his smile and turned to see Diego standing at the top of the stairs, frowning in confusion, shirtless and darkly unshaven with tussled black hair. Smooth olive skin covered his subtly athletic build, his big green eyes clearly visible from the foyer. The man was annoyingly attractive.

"Clean yourself up," Pierre called up to him in Spanish. "We're going on a date." He then turned to Bernard and spoke French, "Some eggs, coffee, and toasted bread, please."

Bernard quivered with nervousness, bewildered by the visitor and his master's reaction to him. "Of course, monsieur," he said as he withdrew into the kitchen.

Claudette was beginning to feel foolish. Lavinia had insisted that she prepare herself and be ready by noon. "You don't want him to surprise you if he comes early. What if your hair isn't done?!" she warned.

"Pffft! That would be his fault then," Claudette answered.

"Don't be so flippant, child!" Lavinia chided. "You think you'll be pretty forever? Do not push a good man away when you have one in your grasp. Don't make mistakes out of your youthful folly that you'll regret for the rest of your life."

"But which path is truly the mistake?" Claudette quipped.

"Oh, you're impossible! Sit down so I can brush your hair."

That was hours ago. Now, she was sweating in her clothes, waiting for someone, who, she was beginning to think, wasn't going to show up. *Good!* she thought, then tried to focus on her reading. She didn't get far before she heard the rattle of the carriage approaching.

"He's here!" Lavinia let out before Claudette could even form the thought. "Quickly, let me freshen you up!" she said, then insisted that Claudette retreat to her room upstairs so she could call her down once Pierre had come inside. Claudette felt foolish sitting in her room waiting as she strained to listen to the pleasantries that were being exchanged at the door.

"Won't you come in, monsieur?" she heard Lavinia's deep alto voice say. "I'll go get her." Then she heard the patter of feet coming up the stairs. The door flew open. Lavinia stood there with her eyes bulging, motioning with her head for Claudette to come out. Claudette sighed and rolled her eyes as she hoisted herself from her chair.

Pierre was standing below as she came to the banister. He turned and smiled grandly at her. "Monsieur Godfrey, what a pleasure to see you," she said.

"Please, call me Pierre," he smiled. He was handsome like she remembered from the night before, but the daylight now showed a pallor of skin and dark circles under his eyes. "You look beautiful," he said. "May I call you Claudette?"

"Yes, of course," Claudette smiled softly as she made her way down the steps, holding her skirts so she wouldn't trip.

Pierre held out his hand and helped her down the final steps, then led her to a set of chairs. Lavinia beamed at the sight of the pretty couple. "Shall I bring you some refreshments? Coffee, Tea?"

"Coffee would be great," Pierre smiled, "and for you, my lady?"

"I'll take some too, please," Claudette said shyly.

They talked lightly about weather and art, staying away from politics and other heavier subjects. She found Pierre to be a good conversationalist, but he seemed agitated, fidgeting and checking his pocket watch often. A light sweat formed on his brow at times, which he dabbed lightly with a handkerchief.

"Shall I open a window?" she asked.

"I've got a better idea," he smiled. "I've brought a carriage. Perhaps we could take it to the shore and walk by the sea."

Claudette looked over to Lavinia, who pretended to be lost in her knitting and not paying attention to their conversation. Lavinia looked up and nodded.

"Sure," Claudette returned her gaze to Pierre. "But I should bring Lavinia as a chaperone."

"Oh, you two go ahead," Lavinia stepped in. "You should have time to talk alone. Just bring her back before supper, monsieur. I can only hold off her parents for so long."

Pierre laughed, "Of course, madame."

The open-air ride into town was delightful. The sound of the street and the clattering of the wheels made the silent moments between them more bearable. She couldn't help but notice a man with a wide-brimmed hat was following them on horseback. He was keeping a respectable distance, but looked alert and attentive.

"Is that your guitar player, Pierre?" she asked, turning back to him.

"Diego, yes," Pierre chuckled. "He's also very useful with a sword and pistol. I keep him around for security."

"Security? Are we in any danger?" she asked, somewhat disturbed.

"Of course not, my dear," he took the opportunity to squeeze her hand. "I am a wealthy man. He's merely there to make sure no one takes an opportunity with me on the street."

"I see…" she said, looking back at the grim-looking man that followed them. "Did you say he's Spanish?"

"Pfft, hardly," Pierre chuckled. "He's a Mexican, a *mestizo* even. He claims his family are aristocrats living out there on the very edge of the world, but he's really not much more than a country bumpkin." Pierre stole a glance back at his friend. "Still, that savage blood makes him quite a bodyguard and not a bad guitarist either."

"Savage blood…" she mused, stealing another glimpse at the man who followed them. She had never seen anyone who was truly from the New World. She had heard stories of the colonies and the frontiers where settlers tussled with these mysterious people. Some of the stories were horrific, others were sad, and some, noble. She was fascinated at actually seeing someone who carried this exotic blood.

"How do you know him?" she asked.

"School in Barcelona. The hidalgos in New Spain, or Mexico now, send their mixed-breed sons there to try to turn them into gentlemen. But some of them just can't be tamed," he laughed lightly, stealing another glance at his friend. Diego's eyes narrowed as he began to sense the attention they were paying him.

They left the carriage behind and continued on foot, passing the vendors that lined the boardwalk. Pierre put up a polite hand in refusal as the men with their carts called out to them to try their sweet pastries, savory meats, and iced creams. The two descended onto the beach and walked among the other couples, families, and fishermen who passed to and fro. Claudette took in a deep draft of sea air through her nose, smiling at the sights surrounding her.

The harbor was hugged by high craggy hills and filled with vessels of all sizes. Tiny fishing boats with lateen sails darted in and out of the way of the heavier steamships and tall-masted sailboats.

The city of Marseille sat stacked up on the hills opposite the sea. Its winding roads and bright mismatched pastel houses created a kaleidoscope of confusion and wonderment.

She gazed at the water, watching the soft waves advance and retreat while little birds scurried back and forth, picking into the wet sand with their needle-like beaks. She suddenly had the urge to tear off her dress and run naked into the water. She let out a giggle. *What would he think?*

"What is it?" Pierre asked, noticing her sudden mirth.

"Oh, the little birds," she decided to say, "they are so busy in the waves."

"They certainly have their own business to attend, far removed from the scale and worries of our world," he said, now watching them too.

"I wonder if we are also ignorant of a grander scheme of things happening around us," she mused, watching them.

"Perhaps for the better, I suppose. Just like them, we are merely hunting the waves, looking for something to sustain us…"

He drew silent again, then slowly came to a halt. She stopped and looked up at him, then followed his eyes. His friends were standing on the boardwalk, all three looking grim. The man she knew as Atilla was beckoning him with his hand. Pierre turned and looked back at the man idling some fifty meters behind them and waved him forward.

Diego looked around for a moment as if somewhat surprised to be suddenly acknowledged by the couple. Then, with shrug, trotted up to them.

"¿Si?" he asked as he slowed to a walk.

"Stay with her for a moment," Pierre told him in Spanish. "I'll be just a minute," he said, motioning with his head to his friends who were waiting for him with an air of urgency.

"Por supuesto," Diego said turning his eyes to Claudette. His sudden nearness and direct gaze startled her.

"I'll be just a moment, my dear," Pierre told her in French. She was thankful to have a reason to draw her eyes away from the newcomer. She looked at Pierre with a small amount of fear. "There's nothing to be alarmed about, my dear," he smiled at her. "My apologies, I'm afraid I might have some business to attend, but I won't be long. Diego here will keep you company," he said, slapping Diego on the shoulder.

"Of course," she said. Then watched Pierre walk away to meet his friends. Suddenly, there was a strange silence in the cacophony of seagulls, children playing, and the waves. She could feel his nearness. Fear and exhilaration crept through her. She turned to him. He was still watching Pierre walk to his friends with focused apprehension. She took the opportunity to look him over. She noticed a pistol and dagger hidden in his sash under his waist jacket. She wondered if this man had ever killed anyone. He seemed to become aware of her gaze and slowly turned to her. She cleared her throat and attempted to make conversation.

"*Vous appréciez votre séjour en France, monsieur?*" she asked.

His eyes flickered a brief sense of panic before responding, "*Pardon, je ne parle pas français,*" then switching languages, "*¿Habla español, señora?*"

She giggled lightly, then caught herself, and covered her mouth lightly with her hand in slight embarrassment, but still smiled warmly at him with her eyes. His eyes softened in response. Suddenly, he seemed less frightening. "*No...señor,*" she said, "Do you speak English?" She saw an understanding flash in his eyes. He narrowed them as he looked aloft to Pierre and his friends, then returned to her.

"Yes, I speak the tongue of the heretics," he said with dark conviction.

She stifled another giggle at the overly dramatic response. "I see," she said, then looked over at Pierre and his friends engaged in serious conversation. "Is it a secret, sir?"

Diego followed her eyes and her meaning. He returned them to her. She felt her breath nearly swept away at their brilliance. "It is more of discretion, my lady."

"I see...then I shall be discrete about it as well, my friend," She smiled at him, and for the first time, she saw his serious mask slip away. What replaced it was a full, charming, even boyish smile filled with mischief and warmth. It cut straight through her, unlocking chains she never knew she carried, and opening doors she knew she could never shut again. She shuddered as the change swept through her.

"I thank you for your kindness, my lady," he bowed grandly.

She giggled with embarrassment at the dramatic gesture. "Please, call me Claudette. We are friends now, sir, are we not?"

He smiled as he came out of his bow. "Claudette…" he said, feeling the sensation of speaking her name out loud for the first time. "I am Diego, then, at your service…Claudette."

"Diego..?" she said, saying the name for the first time. "Would that be David in English?"

"James, actually. It is short for *Santiago*, which is short for Saint James."

"Oh, it seems like it would be David," she said, trying to follow the logic.

"One would think, *Little Claudia*," he grinned.

She let out a laugh, "'*Little Claudia*?!' My name is the same in all languages, you silly man!"

"Yes, but it seems it would be '*Little Claudia*' in English, would it not?"

She clutched his arm and laughed. The sensation of touching him for the first time was exhilarating. "Alright, you've made your point. Diego, it is!"

Diego chuckled lightly along with her, "Still, I think I prefer to call you, *Little Claudia*."

"Oh, you're an impossible man!" She squeezed his arm, delighting in the way his Mexican accent emphasized the 'i' in 'little' making it come out 'LEE-tul.'

"He is coming," Diego said, dropping the levity in his voice. She looked up to see his stern mask had returned. She followed his eyes to see Pierre marching toward them. She let go of his arm, suddenly feeling like she had been guilty of something. She struggled to find something natural to be doing with her hands as her suitor approached.

"I'm sorry for the interruption, my dear," he said. "Business sometimes knows no sense of timing."

"It's fine, I assure you," she told him, seeing the worry and agitation on his face.

"Diego," Pierre turned to his friend and spoke Spanish, "please give us a moment, my friend."

"*Por supuesto*." Diego withdrew, walking alone toward the sea. Claudette felt suddenly alone without him.

"Claudette," Pierre softened his voice. She looked back up at him. A tenuous smile spread across his worried face. "It's business that will keep me in high finances, for sure. My family is already wealthy, of course, and my prospects are good..." he paused, searching her eyes.

"I would think so, monsieur," she assured him.

He let out a light nervous laugh. "I'm glad to have your confidence in that," he said. He dropped his eyes to the ground. She looked down too, feeling and absorbing his nervousness. She saw his hands reach out to take hers. She fought the urge to flinch and pull them away. His hands were cool and smooth. He drew her hands up. She followed them with her eyes, then found his big blue eyes looking into hers. "...because I want to ask you to be my wife."

The blood ran from her face. Chills ran through her body, then concentrated in her stomach, leaving a hollow feeling of dread. She took a step back, withdrawing her hands. "Monsieur! We have only begun to know each other. How can you be so forward?!"

Pierre furrowed his brow, caught off guard by her reaction, then looked around to see if any of the passersby were taking note of the unfortunate scene. He caught a glimpse of Diego, off watching the waves, occasionally looking back at the couple to make sure they were safe.

"Yes, yes, I understand. I'm a bit too bold, but things are moving quickly for me, and...you had to know this was coming eventually, whether now or in the weeks or months to come if we did everything properly."

Claudette searched for words. He was right, but she had still hoped to have some time before the inevitable happened. The only thing she could come up with was, "...my parents..."

"I assure you, I already have your father's permission. He would not have allowed us together today if he didn't know my intentions."

"I just don't know...it...it's so sudden."

"I know. I'm sorry," he said, "I am bold. I am a man of action. When I see what I want, I take it. You may not know it yet, but this is what you want too. I'm here to help guide you to what's best."

"What's best?!" she exclaimed, then drew her mouth back in outrage. Tears began to fill her eyes. She pulled her hands to her mouth as she stifled a sob. Pierre looked around to see who was noticing his embarrassing predicament. Diego had turned around and was now watching with intense concern. Pierre shook his head and waved him off, then pulled out a handkerchief.

"Here, please..." he said softly. "I should not have done this here in public. I was wrong to put you on the spot. Please, don't cry, not here...people are watching."

Claudette lifted her tear-blurred eyes at him, smirking bitterly. "Let them watch."

Pierre let out a breath, "Alright, let's go. I was wrong to put you on the spot. I just have so much on my mind, I thought I'd get this taken care of quickly." Claudette stayed silent as they walked back to the carriage. Pierre nodded to Diego to follow. "You can think about it. We have time. I think you'll feel better once you've thought it through logically."

"Logically..." she repeated softly as if she were weighing the word's meaning.

Chapter Eight: Hunters and Prey

They rode back in awkward silence. Pierre did his best to make light conversation but only got minimal responses for his effort. Eventually, he gave up and stared out the side of the carriage. Claudette stared out the other. She watched the street scenes go by, wanting to jump out and disappear into the crowd forever. She wanted to look back. She wanted to see if Diego was still back there, following with his grim-set face, watching over them. She was certain he was. She found comfort in knowing he was there: a protector. The urge to look was overwhelming, but she did not dare.

"Oh, God…" she groaned as they came up the gravel drive to her home. Her parents were there, smiling and waving, so uncharacteristic of them.

"Here are the love birds now!" she heard her father call out. Claudette closed her eyes and squeezed the bridge of her nose with her thumb and forefinger in embarrassment.

"Oh, you two look so pretty together!" she heard her mother say. *That's the first nice thing she's said to me in years!* she thought bitterly. The carriage came to a stop. The coachman sprung from his bench, lowered the step, opened the small door, and offered his hand to her. Claudette brushed past him with tunnel-visioned fury. "Let us take a look at you two," her mother beamed.

"Leave me alone!" Claudette spat as she stormed past them into the house. Bewildered, her parents looked to Pierre who softly shook his head as if to say, "Let her go."

Lavinia was inside smiling grandly, "So…?"

"You were in on this, weren't you?" Claudette blurted, the tears welling in her eyes.

Lavinia recoiled in surprise at the outburst, "Child, we only care for your future."

"My future?! What about what I care for my future?!" she felt the tears run down her face again and a wave of impotent frustration course through her body. "Oh, just leave me alone!" she cried, then ran up the stairs, slamming the door behind her. She flung herself onto her bed and wept. She could hear her father invite Pierre inside. Her parents were apologizing profusely.

"She's still just a child," she could hear her mother say. "She'll come around."

"It's fine," Pierre assured them, annoyingly being a perfect gentleman. "I shouldn't have been so forward..." he said as she heard him entering the house. She pressed her face into her pillow and cried harder. Now she was embarrassed. She had made a fool out of herself in front of him and her parents. Still, the idea that everyone but her had a say in her life filled her with rage.

She sat up and wiped her tears on her sleeve. She had to pull herself together. *This is why they don't trust me to make any of my own decisions*, she thought. She was determined to prove that she wasn't a little girl anymore. She stood up, straightened her dress, and walked to the window, lying to herself that she merely wanted fresh air.

He was there, sitting on his horse behind the carriage. He was looking at her window with deep concern in his eyes. A light laugh escaped her at the sight of him with such a worried look. His boyish smile returned, sweeping away the concern from his face. He was pretty when he smiled, she decided. The late afternoon sun sparkled in his green eyes.

"Are you well, Little Claudia?" he asked, smiling at the attention she was giving him.

"I am now, David," She said

He laughed, shaking his head. "That is fair," he said. "You can call me anything you want." Joy spread through her, and in that moment, all she wanted to do was leap from the window onto the back of his horse, and beg him to take her away.

His smile fell away at the sound of the door. Claudette retreated into her room. Pierre was speaking tersely to him in Spanish. *I hope I didn't get him in any trouble*, she thought, trying to make out what he was saying.

"Tie your horse to the back of the carriage and get in. We need to talk," Pierre said as he emerged from the Moreau house.

"Of course," Diego replied, leaping from his horse. He worried suddenly that the secret fancies of his heart had been revealed. He couldn't bring himself to look at his friend, fearing that Pierre would see right through him. The carriage rocked as he entered and sat next to him. His closeness suddenly felt awkward. The driver gave a slap of the reins and they were off, rolling down the driveway. The crunching sound of the wheels on the pebble stones mercifully filled up the silence between them.

"We have much work to do," Pierre said at last. Diego remained silent. "We must move the guns tonight."

"That's fine," Diego said.

"There's a rat among us, Diego," Pierre said, looking at him at last, his fierce blue eyes burning holes into him, making him wonder if Pierre was referring to him directly. "One of the workers ran his mouth and now the gendarmes are sniffing all around us like dogs running down a fox."

"I see," Diego said softly, relieved it wasn't him who had evoked his friend's fury.

"I'm glad you do," Pierre said, softening his voice, much to Diego's relief. Then his voice sharpened like cold steel. "When we find the identity of this rat, you will kill him, maybe his family too. I want you to cut out his tongue and leave him where he'll be found. That'll teach the rest of them to keep their mouths shut."

They rode out to the old farm where they had been the night before. Thomas, Atilla, and Levi were waiting for them with carts and mules. "*Bueñas noches*," Levi nodded to him with a wink.

Diego leaped from the carriage. "*Buenas*," he responded. The other men nodded to him as well with a new respect since the events of the previous night.

This time the workers weren't there. The five men removed their jackets and waistcoats, rolled up their shirtsleeves, and went to work retrieving the crates and hoisting them onto the carts in grim silence. At last, the work was done. Atilla lit a pipe. It glowed in the darkness, illuminating his piercing eyes. Diego listened intently, trying to pick out any understanding he could as the four spoke French in hushed and hurried voices. The men patted Levi on the shoulder and handed him a jug of wine and a small bundle that appeared to be food before turning away to the carts and horses.

Diego remained, looking quizzically at the man left behind with provisions. Levi smiled humorously at Diego's confusion. "I am your dog sniffing out your prey, Señor Hunter!" Levi laughed in his heavily French-accented Spanish.

Diego lifted an eyebrow, trying to hide his alarm and confusion, "Good hunting, then, my friend."

The days that followed were tense but bearable. Claudette did her best to pretend her outburst never happened. Lavinia and her parents also did their best to reciprocate. An awkward cordialness settled on the house as no one wanted to reignite the passions that had followed her outing with Pierre. As for her suitor, he sent letters and even chocolates and flowers. Claudette dared not open them for fear of reliving her embarrassment, nor did she nibble on even one piece of chocolate, as if doing so would oblige her to accept his proposal. She could barely allow herself to take in the aroma and beauty of the flowers.

The stilted quiet of the house allowed for reading and perhaps reflection. Monsieur Dumas's new story was appearing in the weekly paper. She read with forlorn desire about the young D'Artagnan riding alone to Paris to seek his destiny. *Oh, what it must be like to be a man and master of your own fate!* she swooned, looking out the window at the fields of grapevines and the hills that hid the city from her eyes. Somewhere over those hills was the man with the mess of black hair and green eyes that sparkled in the sun. She could see his boyish smile, so natural and different from the stern face that he carried. She tried to recall his smell from the fleeting moments they spent together.

"He'll probably be at the ball, dear," her mother said, stepping into the parlor. "You really should consider coming."

"Huh?!" Claudette was shocked at her mother's intrusion into her thoughts.

"Monsieur Dumas, of course! I see you're reading his serial in the paper," her mother clarified, seeing the horror and confusion on her daughter's face. "He'll be leaving for Paris soon. This might be your last chance for an autograph."

"Oh, I wouldn't bother him for such a trifling thing," Claudette said, looking back out the window.

"Ah, but all is trifling when you're young and pretty, my dear. You really shouldn't be so dismissive of the opportunities you have now. They will torment you with regret long after you've let them slip away."

Claudette sighed, "I know who we're really talking about, mamá."

"Just be kind, dear, and cordial. He knows he made a mistake. Give him the opportunity to make it better. You'll begin to see him anew."

Claudette knew her mother meant well and was truly concerned for her. There really wasn't a reason to reject Pierre. She certainly didn't want to have another embarrassing outburst in front of her parents or let it be known among the gossipers in town that she was petulant in resisting his suit. Still, she could feel the tentacles of this presupposed future wrapping around her limbs and dragging her down into its abyss.

"I'll come, Mamá," she said softly. "I'll be good."

The sound of horses and marching men broke Levi from his reverie. *Aha! They come at last!* he thought as he blew out his single candle. He was happy it happened on his watch. The friends had been watching over the old abandoned barn for days. They took turns, spending the night in hidden seclusion, waiting for the rat to reveal himself.

Levi tossed down the remains of the wine in his cup and quickly gathered up his sketch pad, blanket, and things. He then dared a peek through the slats of wood in the wall to see a collection of torches working their way up the hill in the evening gloom. He smiled grandly at the sight and then scurried up the ladder to the hayloft above.

The barn door opened. He could hear the clattering muskets and boots entering below. Levi peered from his hiding space. The torchlight flickered in his eyes It glimmered on the bayonets as the blue-uniformed gendarmes entered. Some were holding torches while others held their weapons at the ready. Their sergeant scanned the room, then turned to the open door and called to his commander. "All clear, Lieutenant!"

A man in shabby work clothes stumbled into the room. He had been obviously shoved by someone outside. The gendarmes laughed as the man fumbled for his balance then snatched his soft-knit cap from the ground and clutched it with both hands. Levi's eyes narrowed as he recognized him from the work crew they had assembled to unload the guns several nights before. Then he watched as Lieutenant Saint Cloud strolled in with his bicorne tucked under his arm. His riding spurs clinked as his boots thumped the hard-packed ground.

"Alright, monsieur Basset," he said, stroking his mustache, "show me the guns."

"Of course, monsieur," the man sputtered, twisting his cap with his hands and then shoving it back on his head. He dropped to his knees and began sweeping the loose straw from the ground with his hands. Saint Cloud watched with growing interest as the shape of a wooden door was revealed. Basset stopped and sat back on his knees. "Hmm…" the man said quietly.

"Is there a problem, monsieur?" Saint Cloud prodded.

"The lock…it's missing," the man said. Beads of sweat began to form on his brow.

"Open it then," Saint Cloud instructed. "Let's see what other mysteries lie beneath."

With some effort, the man lifted the door and let it flop open in a puff of dust. Saint Cloud nodded at two of his men. They descended the hidden steps. One led with his bayonet held forward while the other held a torch. Moments later, the man with the torch popped his head up from the abyss. "There's nothing down here, Lieutenant."

"But…but…there must have been about a hundred and fifty crates!" Basset protested.

"Close it back up," Saint Cloud ordered.

"I still get my money, right?" Basset pleaded. "I told you everything I know."

Saint Cloud turned to his sergeant, "Take Monsieur Basset outside and pay him for our time."

Levi grinned at the sound of Basset's squealing protests as the sergeant and two other men dragged him outside and proceeded to pummel him with their fists and boots. Saint Cloud turned on his heel. "Let's go," he commanded. His men fell in behind him and marched out. Levi slid down the ladder, pulled out his dagger, and stepped outside. Basset was already up and hobbling after the lawmen.

"Wait for me!" he cried, "don't leave me alone in the dark!"

Levi hissed at the missed opportunity and then broke into a quiet trot behind them, keeping his distance and moving from shadow to shadow.

The carriage pulled into line behind the others and waited for its turn to pull up to the house and unload its passengers. Claudette suddenly regretted coming. *Everyone is going to know*, she thought as they rolled up to the next position.

"Don't fuss, honey," her mother said, reading her mood. "People want to see you."

That made it worse. She flashed her parents a brief look. They were watching her, smiling with agitated anticipation in their eyes. She quickly looked away, turning her eyes back to the line of carriages inching forward as each one unloaded its guests onto the torch-lit steps that led to the house. Suddenly she felt she was walking into a trap. Everything inside her told her to run.

The carriage moved forward and stopped again in front of the house. "Oh, at last!" her mother huffed.

"Hmm," her father grunted, sliding his pince-nez into his pocket, then folding his newspaper, and dousing the lamp.

The carriage door opened. Claudette took the hand that offered to help her down. "Huh!" she gasped at the sight of the man helping her. Pierre's big blue eyes sparkled in the torchlight. He looked splendid in his blue velvet vest and black coat.

"Please tell me you're not unhappy to see me, my love," he smiled.

"Of course not," she answered quickly, bewildered by the surprise. She stole a look at her parents who were grinning mischievously to each other, a rare moment of acknowledgment and affection between the two.

"Then I hope you have forgiven me for my indiscretions. I've been waiting eagerly for your reply to my letters, my dear."

"Of course," she said softly, embarrassed by the moment and the memory of the last time they were together. Her parents began climbing the steps.

"Shall we?" Pierre smiled at her, gesturing with his hand to the steps. She nodded softly, taking his arm as they climbed.

A servant called out as they entered the room. "The Monsieur and Madame Moreau!" a few people turned and smiled at her parents, who waved and then walked a few steps down to the dance floor. They turned and looked up, beaming with pride at their daughter and the gentleman escorting her. "The Monsieur Godfrey and the Mademoiselle Moreau!" the servant called out again. Claudette blushed ferociously. Several of the guests started turning their heads to see them enter.

"To the beautiful new couple!" someone shouted, raising a glass of champagne.

"Hear, hear!" called another. A light round of applause rose above the music. Claudette covered her mouth with her hand in embarrassment. Pierre smiled grandly and waved as they descended the steps to a small crowd of well-wishers. If a hole had opened up in the floor at that moment, Claudette was sure she'd jump in. Instead, she suffered through the congratulations, as ladies kissed her cheeks and men kissed her hand.

At last, Pierre took her to the floor, where she no longer had to acknowledge the congratulations and kind-hearted questions about their assumed betrothal. Still, the dance floor offered no escape as people stopped to admire the beautiful couple execute the well-practiced steps of the quadrille.

After several sets, Pierre led her off the dance floor where they joined the crowd watching from the side. "Ah, perfect timing!" he said happily, taking two glasses of bubbly white wine from a passing servant. She was happy to have something to do with her hands. She took a sip. It was crisp and tart. It tickled her throat and then entered her belly with a calming warmth. Pierre was waving to his friends across the way. "If you'll excuse me for a moment, dear," he said, turning to her

"Of course," she said, trying not to seem too eager to see him go. She sighed in relief as she watched him move across the floor. Perhaps this was what her life would be, something tolerable. There would be moments like this, moments of peace.

She looked around the floor, wondering if he had brought Diego and what she would say to him if anything. Plenty of the young men Pierre associated with were there. She could see them laughing and patting him on the shoulder, probably congratulating him on the proposal that she had yet to accept. She let out another sigh. Did she ever have a choice? She looked among the gallery of young men, disappointed not to see the mysterious dark man from the exotic place far away. Suddenly she worried he'd gone back already, that she'd never see him again.

"Ah, the beautiful Mademoiselle Claudette Moreau," a friendly and familiar voice said.

"Monsieur Dumas," she turned and smiled. "I was worried I'd miss seeing you before you left for Paris."

Dumas beamed, taking her hand and kissing it with a low and stately bow. "I could not bear leaving without taking in your beautiful countenance one more time."

"Oh, monsieur, you unduly flatter me," she blushed with a slight curtsy.

"No, my dear, merely being in your presence, it is I who is flattered," he smiled mischievously.

"Now you mock me, monsieur!" she giggled, slapping him lightly on the chest.

He drew his hand to his chest with a feigned look of hurt surprise that seemed to say, "Who, me?!" The sly grin returned to his face, "I suppose I should congratulate you."

Claudette sighed in annoyance then quickly regained her composure. "Thank you, monsieur," she said, slightly embarrassed at the slip. Dumas's large eyes narrowed as he examined her more closely. Claudette laughed nervously, "What is it?"

He looked at her for another agonizing moment of silent inspection before speaking in a low voice. "Something about you has changed…" he said, searching her eyes.

"I assure you I am the same as I was the last time you saw me," she said, now a little worried at what he was seeing.

"Hmm…" he mused, then his eyes lit up with revelation. "You're in love! I can smell it on you."

"Monsieur, I…" she sputtered.

Dumas turned to look at Pierre, who was smiling and making conversation with his circle of friends. Claudette looked as well. Dumas turned back to her, drawing her eyes again to his. "But perhaps the fortunate man isn't here, is he…?" he smiled slyly, his eyes twinkling with devilish delight.

Claudette stared at him with opened-mouth shock, "Monsieur Dumas, I..I…"

He squeezed her arm gently and smiled, "It's okay, child. Your secret is safe with me. I'm just sad I'm not the one."

Claudette blinked at him for a moment and then smiled bashfully before dropping her eyes to the ground.

"There you are, you devil of a man!" Veronica's voice cut through the moment. "Leave her alone! She's spoken for!"

Dumas stole one last glance at Claudette before her bombastic friend was upon them. "You're about to have quite an adventure, my dear. I would like to know about it someday. I'm sure it would make a good book!"

Claudette looked back at him and smiled. Dumas's eyes twinkled warmly in response. Veronica threw her arm around him. "I, on the other hand, am sadly without a dance partner!" she said.

Dumas's eyes widened with comical surprise as he drew his mouth into a silent, "Ooh!" He turned to her and smiled grandly. "Then I shall remedy that immediately, mademoiselle!" He turned back to Claudette and gave her a wink. She smiled at him and then watched the two disappear into the swirl of dancers.

The ball turned out to be not as dreadful as she had feared. There was the initial embarrassment of being announced with Pierre as if they were already a married couple. Then there were all the well-wishers, congratulating them on the wedding they assumed would come soon. But the wine softened her frustration, and it was good to see so many friends. It was especially nice to spend a moment with the famous Alexandre Dumas before he left for Paris.

She sighed as she sat on her bed. Looking out her window she could see the faint glow of Marseille over the hilltops and under the canopy of stars. She wished she could go to Paris with Monsieur Dumas. Anywhere but here would be grand, maybe even…Mexico.

Diego crept back into her mind: dark and mysterious, charming and boyish. What would it be like to lay with him under the stars in the desert of his homeland? "Ca-li-for-n-i-a," she said softly, feeling the pronunciation of the Spanish name for the first time in her mouth.

The lonely sound of a single violin drifted through her window. She smiled, *She's calling me!* A pang of guilt ran through her. They had not spoken much since her outburst. Lavinia had since kept on with her duties with quiet humility. Normally, she would have been waiting for her late into the night to help remove her corset and to hear the gossip from the ball. Now she was playing coy, Claudette decided. *Fine. I shall go to her then.*

Dressed in her corset and drawers, she crawled out of her window, climbed down the ivy, then followed the music to the kitchen house like she had done so many times before. The thrill of sneaking out into the night air tingled through her and ignited a sense of warm nostalgia.

The window there flickered from a single candle. Lavinia stopped playing as soon as she sensed Claudette had come through the door. "I hope I wasn't keeping you awake, mademoiselle," she said, setting her instrument on the table and lighting her pipe from the candle.

"Of course not," Claudette said. Lavinia turned to her, first with apprehension, then smiled as she read the warm friendliness on her face.

"How was the ball?" she asked, taking a puff from her pipe.

"It was fine," Claudette said, slumping into the other chair. "Everyone congratulated me for the wedding I didn't know I was participating in."

"Hmm…" Lavinia said thoughtfully, guarding her thoughts.

Claudette frowned as she regarded her. A tear formed in her eye. "I'm sorry I spoke to you harshly."

"It's fine, child. I know these are difficult times for you. Your heart is still young and wild. I only want your enduring happiness."

"I know," Claudette said, reaching out and squeezing her hand. "All I want is the truth. What is it that you see when you read my cards that you won't tell me? What is it that scares you so?"

"The cards are nothing more than a parlor game, child. Divination is the art of reading people, not the cards or crystal balls."

"Yet you read the same thing every time. I've seen it in your eyes. I want to know what it is."

Lavinia drew in the smoke from her pipe, eyeing the young woman carefully, then exhaled. She leaned forward, focusing her eyes deeply as she peered into Claudette's. "It is the fool, child, the disrupter. He will lead you astray, down a path that leads only to despair."

"Pierre?" Claudette asked, feigning ignorance.

Lavinia narrowed her right eye and dug in deeper, "You know who. He is the shadow that haunts you."

Claudette sat back in her chair, recoiling from the truth of what she already knew. It had just been laid bare before her. "What about love? Does not love matter in a woman's life?"

"Hmph!" Lavinia snorted. "Love is for girls to swoon and break their hearts over. Marriage isn't about love, child. It's about security. It's about having children and building a family. Tame your wild heart, girl, before it leads you to ruin."

Claudette eyed her for a moment, digging deep into her eyes and finding what she was looking for, "Did you not love your husband then…?"

A carousel of emotions flashed through Lavinia's eyes: surprise, anger, then pride in the girl she had been teaching for so long. She closed her eyes and smiled as she sat back in her chair, then opened them again as she relit her pipe. "That was different. We were, as your people call us, poor dirty gypsies. All we had was love."

Claudette leaned forward, her dark eyes wild with passion, digging deep into Lavinia and breaking through her defenses. "Then isn't love everything?"

Diego rode out to the barn at dawn. He brought a second horse just in case their work was done and the night watcher could return with him. Otherwise, Levi could take both horses back and Diego would stay until Thomas relieved him the next day.

He held his face up to the sun and let it splash over him. The warmth was invigorating as he rode past the small patches of fog that still hovered over parts of the fields and lingered in the woods.

He hadn't slept much. He started the evening idly playing the guitar Pierre kept in his parlor. Then read and drank wine until he was drowsy enough to sleep. But that only lasted for a few hours. He woke soon after, burning with running thoughts as he shifted time and time again in bed. He had escaped a trap in Barcelona. Now he was sinking into a new one.

Pierre had been good to him. He gave him a place to stay, food, clothes, a sword, and pistol, but this business with the muskets was getting dark. Did he really expect him to kill someone? The kind welcome he had received was beginning to turn into something else. Asked favors started feeling more like commands.

Diego had been happy not to go to the ball. It would have been an awkward evening of fake smiles and barely understanding conversations. Still, he was never invited. Diego, after all, was a *caballero* of a noble family, just like Pierre. Was he not an equal? They seemed to be the same in Barcelona, two young noblemen in a foreign land. Certainly, Diego's family's hacienda in the Pueblo de Los Angeles rivaled, if not surpassed, Pierre's family's home in Marseille. Of course, the Godfrey estates in Normandy could also be grander beyond his comprehension.

He frowned at these returning thoughts as he rode in the morning light then shrugged. Diego was also a wanted man in Spain for assaulting and robbing a clergyman. Parading a fugitive friend around the Marseille elites was probably not a good idea...or was he merely keeping his personal killer's identity a secret?

Still, he would have liked to have gone to the ball and seen the pretty girls in their dresses. Would he have been brave enough to talk to any of them? Maybe some lonely girl spoke Spanish or even the guttural-sounding English. Maybe he could have spoken to her again...*Little Claudia.*

He smiled and shook his head. The thought of her had crept in again. It tormented him last night as he tried to sleep until finally satisfying his burning arousal calmed his mind enough to fall asleep again. Now, the thought of her beautiful face and the sound of her voice warmed him as he rode through the cool morning air.

The barn loomed ahead, quiet and imposing. He raised an eyebrow and examined the ground with increasing concern. There were hoof marks and boot prints everywhere. He looked around carefully as he dismounted and tied the horses.

The large door groaned as he dragged it open, spilling daylight onto the hay-strewn floor. The hay that had covered the trapdoor to the cellar had been brushed aside. He looked up and examined what he could see of the loft above. Slices of light from the slats in the wall fell on the hay above but illuminated little else. The ladder creaked as he climbed. There were no signs of anyone having spent the night up there. The mounds of hay and the wooden walls dampened the sounds of the birds outside, creating an eerie silence. He slowly scanned the hay. His eyes stopped at a man's head laying on a mound. Its eyes and mouth popped open as it shouted in Spanish.

"I am just a head!"

"¡*Por Los Santos!*" Diego gasped, whipping out his sword. Levi emerged from the hay bursting with laughter.

"Your face! Ha! I'm dying!" he cried.

"You almost did, had I drawn my pistol," Diego said, sheathing his sword, trying to collect his nerve.

"Ha! You would have missed," Levi sighed from the heavy laugh.

Diego frowned, pushing his lower lip into his upper. "Maybe…"

"I saw him, Diego! I know where he lives!" Levi said in his heavily accented Spanish. "But first, did you bring food? I'm starving!"

"Of course, my friend. Start the fire. We'll make coffee." Diego patted his arm. The two slid down the ladder and went to their tasks. Diego went to his horse and untied the bundle he had wrapped in a blanket behind the saddle. Levi lit the small forge next to the barn. Soon the little kettle Diego brought bubbled with hot coffee which the two shared in a single tin cup along with bread, apricot preserves, cheese, and cold sausage.

"You think of everything, Diego," Levi said with delight, sipping the coffee to wash down the bite of bread, cheese, and preserves.

"I spent plenty of cold hungry nights on cattle drives to know to be prepared," Diego said, accepting the hot cup of coffee from his companion. Levi's eyes flashed with excitement.

"You're a *vaquero*!" he said with glee.

"Only when I have to be," Diego smiled slyly.

"What's it like?"

"Well, you spend all day in the saddle keeping the beasts in line, then you sleep under the stars."

Levi's eyes twinkled as he looked off afar. "I would like to see California someday and be a *vaquero*!"

"Come," Diego shrugged. "We'll put you to work."

The two rode into town wearing their hats low, shading their eyes. Their capes were wrapped around them, even as the day began to warm. Far away from where the grand houses sat on cobbled stone streets, they moved through the narrow muddy back ways of the working-class neighborhood, careful not to be splattered as wives dumped their chamber pots from apartment windows above.

"There," Levi said, indicating an old rundown building with women sitting on the front steps cleaning fish and throwing the guts into the roadway. "That window on the second floor...I think is his." Diego looked up and marked it well. *Do they really expect me to kill this man?*

Next, they rode to the quay. They left their horses at a stable nearby and paid the workers to clean the filth off their hocks.

It was easier to move and blend in with the crowds on foot. They moved through the throngs of dockworkers, sailors, and passengers like cats soft-stepping nimbly toward their prey. Their cloaks and hats obscured their faces, yet their martial and aristocratic demeanor was enough for others to keep their eyes humbly away while steering clear of the two men.

"There he is," Levi said in a low voice. As if hearing the words, a paunchy man in a knit stocking hat stole a look at the pair as he stepped onto the dock with a crate he had carried off the gangplank from one of the ships. A flash of white fear spread across his face before he quickly looked away and carried his load to a waiting cart at the end of the quay.

"That is your target, Señor Hunter," Levi said quietly.

Diego noted the bruises and black eye the man bore. "The gendarmes certainly did some work on him," he said.

"Nothing compared to what you'll do," Levi said grimly.

Diego grimaced as he watched the unfortunate man disappear into the crowd.

Chapter 10: The Angel of Death

"Kill him," Pierre said in Spanish, turning his eyes to Diego. Levi had just finished telling the story. Pierre was still in his robe, drinking coffee with his leg crossed over his knee in the grand leather chair of his study. Levi smiled, turning to Diego with wild anticipation in his eyes. Diego stood silently, gripping his wide-brimmed hat. Pierre continued. "We have another shipment coming tomorrow night. There will be more after that. We can't do it all ourselves. We need the workers. Once we make an example of one, we won't hear a peep from the rest."

Diego stood silently, not sure what to say. Pierre shifted in his chair, then uncrossed his legs and leaned forward. "Look, I know I ask a lot. That man would have put us all in jail and denied your countrymen these arms to defend themselves against the American imperialists. This is a war by all accounts but name. Basset is a traitor. It's justified. You'll be doing your country and your friends a great service. Soon, I'll be sending you home with a ship full of guns. You'll be a hero to your people. Can I depend on you?"

Diego paused for a moment, then spoke, "Sí."

"There's our killer!" Levi gripped his shoulder. "I'll help!"

"No," Pierre said. "Diego is unknown and will soon be gone. He must be the only witness and our only connection to the killing. He must do it alone…tonight."

Henrí Basset felt the presence of a shadow hanging over him all day. He had taken a lot of teasing from the other workers for the black eye and bruised face. "I was drunk and fell down the stairs," he told them.

"Quit lying! We know your wife beats you!" one of the men shouted, earning a round of laughter from the others. He shrugged, grateful that the taunt had put a stop to the questions as the men came up with more and more ridiculous and embarrassing reasons for his injuries. Eventually, and much to his relief, the banter moved on to other topics as they worked.

Only a few knew about the well-paying night work in which he and some of the others had been involved. Those others could never know that he had tried to betray their aristocratic employer for reward money. It was a dishonorable business decision, for sure. But the wealthy didn't care about him or the family he had to feed with his aging and aching back. So why should he care about them and their late-night schemes?

It didn't matter. Someone had gotten wise and moved the guns before he and the gendarmes arrived. For all his effort, all he got was a beating, humiliation, and no money. Most of all, it earned him this nagging fear that he was being watched.

He feared the others would find out about his betrayal and exact revenge for the loss of further income from this eccentric nobleman. But worse, he feared this nobleman would send his Spanish devil in black to kill him and his family.

His fears subsided by mid-morning. The sun came out in earnest and the work was brisk. There was plenty to load and unload. Even the taunting had died down as his fellow workers got more and more involved in their tasks.

Then he saw them: two strangers in capes with their hats pulled down low to shadow their faces. It was a fleeting glimpse, but he was sure he recognized the grim face of the Spanish demon. A cold sweat broke across his body as he quickly looked away.

He carried his load to the wagon at the end of the quay and returned for more. He was careful not to seem obvious as he scanned the crowd for the two mysterious men. They were gone. He wondered if he had been dreaming. He shook his head. Perhaps his guilt was playing tricks on him. Still, he couldn't shake the uneasy feeling that someone was watching him and that those around him knew his crime, that justice was stalking him.

He followed the others at dusk to the tavern, seeking safety in numbers rather than braving the dark winding streets alone. Once again, men teased him about his black eye and bruises before moving on to other topics. The music from the accordion, boisterous stories, and laughter mixed with cheap watered-down wine helped ease his feeling of dread that ate away at his stomach.

At last, the last of the workers cleared out and he was low on money. It was time to go home.

The alley seemed strangely empty as if all living creatures knew to stay away from the impending danger. Henrí looked both ways, expecting to see the dark figure out there waiting for him. He turned up his collar and pulled his knit cap low before stepping off into the alley. His feet sloshed in the mud making a rhythmic sound as he walked. He found himself falling into a trance while listening to it.

He stopped.

There was another sound following him. He turned quickly. There were only a few slumping drunks in the alley behind him. Even the whores had turned in for the night. He started walking once more. He heard it again. He stopped, this time looking up, wondering if the cheap wine had affected his senses. He shook his head. He just had to get home and sleep. Hopefully, his wife would be already sleeping and not waiting to scold him for spending his day's wages on wine.

The doorway to his building was in sight now. He let out a sigh and smiled. He was being foolish. He'd forget all of these troubles in the days to come. They would fade like the bruises on his face. Honest work and less drinking, he resolved, would be the rule of his new life, the new life he planned to start living tomorrow. The thought invigorated him. Maybe his wife would be up when he got home. Maybe she'd be up for a little dance in bed tonight. He smiled, suddenly feeling aroused. He was smiling grandly as he put his foot on the first step to his door. He had made it.

A ruffling sound caught him mid-step. He looked up just in time to see a black form descend upon him from the roof. He tried to scream, but the creature enveloped him quickly in its black cape, knocking him to the ground. A gloved hand covered his mouth, then grabbed his collar and drew him to the needle-like point of a dagger.

He quivered as he looked up at the dark creature clutching him in its deadly grip. The lower part of the demon's face was covered with a black scarf, revealing only its terrible green eyes below its wide-brimmed hat. Henrí quickly clenched his eyes shut at the horrifying sight of this dark angel of death. He shuddered violently, waiting for the blade to take his life.

"Papa!"

The voice of a child stopped his shaking. He popped an eye open. Above the creature was his little girl, Claire, leaning out of the second-floor window. She was watching with wide-eyed confusion.

Henrí's fear-ravaged face softened into a bittersweet smile. "Look away, my love," he told her.

The creature turned and looked at her, then back to its victim. Its green eyes narrowed as it drew Henrí's throat further into its knife. Then it stopped, holding him at the point of death in a frozen moment that felt like an eternity. Its eyes suddenly softened. It slackened its grip on Henrí's collar and eased him back down.

Henrí blinked in confusion at the black figure towering over him. At last, the creature spoke in simple French heavily accented with New World Spanish. "Take your family and run," it said, releasing him from its grip.

"*Oui*, I mean *sí, señor!*" Henrí blurted as he bumbled to his feet. He grabbed his cap and clutched it to his chest with both hands. "*Gracias! Gracias!*" he huffed. The man in black stepped back and watched him silently. Henrí stole one last look at the frightening figure before turning to his door and running up the stairs to his family's apartment.

His wife was awake, holding Claire in her arms. Her eyes were wide with alarm. "What is it, Henrí? What have you gotten yourself into?"

"There is no time to explain," Henrí said, frantically looking around the room for what they could manage to take. "We must leave at once! Our lives are at stake!"

Seeing the ghostly fear on his face was enough to convince her that this was no time to argue. She set the child down and joined him in packing. At last, she and the child were dressed. The few items they could carry were strapped to their backs. They made their way down the steps toward the dark world outside.

"Wait," Henrí whispered. "I'll see if it's clear." He peeped his head through the doorway and scanned the alley, then stepped out and turned to look toward the roof where the creature had appeared. He let out a breath, then turned his eyes to his wife. "Alright, let's go." He smiled at her as she waddled through the door, laden with her load. He turned back toward the alley.

"Going somewhere, Monsieur Basset?" The familiar voice sent chills through him.

Lieutenant Saint Cloud stood before him with a handful of armed gendarmes.

"I…I was…" Henrí stammered.

"Spare me the lie, Henrí. You're not out of this yet, my friend. You may still be of use to us, that is if you still consider yourself to be on the side of the law."

"Of course, monsieur," Henrí said, then turned to his wife and indicated with his head to go back upstairs.

"Good! Prison's no place for women and children," Saint Cloud said, smiling broadly. "I'd much rather pay you a reward than see you in chains," he laughed, eliciting a sinister chuckle from his men.

Henrí laughed nervously along with them. "How may I be of service, monsieur?"

Saint Cloud dropped his smile. "I have word that the British smugglers are bringing another shipment of arms tomorrow night, once again, avoiding our customs inspectors at the quays." He paused for a moment to look into Henrí's eyes for a hint of pre-knowledge of this coming event, then smiled warmly again. "I mean, if they're going to arm Republican dissent in this country, they could at least have the decency of paying our taxes," he said with a laugh. His men laughed darkly with him.

"Monsieur," Henrí pleaded with his hat in his hands, "I believe the weapons are for some foreign adventure, not for any mischief here in France. Furthermore, I think I've been discovered as an informant. Just tonight, they sent a man to kill me and my family. It is why we were attempting to flee. I've had no word of this shipment which must be further proof that I am no longer trusted."

"All the more reason for you to help us," Saint Cloud responded. "Work your sources, find out where and when the drop will be, then lead us there. Once we arrest these pirates, you and your family will be safe and absolved from any wrongdoing." Then the smile fell from his face once more. "Try to flee again, and I'll have your whole family in chains."

Chapter Eleven: The Date

Pierre sucked in his breath at the sound of the door opening below. He looked up from his late-night letter writing and listened to the soft clacking of boots on the marble floor. He then looked to his candle, wondering if it were too late to blow out. He realized it was much too late. Diego would have already seen the faint glow from outside and knew he was awake.

Pierre listened to the footsteps come up the stairs. He heard the door open to the room where Diego had been sleeping and then finally close. He let out his breath and chuckled lightly at himself, shaking his head. There was no reason to be afraid of his friend. Still, he did not want to see the bloodstains on his clothes. He did not want to be a witness to any incriminating evidence. The less he knew of the killing, the better.

He poured another glass of brandy and sat back in his chair. He was done writing for the night, even though there was still much to manage. The next shipment of arms would be coming the following evening. It would be a delicate game of making the rendezvous with his British suppliers somewhere along the dark shore while evading the gendarmes.

Then there was the quickly approaching wedding date. The bride-to-be still wasn't aware. She hadn't even said yes yet. The Moreaus assured him that they'd bring her to her senses, but that did nothing to ease his nerves in these wee hours of the night.

He threw back the brandy and blew out the candle. He'd work all this out tomorrow, he decided as he threw off his robe and laid himself in bed. *There's no use losing sleep over all of this*, he thought as he stared wide-eyed at the ceiling.

Full sunlight was pouring into the room when he finally roused himself from bed. It had been a fitful night, but he must have found some sleep in the early morning. He checked his pocket watch and sighed. Bernard would most likely be away running errands by now.

Pierre threw on his robe and crept downstairs in search of coffee. He found Diego sitting at the kitchen table, staring at nothing. A cup of coffee sat in front of him. Pierre nodded as he passed. He wasn't quite sure if the gesture had been returned. He smiled with relief at the weight of the liquid left in the pot.

"You did the right thing last night," Pierre said as he poured himself a cup. He didn't turn to see if his words were having any effect. The silence was enough. "That man would have been our ruin if left alive."

He took a sip and frowned at the bitter, lukewarm liquid. "I thank you," he said, finally turning around to face his friend. "It was a lot to ask, I know…" Diego was staring at his coffee. "I'm afraid I'm going to need to ask more of you." Diego looked up, acknowledging Pierre for the first time that morning. Pierre could see the distress in his eyes. "You will go to the rendezvous with the British in my stead tonight. I will be out with Mademoiselle Moreau and making a very public show of it. I'm being constantly watched. I have to throw the authorities off my trail or we'll all be in peril." He paused, trying to read the pained look in Diego's eyes. "Can I depend on you?" he asked at last.

"Yes," Diego said, then looked back into his coffee.

Henri Basset showed up at the docks for work before dawn, just like he did every day except Sundays. He had not slept the night before. He shuddered. He wasn't sure if it was from the cold morning air or the fear that clung to him. He wondered if the others would be surprised to see him. Did they know he had betrayed his friends and their clandestine employer? Did they know he had been marked for death the night before?

"What…?" he finally asked one of the inquisitive faces that greeted him.

"You look like you've seen a ghost, Henri," his fellow worker told him.

"I was up with a sick child," Henri offered, hoping it would be enough.

The man stared at him for a moment, then shrugged. "Children can be such worry," the man offered.

"Yes, yes, mine is more worrisome than others, I suppose," he shrugged as well. The man seemed satisfied and turned to others for conversation. Henri let out a sigh. Hopefully, little Claire and her mother were well on their way to his mother-in-law's home, far away from the gendarmes and murderous Spanish demon.

He quickly warmed as the work began. He kept quiet and listened to the conversations of others as he climbed into the hulls and emerged with crates to load onto the carts that lined the quay. If there was night work this evening, he was yet to be invited. Did they know? he wondered. Had he been excluded or even dismissed as already being dead?

These worries grew as the day wore on. He paid particular attention to Maurice, the man who had invited him to the late-night work before. Maurice seemed particularly coy. *Was he expecting me to be dead?* Henrí wondered every time the man avoided his gaze.

At last, the work for the day was done. Henrí shifted nervously from foot to foot, waiting for his pay. Maurice paid him without making eye contact. Instead, he looked nervously around as he whispered, "There's work tonight if you care to join us."

Henrí's eyes lit up in response. "Yes, of course," he said quickly under his breath.

Maurice described the small cove where the work would take place. "Do you know it?" he asked.

"Yes, I know it well," Henrí answered, looking around nervously for anyone else listening.

"Good. We'll meet behind the tavern after dark. Tell no one. They are very nervous about leaks," Maurice told him.

"Of course…" Henrí was quick to reply.

Claudette felt like she had a rock in her stomach all afternoon as Lavinia fussed over her hair, make-up, and dress. It didn't help that her closest confidant was also nervous and careful not to broach the subject that had seemed to have driven a wedge between them. Claudette finally let out a sigh. "I'm not going to make a fool out of myself again, I promise," she said, annoyed at her friend's silence.

"Of course, child," the Romani woman mumbled while still managing to hold hairpins in her mouth. Claudette looked at her in the mirror. She was standing behind her, working intently on the complicated stack of hair she was creating on the back of Claudette's head while still allowing curled strands to fall gracefully from in front of her ears and land delicately on her bare shoulders. *How am I supposed to move my head with all of this?* she wondered as she looked at the elaborate hair sculpture Lavinia was creating.

"I promise, I won't ruin the evening. I'll be pleasant as pie," Claudette insisted.

Lavinia looked up from her work, focusing her eyes on Claudette's in the mirror. She let out a small sigh, "I just want you to enjoy yourself, child. You might find you actually like him," she said with a shrug.

"I will do my best," Claudette said with a wink. Lavinia gave her an incredulous smirk. She dropped the smirk at the sound of a carriage coming up the drive.

"He's here!" she gasped, widening her eyes.

"It's okay," Claudette smiled slyly, "it's customary to make them wait a bit. Finish. We've got plenty of time."

"It's simple," Pierre stated, pausing to sip his glass of gin and tonic. He sat in one of the leather chairs of the Moreau parlor. "If the Moroccans insist on harboring Algerian rebels, then they can consider themselves at war with France. We'll be building gin palaces in Casablanca in a week."

"Bah!" Monsieur Moreau scoffed. "Why would we want more territory in Northern Africa? The land is useless unless they're hiding something precious underneath the sand. I say, leave North Africa and the Levant to the damn Saracens and their fanaticism."

Pierre shrugged, pressing his lips into his inverse smile while looking into his glass for a response. A door opening above interrupted his thoughts. He set his glass down and stood, straightening his jacket as he looked to the top of the stairs. He smiled at the sight of her. Claudette allowed a flicker of a smile in return. She held the skirt of her dress in one hand and the banister in the other. Pierre drew in a breath as he watched her descend. For all the trouble she caused, she was certainly beautiful, he thought as he let out a whisper of a sigh.

"You do me great honor," he said with a slight bow, "allowing me to stand in the shadow of your beauty."

Claudette let out a small laugh, "Now you're just being silly."

"Perhaps," he smiled, "but I am rendered a fool by your loveliness."

Claudette responded with a shy giggle, looking away quickly from his brilliant blue eyes.

"Don't you both look splendid!" Monsieur Moreau beamed, touching both of their shoulders as he spoke.

"My, what a vision of youth, beauty, and love!" Madame Moreau exclaimed as she walked into the parlor. "The town will seethe in jealousy at the sight of you!"

"Well, I certainly plan to make a show of it," Pierre said, bowing deeply to her.

Certainly a man of his word, Claudette mused as the evening progressed. It seemed Pierre made a point of acknowledging everyone they encountered on the streets, and during their seemingly endless tour of cafes. He seemed to especially go out of his way to tip his hat to every lowly gendarme they passed. "Keep up the good work, boys!" he called to a group of them, standing outside the *Grand-Théâtre.*

"One would think you're running for office," she chided him as they climbed the stairs.

"I just want our brave law enforcement to know they have my support and gratitude," he smiled. "They're our only bastion against chaos and anarchy."

What seemed even more peculiar that evening was the congratulations they received nearly everywhere they went. Pierre had a way of brushing it off and quickly changing the subject each time. She thought she caught him once even shaking his head subtly as if to signal to their well-wisher not to pry further.

These thoughts troubled her as they made their way up the stairs and down the hall to their box. The view of the stage and the crowd below was breathtaking as they entered. She fanned herself in an attempt to shoo away the exhilarating feeling of vertigo as she sat. A wave of damp warmth rose from the mass of spectators below and washed over the balustrade. She suddenly wished she had eaten more and drank less during their dash through the many cafes before the show.

Out of the corner of her eye, she detected the movement of a man standing up among the seated crowd. She turned to look. The woman next to him stood, too. Both were looking right at her and

Pierre. The man lifted his hand to his mouth and called out, "*Félicitations pour vos fiançailles!*"

"What?!" Claudette gasped. People began to stand and clap as blood rushed to her face. "What is this?!" she gasped again.

"Stand up and smile, dear," Pierre said, standing himself. "They're just being nice." He took her hand and helped her to her feet, waving at the people below and smiling grandly with his upside-down grin. Claudette stood wide-eyed and waved limply back at them. "Smile!" she heard Pierre say. She did her best to comply.

At last, the gaslights began to dim. The crowd mercifully began to quiet and sit in their chairs. The strings began with a jaunty martial tune that ended in a sudden pluck. Then, they settled into a rolling and mysterious melody. Claudette's mind raced as the orchestra ran through the themes and melodies that would accompany the evening's romantic comedy. The curtains opened and a chorus of actors dressed as peasants began to sing in Italian. Then the music settled and a man began to sing alone, "*Quanto è bella, quanto è cara!*"

Pierre turned to her with a sly smile, searching to see if she recognized the song from his serenade below her balcony. She rolled her eyes at him, "I see what you did there," she whispered. He grinned boyishly, then sat back in his chair with satisfaction.

Claudette turned her eyes back to the stage and listened to the singer profess his love for a seemingly unobtainable object of his affection. It was hard to follow the Italian lyrics, but she understood the sentiment.

Her mind then followed the melody coming from the orchestra. She remembered how it sounded on a guitar. She thought of the guitar player: a proud man below her station. Did he have such aspirations of impossible love beyond his race and class? What kind of woman would stir such a longing in a man like him? She would have to be very attractive, Claudette decided, to elicit this kind of passion from a man as pretty as Diego.

She suddenly felt a hot wave of jealousy wash over her at the thought of such a woman. She scoffed at her own foolishness. Pierre turned and looked at her with concern. She smiled at him and shook her head to say it was nothing, then turned her attention back to the absurd story being played out below. She tried to concentrate and listen for any comprehension of the words sung in Italian. It was nearly impossible as her eyelids got heavier and heavier.

At some point, she startled herself awake with a snore. Horrified, she quickly straightened herself and wiped away the slobber that had built up in the corner of her mouth. She stole a glance at Pierre. He turned, gave her a knowing smile, and patted her hand before returning his gaze to the show. Warm embarrassment rushed to her cheeks, thankfully hidden in the dim light.

The singers were all on stage now belting out *"Addio! Addio!"* to the frantic flourishes of the orchestra. Then it was over. Applause broke out as the curtain fell and opened again. People stood and cheered as the singers took their bows. Claudette stood and clapped, grateful that any attention anyone might have been paying her was now focused on the stage.

The fresh air revived her fully as the current of people swept them from the stuffy theater into the streets. The nights in Marseille were becoming warmer as spring progressed. Cafes filled the sidewalks with closely packed diners and waiters. Despite the crowds, they found a table and enjoyed fish stew with fresh bread and a bottle of wine hearty enough to stand up to the heavy use of garlic. Still, more well-wishers stopped by and congratulated the couple as they ate. Pierre was quick to rekindle their conversation after each interruption.

After dinner, they rode in Pierre's open carriage along the shore. The stars twinkled as they reflected on the calm waters. Claudette sighed with satisfaction. The warm stew and red wine settled peacefully in her stomach. Pierre took note of her contentment.

"See, I'm not so bad, am I?" he said, smiling at her coyly.

"I never said you were," she replied, gazing at the sea.

"I'm glad to hear it. I think people would be disappointed if we were at odds," he said. There was something in his tone that awoke her earlier concerns. She felt her contentment slipping away.

"Why were people congratulating us tonight?" she asked, still watching the sea.

"Because we make a handsome couple," he replied. She turned to look at him. Pierre let out a nervous laugh. "Well…to be honest…" he started, rubbing the back of his neck. She cocked her head and lifted her eyebrows. "We didn't expect your reaction to my proposal and..." Her eyebrows drew nearer to each other as she sharpened her eyes. "Well, to put it plainly...you and I are to be married in two weeks. The date has been set."

She blinked at him as he offered her a weak smile. "I have not consented to your proposal," she said flatly.

"An overlooked technicality, for sure, but much has gone into the planning. We've sent invitations. We can't withdraw them now. Think of the scandal."

She could feel the rage building inside her as she fought for words. "What about me? Do I not have a say? Is it not my choice?"

Pierre let out a sigh and fell back into his seat. "Yes...yes...it's your choice, of course," he sighed in frustration. "So what will you choose, then?" He sat back up, focusing his eyes on her. "Will you choose a happy marriage with a wealthy, kind, and if I may say, not too hard to look at nobleman...or will you choose scandal and humiliation for you, me, my family, and your parents?"

Claudette glared back at him, holding her fury down in silence.

He continued, "And after the scandal and humiliation, who do you think will come along and offer you the same? No man would dare risk his good name on taking such a chance on a petulant child again!" He paused to see the effect of his words. Claudette could feel the angry tears well in her eyes. Pierre lowered his voice and spoke firmly, "Do not let this childish petulance be your permanent ruin."

Chapter Twelve: The Ruin

Claudette looked away in frustration. A silence grew between them. It was on the verge of being unbearable. She suddenly felt the urge to scream like a wild animal. She wanted to leap from the carriage and run until she could run no more.

"What's this?" Pierre broke the silence. Claudette could feel his muscles tightening next to her. She turned back to see what he was looking at. Four horsemen were galloping up the road toward them. She instinctively clutched his arm in fear. She felt his muscles relax slightly as he let out a breath. The riders reined in their horses as they neared and now she could make out the faces of his friends. She found herself unthinkingly scanning them to see if Diego was among them. His eyes were already on her when she found him. She smiled softly. A brief smile flashed across his face before he looked away and returned to his stern demeanor.

"What is this? What's happening with the shipment?" Pierre asked.

"The gendarmes found us," Atilla spoke. "They swarmed the beach and captured most of the workers. The British barely escaped in their boats. There were shots fired...perhaps casualties."

"They got the first load of muskets brought ashore, maybe two hundred of them," Thomas followed.

"We would have been captured ourselves, had it not been for our horses," Levi added.

Pierre sat upright in the carriage and looked up the road as if expecting to see the gendarmes charging toward them at any minute. "Where are they now?" Pierre asked, barely concealing his alarm.

"We scattered in several directions to confuse them, then rejoined before coming to you," Atilla assured him. "Most of them were on foot. Just their leader was mounted." Atilla paused, then let out a breath, "Pierre...they knew we'd be there."

"Damn it..." he muttered to himself. He turned back to his friends and spoke in Spanish. "Diego, give me your horse. See that she gets home safely," he said, indicating to Claudette with his hand. He then sprung from the carriage and took the reins as Diego leaped from his horse and handed them off. Pierre stepped into the stirrup and bounded into the saddle, reining in the horse as it nickered and side-stepped in agitation from the commotion. He then turned to the others. "Let's go!" he said, giving the horse a light kick with his heels, setting the beast into motion. The others followed, kicking up a cloud of dust as they hurried away.

Diego watched them go. As the sound of pounding hooves faded, he slowly became conscious of the young lady sitting in the carriage behind him. He suddenly became nervous. Almost afraid to turn and face her.

"Well," she broke the awkward silence with her accented English, "are you going to walk or get in with me?"

A smile broke across his troubled face. He turned to her. Her eyes flickered with delight at the sight of his boyish grin. "I would join you if you would have me, *Little Claudia*," he said with a slight bow.

"Of course!" she said, slapping the seat next to her. "We are friends, are we not?"

"Always, my friend," he said, removing his sword belt with glee before climbing into the carriage and plopping down next to her. He placed his sword on the opposite seat. He smiled at her, then suddenly felt embarrassed by the arousal caused by the sudden closeness of their thighs pressing together in the little carriage. She smiled back bashfully, dropping her eyes for a moment before lifting them to the driver. She told the man in French to return to her home. The man gave the horses a slap of the reins and the carriage lurched forward. The two fell back into their seats and then giggled madly at having been startled by the sudden motion.

She sighed, looking at him as she recovered. She wondered what would happen if she just leaned forward and kissed him. He blushed as if he read her thoughts. Suddenly, the thought of this man returning to his side of the world saddened her, but at the same time, the faraway land seemed so exotic.

"Tell me what Mexico is like," she swooned, fluttering her eyes at him.

"Not too unlike, Marseille, but the land and the people are wild. It can be very dangerous if you are in the wrong place with the wrong people."

"Is that why you are such a fighter? I know Pierre and his friends see you as some kind of exotic warrior."

"Ha!" he chuckled. "I'm a lover too, you know." He laughed nervously, wondering if he had gone too far. "But I suppose it is in my blood. My grandfathers were both great warriors. They rode together and fought side-by-side against injustice. They came from the two nations that became one…Mexico."

"Mexico…" she repeated with awe. He had said it with such reverence she that couldn't help but feel it too. "What nations? I know Spain, but…what else?"

"*Aztlán*," he said. His large green eyes were full of exotic mystery. She felt a chill as if the mists of this faraway ancient empire swirled around her and tickled her skin. The world outside the carriage faded away as it clattered toward her home. It was replaced by a land of wild and vibrant colors, filled with pretty people like Diego, savory smells of spicy foods, and the sounds of lively music filling the desert air. She could have listened to him talk all night about his homeland as she swooned. She found herself clutching his arm, pressing her body up to him, and feeling his warmth.

The familiar sights of her approaching home pulled her back into her own world. She dreaded the end of their journey. Such excitement and happiness she felt with this dark passionate stranger. The carriage pulled to a stop. Diego leaped over the side so that he could lower the step and open the door for her before the driver could even start to climb down from his bench. He took her hand and gently helped her step back down to earth. She looked at his large green eyes which dazzled in the flickering lamplights.

"I wish you could come in with me," she said before she could stop herself. Wild excitement flashed over his eyes. She was suddenly embarrassed by her unthinking boldness. "I would feel safer in your presence," she tried to qualify her statement.

He smiled slowly with boyish mischief. "Don't worry, *Little Claudia*, I will keep you safe."

She smiled softly at him, then looked away as she felt the blood rushing to her face. "I should go in then…" she said softly. "My parents are already in bed."

"Of course," he said, stepping aside, clearing the path to the door.

She took a few steps, then turned back to him, "I really enjoyed hearing about your homeland, Diego. Perhaps you could tell me more sometime."

"I would like that," he smiled warmly at her. She could feel herself blush again. She let out a quiet nervous laugh as she turned away and opened the door. She closed it behind her, leaned against it, and shut her eyes. She could hear the carriage pulling away. Wild feelings of excitement and dread swirled inside her.

She sighed as she opened her eyes and looked about the dark house. She would sort out her thoughts and feelings in the morning. But how could she sleep in such a state? She decided to take some drinking water and a candle with her. The thought of snuggling up in bed with a book felt welcoming.

She carried an ewer and mug to her room and set them next to her book by her bed. Then turned to the dark figure in the mirror, looking herself over in the darkness. She'd wait until she got in bed to light the candle, she thought, as she pulled the pins from her hair and loosened the ties of her dress. It would be easier to get undressed if Lavinia was up to help, but she was grateful to be alone with her thoughts. Here in the darkness, she could let her fantasies run wild without Lavinia constantly bringing her back to earth with her practical advice.

She pulled off her dress, then removed the petticoats until she stood in the mirror in her corset, short linen drawers, and stockings, which were tied just below her knees with silk ribbon garters. *What would he think if he saw me like this?* She wondered mischievously, admiring her own figure in the mirror. Then she saw the dark-caped figure standing behind her, outlined by the window.

"Huh!" she gasped as terror spread through her. She covered her mouth to stifle a scream. It never came. The realization of who the intruder was swept away the terror and replaced it with relief and then wild excitement. She stepped to him. He opened his arms and she fell into them. She found herself kissing him madly as if stopping would cause her to wake from this dream only to find herself alone in the darkness.

His hands found the delicate small of her back and the line of her shoulder. She groaned as she lifted her leg and wrapped it around him, feeling the muscles of his back with her hands. He gasped in ecstasy as he clutched the bottom of her thigh, hoisting it higher as he pressed his arousal against her. The warmth of it pressing against the crux of her legs and the flat of her belly filled her with shuddering excitement. She could feel the thin layer of linen between them dampen with her arousal. "Oh, Diego..." she gasped softly, kissing his neck and nibbling on his ear.

Sudden resolve course through her. She shoved him away. He looked at her with pained surprise. She smiled devilishly in return as she reached around her back and began to undo the laces of her corset. Then let out a snort of frustration as she turned her back to him. "Help me," she whispered. She could sense his hands lightly brushing up against her back as he worked the laces. She couldn't help but press the subtle fleshiness of her rear against his raging stiffness.

He gasped in excitement as she reached back with her arms and felt the back of his neck and the line of his jaw. Done with loosening her laces, his hands moved around to her belly then glided along the surface of her corset to the outward curve of her small rounded breasts.

She turned and pushed him away again. He stood there in the gloom, watching as she undid the hooks of the busk in the front of her corset, one by one. He sighed longingly as the garment fell away, revealing her slender white figure. Enraptured, he stepped forward again, sliding his hand down the back of her short linen drawers and feeling the nakedness of her chest with the other.

She untied his cape and let it drop to the floor. Then unbuttoned his waistcoat. He hurriedly untied his cravat, tossing it to the floor, then freed himself of his waistcoat and suspenders as she untucked his shirt from his trousers. He pulled it off over his head and threw it to the ground. Then threw his arms around her again and kissed her, feeling the naked flesh of her upper body pressing against his.

She pushed him toward the bed, unbuttoning the front flap of his trousers, wanting to feel that warm stiff thing that had been pressing against her. "Little Claudia," he gasped softly. Her cool hand found it, feeling the smooth warmth of its skin as it pulsed with raging desire. He quivered and groaned at her touch. "Maybe we should stop," he said softly, his voice betraying his inner battle between lust and morality, "I don't want to ruin you."

She groaned in ecstasy in response, pushing him onto the bed then climbed on top of him, grinding the thin damp linen of her drawers against his raging erection. "Claudette...I..." he gasped, reaching out, clutching her rear with one hand and feeling her delicate small breast with the other.

She stopped for a moment, feeling him throb beneath her. She looked down at him. His face now seemed young, innocent, full of apprehension and desire. She touched his cheek with her hand and smiled softly at him. "You are sweet, Diego. I want you to ruin me." He blinked in the darkness, trying to comprehend.

"I want you to ruin me," she said again firmly. "They think I am nothing more than a product to be bought and sold like a cask of wine to the highest bidder. This is my body. I decide to whom I give it, not them." Diego sat up, cupped the back of her neck, and kissed her. "I give it to you..." she gasped.

He pulled her back into him as they lay back down. He kissed her, clutching her rear and the small of her back, grinding her further into him. They rolled over. She untied and shimmied off her drawers as he frantically removed his boots and pants. She groaned, feeling him slide up against her wetness. She wanted more, she wanted all of it. She felt something pop as he plunged into her. A brief point of pain followed by waves of ecstasy as her inner muscles clung and pulsed with him.

She wanted to scream. She clung to him and buried her teeth into his shoulder, trying to stifle her urge to call out. It was too much. She couldn't bear it any longer. She gripped the smooth skin of his back, pushing him deeper into her as she threw her head back and fought the need to scream.

Then it came like an explosion of flowers filling the sky with colors. She wanted to laugh, cry, and shout out her existence to the universe. He shuddered and groaned. She could feel him exploding inside her, then collapsing into her arms.

He lay there on her, breathing sweetly. She held him, running her fingers through his rich black hair. She could feel herself glow. They were glowing together in the darkness. She hoped the sun would never rise again, that they could lay there together in the darkness and feel this way forever.

She wanted to tell him, to say the words. She worried it would ruin the moment, that it would force him to say something he didn't mean.

"*Te amo…*" he said softly. She smiled, understanding the simple Spanish phrase. Warmth radiated from that smile and spread through her.

She squeezed him and kissed his forehead. "I know, I love you too."

The two bolted up in bed as the door opened with a burst of sound. The room was full of daylight.

"You're so late getting out of bed I thought I'd bring…" Lavinia stood in the doorway holding a wooden tray with food and coffee. Her eyes bulged as she stared at the couple clutching sheets to their chests to hide their nakedness. She scanned the trail of clothes strewn across the floor, following it back to the lovers in bed. Her eyes rolled off to the side as her mouth drew into an ironic frown.

"Alright," she said, setting the items from the tray on the dresser. "I'll make more eggs then." With that she withdrew from the room, closing the door behind her.

The two turned to each other in open-mouth shock. Claudette broke into a laugh. Diego smiled cautiously then let out a nervous chuckle. "Oh, your face!" she laughed. "It's alright. She's a friend. Come, let us have some coffee." She slid out of bed. Diego sighed as he watched her loveliness move across the floor wearing nothing more than knee stockings and garters. "Here," she said handing him the cup.

He took a sip, feeling its warmth run down his throat and radiate through his body. "What am I going to say?" He looked at her with concern.

She stroked his cheek then rested her hand on the back of his neck. "Maybe nothing," she said, "maybe he won't notice you didn't return last night." He frowned, then looked down at the coffee. She could see the worry on his face. She took the cup and set it on the nightstand. "Kiss me," she said. "I want to know it wasn't a dream."

He smiled, turning to her and clutching her hip. She drew his face to hers and kissed him as they laid back in bed, rekindling the passions from the night before. The thought that Lavinia could return any minute made the hushed lovemaking even more enticing. She stifled her groans as she wrapped her legs around him, worried that their motion was making too much noise. At last, they were done, panting, and clinging to each other in the morning light.

She was just about to doze off again when a light knock at the door roused her. "Come in," she said in French.

Lavinia entered, trying not to look at the couple as she brought the food to the nightstand. "Your parents are out, but I would not let him linger too long." she said, then stole a look at the couple and smirked."He is pretty," she said, turning away and moving to the door.

Claudette giggled and then watched the woman leave with affection, "Thank you, Lavinia."

Lavinia sighed and turned. "I do you no favors, child, but stand by while you ruin yourself," she said, then let herself out, closing the door behind her.

"What did she say?" Diego asked.

"She said you're pretty," she smiled at him. He smiled back bashfully, then looked down at the sheets. "Come," she squeezed his hand. "Let's eat. I'm starving!"

Chapter Thirteen: The Reckoning

Diego pulled the brim of his hat low to hide from the prying eyes in the street. His black clothing had obscured him well during the night before but now made him a spectacle as he hurried his way through the sun-splashed streets of Marseille. He was hot and clammy under his cape but dared not take it off. It hid his sword and pistol, which would certainly bring more unwanted attention.

It seemed everyone was watching him as if they knew he was a would-be murderer, a smuggler, and that he had just slept with his best friend's fiancé.

The sweat that covered his body turned ice cold at that last thought. *What am I going to say?* he fretted, letting out a light and panicked gasp. The thought of facing Pierre now filled him with dread. *He's going to know,* Diego assured himself. *He'll see it in my face.*

The Godfrey house loomed grand and imposing before him. The sun hit the white-washed walls and made them glow with authority. He considered climbing through the back window that led to his bedroom but realized he'd look like a ridiculous giant black spider in the broad daylight. He let out a sharp snort and chided himself for cowardice. No, he'd walk through the front door and face whatever he had to like a man. His knees suddenly seemed to weaken at the thought.

He eased the door open carefully, trying not to disturb the eerie silence that enveloped the house. Popping his head in, he scanned the foyer before stepping inside. Every clack of his boots on the marble floor made him cringe. He was becoming more at ease as he reached the stairs and started to climb. For now, it seemed he was alone. All he had to do was get in his room and close the door. Then he could get his thoughts together and decide what to do next.

His room, and the sanctuary it promised, sat before him. With great relief, he stepped through the portal and closed the door with a great sigh. He took a step toward his bed, remarking how neatly made it was, clearly untouched since Bernard must have made it the day before.

"Where were you last night?" the voice behind him said.

"*¡Por Los Santos!*" he yipped, spinning around and drawing his sword.

"So you prefer to stab me in the front now instead of the back this time," Pierre said, "refreshing…" He was sitting in a chair next to the wall by the door.

"You startled me. That's all," Diego said, sheathing his sword.

"Well, you're not the only one who can surprise people in their bedrooms," Pierre returned.

Diego pondered the meaning of that in the pained silence that followed. "Perhaps I should reconsider my tactics, then…now that I know how it feels…" he said limply. Pierre sat in silence. His large blue eyes were sharp in the dim-lit room. Diego searched for more to say.

"I think there's a lot you need to reconsider, Diego," Pierre said at last.

Diego blinked at him, waiting for him to continue until the silence became unbearable. "Like…?" he said at last. Pierre watched him silently. Diego could feel him reading all the guilt he could not hide from his face.

"You betrayed me," Pierre said flatly. Now it was Diego's turn to fall silent. Pierre's lips slowly drew into a smile. "At least you're sparing me the tedium of denying it."

Diego stared at him dumbstruck, his mind racing over all the possible meanings.

When Pierre was sure Diego was not going to speak without further prompting, he started again. "Henrí Basset was alive and well last night. He led the gendarmes right to the rendezvous." Diego blinked in silence. "Why didn't you kill him like I told you?"

Diego paused, then spoke softly, "He had a child. She was watching…"

"Oh, thanks for telling me," Pierre said. "I'll make sure she has the same accident as her father."

"What happened to him?" Diego asked.

"He fell on a knife…multiple times. It was very tragic." Pierre stared at him unblinkingly.

"I'm not a killer, Pierre," Diego said at last.

"You're not a lot of things, I'm finding," Pierre said, standing up. Diego took a step back. "But are you a liar?"

Diego blinked in confusion, "No, I am not."

"Then I will ask you again," Pierre said, tightening his voice as he took a step forward, "where were you last night?"

Diego blinked a couple of times, "I was with a woman."

"Ah, the truth! You smell like you were," Pierre said, widening his eyes with menacing mockery. Diego unwittingly pulled his collar to his nose and sniffed it. Pierre let out a scoffing laugh. "Must have been a good night for sure!" Diego let go of his collar, immediately feeling foolish.

"So let me think this through..." Pierre continued. "The last I saw you, you were with...my woman..."

"I took her home."

"Very heroic of you. Then what?"

"She went to bed."

"...and you?"

Diego tightened his jaw and straightened himself. Pierre's shoulders dropped in defeat. The anger in his eyes seeped out as tears began to well. Diego felt his own heart breaking. "If you knew it would hurt me," Pierre said meekly, trying to control his urge to cry, "why did you do it?"

"Pierre...I'm sorry..."

"Eeeeyaaaaaaa!" Pierre screamed as he reached around and pulled a pistol from behind his back. Diego's eyes widened with shock. He stepped forward, sweeping his left arm out to stop the pistol from swinging around fully and pointing at him. The gun went off with a shockingly loud explosion, filling the room with smoke and the stench of rotten eggs. The ball smashed into the wall with a puff of plaster dust. Pierre shifted direction with Diego's blocking motion. Then brought his left fist crashing into Diego's face.

Diego stumbled back from the blow and instinctively pulled his sword as he caught his balance. "Are you mad?!" Diego shouted.

"With the flaming rages of hell!" Pierre shouted back. "Give me back my sword, you damn traitor!"

"Not while you're trying to kill me!" Diego returned with incredulity.

"Fine! I'll kill you with something else!" Pierre said, tossing his pistol down and storming out of the room. Diego stood up out of his defensive crouch, wondering if he should draw his own pistol. He could feel his right eye begin to swell. Blood trickled from his nose. He wiped it with his sleeve, then remembered the bag of coins he had taken from Frey Alfonso's chambers. He sheathed his sword and snatched the bag from under his mattress, then tucked it into his pants.

Pierre's emphatic footsteps were returning. Diego realized it was foolish to wait to see what he'd return with. There was no point in fighting. Even if he won, Pierre was a nobleman and Diego was a fugitive of Spain. It would be considered nothing less than murder by the French authorities. He grabbed his hat and climbed onto the window sill.

"Stay here and fight, you fucking coward!" Pierre stood in the doorway with a sword in his hand.

"Not today, my friend," Diego said with sorrow building in his voice. "I am not in the right here and I cannot defend it." With that, he slipped out the window. He could hear Pierre scream in frustration as he scurried down the wall to the courtyard below.

"Come back here, you coward!" Pierre shouted from the window. Diego turned to see him in the window, ramming another ball into his pistol.

"¡Por Los Santos!" Diego gasped as he ran toward the stables. A shot fired and smacked against the wall as he ducked inside.

"You son of a bitch," Pierre mumbled, holding a percussion cap between his lips as he frantically rammed another ball into the barrel. He threw the ramrod to the floor, took the percussion cap out of his mouth, set it on the nipple, then pointed the gun out the window, waiting for his target to reappear.

Diego burst from the stable on the black horse Pierre had lent him. Pierre closed an eye and sighted the pistol at the rider, then let out a frustrated gasp. He couldn't risk shooting such an expensive beast. "Hey! That's my horse, you fucking thief!" he shouted. Diego bolted past, rounding the corner of the house. "Damn him," Pierre huffed. He ran down the steps, hoping to catch him before Diego could ride through the gate. *He'll have to dismount to open it*, he thought with some satisfaction.

Pierre burst through the front door and leveled his pistol at his erstwhile friend. Diego gave him a frightened look before leaping back into the saddle, then urged the animal through the portal with a kick of his boots. Pierre took aim, then yelled in frustration as he lifted the barrel toward the sky and fired into the air. The birds in front yard trees took flight, squawking in protest at the noise.

Pierre dashed back into the house and slammed the door behind him. He ran upstairs to collect his ramrod, powder horn, and a sack of lead balls, then scurried back down the stairs. If he hurried, he thought, he might still be able to ride him down. A knock at the door froze him in his tracks. "What in the world…?" he mumbled, then smirked, *The fool came back!* He quickly reloaded, then threw open the door and aimed.

Lieutenant Saint Cloud's eyes widened in shock as he took a step back and reached for his own pistol.

"Sorry! Sorry!" Pierre said, quickly pointing the gun in the air. "I wasn't expecting you."

Saint Cloud's shocked look oozed into a knowing smirk. "Who were you expecting?"

"Uh…" Pierre searched his mind quickly, "no one…you just can't be certain these days in Marseille."

Saint Cloud smiled broadly, twisting the waxed end of his mustache, "Sadly true, monsieur. It would seem there are criminals everywhere."

Pierre let out a nervous laugh, looking quickly to the floor, then finding his composure again, he looked back into the lawman's eyes. "What brings you here, Lieutenant?"

"Well, I was passing by, considering whether I should stop and ask for your help with that smuggling case when I heard gunshots. I came as quickly as I could. Are you alright? Have you been shooting at someone?"

"Oh," Pierre said with a light chuckle, looking at his pistol, then back at Saint Cloud, "I…have squirrels…getting into my bird feeder again."

"I see…" Saint Cloud said, eyeing him carefully, "a perfectly reasonable solution, for sure." He paused for a minute, then shifted his stance, "We arrested a gang of dockworkers last night. They were taking a shipment of old British flintlocks on a deserted beach outside of town."

"Well, I can assure you that hundreds saw me last night attending the opera and visiting the cafés with my fiancé," Pierre said stiffly.

"Monsieur!" Saint Cloud said with feigned surprise. "You are quick to assume my line of questions!"

Pierre sighed in frustration at his own lack of control. "I'm sorry, Lieutenant. Please continue."

Saint Cloud regarded him with a raised eyebrow for a moment before speaking again, "We captured the workers, but four men escaped on horseback. Noblemen, judging from their dress and mounts. Did you notice any prominent young men missing from theater boxes and cafés last night?"

"No, I didn't bother taking attendance," Pierre said flatly, allowing his annoyance to seep back into his voice.

"I see," Saint Cloud said with a light chuckle and mirth in his eyes. "We had an informant among the workers. We had to lock him up with the rest to hide his identity." Pierre just blinked at him in response. "He didn't survive the night," Saint Cloud continued, after giving Pierre space to comment. "Seems he was stabbed multiple times in a crowded cell, yet there were no witnesses."

"Tragic…" Pierre let out before stopping himself.

Saint Cloud eyed him carefully, then continued, "Yes, tragic indeed. He was our only conscious asset in the case." Pierre blinked, trying to hide his surprise and curiosity at Saint Cloud's implication. Saint Cloud waited for the question. When he was sure it wasn't coming, he continued. "One of our musket balls found one of the smugglers before he could get away in one of their launches. An Englishman, for sure. I'm sure he'll have quite an interesting tale to tell if he recovers."

"Let us pray for his health then," Pierre replied. The two men eyed each other for a moment. Pierre spoke again at last. "I'm a very busy man, Lieutenant. If you have no more need of me at the moment, I'd like to attend my own business."

"Of course, monsieur," he said grandly, then fell into a sly smirk. "You have a rodent in your feeder. It may cause you all sorts of trouble."

Chapter Fourteen: The Difference

Everything was different now.

What once felt like a world conspiring to lock her away, was now wide open, full of endless wonderment and possibilities.

She had walked him to the door. There was no point in him crawling out the window like a thief in shame. She wanted the world to see him, to see them together. She stopped along the way to gaze at him standing next to her in the mirror. He smiled bashfully, looking away from his own image. She couldn't help but beam at the sight. She held his hand up and looked at the contrast of his olive skin interlaced with her delicate white. She wanted to imprint this image of them: disheveled, greasy, young, and beautiful together in her mind forever.   She stopped him at the door and kissed him, feeling the full sunlight wash them in glory. He murmured a farewell, then turned and walked away.

"Come back," she told him.

He turned, giving her a soft half-smile that tickled her with delight. "I will," he said with his usual dark drama. He then turned and walked down the gravel drive that split the vineyards. She listened to the crunch of his boots on the small stones. A hand gently laid on her shoulder.

"Come, child," Lavinia said softly, "let's get you cleaned up before your parents return."

Lavinia was quiet while she helped her bathe. Claudette was grateful for it. What could she say now? It was done. There was no going back. She smiled with satisfaction as she sat back in the tub while Lavinia poured warm water over her shoulders.

Everything was different now.

Her parents could see it too. They eyed her nervously, then returned the smile she gave them. "You seem particularly happy, dear," her mother offered over dinner.

"I suppose I am," Claudette said, taking a sip of wine.

"Your evening with Monsieur Godfrey must have gone well, then," her father added.

She giggled mischievously, causing them to look at each other with apprehension, then back to their daughter with forced smiles. "Better than I could have dreamed," she told them, smiling slyly.

Her father paused to regard her as he dabbed his mouth with his napkin, then looked to his wife for guidance. She shrugged. He returned his gaze to his daughter. "Have you considered Monsieur Godfrey's proposal?"

"I have," she said with her own shrug, then returned her attention to cutting her meat.

Her parents looked to each other again before looking back at her.

"And…?" her father asked at last.

"I let you know soon."

Claudette climbed the steps to her room, reveling at the image of their faces when she told them she'd "let them know." It was invigorating to be in control of her own life.

Lavinia was waiting for her at the top of the stairs with wide eyes and a face full of concern. "What is it?" Claudette asked quietly. Lavinia rolled her eyes and motioned with her head to Claudette's bedroom door. Claudette blinked at her for a moment, then turned to the door and entered.

He was sitting on the bed with slumped shoulders. His face was turned away from her. He didn't bother to turn and look when she entered. "Diego!" she said in a hushed voice as she dashed to his side. She put her hand on his shoulder and felt him weaken under her touch. She gasped as he turned to her. His eye was blackened and swollen shut. His nose was swollen too with remnants of blood crusting around the rim of his nostril. What was most startling was the pain and sorrow in his one good eye. "My God, your eye! You're hurt!"

"A lucky shot, for sure," he shrugged. "I'm fine," he said, then looked back at the window. Claudette turned and nodded to Lavinia who standing at the door. Lavinia sighed, nodded back, then withdrew into the darkness of the hall, closing the door gently behind her. Claudette turned to the broken man on her bed. She squeezed his shoulder. "What happened?"

Diego sighed, then spoke. His voice was cracking with sorrow. "I'm so sorry for the trouble I've caused you."

"Diego," she said, wrapping her arm around him and drawing him to her. She kissed his neck and took in his intoxicating smell. "What happened?"

He turned to her, his large green eye brimming with tears. "He knows…" he said, shaking his head in disbelief. "I tried to keep it from him. He…he read right through me. I came to warn you. I came to… say I'm sorry."

Claudette stared at him in wide-eyed shock, her mouth wide open too. Diego forced himself not to look away, but to face his shame and failure. Claudette's wide-open mouth fell slowly into a smile. The pain in Diego's eye turned into confusion. He lifted an eyebrow. This caused a ripple of giggles from Claudette, "My God, your face right now!" she laughed. Diego let out a nervous chuckle, still bewildered by her reaction.

"Are you not angry with me?" he asked.

"No, my sweet," she hugged him and kissed his cheek. "I'm glad he knows. Now I am free. What use am I to him now as a wife?" Diego blinked at her in quiet contemplation. She took his face in her hands, "Do you love me?"

He blinked at her for a moment, then the confusion in his eyes turned into something different, something softer, something sweet. "More than I ever thought I was capable of," he said with that dark dramatic conviction returning to him.

"Then take me away with you. Take me to your beloved Mexico, my love." He blinked at her for a moment. "What is it…? Do you not want me with you?" she asked, suddenly worried.

"Of course I do," he clutched her hand. "I'm just not accustomed to such happiness." Claudette smiled bashfully and looked away. A light tap came to the door.

"It's me," Lavinia whispered in French.

"Come in," Claudette told her.

She came in with a chunk of ice she held in a bowl and a rag, "I chipped some off from the icehouse. There's still plenty to get us through the summer." She explained as she wrapped the rag around the ice and applied it to his eye. Diego let out a hiss in pain. "Easy, child, this will take down the swelling."

"*Merci*," Diego replied, not understanding her words, but understanding her intent.

"He's very sweet," Lavinia turned to Claudette, realizing that he didn't speak French, "but he stinks. We need to wash him. I'll draw a bath."

They stripped him of his clothes and helped him into the warm tub of water. Claudette gasped at the scars that covered his rear. "A Catholic education," he said, noticing her shock.

"Looks like he's a hard learner," Lavinia said in French, having understood his words in English. She took his black clothes to wash, leaving him with a nightshirt borrowed from Monsieur Moreau's wardrobe. She returned moments later with a plate of bread, dry sausage, cheese, a small jug of wine, and a cup. Claudette giggled at the boyish delight that flashed across his face.

"*Merci beaucoup!*" he whispered, taking the plate with famished enthusiasm. Lavinia smirked and looked to Claudette.

"Make sure he doesn't stay too long," she said. "We can only hide an appetite like his for so long."

Claudette smiled at her warmly "Thank you," she said, "for everything."

"I do you no favors, child. I only help you to your ruin," Lavinia said as she withdrew.

Diego offered her a piece of bread with cheese and sausage on it. She shook it off, taking a pull from his wine instead. He smiled. "Will you take me to Mexico with you?" she asked, afraid of what the answer might be.

"Of course!" he said, still chewing his mouthful. He paused to swallow, then took a drink. "One look at you, and my father will not be able to stay angry with me."

"Is your father upset with you?"

"If he isn't already, he will be once he finds that I'm no longer studying at the university at Barcelona."

"Why did you leave?"

He thought for a moment, then shrugged, "I suppose Catholic education didn't suit me."

"I can see why," she giggled, then sighed, watching him eat and drink. "Diego," she said at last. He looked up from his food, realizing she was waiting for him. "Will you marry me?" she asked.

He paused for a moment then smiled, "Aren't you supposed to get on one knee and give me a ring or something?"

"I'm serious!" she slapped his arm, laughing. "If I reject Pierre's proposal, ruin my name, run away with you...will you marry me?"

His smile faded into something more serious, filling her with dread at what he might say. He took her hand and held it as he peered into her eyes. "Of course," he said with gravity. "It is the only way God will forgive us." She let out a breath with a light laugh as tears welled in her eyes. "And it would make me happier than I ever thought I could be," he finished.

"Oh, Diego!" she gasped, wrapping her arms around him and kissing him, her hot tears smearing between their cheeks. Diego gently set his plate to the side as she smothered him in a rush of passion. He hissed as her kisses touched his swollen eye. "I'll be gentle," she whispered as she pushed him down on the bed and lifted his nightshirt. She slid her damp desire up and down against his arousal. He groaned and arched his back in ecstasy. She ran her hands through his hair, kissing him, then brought her hand down to guide him fully inside her.

They lingered in bed through the morning hours, snoozing, making love, then falling back asleep in each other's arms. At last, Lavinia brought them breakfast, Diego's clothes, and a warning, "You need to get him out before your parents come to check on you. It's ten o'clock already!"

"I know..." Claudette told her, knowing the moment she'd been dreading was upon her.

"I should go," Diego said in English, understanding Lavinia's tone more than her French words. "There is much to arrange before we make the crossing."

"I know..." she said to him, now in English.

"Listen to him, God help you," Lavinia said in French, pointing at Diego, "and tell him his clothes are still damp. They'll dry as he wears them." With that, she withdrew.

Diego slipped out of bed, removed his nightshirt, then shimmied up his black trousers over his hips. "Do you trust me?" he asked, bending over to put his foot into a boot

"It's a little late now if I don't," she quipped, watching the lean muscles of his arms and chest flicker as he pulled his boots up over his trousers.

"I need time to find us passage home: time and money. I have made an enemy out of Pierre and most likely his friends. I have to disappear for a while, but I'm coming back. I'm coming for you. Do you understand?"

She nodded then looked at the ground, overwhelmed with a sudden fear of losing him and never seeing him again. He stepped toward her, wrapping an arm around her. He raised her chin with his free hand. "I promise, I will come for you. You have to trust me."

"I do," she said, looking into his eyes and offering a weak smile.

"*Por Los Santos*, I love you so. You are all that matters to me now," he said and kissed her. He then moved to the window and began climbing out.

"No," Claudette stopped him. "Come with me," she said, gently leading him to the door. Diego followed, not quite sure where they were going. He stopped at the open door to the hallway. "Come!" she said, smiling. "It's alright."

After a short pause, he shrugged and followed her out of the sanctuary of her room and into the hallway outside. He grimaced at the sound of his boots on the floor. He stopped at the top of the stairs. "Come," she said, "this is the way."

She held his hand and led him down the stairs. He could see the tops of her parents' heads. Monsieur Moreau was the first to turn and look. He immediately sprung from his chair, dropping his paper to the floor. Madame Moreau let out a frightened gasp as she turned as well and saw the armed man dressed in black accompanying her daughter.

"Mother, father," she addressed them in English, "I have decided."

They blinked at her in silent bewilderment. Diego suddenly didn't know what to do with himself, standing before them.

"I will not marry Monsieur Pierre Godfrey." She paused, waiting to hear any protest her parents might offer. They remained silent in their stunned stupor. She smiled, satisfied she was in control of the room. They followed her hand as she motioned to the dark figure standing next to her with the black eye. "This is Señor Don Diego de la Vega," she continued. "He comes from a family of wealthy landowners in Alta California, Mexico."

"How do you do, sir?" Monsieur Moreau mumbled in English, nodding to the black-caped man next to her.

"Fine, thank you, sir," Diego mumbled back, suddenly feeling strange in his all-black clothes.

"He's the man I'm marrying," Claudette announced.

"Have you lost your mind?" Madame Moreau said in French at last.

"No, mother," Claudette insisted on speaking English, "just my innocence, or rather, I gave it to this man." Diego could feel the blood rush to his face at the implication.

"Oh!" her mother gasped, clutching the fabric of her dress at the breast. She stumbled to her chair and fanned herself weakly.

Her father dashed to her, held her other hand, then looked back at his daughter in pained fury. "What have you done?!" he asked in French.

"I have set myself free," Claudette answered in English.

"You have ruined your name!" he responded in French.

"It won't matter when I'm reborn in the New World," she said, glaring at them.

"You have ruined us…the Godfreys…what will they say?" he said weakly, now matching her in English.

"The De la Vegas will be better trading partners, anyway," Claudette answered, knowing her father's motives for her marrying her into the Godfrey family. "Imagine our wines flowing into California. We could even grow our vineyards there!"

"Grapes grow very well in California, sir," Diego offered meekly.

Her father looked at him for a moment then spoke, "If you don't mind, sir, we are having a bit of a family emergency here."

"Of course," Diego bowed slightly, "my apologies, sir." Monsieur Moreau glared at him in silence. "I…uh…will see myself out then." Diego turned and walked to the front door, cringing at the sound of his boots on the marble floor. He turned the knob, then bumped into the door. "Uh…it…um…opens inward…I see," he said, opening the door toward himself, then had to get out of its way.

"Diego, wait!" Claudette called to him. He stopped in the threshold, the daylight outlining his silhouette. She dashed to him, clutching his hands in hers. "I'll be waiting for you," she told him.

He smiled at her. "I'll come for you," he said. She popped up on her toes as he leaned in and kissed her. He stole one last look at her parents who were still glaring at him in silence. He nodded to them, then walked out into the sunlight. Claudette watched him dash off. Moments later he reappeared on his stolen horse, reining it in as the animal reared onto its back legs, kicking its front legs as it neighed. "I'll come for you, my love!" he shouted, then with a kick of his boots, he sent the horse charging down the gravel lane.

Claudette closed the door and looked at her parents. They stared, still dumbfounded with shock. "I'll be upstairs," she told them. Then returned to her room.

Chapter Fifteen: The Help You Need

Claudette leaned back against the door after closing it. She smiled. She had done it. There was nothing they could do now but let her live the life she chose. She dashed to the window. Holding onto the sill, she leaned out, hoping to see one last glimpse of her Mexican rider, dashing down the road to Marseille. All she saw was the trail of dust settling in the sunlight. She shrugged. At least he was making good time, she thought, all the quicker to return with their travel plans.

She lay on the bed and stared at the ceiling, trying to imagine life in Mexico. She'd have to learn Spanish for sure. She let her mind run wild with all the possibilities life could be there. The sound of someone in the hallway pulled her back to earth. She dreaded having to talk to anyone, even Lavinia. She was done defending her decisions. She just wanted to be left alone with her fantasies.

Those fantasies ran dry within an hour. Now she wondered why Lavinia hadn't come to talk to her. Where were her parents? Clearly, they would have more to say on the matter. She lay there listening to the sounds of the house. Occasionally, she heard footfalls on the floor below or a muffled exchange of words, but other than that: nothing. Now she worried. Were they just going to let her go? Where was Lavinia? Why hadn't she come to lecture her? Claudette's worry deepened. Did she get her in trouble? Did her parents consider her complicit in Claudette's tryst?

She was relieved at the light tapping on her door that afternoon. "Come in," Claudette said, sitting up in her bed.

"You should dress and eat something, child," Lavinia said, opening the door. "You cannot stay in your room all day."

"I know," Claudette said, looking at the floor. "I'm sorry if I got you in any trouble…"

Lavinia shrugged, "They suspect I knew, but they haven't asked me yet." She brought in a plate of bread, fresh cheese, and preserves with a glass of water.

"What will you say?" Claudette asked, taking the water and drinking it greedily.

Lavinia frowned, looking off to the side, "I don't know. I need this job."

"Well, I won't say a thing. I promise!" she assured her.

"Come, now's not the time to talk of such things," Lavinia picked up a brush and started working on her hair. "What's done is done. Now we wait for the effect."

"Have they said anything?" Claudette asked.

"They've been very quiet. Your father has been out most of the day."

Claudette finally found the courage to join her parents for dinner. They were overly polite, straining to hold their smiles as they made light conversation. At last, her father broached the subject. "Crossing the Atlantic is an arduous task, even for the young. Do you think you'll endure it?"

Claudette blinked at him for a moment, then dabbed her mouth with a napkin. "Well...yes. People have been doing it now for centuries. I suppose I will do just as well."

Monsieur Moreau looked to his wife, who returned his look with eyes full of caution.

"I suppose you will, dear. Still, your mother and I think you should be examined by a physician before you set out on such a journey, just to be safe."

"Father, we don't even know when I'll go. Isn't it a bit early?"

"Well, it's never too early to start planning," he told her. "We care greatly for you, my dear. We'd feel much better if we knew you were in top shape for your voyage."

She looked at her parents, trying to discern this change of attitude. "Please, honey," her mother stepped in, "we know we can't change your mind. At least give us the peace of mind that you are in good health to travel."

"Um...alright," Claudette said at last.

"Excellent!" her father said. "I've gone ahead and arranged for an examination. A carriage will be here tomorrow at ten to take you to the doctor's office."

"Why doesn't he come here?" she asked.

Her parents looked to each other before turning back to her. "He's able to do a more thorough examination at his clinic. Modern technology, my dear, it doesn't load so easily onto a carriage."

Lavinia made sure Claudette was up, fed, washed, and dressed well in time for her visit to the doctor's. Claudette's attempts to draw her into conversation fell flat with shoulder shrugs and short answers. *Is she mad at me?* she wondered as Lavinia went through her tasks in silence.

Claudette tried to put these thoughts from her mind later on as she read her copy of Dumas's *Captain Pamphile.*

What would Monsieur Dumas think of me now, she wondered, *now that I've liberated myself?*

She realized she had been merely scanning the last few pages without absorbing a single word. She sighed and flipped back to where she had lost her concentration. Her thoughts crowded her mind, making it nearly impossible to read. Worse was the feeling of undefined dread creeping into her stomach and a vague fear of impending loss.

The sound of the approaching carriage broke her from her thoughts. She got up and watched it come up the drive from the window. It was black, boxlike, and foreboding. Its small dark windows were hard to discern against the dark interior inside. Two grim-looking men sat on the driver's bench.

"Oh, good. Your carriage is here," her mother spoke up behind her. "Be a good girl and listen to the doctor's advice. He's there to help you."

"Of course, mamá," Claudette turned to her, then looked back at the sound of one of the men lifting the heavy lever to the carriage door and swinging it open.

"That's my girl," her father said. "Come! Let's not keep the doctor waiting. I'm sure he's got a full appointment schedule today."

"Of course, Papá," Claudette said softly. She stepped outside, feeling the hot sun strike her as she stepped onto the pebbles with a light crunch. The two men stood by the carriage door, watching her approach. She turned back to her parents. Her father beckoned her to go on with his hand. Both of them held forced smiles on their faces. The carriage leaned with her weight as she stepped inside. It was dark and stuffy. The walls were padded leather with a simple bench. At last, she was able to make out the tiny window. It had iron bars on it.

"Wait!" she called out, turning back to the door. With a grim smirk, one of the men slammed it shut. She heard the other placing a padlock on the lever. "Mamá! Papá! What are they doing?!" she screamed through the window, thrashing and pounding on the walls. Horror, frustration, and rage coursed through her as she screamed. She could no longer see her parents from the angle of the tiny window. "Let me out!" she screamed as she pounded against the padded walls.

Suddenly, a face appeared at the window. Its big blue eyes regarded her with satisfaction.

"You!" she gasped.

"We're getting you the help you need, dear," Pierre told her. "Hopefully, they'll be able to beat the wild petulant beast out of you before our wedding."

"I'm not marrying you!" she screamed.

"Well, I'd hate to postpone the wedding, but I'm willing to endure until you come to your senses. In the meantime, you won't be able to humiliate me any further with your filthy Mexican bandit while you go through treatment." He then stepped down from the running board and turned to the drivers. "You may take her. Make sure they don't mark her up too much. I still want her pretty for the wedding."

The carriage lurched forward with a slap of the reins, jolting her to the floor. "No!" she screamed as she scrambled back to the window. "Mamá, please!" She broke down into sobs, then rage shot through her again. She screamed with all her might, kicking at the door with her feet as the carriage rolled along.

At last, it came to a stop. She huffed, trying to catch her breath. She could hear the padlock unlatching. She smirked with satisfaction as the door opened. The men outside were not smiling. They lurched inside and grabbed her by her arms. "No!" she screamed as they dragged her out. She looked for her house. It was gone now, hidden behind the hill.

"Hold her," one of the men said. He held a leather paddle in his hand.

"No! You wouldn't dare!" she screamed.

The other man held her by her arms. She could feel his erection pressing against her as the first man lifted her skirts and pulled down her undergarments.

"No, you animals!" she screamed.

WHAAP!

"AAAAAIYYYEE!" she screamed. The blow to her bare bottom sent a thousand needles of pain through her body.

WHAAP!

"Stop it!" she screeched

WHAAP!

"AAAAIYY!" she screamed as the blows kept coming. "Please, stop...," she whimpered softly. Her tears, snot, and slobber ran together and hung from her mouth. Large globs broke off, fell to the ground, and soaked into the dust. She shuddered with pain as she sobbed. She could feel the sudden wetness in the man's trousers who was holding her. He had lost control of his desires.

"Will you be quiet?" the other man holding the paddle asked. He was panting from the exertion.

"Yes..." she cried, "please stop hitting me..." She shook with sobs.

After a moment of catching his breath, he spoke again, "Put her back in."

The man who had been holding her loosened his grip, then eased her back up before letting go. She looked at him with disgust as she pulled up her undergarments over her throbbing rear end. His face went red with shame as he looked down. He crouched over to hide the wet spot in his trousers as he tried to help her back into the carriage. She threw his hand off her and climbed in on her own, then lay on the floor. The door closed behind her. She could hear the lock click shut again. They began moving once more. She lay on the floor of the hot dark box, rocking with the motion of the carriage, softly crying.

The carriage rolled to a stop once more. She lifted herself up on her arms to listen. *Have I been sleeping?* she wondered. She was groggy. Her face felt puffy. It was crusted over with dried tears and snot. She wiped it with her sleeve, then covered her eyes as sunlight came slashing through the opening door. Rough hands were on her again, dragging her out. She flinched and squinted at the searing sunlight.

They were inside a building now. It smelt like urine, excrement, and decay. She could hear women crying and somewhere far off, a woman was laughing. Filthy women were laying around on the dirty floor looking at her with dazed indifference.

They brought her into a room with dirty tile and started stripping off her clothes. In the center of the room was a tub filled with cloudy water. Now completely naked, they began leading her to the tub.

"No!" she gasped as she tried to stop by locking her legs.

WHAAP!

She yelped, then hissed in pain as the tingles spread from her bare behind to the rest of her body. The sudden blow from the paddle unlocked her knees. Now she was stumbling along as they dragged her to the tub. They lifted her by her arms and set her in it. She howled from the icy cold as they shoved her down into the water. Goosebumps spread across her tight white flesh. Her butt stung once the cold water hit the tender bruises. She screamed as a bucket of icy water was dumped over her head. Then rough brushes went to work scouring her as she screamed and cried.

At last, they pulled her out. She shivered uncontrollably, clutching herself tightly, trying to hide her nakedness from the rough men handling her. Someone shoved a piece of cloth in her hand before pushing her into a room and closing the door behind her. She heard the lock clicking in place. She shivered, standing awkwardly in the room with her arms wrapped around herself. Sunlight poured in from high windows casting the pattern of iron bars on the floor. The walls were padded. She looked down at the cloth in her hand. It was a simple cotton shift. She quickly pulled it on, then found a place next to the wall to sit.

"Ow!" she hissed as her tender rear end touched the floor. Too painful to sit, she laid on her side, softly feeling the welts on her butt with her hand.

"A Catholic education..." she said flatly, staring at the floor.

A smile slowly formed on her face. The smile turned into a light chuckle, then grew until she found herself laughing hysterically. She could see eyes peering at her through the small window in the door. "What?!" she shouted at the observer while still laughing, "I'm supposed to be crazy, right?!"

Chapter Sixteen: Brides and Bandits

She lay on the floor, listening to a woman screaming somewhere. She knew what was coming next. She had learned the lesson very early: outbreaks bring paddlings. She had her share in the first few days at *l'Asile des Aliénés de Marseille*. Acting out only gets you a swift paddling, an ice bath, or put in restraints for hours. She cringed when she heard the poor woman begin to yell and beat on her walls. They'd be coming for her soon. She could hear them unlock her door. The woman's angry shouts turned into pathetic cries for mercy, then came the sickening whacks of the paddle and the screams of pain followed by the soft sobbing after.

She shook her head, listening to the familiar ritual play out. She had learned that the overworked staff was happy to leave you alone so long as you kept quiet. So Claudette lay on the floor listening to the rhythm of the asylum outside her door, day after day. It was hard to know how long she'd been there or when days even began or ended. She'd cry herself to sleep and then wake up in the darkness. Sometimes laying there for hours, waiting to hear the birds announce the coming day.

Food came at intervals. They emptied her bucket once a day. A doctor had visited her, asked questions, but answered none. A priest came too. He took her confession and then ordered her to repent and pray for forgiveness. They kept her in her room most of the time, away from the other patients. She was grateful for that. So she spent her days lying on the floor, thinking, and crying.

Has he forgotten me by now? she wondered. *Does he even know where I am or what happened to me?* The thought of never seeing him again filled her with sorrow. Once again, the tears came. She did her best to stifle them, lest she earn herself another ice bath.

She woke to the door opening. How long she'd been sleeping, she didn't know. It could have been minutes, hours, or all day. Time was immeasurable here.

"Oh, child!" the familiar voice gasped in pity. Claudette turned to see the pained sympathy on Lavinia's, face and immediately dissolved into sobs. "Oh, child!" Lavinia rushed to her and wrapped her in her arms. "I'm here, my child, I'm here…"

Lavinia let her cry, holding and soothing her, then spoke at last. "I'm here to clean you up for the ceremony. I brought your wedding dress."

Claudette sniffled, "But I don't want to marry him…"

Lavinia looked at her proddingly, forcing her to return the gaze into her eyes, "Do you trust me?"

"Yes…" Claudette said softly.

"Then do as I say, and I promise you, things will turn out fine."

Lavinia insisted on cleaning the tub the hospital provided first before filling it with warm water. "Honestly, how does anyone get properly clean here," she huffed as she scrubbed. Once it was ready, she helped Claudette out of her stained shift and threw it to the ground. "It should be burned…" she said in disgust.

The soap, warm water, and loving hands were a comfort, like a distant memory suddenly recalled. Lavinia combed her wet hair, meticulously picking out the lice that had found their way into her scalp during her stay at the asylum. Claudette felt her humanity slowly returning as Lavinia helped her into her petticoats and corset.

At last, Lavinia gave her a mirror to see the result. She was surprised to see a beautiful woman in the reflection after having endured the degradations of her hospital stay. But the youthfulness that once resided on her face was now replaced with stern hardness. The makeup could not hide the dark circles under her eyes from days of crying and sleepless nights.

She followed Lavinia out of her room and walked through the hospital in her wedding gown. Patients and staff alike stopped to watch the vision go by: an angel walking through the pits of their purgatory. *Perhaps, I'm dead*, she thought.

Pierre's open-air carriage was waiting outside. The coachman leaped from his bench and opened the small half-door for her. She stopped and looked at him, "I was rude to you…the night Pierre first proposed…I'm sorry."

He smiled softly, then flashed a look to Lavinia who gave him a knowing nod. He looked back to Claudette, "It's fine, mademoiselle. I know the person you really are. We only want you to be happy."

Claudette fought back the tear welling in her eye. "Thank you," she said softly, then offered him her hand. He took it and helped her into the carriage. Lavinia climbed in next to her. Claudette stared off at nothing as the carriage rolled away from the asylum and into the woods on the way to town. She was numb. She thought she should take this last chance to run away, but could not bring herself to do anything but stare as they rolled toward her fate. What could she do? Could she ever find happiness after this day? Where was Diego?

The carriage clattered to a stop. "Oh, no," the driver said flatly, "it's a bandit…"

"What?!" Claudette said, sitting up suddenly.

"I certainly hope he isn't here to steal you away…" Lavinia added, matching his tone.

Claudette looked up to see the masked man on horseback blocking the road. His black clothes and mount made him hard to see in the shade from the canopy of trees that covered the road. He held a pistol in one hand and the reins in the other.

"Please," the driver said dispassionately, as he raised his hands, "don't shoot…"

"You!" Claudette turned and looked at Lavinia in shock, "You did this!"

"I have no idea what you're talking about," she said flatly.

"Why?" Claudette persisted.

Lavinia let out a sigh and smiled, "You were right, child, love is everything. Now go to him. You'll have little time to get away once we show up to the wedding without a bride."

Claudette stared at her in stunned shock, then broke into tears, "I may never see you again."

"But you will always carry my love and the things I've taught you. Now go, child, and be happy. It's all I've ever wanted."

Claudette hugged her and kissed her cheek. "I love you," she said softly through her tears.

"I know," Lavinia said, pushing her away, "now go."

She climbed out of the carriage and ran clumsily to him, the mud staining the hem of her dress. Diego put his pistol away, took her arm, and hoisted her onto the back of his horse. The animal danced in a circle as it adjusted to the new weight. Diego regained control, then nodded to Lavinia and the coachman before giving the horse a tap of his heels and sending it charging its way to the quay.

Pierre drummed his fingers on the pew. He looked at the ceiling of the old cathedral. *Is it even safe to be in here?* he mused, then shook his head. The ancient cathedral crumbling on top of him and his hundreds of guests was the least of the disasters looming over him. He was annoyed with himself for being so nervous. Still, he wondered if it had been a mistake to wait until the last minute to have Claudette fetched from the hospital.

The doctor said she was well-cowed by now, but Pierre felt that bringing her out any earlier would have invited all sorts of opportunity for mischief. Still, it would be nice to know her mind before meeting her at the altar. He hoped the stay in the asylum had softened her up enough to at least get through the ceremony. After that, he'd have a beautiful wife along with the inheritance of a profitable vineyard to look forward to. He'd learn how to tame her along the way. *Even the best of horses need breaking,* he thought.

Then there were his British trading partners and the French gendarmes. The British wanted payment for the seized guns and answers for their dead sailors and the injured man currently held by the gendarmes. His simple scheme of buying surplus guns from British smugglers and selling them to Mexico was unraveling before his eyes and could very well turn into an international embarrassment for everyone involved. It all pivoted on the injured man. All their secrets were held in his unconscious mind. Pierre had hoped he would just conveniently die before waking. But he must have recovered.

Lieutenant Saint Cloud had come to the house early one morning with armed men, demanding to see Pierre. Thankfully, Bernard had the sense to lie and say he was out. Since then, they'd been hounding him, appearing in places he frequented looking to arrest him for sure.

This wedding was the first time Pierre dared to show his face in public since. With all the planning and cost involved, he certainly couldn't call it off without creating all sorts of humiliating scandal. So he had to endure and hope Lieutenant Saint Cloud would have the decency not to arrest a man at his wedding.

He was just now fighting the urge to check his watch again when the carriage came clattering up the street. A mob of commoners crowded the doorway hoping to catch a glimpse of the beautiful bride and the opulent ceremony denied to them and their class. He smiled as he stood, taking his place at the altar.

The music didn't start. Instead, the cheers quieted and turned into gasps. A woman outside screamed. Now he was concerned as it seemed something had startled the crowd. He took a step forward, stepping down from the altar, walking cautiously through the nave toward the opened doors. He started hearing the words rumble through the crowd in hushed tones: "kidnapped," "bandit," and "the *Fox*!" He stopped at the sight of the carriage surrounded by the mob. He could see the feigned concern on Claudette's servant and his own driver's faces, but no Claudette.

"Damn you, Diego…" he mumbled.

"Monsieur Godfrey!" a voice shouted from outside, rising higher than the rest. "Stay where you are!"

Pierre could see them now, Lieutenant Saint Cloud and his men armed with bayonets and muskets were pushing their way through the crowd.

"Damn it!" Pierre hissed, then turned back toward the altar.

"What's going on?" the priest asked.

"Out of my way, Father," Pierre brushed him aside. He had to get out the backdoor and find his horse.

Claudette clung tightly to Diego's waist as they galloped into town, then slowed to a trot. He took off his mask and shoved it in his shirt, but that did nothing to stop people from staring at the dashing armed man in black on a black horse with a beautiful woman in white clinging to him. She still held him tightly as they wove through the crowded street. After thinking she had lost him forever, the exhilaration of touching him again was overwhelming. She was drunk on his scent, breathing him in as she pulsed her hips to the rhythm of the horse. *Let them gawk*, she thought, seeing the people stare at them. *This is what love looks like!*

It occurred to her that she barely knew him. He was nothing more than a dark enigma she had thrown her life away for. *What happens now?* she wondered, then realized she didn't care. She was young, alive, and in love. She was willing to go anywhere he took her.

They rode up to the stable near the quays. Diego got down then grasped her by the waist and lowered her to the ground. She felt her body sliding against his as he did. She kissed him impulsively. "We'll get to that soon, I promise, my love," he smiled, then turned away, leading her by the hand and the horse by the reins.

"She belongs to Monsieur Godfrey," he told a stablehand in broken French. Claudette recoiled for a moment until she realized he was talking about the horse, as he handed over the reins. He then handed the man a coin. "Make sure she's well cared for and returned to her owner." He then turned to her and spoke in English, "Come, we have little time." He took her by the hand as they ran along the dock. They stopped at a small felucca. The two Arabs aboard looked up at them and smiled.

"We're crossing the Atlantic in this?!" she exclaimed.

"No, just the Mediterranean for now, my love. Get in. I'll explain later," he told her.

"Stop!" someone shouted in Spanish. They looked back to see Pierre running toward them from the foot of the dock.

"Quickly, get in!" Diego told her in English. She looked down at the two Arabs who were smiling and holding their hands out to receive her.

"Push off and I'll catch up!" Diego told them in Spanish.

"Unhand my woman!" Pierre shouted, unsheathing his sword as he trotted up. Diego pulled out his own. "…and give me back my sword, you thief!"

"Not while I have to defend myself and the woman I love," Diego told him.

"Pfft!" Pierre scoffed, "You're the only one who's in danger here, you fool!"

Diego turned to the boat. "Go!" he shouted. The Arab brothers untied the boat and pushed away, using the paddles to move the small sailing vessel along the row of boats and ships. He turned back just in time to deflect Pierre's first thrust with a roll of his wrist to the left, then countered with his own. Pierre circled his blade underneath catching Diego's, then flicked it up and away creating an opening.

"Halt!" someone called in French. The two combatants turned to see blue-uniformed men with bicorne hats surging onto the dock.

"Damn it!" Pierre gasped at the sight, then turned just in time to see Diego's fist finish its journey to his jaw. The blow sent him reeling back. Then a boot buried itself into his stomach, knocking him to the wooden planks. Diego was upon him before he could collect himself.

"I believe this belongs to you, my friend," Diego said, drawing his sword back and then thrusting it forward. Pierre cringed, waiting to feel the pain of the blade entering him. Instead, it drove through his clothing, pinning him to the wooden dock. He tried to sit up but was slammed back down, caught by the blade.

"EEEYYAAA," he cried in frustration, grasping the blade and yanking it out of the plank, cutting his hand in the process.

Diego ran along the dock, keeping pace with the felucca. Without missing a step, he threw himself headfirst into the water. He quickly came to the surface and started swimming toward the boat with powerful plunging strokes. Claudette and one of the brothers helped pull him in. He turned and looked back at the dock just in time to see Pierre leveling his pistol. His long blonde hair was wild and hanging in strands around his face. Then he was enveloped by the men in blue uniforms. They grabbed his arm as he fired causing the round to fly high. Claudette yelped in fear at the sound of the pistol.

"Claudette!" Pierre screamed as the uniformed men tried to restrain him, "You're in love with a madman!" The other brother hoisted the sail, and now the little vessel was moving with the wind. They watched as the gendarmes dragged Pierre from sight. Diego turned to the brothers and spoke to them in Spanish.

"Thank you, my friends. Once again you have saved my life. Here is the rest as promised." He handed one of them a small sack of coins. He then turned to Claudette and spoke English, "These are my friends, Nassar and Akbar. They have saved me before."

"*Muchas gracias,*" Claudette attempted.

"*De nada,*" Nassar smiled at her.

Akbar said something in Arabic, causing Nassar to laugh.

"What did he say?" Diego asked.

"He wants to know if you always leave countries this way," Nassar chuckled.

"It's a bad habit for sure," Diego replied.

Part II: The Crossing

Chapter Seventeen: The Best Day

Claudette stared silently at the dock as they drew farther away. She was really staring at nothing at all as she rocked involuntarily with the boat fighting its way through the waves. She was completely lost in her thoughts. The reality of her situation came crashing down on her. She had just run away from a comfortable life, her parents, and everything familiar to her, to be with a man she barely knew. Now she was on a tiny boat sailed by Arabs headed for Africa. Yet somehow, it all felt familiar.

"Say goodbye to your prison," the one she knew as Nassar spoke to her in French.

"What?" she asked, roused from her thoughts. She looked at him and smiled nervously.

He smiled back and pointed behind her, "There! *Le Château d'If*! Do you remember?"

She turned to see the foreboding prison island sitting on their left as they came out of the harbor. "Yes, of course!" she said. "You and your brother took us to the island with Monsieur Dumas! I thought you looked familiar!"

Nassar smiled, "Yes, yes, let's eat!" The brothers unpacked a lunch of sardines, flatbread, olives, cheese, and chickpea paste that carried a heavy smell of garlic. Akbar drizzled it all with olive oil and freshly squeezed lemon wedges. Diego offered them wine, but the brothers politely refused. The Arabs quickly mumbled a prayer after which Diego absently crossed himself.

Claudette decided to cross herself too before digging into the humble but delicious meal. She was grateful for the wine to wash down the heavily spiced food. She watched Diego eat as he watched the shoreline go by. She could see he had brought the wine, some bags, and two small bundles of clothes. One was hers. Tied to the top of her bundle was the copy of the novel she had been reading, *Le Capitaine Pamphile*. She smiled warmly. He had thought of everything. She wanted to wrap her arms around him and kiss him. But she felt it would be odd in the little open boat in front of the brothers. So she just smiled and watched him watch the world go by.

The journey took over a week. Not daring to take the small craft into open waters, they hugged the coastline as they made their way south and west, stopping several times to unload their cargo and take on new. Diego threw himself into the tasks of running the small bartering craft, helping with the cargoes and the sails.

"We'll find passage across the Atlantic once we get to Morocco," he told her, "away from Spanish and French authorities."

She swallowed at that. She knew he was a fugitive from Spain. She figured he'd now be wanted for banditry and kidnapping in France as well. They watched with dread as French warships passed them. The large gunboats were on their way to Algeria. Diego seemed particularly on guard once they passed into Spanish waters. He kept his pistol and dagger tucked into his trousers at all times.

Claudette spent much of the time reading or practicing her tarot cards. Diego and the brothers watched with slightly disturbed frowns as she turned over the cards and read their meanings. It made her laugh. She was delighted to find the cards packed among her things. Lavinia must have given them to her as a parting gift. Claudette was now determined to learn and continue her studies of the dark arts, even if it alarmed the Muslim brothers and her stoutly Catholic lover.

Being with her lover, at last, was the most frustrating part of the journey. She wanted to squeeze and kiss him, to let her passions run wild. But they were never alone. They were trapped on an open boat with two other men. The best she could do was enjoy the nights when they cuddled together under the canvas tarp the brothers strung over the boom like a tent to protect them from the rain. She lay there listening to the water lap against the hull. The larger ships docked around them creaked and groaned in their slips. Sometimes she could feel his arousal pressing against her and the small gasps and groans that escaped him. She smiled in the darkness. It was hard for him too. *Soon, my love,* she thought, then slipped into a soft honeyed sleep.

At last, she could see the large promontory looming in the haze ahead. The setting sun gave it a halo of orange and pink ribbons that extended across the sky. The water around it was filled with vessels of all types and sizes, carrying the flags of dozens of nations. The most prominent were the warships flying the Union Jack.

"The Rock of Gibraltar," Nassar pointed, noticing her fixation on the monolith which commanded the sea around it. "It's from there that the English look down and watch over all of us."

The sight of it brought waves of dread and awe. It seemed as if the power of France's ancient enemy radiated from it. But it wasn't the British warships that worried her so much. It was the ones carrying the Tricolors of her own country, a country they had fled. Diego watched them too with silent reservation.

"It is best we follow them and make the crossing tonight," Nassar said as if reading their thoughts. "Moroccan customs agents are more forgiving than the British," he said, nodding toward the enormous rock formation that jutted into the sea.

"Anywhere is better than Spain," Diego mumbled in agreement.

Nassar nodded to his brother who then pulled the tiller to the right, causing the little boat to turn south and away from the wind. Nassar let out the sails. They billowed as the wind was now filling them from across the beam. Claudette drew in a breath as the small craft found a place among the warships sailing to Africa.

Akbar mumbled something in Arabic as they approached the Port of Tangiers, to which Nassar mumbled something back that sounded like an agreement. "What did he say?" Diego asked.

"He says it looks like an invasion," Nassar told them. The harbor was filled with French ships. Their gas lamps glowed eerily in the twilight.

"But France is at war with Algeria, not Morocco," Claudette said in English, understanding a little of the Spanish spoken between Diego and Nassar.

"Yes," Nassar answered in the same language, "but European invasions spread quickly in Africa."

"Perhaps we should make our own invasion somewhere away from the port," Diego added, now in English as well.

"I think you're right," Nassar said softly, looking at the warships looming ahead. He turned to his brother and spoke in Arabic, to which Akbar nodded and turned the craft back toward the east. Nassar let the sails out further. The wind from behind puffed them out like balloons.

They sailed along the African coast until there were no more lights or any sign of civilization. "Here, I think is best," Nassar said to Diego in Spanish. Diego nodded. Nassar then spoke to his brother who responded by dropping the sail, then using a staff, tested the depth of the water. Akbar spoke in Arabic again. Nassar then turned to Diego and Claudette, "The tide is out. He says it's shallow enough for you to wade ashore from here."

"Let's see," Diego smiled at him in the darkness, then pulled out his pistol and handed it to Claudette. The wood and iron weapon felt surprisingly heavy in her hands. She suddenly felt an alarmed exhilaration at holding such a thing for the first time. Diego grinned, reading the alarm on her face. "It's alright," he told her in English. "Just don't point it at anything you don't want to shoot."

She giggled nervously, "I'll do my best." He laughed at that, then cupped her cheek with his hand. He looked at her with a heart-melting softness in his eyes. She blushed, which caused him to smile. He ran his hand through her hair, tussling it before turning to the edge of the boat. He put his hip on the gunwale, swung his legs over, and dropped into the water with a splash. He spoke Spanish to Nassar, who responded by handing him their bundles and bags.

"I'll be back in a moment," he told her, then waded off into the darkness. Suddenly, she realized she was sitting alone on the boat with the two Arabs. She gripped the gun with apprehension. They smiled at her in the darkness.

"It's alright," Nassar assured her in French. "He'll be back soon."

She giggled nervously. "Of course, thank you," she said, embarrassed for showing her fear of being alone with them. She sat there, awkwardly listening to the soft laps of water hitting the hull and the creaks of the boat. At last, she could hear Diego splashing his way back. She let out her breath as he approached.

"This will do," he said as he came into sight. He held out his arms and the brother helped Claudette into them. Parts of her dress were already lying on the surface, slowly sinking as they absorbed the water. He cradled her in his arms. He looked up at the brothers and spoke, "You have saved us. I cannot thank you enough."

Nassar smiled, "Well, this time we let you pay."

"You could have gotten more by selling us to the slavers," Diego replied.

Nassar laughed, "We are Arab traders, not Berber pirates, my friend."

"Well, once again, I live because of you. I thank you and your brother," Diego replied, nodding to Akbar.

Akbar said something in Arabic. Diego looked to Nassar for translation.

"He says, 'go with God,'" Nassar told him.

Diego nodded, then looked to Akbar again and repeated, "*adhhab mae Allah*," with a short bow. With that, he turned and waded toward the shore. She lay snuggled in his arms, holding the pistol as he carried her. The nearness of him and the strangeness of their predicament was suddenly overwhelming. She found herself clutching his hair and kissing his neck as they went.

At last, he set her down on the dry sand. She realized that, for the first time in her life, she was not only outside of France but on an entirely new continent. The idea of it filled her with fear and excitement.

"Are we safe here?" she asked, trying to see their surroundings in the dark.

"I don't know," he said. "Perhaps we'll see better in the morning."

They picked up their bundles and stumbled up the beach in the darkness. "We have to get off the sand or we'll wake up in the water when the tide comes in," he told her.

She could make out a towering form looming ahead in the darkness. Looking at it caused her to trip over a rock and stumble. He was quick to catch her. "Here," he said, offering his hand. He led her toward the dark towering form that slowly revealed itself to be a rocky cliff wall as they got nearer. They found their way onto a small footpath that twisted and turned as it climbed through the crags and rocks, some of which he had to hoist her onto, then climb himself.

At last, they found a small perch and cubbyhole in the rock wall. "I think this is high enough," Diego said, looking down at the progress they had made from their climb. He shimmied off his boots and set them out to dry. Then did the same with his pants. Claudette watched him and then decided to get out of her dress.

"Help me out of this," she turned to present the laces on her back. She smiled as she felt his hands on her, loosening the binds.

"We'll be warm under the blanket," he said nervously. She smiled at his self-consciousness.

"Only if you hold me tight," she told him with feigned earnestness. "We must combine our body heat to protect us from the cold."

"Of course," he said softly. His sudden shyness filled her with delight. With their clothes hung to dry, he dusted off a spot in the cubbyhole for their blanket. He lay on it, then reached out to her, inviting her into his arms. Claudette snuggled up next to him, feeling his warmth as he wrapped her in the blanket and his arms. She could feel his arousal pressing against her rear. She smiled in the darkness, sensing his sweet agony at their closeness.

She closed her eyes and tried to sleep. She could hear him let out a light, tormented gasp. It filled her with devilish delight. Suddenly she felt his lust seeping into her. She pressed her rear into him further, squirming with desire. Finally, it was too much. She turned to him and gasped, "Kiss me!" They were at once diving deep into each other's passion, kissing and caressing each other frantically. "Oh, I've waited so long…" she gasped, feeling him slide up against her wetness. She moaned in ecstasy and then he was inside.

They made love with frantic abandon until they lay exhausted in each other's arms. Claudette smiled softly with her eyes closed. She was snug with the blanket and his arms wrapped tightly around her. She listened to his soft breathing. He was already asleep. She could hear the light breeze outside of the rock walls of their cubbyhole and the sound of the sea below. Somewhere in that contentment, she fell asleep.

She woke to the sound of the waves crashing below. Pink and amber ribbons of light stretched across the dim sky. Sensing her consciousness, Diego squeezed her. He kissed the space behind her jaw and ear. "Mmmmm…" she said, closing her eyes in satisfaction. "It wasn't a dream…"

"No, my love, it's all real," he told her.

"Hmph," she turned to him with a smirk, "prove it!" He smiled and pulled her to him, kissing her softly at first and then more passionately until they fell back into making love.

They lay there afterward, listening to the sea and watching the dark forms around them slowly reveal themselves in the morning light.

"I'm starving!" she said at last.

"Me too," he said, sitting up. "Thankfully, we still have some bread and cheese," he told her, as he unfolded a small bundle wrapped in cloth, "but we'll have to find more food before we make our way to Tangiers."

They enjoyed their breakfast as they talked about their plans and what life would be like in Mexico. Finding fresh water was first among their tasks, as their breakfast took most of what was left in their waterskin. "Rivers always reach the sea," he assured her, but she soon began to worry as they explored the beach for more than an hour.

"There!" he said at last with thinly veiled relief in his voice. She followed his pointing to a trickle of water that bounced and splashed down the rocks and then soaked into the sand below. She ran to it and filled her cupped hands, drinking greedily while splashing most of it on her face.

"Ah!" she smacked her lips. "It's fresh!" They drank and filled their water skin. "We should wash the salt from our clothes," she told him, then pulled her dress off. Diego's eyes went wide as he watched her rinse her clothes in the cascading water. "Come!" she beaconed. He shrugged and began taking off his.

They washed their clothes and bathed, stopping from time to time to hold each other and kiss as the water splashed over them. They laid their clothes on the hot rocks to let them dry, using just a few scraps of cloth to cover themselves. She ran a cloth between her legs and secured it with a string that she tied around her hips so that a just small triangle covered her in front and rear.

Diego sharpened a stick with his dagger, then led her out to the rocks among the retreating tide. She smiled at the sight of him with a spear in his hand and a dagger tucked into the back of his loincloth. The sun beamed on his olive skin as he crawled among the rocks. She imagined this was how the first people lived.

"Gotcha!" he shouted, driving his spear into the water at the base of one of the rocks.

"Ew!" she drew her face back in disgust as he reached in and pulled out an octopus which squirmed in his hand.

"Here!" he shouted, tossing it to her, "our first of the day!" She screeched as she involuntarily caught it, then looked at it in horror as her knees buckled into each other. The creature began wrapping its tentacles around her arm. Diego broke into a laugh, and soon she was laughing too with a mixture of mirth and mortification.

They continued to hunt, catching crabs and prying limpets off the rocks. Diego managed to spear some fish as well. Once satisfied with their bounty, he built a fire and set a stone in the center. After a few moments, he tested the stone with a trickle of water which hissed and bubbled upon contact and evaporated. He used it to cook most of the food, handing her cooked morsels as they were done and putting a few in his mouth. It was salty and delicious. Thankfully there was just enough wine left to wash it down. Finally, he strung up the fish over the smoldering ashes and allowed the smoke to slowly cook them.

"Where did you learn to do all of this?" she asked, looking at the glowing embers as they sat near the fire.

"You learn where the food is and how to cook it on long cattle drives. The sea here is not much different from California," he said as he inspected the cleaning job he was doing on his pistol.

She watched him for a moment, then spoke again. "I should learn to shoot," she said, "in case I need to someday."

He lifted an eyebrow and regarded her for a moment before speaking. "You should," he said, then stood and reached his hand out to her. She looked at him for a moment, not sure if she was ready to learn at that very moment while being almost completely undressed. She gave him her hand and allowed him to pull her to her feet. "Don't be scared," he smiled, reading her expression. He pulled her into his arms and kissed her neck as he played with the string tied just above her hip bone with his finger.

"You should respect firearms but not fear them," he told her. "Unless they are being held by your enemy," he added with a chuckle. He handed her the weapon. Once again, it felt surprisingly heavy. "Pull the hammer back to the full-cocked position," he told her. It was hard to do so. She had to use both thumbs to draw it back until it clicked. He held her arm up with his right hand while cradling her with his left arm wrapped around her hip. "Now close your left eye and line the sights with your right. Find a spot to shoot among the rocks."

He let go of her and took a step back. "When you are ready, squeeze the trigger as you exhale. Keep your arm loose. Let it recoil flow naturally."

She grimaced as she took aim. She could already feel her heart pounding against her chest. "*Mon Dieu!* I can't do it!" she gasped.

"Just shoot, my love. It'll be fine."

She sighted the gun once more, slowly squeezing the trigger as she exhaled.

She squealed in horror as the thing went off, jolting her arm upward and dousing her with smoke that smelled like rotten eggs. She immediately broke into a peal of laughter. Diego wrapped his arms around her. "See? It's not so bad," he said.

"It's the expectation more than anything," she said.

"As is with most things," he agreed. "Let me show you how to clean and load it."

"Yes, I think I'm done shooting for today."

They lay next to the fire, gazing at it while in each other's arms. The sun had crossed over them and was now finding its way westward toward the new world. The world around them was quickly dimming. "I should put it out before it gets too dark," Diego said. "We are marking our position for miles around us now."

"Just a little longer, my love," she cooed. "Let us worry about the outside world tomorrow." She had stopped him from dressing earlier after they had swum that afternoon as well. "I'm not ready to be civilized yet," she had told him.

Now Diego stared silently at the flames. She snuggled up next to him, sensing his unrest. At last, he let out a sigh, squeezed her, and kissed the side of her face.

"I suppose," he said. "Tomorrow will come soon enough."

She sat up and looked at him for a moment. "I want to thank you," she said in earnest, squeezing his hands in hers.

He looked at her with a raised eyebrow. "What for?"

"…for giving me…the best day of my life," she said, looking at him with new conviction.

He looked back at her with some confusion.

"Just to be with you…" she tried to explain, "has given me the best day of my life." A tear began to roll down her cheek. He drew her into him and held her. She breathed him in, clinging to him tightly as undefined dread began to spill into her stomach.

She woke several times that night. Sometimes from some undefined terror or from a dream in which she was lost in a crowd and couldn't find him. But each time, she'd feel his warm body next to her and hear the soft sounds of his breathing. She'd snuggle up next to him again and go back to sleep, listening to the waves below and feeling the cool night breeze brush over the top of their blanket.

Diego's sudden movement jolted her awake. He whipped out his pistol and dagger and pointed them upward as he lay next to her. She turned, opened her eyes, and screamed. Musket barrels and swords pointed closely at their faces from all directions. Above them were dark faces, some partially covered with scarves that cascaded from headdresses. They gripped their weapons with newfound aggression at Diego's sudden movement and barked at them in an angry guttural language.

Chapter Eighteen: Abd al-Qādir

"Diego, don't fight!" Claudette pleaded, unwittingly digging her nails into his arm. "I'll be alone and lost if they kill you!" The men shouted in Arabic, shaking their guns and sabers at them. Diego was still lying flat on his back, holding his pistol and dagger straight up, promising death to the first man to come for them.

"Diego, please…" she said softly, then sucked in a sob.

The men around them began to quiet, waiting to see what he'd do.

In a blur of action, he spun both weapons in his hands. The men shouted. Muskets rattled as they once again pulled them to their shoulders. A new quiet fell over them as they looked on with fear, only to see that Diego was now offering his weapons to them, handles first. One of them started laughing, then another. Soon they were all laughing as they lowed their weapons. Claudette couldn't make out the language, but the tone seemed to say that they were impressed by the trick.

"You almost got us killed with that!" she hissed.

"I just wanted them to know who they're dealing with," he said as hands reached in and relieved him of his weapons. One of the young men tried spinning his own pistol. It flew out of his hand and bounced around in his arms as he tried to regain control. It clattered to the ground and fired. Claudette screeched. The man next to the bumbling youth yelped and clutched his foot, hopping around in agony. Another man swatted the youth in the back of the head, knocking off his headscarf as he yelled. This caused another round of uproarious laughter from the desert men.

"*Mon Dieu*, you men are all idiots!" she said. "We won't survive the day at this rate!"

Hands reached down to help them up. The blanket fell away as Claudette stood wearing nothing but her tiny string and cloth garment. This caused another uproarious commotion from the men. Many turned away, shielding their eyes from her near nakedness. Someone quickly covered her with a robe, then wrapped a scarf around her head, leaving only her eyes uncovered.

They whisked her away and set her on a horse. The small band of men moved out at once. She kept looking back, hoping to catch a glimpse of her lover as they moved through the trees, the scrub brush, and finally, into the open wasteland of the desert. She saw him at last. His hands were bound in front of him. He stumbled along as the rider holding the other end of the rope tugged mercilessly at it and yelled at him in Arabic to keep up. The hot sun sparkled on his sweat-soaked body. "They'll kill him," she gasped under her breath.

Much to her relief, they eventually covered him with a robe and headscarf during their first stop. Diego caught her eye and nodded as if to say all would be alright as he accepted water from their captors.

They stopped again that evening. They gave her bread and water and had her lay in the sand as armed men took turns guarding her through the night. Already, she missed the nearness of her lover laying next to her. She took comfort knowing that he was still alive and somewhere nearby. But it was agony not being able to go to him, to feel the comfort and security of his arms

The men knelt and prayed before sunrise, all facing the same direction as they did the night before and several times throughout the previous day. Once done with prayers, they ate and set out once again. At last, she could see what appeared to be a village made entirely of tents in the distance. There were palm trees interspersed among the tents. The encampment was a busy place. Horsemen came and went. Men moved in and out of the tents with swords and daggers tucked in their sashes, and muskets slung over their shoulders. Women carried jugs on their heads or sat in circles under canopies, mending clothes and kneading dough. Their faces were covered with scarves like hers. She did not see where they took Diego. She feared he'd be tortured or killed outright. She feared she'd be sold as a slave or simply turned over to these rough men to do as they pleased.

Instead, they led her to a tent full of women. One of them barked orders in Arabic at her and at the others. Claudette tried to understand what she wanted. The woman appeared to be in her mid-fifties and carried an air of authority over the other women. Eventually, some of the younger ones stepped in and started removing Claudette's robe, which now seemed to be the woman's wish.

They washed her with rags they dampened from bowls of water. The woman in charge continued to talk at her in harsh tones which were matched by a hardness in her eyes. Claudette tried to understand what she wanted. "I'm sorry...I don't understand..." was all she could say in return. The woman felt Claudette's forehead, then put her hand on her belly. Her eyes softened a bit. She said something to one of the girls, who then brought her a cup. The woman thrust it into Claudette's hands and mimed what she wanted her to do.

"You want me to...pee in it?" Claudette asked nervously, trying to repeat the mimed movements of the woman.

"*Naem! Naem!*" the woman repeated, nodding her head, showing somewhat of a smile in her eyes for the first time. Claudette blinked at her for a moment. The women around her nodded their heads as well. After waiting a moment to make sure she was interpreting this request correctly, she squatted over the cup and filled it as the women watched with interest. She handed it to the woman as she stood again. The woman looked at it closely, then sniffed it. At last, she dipped her finger in and tasted it.

I must be dreaming, Claudette thought, as her knees buckled beneath her. The women caught her as she collapsed. The world spun and dimmed as they carried her to a low-sitting armless sofa and laid her down. She could hear the woman give the others orders. The woman then came and squatted next to her. She was smiling now. There was kindness in her eyes as she spoke softly, stroking Claudette's hair.

Claudette slept, waking to waves of nausea which caused her to retch over the side of the sofa. A young girl was quick to bring her a bucket. Another brought her a warm cup of mint tea that soothed her roiling stomach and helped her sleep once more.

She woke again in the early morning darkness. Someone was calling out, chanting in rhythm. The women rose and found places on the ground to kneel. She got up too. Some of the girls motioned for her to kneel with them. They murmured their prayers and bowed their heads to the ground. Claudette crossed herself and tried to follow their example.

Once done, the women went to work, preparing a meal for the camp, which was already coming alive. Horsemen galloped in and out of the circle of tents. She could hear men barking orders at others in the harsh guttural language. *Where are they keeping him?* she wondered, worried about what these rough desert men may have done to his pretty face.

She sat under the canopy with the rest of the women after breakfast. They were busy cracking barley with stones. It was part of the endless task of creating food for the warriors and the mobile village that supported them. Her eyes began to grow heavy in the mid-morning heat and the monotony of the work. She shook her head to ward off the sleepiness, then saw the two warriors coming to her with much purpose in their step. They barked at her in the strange language. She flinched and drew her hand to her breast as if to say, "Me?" The older woman stood up and spoke to them harshly. This quieted the two men as they bowed their heads to her. She then turned to Claudette and beckoned her to stand.

Claudette took her arm. They followed the men through a maze of tents until they came to the center of this small temporary city. There stood a grand tent guarded by men with bayoneted muskets and curved swords at their sides. The sight of it, and the power it seemed to radiate, filled her with dread. The woman tugged at her, beckoning her on. The guards bowed their heads to them as the woman pulled her through the flaps.

The dim light emitting through the canvas contrasted greatly with the sunlight outside. It was difficult to see at first but she could make out the forms of men sitting on the rugs that made up the floor. They all seemed to be focused on a man sitting cross-legged in the center. The woman guided her to a spot in front of this man and pushed her to sit down like the others.

Claudette widened her eyes to adjust to the dim light as she scanned the room. "Diego!" she gasped. He was sitting nearby. This caused a bit of a murmur among the men in the tent. The woman next to her immediately grabbed her shoulders to keep her from getting up and going to him. Diego smiled and winked at her, drawing his lips together to create a silent, "Shhh…"

Relief at seeing him alive and well washed over her. Diego motioned with his head to look forward at the man seated in the center of the room. She turned to see the man's deep-set brown eyes regard her with interest. His silent demeanor was regal and frightening. He was an Arab in his mid-thirties with olive skin and a full beard. He wore a simple white robe and headdress. As terrifying as he seemed, there was a depth to his eyes that she found compelling and irresistible.

"You are in the presence of Emir Abd al-Qādir, Leader of the Faithful," a man sitting near him said in perfect French. "Please refrain from further outbursts."

Claudette focused on the man speaking. He was bearded like the rest of them but wore a small skullcap that covered the back of his head instead of the full headscarves that most of the men around him wore.

"You're a Jew!" she gasped in surprise. This caused another round of agitated murmurs. Some of the men began to rise to redress this outburst.

The emir smiled with a light chuckle. He put his hand out to calm them and to say it was fine.

The man who had been speaking took that as a cue and smiled as well, "I hope you don't find it too distasteful to speak through a man of my faith."

"Of course not!" she said, realizing her misstep with embarrassment. "I thought the Bedouins despised your kind."

"Not if we're useful, my dear," he said. That brought a chuckle among some in the room. "I am Judas Ben Duran. I translate for the emir."

"My apologies, monsieur. I meant no insult," she said, bowing her head in embarrassment.

"None taken, my dear," the man assured her. "We've even had priests at one time to attend to our Christian prisoners. We lost them once the French overran our camps in Algeria. You'll find the emir can be quite tolerant so long as you're respectful in return."

"I see..." she said softly, stealing another look at the emir's dark eyes.

The emir spoke at last in a soft but deep voice that carried easily across the room.

"He asks if you are French," Ben Duran said.

"Yes, but…we are fugitives of France," she answered.

The emir said something that brought a round of chuckles.

"'Aren't we all,' he says," Ben Duran translated. "The man you are with, he is not a Spaniard?"

"He is Mexican, monsieur, from the New World. We are trying to get to his home," she told him.

This brought another round of murmurs in the tent as the Arabs mumbled the word, "*Miksikiun*," with some awe as they looked at the man before them as if he were some kind of exotic creature.

Ben Duran said something to Diego in Spanish, to which Diego replied.

Ben Duran turned to Claudette. "He says you both speak English," he said in the same language.

"A bit, yes," she replied in kind.

"Ah," he said, "that'll be a bit easier than switching between Spanish, French, and Arabic. Why are you running from France?"

Claudette looked to Diego, who shrugged, then turned back to Ben Duran, "We are in love. I was to be married to another man, but we ran away together."

Ben Duran relayed the story to the emir. There was much mumbling among the men seated around them as it was translated to Arabic. The emir sat quietly, listening, switching his gaze between the two lovers before him. There was silence as Ben Duran finished. The emir spoke at last. A man got up and approached Diego. He pulled out a dagger and pistol tucked in his robe. Claudette let out a gasp, then covered her mouth with her hand at the sight of them. They were Diego's.

The emir spoke.

"Do the trick," Ben Duran translated.

Diego smiled slowly. "*Gracias*," he said as he stood and accepted the weapons. The Arabs leaned in with anticipation of what this wild New World man would do. With a show of indifferent effort, Diego began to spin the two weapons in his hands, twirling the knife among the fingers of his left hand while spinning the pistol in various directions with his right. A murmur of delighted "oohs" and "ahs" spread among the room.

Then, with suddenly surprising speed, he chucked the dagger across the tent. It stuck into the tent pole near the emir with a loud "thunk!" Men gasped and reached for their weapons, springing to their feet. An unbearable silence ensued. Claudette was sure their deaths were near. The emir started to chuckle lightly. Soon, all of them were laughing, some even patting Diego on the back. The emir put his hands out and motioned everyone to sit before he spoke again. Ben Duran translated.

"The emir says you can travel with us to Tangiers. There, you'll find transport to the Americas. Until then, you are expected to do your part as members of the *smala*."

"Of course, thank you," Claudette said softly. The emir looked at her and smiled. He then spoke to the woman next to her before returning his eyes to her. He spoke again. Ben Duran translated.

"The emir's mother says you are with child. Are you aware of that?" he said.

Claudette felt the blood flee from her face. The dark stuffy tent began to spin as it dimmed until there was nothing but darkness.

Chapter Nineteen: The Hat Dance

"Mamá…" Claudette mumbled. She wasn't sure where she was, only that it was hot and someone was fanning her. She sat up and blinked. There were concerned faces around her. She was in a tent. Diego was smiling madly as a tear rolled down his cheek. An older woman was speaking to her softly in a language she couldn't understand. The woman was urging her to drink. The cool water was a relief. She could feel her senses return as the water ran down her throat.

"Are you alright?" Judas Ben Duran asked her.

"Yes…I'm sorry…I must have fainted," she said.

Al-Qādir's mother said something. Ben Duran translated, "She says it's common for women in your condition."

"Yes, of course," she said, bewildered. She stole another glance at Diego, wondering how he was taking this.

"…My love," he mouthed softly, shaking his head, tears welling in his eyes as he smiled.

Abd al-Qādir watched him carefully, then spoke. Ben Duran translated.

"The emir says he can't quite understand the libertine ways of you Europeans. Though he tries to be tolerant and merciful, as God commands, he cannot allow you to live in sin among his people. He insists that you marry immediately. Do you consent?"

Claudette blinked in shocked silence. Diego spoke first.

"I do," he said with resolve.

"Yes, of course!" Claudette added.

The emir smiled softly, then spoke again. A dark chuckle rumbled through the tent. Ben Duran let out a slight scoff, then smiled mischievously.

"The emir says that is well. It'll save us the effort of having you flogged and stoned to death." Claudette blinked wide-eyed at him, clutching her hand to her chest as she wondered just how much he was kidding. With a nod of the emir's head, she was whisked away, still reeling from all that had happened.

"Diego…" she gasped, reaching out to him as she was pulled from the tent.

"Do not fear, my love!" he called to her as the men sitting in the tent converged on him, obscuring him from her view.

The sun outside blinded her. The women from the tent where she had been staying crowded around. The emir's mother spoke to them. One started yipping in a high-pitched voice and soon all joined in like shrieking banshee crickets, "Yulululululululululululul...!" Hot air rushed over her face, and once again, her knees gave out. Many hands caught her. They lifted her off the ground and carried her high in the air, shrieking their rhythmic chant. She could hear the bleating sounds of oboes and flutes joining in. Drums and tambourines started to beat, driving the strange music.

They carried her back to their tent, stripped her of her clothes, bathed her with damp rags, then covered her in white linens embroidered with intricate patterns made with golden threads. The women busied themselves drawing intricate patterns on her hands and feet using quills to apply a paste made from crushed henna leaves and rosewater. Others applied makeup to her face, accenting her eyes with kohl and painting red circles on her cheeks.

Claudette's bewilderment eventually eased into comfort and pleasure as the women tended to her while sharing mint tea and sweet pastries. Finally, they placed a gold conical hat on her head adorned with silk veils and strands of beads that hung from the side. The women stood back and admired their work. The emir's mother looked fondly upon her, said a few kind words, then turned to the others and gave orders. The women covered her face with a veil, then picked up her chair and brought her outside, hoisting her high on their shoulders once they cleared the tent flaps.

Men fired muskets into the air and pranced around on horseback. The crowd cheered. The music bleated on at a fever pitch. Twilight was creeping in, cooling the desert air. Torches flickered and glowed as people danced to the relentless rhythm. They set her chair down in the sand. Dancers filled her view as they clapped and shimmied to the music.

The crowd began to separate as a column of horsemen approached. Suddenly, she realized that Diego was leading them. He was dashing in his white robe and headdress from which his black wavy locks spilled and lightly touched his olive cheeks. His green eyes flickered in the torchlight. His slightly crooked smile beamed with confidence as he rode like a desert warrior, born to the saddle.

The men behind him held their muskets high in the air. They fired, causing her to flinch. The women chanted their high-pitch "yulu's" as men came to Diego. They lifted him off his horse and set him on a chair they held high on their shoulders. Claudette fell back in her chair as it was swooped up into the air once again and carried toward him. Diego smiled with boyish delight as he leaned over and lifted her veil.

"You are the most beautiful thing I've ever seen, my love," he said, looking into her eyes. She blushed and looked away. He leaned in and kissed her forehead. Cups of white liquid and plates of figs were hoisted up to them. Judas Ben Duran appeared below in the crowd.

"Drink," he said. "The milk represents purity, the figs: the sweetness of life."

The crowd cheered as they ate their figs and drank the milk, then slowly began to quiet as the two were lowered to the ground. The music stopped and the crowd began to separate as they murmured quietly to each other before completely falling silent. The light breeze and the flickering torches were all she could hear.

Emir Abd al-Qādir emerged in the void left by the crowd. He approached with stately grace. He held his face flat and devoid of emotion, but his deep-set eyes betrayed a sense of peace as he gazed upon the lovers.

Claudette made to stand, but the emir gestured with his hand for them to stay seated. He spoke to the crowd. Judas Ben Duran translated to them softly in English.

"The people of France and the Christians at large are not our enemies," he told the crowd. "Our enemies are their leaders who send them here to fight and subjugate us." He took a moment to scan the eyes around him. "Believe me," he continued with a smile, "they send them here to die. We will fight every Frenchman and Christian they send with holy vengeance. But God also commands us to show mercy to the vulnerable. Today, we accept these two castaways into our *smala*. We celebrate their love as they celebrate one of God's greatest gifts: marriage."

That brought a round of cheers from the men and "yulus" from the women. A few fired their muskets into the air. The emir raised his hand to quiet them, then extended it to Claudette. She looked around nervously until Diego nodded for her to take it. She stood with a slightly nervous giggle. The emir looked at her with his deep penetrating eyes. He spoke softly, yet she could feel his deep voice rattle against her ribs. Ben Duran translated, "It is Islamic law that a woman cannot be married without her father's or guardian's consent. The emir asks if he can stand in as your guardian."

"Uh…" she said looking at Ben Duran and then to the emir, "yes, of course."

The emir smiled at her and motioned with his hand for her to sit. Then with a nod of his head, a small writing desk and chair were brought and set before them. He sat. An aide brought paper, a pen, and an inkwell. The emir started writing, stopping twice to ask each their names through his interpreter. Each time, he paused to consider the answer, then wrote them out in Arabic script. He then handed it to Ben Duran, who wrote the English translation of the marriage contract below the emir's Arabic script.

The emir looked over Ben Duran's work with satisfaction, then looked up at Claudette and spoke. Ben Duran translated, "Do you offer yourself in marriage to this man in accordance with the Holy Koran in the name of the Holy Prophet, peace and blessing be upon him? Do you pledge, in honesty and with sincerity, to be an obedient and faithful wife?"

"Yes," she said. He asked again. "Yes, I do," she responded. He asked a third time. "With my whole heart," she answered. He smiled and turned to Diego. Once again, he asked him three times. Each time Diego consented with boyish earnestness. *How sweet he is!* she thought as she watched him answer.

The emir turned the paper toward them and spoke as he handed Claudette the pen. "Sign the marriage contract, please," Ben Duran translated. She did, then handed the pen to Diego, who took it, and wrote his name with large sweeping strokes to make the first letters of his names, "Diego de la Vega." She giggled softly. Everything he did seemed to exude this dark drama that she found both silly and alluring.

The emir then took Diego's hand, set a gob of henna paste in his palm, and clasped it together with Claudette's. She could feel the warm wet substance squish between their flesh and run down their fingers. The emir spoke with Ben Duran translating, "I now pronounce you husband and wife before God and His Prophet, peace, and blessing be upon him."

A woman started yelping out, "Yulululul..." and soon, they were all joining in as the oboes and tambourines started anew. Muskets fired into the air. She felt the earth fall away once more as the crowd hoisted their chairs in the air. She could see the emir leaning over and signing the document. He then turned it to Judas Ben Duran, who signed it too.

The music and dancing went on for a while. Eventually, much to her relief, the two were brought back down. They ate in the emir's tent with dozens of others. The meal consisted of roasted lamb and chicken served on mounds of couscous with green olives and lemon wedges with freshly baked flatbread. It was salty and heavily spiced with garlic making Claudette wish for a glass of wine.

Jugglers and sword dancers performed in front of them as they ate. Diego seemed most mesmerized by the strange pear-shaped instrument with which a soloist played and sang a haunting tune as the plates were taken away. It had a flat top and a pronounced rounded back. The neck was short and fretless. The headstock bent backward at almost a ninety-degree angle. The strings were arranged in double courses which the player plucked with a plectrum.

"The oud," Ben Duran leaned in and whispered to him, "not unlike the guitars of Spain." Diego nodded and watched as the player's fingers danced along the fingerboard, playing rhythmically using some dark and exotic scale.

The emir watched Diego's fascination with a smile. He whispered to one of his attendants who nodded swiftly and scurried away. Once the music was done, he spoke. Ben Duran translated, "He asks if you are a musician."

"I play some guitar," Diego responded. The emir spoke again. The oud player handed Diego his instrument and plectrum.

"Go ahead," Ben Duran urged him, "try it!"

Diego gave Claudette quick a look as he took the instrument before returning his eyes to the musician. "*Shukran*," he mumbled. It was fleeting, but she could see a flash of panic in his eyes. She drew her hands to her mouth, worried for him, knowing the dread of being put on the spot.

He politely waved off the plectrum, choosing to plunk at the strings with his thumb and fingers. A few giggles passed around the room as he experimented with finding notes on the fingerboard.

Claudette felt her stomach tighten in a knot. Then the plunking started to form a simple melody. The melody found rhythm, and soon, it was a delightful little tune filled with the rich colors and flavors that she imagined filled the streets of Mexico. The tambourines and drums found the beat and joined in. Even the flutes and oboes picked up the simple chord changes. Soon, everyone was clapping along, smiling, and rocking back and forth with the beat.

Diego finished with a flourish, a hard strum, and shouted, "*Olé!*" The room broke into a cheer.

"That was wonderful, my friend!" Ben Duran told him. "What was that?"

"It's a popular dance tune in my country," Diego told him. "It's called *Jarabe Tapatío*. It's the Hat Dance."

Ben Duran translated his words into Arabic for the room. Once again, people repeated the word "*miksikiun*" with awe. Many leaned in to get a better look at this exotic man sitting in their presence. Claudette dropped her hands to her chest in relief. She smiled, tilted her head, and sighed in admiration at the boyish man she was learning to love more and more every day. He turned and gave her a wink which made her swoon in delight.

The room quieted as the emir spoke again. Ben Duran translated, "The emir says you play the music of your people wonderfully. As your wife's appointed guardian, he is obligated to pay a dowery to you. Of course, we are poor fugitives ourselves, but the emir asks you to accept these simple gifts."

With that, the emir nodded his head to someone standing outside the tent. His attendant reentered with another oud and presented it to Diego. Diego gazed at it with reverent wonder as he took it into his hands. "*Shukran*," he said, bowing deeply to the emir.

"*Afwan*," the emir replied with a dismissive wave of his hand, then said something that brought a round of laughs to the room.

Ben Duran chuckled as he translated, "He says it's one less thing we have to lug around."

Next, an attendant brought Claudette a gold bracelet. "It's beautiful!" she gasped as she clasped it to her chest. "Thank you," she said with a bow toward the emir. He smiled and spoke more.

Ben Duran translated, "The emir has arranged for you to have your own tent and bedding, as well as a horse and mule while you travel with us." The couple bowed and uttered their thanks. "One more thing…" Duran translated for him again. The emir nodded to one of his attendants, who hurried out of the tent and then returned with a bundle wrapped in cloth. He sat in front of Diego and unrolled it.

Diego raised an eyebrow and leaned forward to examine the two items. One was a long and slender musket with a short stock and bell-shaped butt. Next to it was a sword. The single blade had a pronounced curve. The hilt had a short crossguard and pommel that curved downward away from the hand. Diego picked it up and tested the weight.

"The scimitar is balanced for cutting from horseback. It'll take a man's head off with the right stroke," Ben Duran told him. "The *moukahla*," he said, pointing to the exotic-looking gun, "is well balanced for shooting from horseback and accurate for shooting across the expanse of the desert."

The emir spoke again. Ben Duran translated, "You are welcome into our *smala* until you reach your destination, but you must do your part and share in the responsibilities. This includes protecting our families from the French invaders. If called upon, you must fight. Do you accept?"

The room went silent. Diego looked to Claudette whose eyes were large with fright. He turned his gaze back to Abd al-Qādir and spoke, "I know what it's like to have my country overrun with invaders, Your Highness. I will fight with you." Duran translated that to Arabic. A round of cheers broke out in the tent and soon, the music started again as the guests helped themselves to dates, toasted almonds, and sweet pastries.

Diego looked back to Claudette whose eyes had grown even larger with incredulity. Diego shrugged. "What else are we going to do?" he said, then popped a date into his mouth.

The party came to an end with plenty of hugs, well wishes, and pats on the back. At last, they made their way out. An attendant guided them through the concentric rings of tents until they got to the outer edges near the horse corral and sheep herd. There, was a small tent, just large enough for the two to lie together and store their things

After bowing and thanking their guide, they took off their robes and lay on the rugs and blankets inside. For a moment, they stared at the ceiling in silence, then suddenly turned and fell into each other's arms.

"Oh, Diego…I thought I'd never hold you again," she gasped in among the frantic kisses. They fell into frantic lovemaking. Claudette bit her lip to keep from calling out in ecstasy for fear of being heard by their neighbors. At last, it was done. They lay next to each other in the darkness, their pinkies intertwined as the sweat on their bodies cooled in the night air.

Claudette finally broke the silence. "Would you really fight against France?"

Diego lay silent for a moment, then spoke, "If need be."

She thought for a moment, then asked, "Could you truly kill Frenchmen? Christians?"

Diego turned to her and put his hand on her bare stomach. "I'd do anything to protect our family."

She turned to him. Even in the darkness, she could make out his large green eyes looking into hers with stark conviction. "Of course," she said softly, kissing him on the cheek. She turned away onto her side, grabbing his hand and wrapping it around her as she did. She snuggled deep into him. He squeezed her tight, drawing in the scent of her hair, then kissed her softly behind the ear before loosening his grip. Claudette closed her eyes and smiled softly in the darkness as her consciousness slipped away.

Chapter Twenty: The War with France

"*Allāhu akbaru....!*"

Claudette opened her eyes at the sound of the lone voice calling out in the darkness.

"*Ašhadu al lā ilāha illā -llāhu...!*"

She sensed Diego stirring next to her. He was rising to his knees as the voice continued to call out from somewhere in the camp. She could see the whip marks on his rear end and lower back as he knelt and crossed himself. She knelt with him. He held his rosary in his hands and muttered softly once the caller finished. "*Pater noster...qui es in caelis...sanctificetur nomen tuum...*"

He crossed himself again once finished.

"Amen," Claudette repeated and did the same. She looked at him quizzically in the darkness.

Diego shrugged, "God is God, regardless how you pray to him..." She smiled at his openness to the strange religion of their hosts, "except for the devil the Anglo heretics pray to," he finished with a smirk. Claudette pursed her lips and slapped his arm.

"Oh, you are impossible!" she chided as he laughed.

"Come," he said, "let's get dressed and find breakfast. I'm starving!"

Claudette settled into camp life in the weeks that followed, throwing herself into the tasks shared by the other women: cooking, mending clothes, and tending to the sick and injured. She found it awkward at first after a lifetime of having servants do these things for her, but she was fascinated by these new skills the wives and mothers of the *smala* did so naturally. She endeavored to learn everything she could with great zeal. Soon, her days were going by quickly while making bread, stitching clothes, and even men's wounds.

The women of the camp accepted her as a sister, some even spoke a smattering of French, and she was quickly learning Arabic words. They communicated using a combination of the two languages and a lot of miming.

A cool breeze drifted through their canopy as she kneaded dough with her new friends. She lifted her chin and closed her eyes, embracing the small reprieve from the hot afternoon air. The women around her were chatting softly as they worked. She opened her eyes and smiled as she looked around. Never did she think, in all those lonely years locked away in her bedroom, that she'd be so happy to be living in a tent, making bread.

Being in love helped. She was so excited the first day that she managed to make a meal and have it ready for her man when he came home. She barely knew what to do with herself once she was done and had to wait for him. She had already arranged their things in the tent twice that day. After a moment of trying to sit still, she rekindled their small fire and made tea, just as her friends had taught her. It was strange, she thought, that such a hot beverage could be so soothing in the desert heat.

Soon the smell washed over her as she tended to the small kettle, making sure it didn't boil over. She poured some into her cup and blew on it before taking a sip. She could see him now through the vapors rising before her eyes: her dust-covered Bedouin warrior. His image shimmered in the hot air between them. His musket was slung over his shoulder and his sword hung at his side. His red robe and white headdress marked him as part of the emir's cavalry.

She poured him a cup, got to her feet, and ran out to greet him. "You are limping!" she said after he took his first sip and then walked with her back to the tent.

"I fell off my horse again," he said. "I'm fine, though."

"Oh…" she cooed. "Come, let me help you clean up and you can tell me about it. I made you dinner. You'll feel better once you've relaxed and eaten."

She knew the spills from his horse wounded his pride. He had told her about growing up on cattle drives in California, living in the saddle for days. Horseman skills were the pride of the *vaqueros*. He was an accomplished fencer too, although he said he preferred the épée to the saber. "The point is deadlier than the blade," he told her. The thought of either made her cringe, but she tolerated his passion as he rambled on about honor and the martial arts. The overtly curved scimitar with its tip pointing up and away from the opponent felt foreign in his hand. He struggled with his musket too, although he admitted, he was never much of a shot with the "Devil's weapon," as he put it.

"Maybe they can find some windmills for you to joust with instead," she told him.

"You mock me, woman," he replied with some humor.

The Arab way of fighting was challenging to him but he was an eager student. She could see his excitement as he left in the morning. It hurt her to see him come home disappointed. She knew it was all in his head. The Arabs seemed to have taken a liking to him and even admired his skills.

He had worried he wouldn't have the chance to show any of those skills at first. They had sent him out into the fields to help with the herd in the early days. But his naturalness in the saddle and his prowess with a blade soon became apparent. Abd al-Qādir had lost most of his men in Algeria and now he needed every man who could ride for his small cavalry. Diego was more than happy to leave the sheep behind and train with the warriors.

They practiced their swarming cavalry attacks, riding in hard on a target with their muskets held high in the air. Then, using only their legs to guide their horses, they fired and then turn away at the last moment. Some of the men were even able to reload and shoot again as they rode off. Of course, Diego, not to be outdone by any man, tumbled from his horse as he tried to reload and turn at the same time. This earned him a good round of laughs from the others.

He was much better with the saber attacks. They practiced riding up on straw dummies and slashing them with their scimitars as they passed. Diego, preferring the point to the blade, rode leaning low in the saddle. He turned his wrist over, inverting the blade so that the edge faced upward, then drove the curved point downward into his target, running it through as he passed. This got a round of cheers from the men and soon, several of them were trying the same attack with varying degrees of success. He was happy to show them the technique. Before long, he found himself teaching fencing lessons to some of the men.

Within weeks, he could understand and even say a few words in Arabic. Some of the men could speak a little French too. Even though he didn't understand the language well, it was easier than Arabic. The men were learning to trust him and his abilities as well. Soon, he was invited on patrols, much to Claudette's dismay.

He'd be gone for days, causing her to worry as she slept alone, cradling the ever-swelling bulge in her tummy. She'd wait with the other wives, hoping for their men to appear on the horizon at any minute, riding home alive and well. It made the time he was home precious, a celebration each time he returned. They made sure the nights before he'd leave were special too.

Then came the alarming news. "I'm only home for tonight, my love," he told her. They had just gotten back to their tent after his patrol had returned. "The French have crossed into Morocco. We spotted a column of men marching through the desert. The emir has decided to attack them in full force. We ride tomorrow."

"*Mon Dieu!*" she gasped. "You are going to fight Frenchmen?!"

"Well, they should have stayed in France if they didn't want to fight," he said grimly.

They were quiet together that evening. She tried not to let the bitterness seep in and ruin this night. It could be their last. Still, the thought of him killing her countrymen haunted her, and the thought of him dying filled her with dread. "Why must you fight?" she wanted to ask as she helped him wash. Certainly, he could be just as useful tending to the herd. But she knew it was useless to argue with him. She could never understand this boyish thing that pushed him toward adventure which ultimately led to violence. Instead, she tried to make the mood light. She took his arm and wrapped it around her as they lay in the darkness, wanting to show him that she loved him, even though she wasn't happy with what he was about to do.

She was awake before the call to prayer. They got to their knees, crossed themselves, and recited the *Lord's Prayer* together softly. She reached out and squeezed his clasped hands, smiling at him as he looked up. He smiled back, leaned in, and kissed her cheek, then got up, put on his robes, and slung his weapons. "Come back to me," she said as she hugged him once more.

"I will," he said, then kissed her, took his pack, and walked off into the twilight.

"Ah, there you are, our Mexican warrior!" Diego heard Judas Ben Duran call to him in Spanish as he mounted. He turned to him, reigning in his horse as the beast pranced around in agitation at all the commotion. Dozens of men were mounting, checking their muskets, and slashing the early morning air with their swords.

"At your service, señor," Diego told him, looking down at the smiling man from his saddle.

"The emir asked me to find you. He asks that you ride in his entourage during the raid."

"Me?" Diego asked, putting his hand on his chest.

Ben Duran smirked, "The emir is somewhat a collector of exotic men. We've had Nubians, Turks, Poles, even Frenchmen fight with us, each in his own way. He wants to see how a Mexican fights."

"Like a bull with his balls on fire," Diego told him.

Ben Duran blinked at him for a minute, "…like a what?"

"Like a bull," Diego said again, using his fingers to mimic horns on his head, "with his balls on fire." The bravado seeped away from his voice as he finished.

Ben Duran looked at him for another moment, "Well…I'm sorry I'll miss that…Anyway, please find a place among the emir's guard. He looks forward to watching you fight."

Diego nudged his horse through the gathering of men until he found the emir sitting on his horse with his retinue mounted around him. His men looked at him grimly, but the emir smiled and uttered, "*Gracias, amigo.*"

"*De nada, Su Alteza,*" Diego responded with a short bow of his head. The emir gestured with his hand for him to join his small detachment of mounted guards. Diego nodded and moved his horse in line with them behind the emir.

The one who seemed to be the leader of the squad spoke to him in Arabic, of which Diego understood none. The man gestured with his hands, and at last, Diego understood he wanted to see his musket. He handed it to him. The man inspected it and then handed it back. He motioned for Diego to show him his scimitar, his pistol, and then his dagger. Once satisfied, the man mumbled something that got a dark chuckle from the other men. He gripped Diego's shoulder and then patted it as he spoke. This got a few nods and murmurs of agreement from the men. Diego decided that regardless of what the man was saying, he must have passed the inspection.

The men meted out cartridges for their muskets and pistols, then rationed the food and water. Diego lifted one of the soft barley cakes to his nose and sniffed it before putting it in his saddlebag with a shrug.

A call went out and soon, the column moved forward into the desert as the sun began to rise above the dunes. With a forward motion of the emir's arm, a squad of horsemen galloped ahead and out of sight over the hills and dunes to take up the advanced scouting position. Diego watched similar parties ride out to each side and to the rear. These men would be the eyes of the column and screen them from the eyes of the enemy.

The heat rose quickly as the day dragged on. They rode over the scrub brush-covered hills and through the open desert valleys. Diego hid his discomfort from the men around him, only taking drinks from his waterskin when they did. By the afternoon, the heat was causing his eyes to grow heavy as the column trudged on. He shook his head, trying to rid himself of the sleep demons prying on him. He opened his eyes wide and blinked hard, trying to stay awake.

Then he saw them. Two of the scouts came galloping toward them from the next ridge ahead. Abd al-Qādir put his hand up and the column came to a stop. Diego could hear the scouts speaking breathlessly to the emir. One dismounted and started drawing in the sand with his scimitar. The emir watched with great interest. Once the scout was done speaking, the emir sat silently for a moment, regarding the schematics drawn in the sand. The men around him watched him intently.

At last, he spoke softly. Men immediately turned on their horses and rode back along the column, barking orders. Soon, the column spread itself into two horizontal lines. The men in the first line unslung their muskets. They held them in one hand and their reins in the other. Diego and his troop crowded around the emir, who sat in the center of the second line. With a few words and a forward motion of the emir's hand, the two lines trotted up the incline and then stopped before cresting the top of the ridge.

A few men dismounted, crawled to the top, and peered over. One of them turned and nodded to the emir. Abd al-Qādir raised his right-hand high. The men scurried back down and got back in their saddles. All eyes were on the emir. He looked to the heavens and spoke, then brought his hand down with a dramatic swoop. A war cry broke out and the first line bolted forward, bounding over the top of the ridge with their muskets high in the air.

Diego's line moved behind them at a measured trot. He could feel his heart in his throat as they crested the ridge. The ground on the other side fell away in a steep decline. Below, a line of wagons and carts stretched as far as he could see in each direction. Tiny men in red trousers, black shakos, and blue jackets scurried around the carts and wagons in panic as the first line of Arab warriors thundered down the slope. A few of the French managed to get off a wild shot before turning and running.

Abd al-Qādir drew his sword and held it high in the air. The entire second line did the same. The emir shouted as he pointed his sword forward. The line lurched forward into a gallop.

Diego barely felt his horse's hooves touch the ground as they bounded down the slope in an almost free fall. Fear and exhilaration swept through him like the passing wind as they plunged. He held the reins lightly in his left with his sword held high in his right. He felt as if he were flying on a winged horse. It seemed they would surely tumble headfirst in their descent, but the sure-footed animal glided down the sand with terrifying speed.

Below, the first line dropped their reins, shouldered their muskets, and fired as one into the mass of confused French soldiers, dropping several of them to the ground. The rest of the French turned and ran as the horsemen plowed through them.

Diego felt the hooves of his mount finally hit solid ground as they bounded off the slope onto the level plane of the valley. The fleeing soldiers looked back in terror as the emir and his swordsmen came rumbling after them. The horsemen funneled around the spaces between the carts and wagons then spread out once more. In seconds, they were upon them. Men screamed as they fell, trampled under hoof, and sliced by sabers.

One of the Frenchmen turned, planted his feet, and braced himself with his bayonet held forward. Diego accepted the challenge. He leaned in low and forward, turning his blade sideways with his point extended past his horse like a spear as they charged. The man lost his nerve at the sight, dropped his bayonet, and turned to flee. It was too late. Diego felt the tip of his blade pop through the wool jacket, pierce the skin, and slide easily between the man's ribs.

He yanked the sword out as he thundered past. The man tumbled to the ground. He pulled the reins in hard to turn and stop. The man lay face-first in the dust, unmoving. Diego frowned. He looked at his sword. Blood dripped from the tip and collected in the sand below. He looked back at the man lying still face down. He had killed him.

The sound of rumbling hooves broke him from his thoughts. French cavalrymen were charging from the rear of the supply convoy. He looked about him in panic, then flinched at the sound of a musket volley. Several of the French fell from their horses as the men of the emir's first line had reloaded, turned, and were now riding and firing into the flank of the charging French.

Suddenly, men from Diego's line were all around him, their muskets now at their shoulders. Diego quickly wiped the blood off his saber with his robe and tried to resheathe it in a frantic effort to follow their example. He flinched again as they fired. Several of the lead French and their horses tumbled to the ground. Before Diego could reach for his musket, the others had slung theirs over their shoulders, pulled their sabers, and were now lurching forward. He gave up on wrangling for his gun, pointed his scimitar forward, and laid his spurs to his horse.

They collided with the faltering French charge in a blur of clanging blades, pistol shots, and screams. The French broke away and fled. Abd al-Qādir put up his hand to stop any pursuit. The Arabs cheered as the surviving French horsemen bolted across the desert floor, leaving a trail of dust in their wake.

Diego panted as he watched them ride away. He looked at his sword. It was dripping with fresh blood.

Chapter Twenty-One: The Evil that Men Do

Diego looked up from his bloody sword to see the men nearby watching him silently. The emir smiled at him and said something that brought a round of laughs. His squad leader patted him on the shoulder and said something more that elicited a few cheers and words of approval. Several of them slapped him on the back and said things before turning their horses back to the work at hand.

They began pulling bodies off the wagons and inspecting the captured supplies with much celebration. Diego tied his horse to a wagon and then pitched in, dragging the bodies to the ever-growing pile. Each time, he avoided the man he had killed, trying his best not to look at him. To his relief, someone finally moved him. He looked to the sky. The vultures were already circling above, waiting for the living to get out of the way. He looked back at the bodies and dared himself to look at their faces, chiding himself for having felt regret. It was weakness.

They corralled the prisoners and their injured into a circle and stripped them of their weapons. Diego grimaced as he prepared himself for whatever terrible thing he'd be told to do to them. To his surprise, the emir let them go. He even gave them wagons to carry their injured, as well as food and water for their long trek back to wherever they came from.

Diego watched the sullen men walk away, pulling their wagons by hand into the vastness of the desert plain. They were defeated, but still alive.

The Arabs, meanwhile, took possession of the supply wagons, horses, camels, and mules. Some of the Moroccan wagoneers volunteered to stay and help drive the freshly won booty back to the emir's camp. Soon, they were moving again, back toward the *smala* as the shadows of the hills and dunes grew longer.

Claudette spent a sleepless night running over, again and again, every scenario Diego would find himself in and wondered if he'd survive with his soul intact. She would have thought she hadn't slept at all if the pre-dawn call to prayer hadn't rattled her from her sleep. Instinctively, she reached out and felt the empty space where Diego normally lay. Dread poured into her stomach as her conscious mind realized he wasn't there.

She could hardly find comfort in her daily tasks. An air of anxiety hung over the women as they busied themselves. Even the ones who still bantered as they worked carried a tinge of worry in their voices.

A rider appeared on the horizon around noon. Several of the women were getting up to see. A few of the men who had been left behind to guard the camp rode out to meet him. It wasn't until the women could see the smiling faces of the men returning that they began to call out their "yulus" in celebration and surged forward to greet them. The news was spreading fast, and by the reactions, it seemed to be good.

Claudette was dying to know more. Clasping her hands to her chest, she watched anxiously as the other women chattered happily. Finally, the emir's mother, who she now knew as Kheira, approached her with a kind smile. "Your husband…is good," the woman said in heavily accented French.

"Oh…I…" Claudette started, then clutched her mouth with both hands and dissolved into tears. Kheira wrapped her arms around her and held her as she shuddered.

"Shhhhhh…" the older woman cooed in place of the comforting words she did not know in French.

The mood was much livelier in the afternoon. The women chatted happily as they prepared the evening meal. Surely the victorious men would be hungry upon their return. Claudette smiled shyly to herself as she kneaded dough. The women nudged her and said things in a teasing tone that brought giggles among them. Claudette could only smile and shrug at the seemingly well-meaning gibes.

It was late in the day when the first sight of them appeared on the horizon. Soon it was apparent why it took them so long to return. They were driving a long line of wagons laden with untold goods and supplies. The women swarmed the men of the advanced guard with their celebratory shrills, "Yulululululululululu…!"

Claudette wandered along the returning procession, searching for her love. She saw Abd al-Qādir sitting upright in his saddle as he approached. He held his chin high with the regal loftiness of a conquering warlord. His opened hands were held out as the camp followers surged forward to kiss them. Claudette looked among the men behind him, scanning their grim faces.

At last, she saw him, scowling with dark conviction. "Oh, Diego…" she gasped and ran to him. The severe look on his face broke when he saw her. It was replaced by that sweet shy boyish smile that melted her heart. He leaped from his horse and opened his arms just in time to catch her as she threw herself at him. "Oh, I thought I'd never see you again…" she gasped.

She squeezed him for a moment, drinking in his scent as he stroked her hair and kissed her head. Then she felt it. There was something strange, something dry and crusty that crackled and crumbled between their bodies. She drew herself back and looked down at her robe in horror. She was covered in brittle pieces of dried blood.

"Huh!" she gasped in disgust. "This is the blood of Frenchmen!" She looked up at him again. He held his face firm, but she could see his eye quiver with wounded pain.

"But at least they are not covered in my blood," he said stiffly.

Claudette looked at him with incredulous revulsion. "They were Christians, Diego…"

"They were invaders," Diego said. The terrifying dark resolve returned to his face.

"*Mon Dieu*, I do not know who you are…" she said, backing away, looking at the ground in fear.

"Oof!" a voice behind her ejected as she stumbled into someone. She spun around to see Judas Ben Duran hold out his hands to steady her. "My apologies, my dear," he said, "I hope I wasn't interrupting…" He looked to Diego, who remained silent. His face was hard and impassive but his eyes were soft with pain. Claudette finally spoke.

"No, I was merely welcoming my husband home," she said softly.

Ben Duran smiled knowingly, looking into her tear-softened eyes. "Well, if I may, I'd like to invite you to my tent for supper. I have something I'd like to share with you, that is if you *Christians* can tolerate dining with a humble Jew." He said the last bit teasingly, hinting that he might've heard part of their conversation.

"Of course," Claudette told him, "don't be silly."

"Good!" he smiled. "Come once you've had a chance to settle and wash. No hurry, my friends."

"Thank you," Diego said softly, to which Ben Duran smiled and gave a slight bow before withdrawing. Claudette looked back at Diego once they were alone again. Diego's face was softer now, his eyes pleading, breaking her heart and softening her fury.

"Come," she said softly, taking his hand, "let me help you get clean."

PUHNK!

Ben Duran pulled the cork from a bottle and immediately the tart and fruity smell tickled her nose causing Claudette to sigh before regaining her self-control. Ben Duran chuckled, "I know, my dear. The desert is dry enough without wine. It's a tragedy we must suffer so!" He filled their cups and then held his high. "*Mazel tov!*"

"*Mazel tov*," Diego and Claudette clinked their cups to his, then sipped. The familiar silky taste brought a wave of warm nostalgia through her body.

"Drink up, my friends. I have plenty!" Ben Duran said with a warm chuckle.

"*Mon Dieu*, that is good!" Claudette gasped after swallowing. "Where did you get it?"

"Well, it was your husband's bravery that got it for us, I should say," Ben Duran laughed. "I'm merely rewarded for doing nothing. Not very fair, is it?"

"You are welcome, my friend," Diego smiled with humor, holding his cup for a toast. Ben Duran clinked his cup to it.

"Actually, I'm charged with selling off whatever the camp doesn't need from the captured goods. The emir allows me to skim a bit for my troubles, including the wine. I'm a Jew, after all. I have to keep up appearances!" He laughed at this self-effacing joke. "It sure is nice to have fellow infidels to share a cup with, even if they're Catholics."

"The pleasure's ours," Diego said, raising his glass again. "I'd rather drink with a Jew than a filthy Protestant anytime."

Claudette gave his arm a backhand slap for this impertinence, causing more laughs from the men. She took a long draught from the wine as a servant brought a plate of couscous, roasted lamb, chickpea paste, and loaves of flatbread. The men immediately reached in and helped themselves. Claudette was slow to scoop some of the food with a piece of bread.

"Still, do you think men should have died so that we can drink?" she asked casually, looking at the food as she scooped, then lifted her eyes, hardening them as she gazed into Ben Duran's.

"No, my dear," he said with patient earnestness, "they should die so that we can live, including the one you carry in your belly, if I may be so bold."

"How so?"

"The French have no problems killing us and taking our lands."

Claudette scoffed, "France is the most advanced country in the world. Surely Africa could benefit from our civilization if they would just stop fighting."

"A civilization that requires a lot of severed heads to maintain," Ben Judas said, lifting a finger and an eyebrow.

"Oh, pooh!" she protested, "*The Terror* was fifty years ago."

"Perhaps in France, but here, it's very much alive," he said, then took a sip of wine. Claudette lifted an eyebrow, urging him to continue. "Like in what once was the village of El Ouffia. French cavalry came in the night. They killed all the villagers as they slept in their tents…and not just the men…but the women and the children too. They slaughtered them like animals, then put their heads on pikes and paraded them through the streets of Algiers for all to see the price of French civilization."

"I see," Claudette swallowed hard, dropping her eyes to the ground, suddenly regretting having pushed the subject.

Diego finally broke the painful silence that followed. "Hey, Mexicans can be pretty bad too," he said, reaching out and touching her shoulder. "Just ask the Indians." She looked up at him and smiled at his kindness.

"I'm sure you could even find a Jew or two who's done something wrong, I suppose," Ben Duran said, lightening the room with his warm-hearted chuckle. "The truth, my dear, is that all men are capable of great evil…and kindness, regardless of their tribes. God judges us for what we do ourselves, not the sins of our people."

"Cheers!" Diego lifted his cup. Ben Duran smiled grandly and met Diego's cup with his own. Claudette shrugged, smiled softly, and clanked her cup to theirs.

"Come, let us talk of other things," Ben Duran said. "How are you coming along with your *oud*?" he asked Diego.

"Fine enough, I suppose, but it is much different from a guitar," Diego said.

"Bring it by sometime while you're in camp. I can help you get started, show you a song or two," Ben Duran offered.

"Thank you, that's very kind of you," Diego told him.

"Bah!" Ben Duran scoffed dismissively. "It'll be nice to have the company of a Catholic bigot for a change instead of all these radical Muslims."

Claudette couldn't help but laugh. The wine, good food, and friendly chatter were slowly pushing away her dark feelings. She clung to Diego's arm as they made their way back to their tent. The sweet anticipation of snuggling in bed with him was intoxicating. She wrapped herself around him as soon as they were out of their robes and smothered him with kisses. Diego chuckled self-consciously, trying to keep up with her sudden passion.

They finished with a gasp, panting and sweating in the cool night air. "Hmmm…" Claudette murmured with her eyes closed and a soft smile. She turned to her side and nestled into him as he brought the blanket around her and held her tight. She lay there basking in the sweet satisfaction, soaking in the contentment as she listened to his soft breathing. He was already asleep. She could feel her own consciousness slipping away. Then, at the very point of crossing over, she could feel the terrible nauseating feeling of loss creeping into her stomach.

She saw a lot of Diego in the days that followed. Abd al-Qādir ordered the tents struck the very next morning. The raid had now given the French a place on the map to search. The *smala* had to move. They set out each day before dawn, taking advantage of the cool air, then stopped in the early afternoons to throw up their canopies and endure the sun's cruelest hours.

Diego spent the days riding out far with the other horsemen to the front, flanks, or rear to watch for French troops and to screen the *smala's* movement from the enemy. He had to spend some nights on vidette duty, but otherwise could join her in camp where they could sleep together. They spent many evenings sipping wine and enjoying witty banter with Ben Duran when he wasn't summoned to the emir's tent. Claudette practiced her tarot cards and listened to the exotic music of the *ouds* as Diego took his lessons.

"Be careful with those cards, my dear," Ben Duran warned, "some of the more zealous Mohammedans will call you a witch and have you stoned." Still, despite the warning, the well-versed man had tips on interpretation. "Sure…the Hanged Man means you are powerless to your fate," he said, pointing to the card she had turned over with a frown, "but once you accept this, there is freedom to find happiness."

Best of all, Ben Duran often sat in consul with the emir, and for this, had privy information about where they were going and what they were going to do when they got there.

"You'll be happy to know we are finally heading to Tangiers where you'll be able to find passage to the New World," he told them.

"That is a relief, but why?" Diego said.

"The bulk of Moroccan forces are moving east to push the French back into Algeria. This leaves the port of Tangiers, which is north and west of us, woefully under-defended. French ships are amassing outside the harbor as we speak. A secondary invasion could be imminent. The emir believes we can cut them down before they can get out of their boats and organize on the beach."

"I suddenly don't feel so relieved," Claudette mumbled, unconsciously rubbing her swelling stomach.

Claudette felt it before she heard it. They had been moving all day, and now it was well past the time the caravan would normally come to a halt. The afternoon heat weighed heavily on her as she urged her donkey on. Bella, as they named her, was pretty well-behaved and usually carried their things with very little prompting, but now she was fighting her bit and refusing to move forward, braying in fear at some invisible danger ahead.

That's when she felt the first one. It was a percussive pulse that pushed against her tummy. At first, she thought it was the baby moving inside her. But the intervals between the pulses got shorter until the thumping was constant.

The other grew quiet as they pressed forward with new urgency. Everyone was listening intently. She could feel it in the ground. The sands shook and cascaded down the dunes. Finally, the pulses became sounds as they neared the city. She could hear the booming of the cannons, the whistling of the shells, and the explosions that followed. Several of the women gasped as they pointed in the air in astonishment. She could see it now too: arcs of light streaming into the twilight then plummeting somewhere beyond the ridge ahead with a loud boom.

There was much chatter among the travelers as they neared the heights. Several of them were now gathering at the summit. Bella stomped the ground and brayed in fear. "Shhhhhhh..." Claudette stroked her velvety ears. "It's alright, sweetie. I'll go look, alright?" The beast looked at her with big doleful eyes as Claudette walked away towards the crowd standing on the ridgetop. The ground shuddered with each boom.

"Huh!" she gasped as the scene revealed itself below. French warships filled the harbor. The explosions vomiting out of their guns flashed in the twilight and added to the clouds of smoke that swirled around them. The shells screamed into the darkening skies, then dropped into the crowded city with a flash and a bang. She flinched as an arm wrapped around her. Diego had found her among the crowd. He smiled softly at her, then turned his big green eyes to the scene below. She could see the fires reflect and sparkle in his eyes as if they were emitting their own light.

She turned back to watch. Countless fires twinkled in the darkness. She could see dark forms scurrying around them. She could hear screams mixing in with pounding guns and explosions.

"*Mon Dieu*, there are people down there!" she gasped, tears welling in her eyes. Diego drew her closer, squeezing her as he kissed her head. "I can't watch anymore," she blurted as she pushed herself away and walked back to the train of carts and animals. Bella pawed the ground and snorted at the sight of her return. "It's alright, sweetie," she cooed as she rubbed Bella's ears and kissed her forehead. "It's alright..." Claudette hugged the animal's neck and cried softly as the bombs continued to fall.

Chapter Twenty-Two: The Unexpected Visitor

The bombardment reached its apex of constant skull-rattling explosions, then finally tapered off, giving way to the soothing sounds of the desert at night. Claudette found peace and sleep in their little tent. The smell of burnt wood drifted through the camp when she woke to the call for morning prayer. She and Diego joined the others at daybreak to see the damage done to the city from the heights above. Black smoke smoldered from several parts. She could see tiny figures moving around the rubble below like ants on a dropped piece of food.

"We should go and help them," she said.

"Not yet, my love," he told her. "It is not safe. The bombardment could resume at any moment." She clung to his arm, squeezing it as they watched the Moroccans dig themselves out of the wreckage.

They waited for days in eerie anticipation. Judas Ben Duran was gone. What they could understand from the others was that he had gone to sell the unneeded loot from the raid and to consult with the Sultan of Morocco on behalf of Abd al-Qādir on how they'd proceed with the escalating war with France.

He returned, at last, with an armed escort and immediately disappeared into the emir's tent for hours. All she and Diego could do was wait in frustration to find out what would happen next.

The order to strike tents and prepare to march came shortly after morning prayers. Claudette and Diego could only look at each other silently with wide eyes and shoulder shrugs as they packed. Neither had any clue as to what was the plan.

Diego held his horse's reins and stood by his wife and their donkey, waiting for the call for the column to move. He had not been ordered to ride out to any of the scouting positions like the other horsemen. Judas Ben Duran found them at last.

"You are not coming with us," Ben Duran told them. "The emir has released you from your service. You are free to go into the city to find your way home. Here," he said, handing Diego a piece of paper. "This is a letter of introduction from the emir. If you take it to the Algerian part of town, you will find sanctuary."

"But is it safe?" Claudette asked, bewildered by the sudden change of affairs.

"Yes, my dear," Ben Duran assured her. "The war is over, at least for you and the Moroccans. The French routed the sultan's forces at the River Isly. Sultan Abd al-Rahman has bowed to the French in order to save his ports. He has renounced his support for Emir Abd al-Qādir and has declared him an outlaw. We can no longer stay in Morocco. We must go back east now and hope to find support among the tribes that have not yet succumbed to the French."

Ben Duran looked at Diego and smiled softly, reading the pained conflict in his eyes. "The emir thanks you for your service, Diego. You have convinced him of Mexican honor and courage. But this is not your war. Go home with his blessing."

"Tell the emir we thank him for his kindness," Diego said with a slight bow.

"Of course," Ben Duran returned the gesture.

"And if you or the emir are ever in California, you'll always be welcome at *la Hacienda de la Vega*."

"*California…*" Ben Duran said, rubbing his chin and looking toward the west. "I can't imagine what life would be like on the very edge of the world." He then turned his eyes back to Diego and Claudette. "Go with God, my friends," he said, then embraced and kissed them both.

Claudette and Diego pulled their animals out of the caravan and stood by as the order came to move out. They watched in somber silence as the train of carts, animals, and people rolled past them and out into the desert. Claudette squeezed his hand as the caravan became an undefined blob shimmering in the distant heat. She could sense the conflict welling inside him. "It is not your war, Diego," she assured him. "You did your part honorably."

They descended into the city with hardly anyone taking notice. The people there were too busy tending to the wounded and dealing with the damage to worry about the two strangers dressed in Beduin clothing coming down from the desert plateau above.

The devastation made for an easy opportunity to blend in and ingratiate themselves to the residents there. No one cared who was who or where they came from as neighbors and strangers helped each other deal with the disaster. Claudette made herself useful in one of the makeshift hospitals using the nursing skills she had learned during her time in Al-Qādir's *smala*. Diego helped clear the streets of rubble and lent himself to repairing and rebuilding damaged homes and buildings.

Within a few days, they found the Algerian quarter, and with Abd al-Qādir's letter, they found welcoming neighbors. Soon they settled into a small, single-room apartment on a crowded street near an open market. It was noisy, but Claudette grew accustomed to the constant sound, taking comfort in knowing she was surrounded by well-meaning neighbors. The Algerians there regarded the couple with kind deference, knowing that they carried Emir Abd al-Qādir's favor and blessing.

"He should be sultan of Morocco *and* Algeria!" some of them told her in heavily accented French. She nodded politely at this, hoping to stay out of such seditious political conversation. Morocco certainly already had a Sultan, who had just turned against the much revered Emir Abd al-Qādir for the sake of peace with the French.

Finding passage to the Americas proved to be harder than they thought. It took weeks to repair the harbor and even longer for trade to pick back up once the French lifted their blockade. Then, it proved to be expensive, costing more than the two could muster, even after selling Bella and Claudette's gold bracelet. Even if they could afford to travel, they decided it was too dangerous for Claudette and the baby. She was too far along to spend weeks cramped in a tiny cabin, tossed by the sea. So they decided to wait for the baby to come and grow strong enough to make the crossing and to save enough money for the trip.

At first, Diego found work at the docks, loading and unloading ships. It was hard work but it paid daily. Diego didn't mind the work as much as he resented the implied loss of status. "I'm a caballero from a noble family, not a day laborer," he told her bitterly, sipping contraband wine over their simple meal of roasted chicken, flatbread, couscous, and cherry tomatoes.

"We are poor refugees trying to stay alive, Diego," she squeezed his arm. "You should be proud of honest work."

"Pft! Maybe you're a poor refugee, but I'm an aristocrat," he said, lifting his glass to her before drinking.

"You're an idiot, is what you are!" she laughed, slapping his arm in humor.

"An idiot in love, my Little Claudia," he smiled, melting her heart immediately.

He eventually found work that he felt better suited his breeding and expertise, that was being a hired sword. He was gone for weeks at a time, riding with caravans along the trade routes, protecting them from bandits. She spent sleepless nights worrying about him. But then he'd come home with money, gifts, and sometimes blood on his robes, making her wonder if he might actually be one of the bandits. She decided it was best not to pry.

"Here, to help you with your devil worshipping," he said with a smirk, then handed her a velvet sack. He had just come home from one of his trips.

"Ooh!" her eyes widened at the sight of it. "What is it this time?!" she asked, taking the sack from him. "*Mon Dieu*! It's heavy!" she said, testing the weight in her palm. She reached in and felt its cool smooth surface. "Oh, it's beautiful!" she said as she pulled the perfect glass sphere from the bag.

"Maybe you could use it to check on me when I am away," he said slyly.

"I'm not sure I want to know what you're doing," she replied playfully. "Come, sit down. I'll pour you a cup of wine and make you a plate."

The crystal ball was a nice addition to her own new-found occupation. Her tarot card reading was one of the best-kept secrets in the neighborhood. All forms of divination were strictly forbidden by Islamic law. But just like the contraband wine, there were plenty willing to pay for the forbidden fruit. The women of the neighborhood paid well in coin, food, and gifts for readings, then brought their friends to the secret parlor, always careful to protect her budding business from prodding clerics and soldiers.

The clandestine work kept her busy and far from being lonely during the times that Diego was away. Between the women who could speak a little French or English, and Claudette's small understanding of Arabic, she could perform readings for just about anyone and quickly became somewhat of a local celebrity.

"Hmm…?" she mused as she laid the Fool card next to the Wheel of Change. The woman sitting across from her blinked her large brown eyes in fearful anticipation from behind a headdress that covered everything else. *Why does this keep coming up?* Claudette wondered to herself. *Surely not everyone has the same fortune today…*

"Well…?" the customer's companion and interpreter asked with some impatience.

"Yes…I'm sorry," Claudette collected herself. "You'll have an unexpected visitor," she told the woman in French as her companion translated. "Perhaps someone who you knew was coming, but you have yet to accept their inevitability."

The translator finished relaying her words. The customer's big brown eyes were wide with fear, then they narrowed knowingly, and then softened with compassion.

That's when Claudette felt it, like something popped inside her. "Huh…?!" she gasped as her robes began to soak. Waves of nausea rushed over her as she looked down at the liquid gathering around where she sat cross-legged on the floor. She reeled as the sharp cramps shot through her body. The customer leaped to her, gently taking her by the shoulders. She said something softly in Arabic as she helped Claudette roll onto her back.

"It's alright," the translator spoke with some worry creeping into her voice. "You're amongst friends. We'll get help."

"*Mamá*," Claudette gasped. Tears rolled down the sides of her face as she clenched her eyes in pain. "Lavinia!" she cried out and began to sob. "Where are you..?!"

"Shhh….*habibti*," the veiled woman cooed, softly caressing Claudette's forehead. Soon there were more women in the room. Swells of cramps and nausea washed over her like waves crashing on the beach. Someone brought her hot tea to sip.

"Diego…my love…where are you…?" she gasped, reeling in agony. "I don't want to be alone…!"

"Shhhhhh, you are not alone," one of the women spoke in accented French. "Now, breathe my child. Breathe steadily. It will be alright."

"Of course…of course," Claudette panted. She looked around at the women gathered in the room. Their headdresses hid their faces but their eyes looked at her with soft compassion. "Thank you..." she began to cry again, "thank you..."

The pains swelled and abated for hours with the intervals in-between ever-shortening until the pain was constant. She gritted her teeth and groaned as it became nearly unbearable. A woman held her hand and muttered a prayer from beneath her veil.

There was a commotion outside. Claudette opened her eyes and looked toward the door to see what was the trouble. A woman came to her hurriedly. "There's a man outside," she says, "he says he's your husband, shall I let him?"

"Yes! Oh, yes, please!" she gasped. The woman smiled, turned, and shouted something in Arabic, causing the other women to make way for the man entering the room. She could smell the desert air coming in with him. The dark form moved across the floor, his saber at his side, his musket slung over his shoulder.

"Oh, Diego," she gasped, "you came for me!"

He took her outreached hand, wrapped his other arm around her, and kissed her sweat-soaked forehead. She could feel the roughness of his unshaven face. "I felt it," he said, "I just knew I had to come home."

"Ughh!" she cried out as the pain returned.

"Breathe," one of the women told her in French, "the child is coming."

Claudette dug her nails into Diego's arm as he held her tight. At last, she was free of the burden. The women cheered as the baby cried out to the world. The women went to work cleaning the blood and afterbirth from the child.

"It's a boy!" one of the women said in French.

"A boy! A boy! Did you hear that?!" Claudette called out to Diego, "We had a boy!"

He squeezed her, kissing her head. "Now, I shall live forever..." he said as one of the women handed them the tiny bundle. Diego smiled grandly, looking down at the child's big green eyes, "... through him," he finished.

They named him Carlos Diego Moreau de la Vega. "Why Carlos?" Claudette asked after Diego suggested the name.

"After Don Carlos María Isidro Benito de Borbón, the true King of Spain," he said with dark drama.

"Pfft!" she scoffed. "What do you care about Spanish politics?" To this, Diego merely shrugged and frowned causing Claudette to burst into a peal of laughter. "Alright, silly man," she said, slapping his arm, "Carlos it is!"

Despite her feigned disapproval, she liked the name. If they were going to live in Mexico and be Mexicans, then their child should have a Mexican name, she decided. She was even more delighted to hear Diego speak to the child in Spanish and call him "Carlito."

"Oh, my sweet Carlito!" Claudette began to say as well to the little olive-skinned baby. Carlito looked up at her in wonderment as she tussled his already thickening black hair. Those big green eyes tore her heart in two until she do no more than smother him with kisses. It seemed to be in an instant that the child went from breastfeeding to taking spoonfuls of mashed vegetables. Soon, he was sitting on his own and then crawling, pulling his little wooden horse on wheels behind him with a string.

It was a gift his father brought back from one of his treks. A trek that had left him bruised and cut with bloodstained clothes. Diego offered no explanation. Claudette knew not to pry, but she was sure that most of the blood was not his own. Diego grew more and more agitated and impatient as Carlito was beginning to hoist himself up and stumble a few steps before plopping back down on his butt. The boy was strong enough to travel now and through his own sweat and blood, and perhaps the blood of others, Diego had raised enough money for their passage. But now there were new problems.

"¡Esos malditos americanos!" Diego spat, throwing the Spanish-language newspaper on the ground as he entered the room. He had gotten the paper from the quays where the big ocean-crossing ships from seemingly all nations came and went. This is where he had hoped to purchase steerage for his tiny family.

"What is it my, love?" Claudette asked in English.

"The Americans are blockading my country making it impossible for us to return. They have seized *Texas* and declared war on *México*, my *México*! I swear I'll kill the first American I see…"

"Diego! They're just people," she chided him squeezing his arm, "people like us."

"They are not like us!" he turned to her glaring, causing her to take a step back in horror at this monster that suddenly appeared before her. "I've seen them, crawling into California, starving, dirty, bearded heathens covered in fleas, begging for help, then turning on us once they're strong again. They won't stop coming until they've taken everything: our lands, our women, our culture. They are vile heretical demons drunk on power." He put his hand on his sword, "I will wipe my land clean of them and wash my sword in their blood…"

Carlito began to cry. Claudette sighed, "Stop being so dramatic. You're scaring the baby," she said, picking up the child and soothing him with kisses.

"Perhaps I should start teaching him to fight so he can kill them with me," Diego said grimly.

Claudette slapped his arm. "Now you're just being an idiot," she said with humor. Diego shrugged with a frown and then sat down to read his paper.

Diego was more determined than ever to make the crossing. "I have to get back," he told her.

Carlito reached out for his mother. "*Umiy*," he called to her in Arabic.

"…our child is turning into an Arab!" Diego gestured to his son with an open palm to further make his case.

Claudette drew Carlito to her and sweet-talked to him in French, which made the little boy giggle with delight. "He says things in French and English, too," she said, turning back to Diego.

"Well, he should grow up speaking Spanish," he said to her and then turned to the baby. "*¿No es así, hijo?*" The child went quiet, dropped his smile, and blinked at his father blankly.

Diego looked back at Claudette with wide eyes, gesturing to his son with his hand once more as if to say, "You see?!"

Diego came home around noon after spending the morning hours around the docks a few days later. He was in a huff. "Pack your things," he told her "we are leaving tonight."

"Tonight?!" Claudette gasped, reaching down, picking up Carlito, and pressing him to her. "But how? Why so sudden?"

"You don't want to know," Diego said grimly.

"Tell me, before I put our son on a boat to cross the sea," Claudette said firmly.

Diego sighed, "It's a smuggler. It's the only chance we have to get past the American blockade, but we have to leave tonight. They are pulling out after dark to avoid unwanted attention."

"What are they smuggling?"

"It's not important," Diego said, then sighed, "My love, this is our chance. It's what we've been waiting for," he said pleadingly.

Claudette sighed, "I have a bad feeling about this."

Chapter Twenty-Three: The Cargo of Sorrow

Diego took her hand and led her through the crowded streets at sunset. There was no time to say goodbye to their friends and neighbors. She carried the baby strapped to her chest and the few things she managed to pack. She stole a parting glance at the alley where they had begun their life as a family. All the memories, the happy nights when Diego returned home, and Carlito's first days were left behind with the cooking utensils and other things they could not carry, left to be found by the first to investigate the now-abandoned home.

"Come, we must hurry," he tugged her along.

The quays were as busy as ever. People and carts full of goods crowded the walkway.

"This one here," Diego said hurriedly, guiding her down one of the docks. Claudette was awed by the mix of people who crowded the way. They were seemingly from every nation she could imagine. Their skin tones and features seemed to have been painted from an endless pallet of colors.

"There it is," Diego said, pointing to a ship, "*O Libertador!*"

The three-masted ship sat ominously low in the water. There was none of the hurried activity on its gangplank like the other ships. There was just the silhouette of a man, smoking a pipe at the top in the quickening evening gloom. The glow from his pipe was the only light she could see aboard the dark ship.

That's when they bumped into him. They were surprised they hadn't seen him standing a head above the crowd, but their eyes had been fixed on the dark ship brooding in the gloom. "*Perdona me,*" Diego mumbled, stumbling back from the tall man he had walked into.

"Huh!" Claudette gasped as she looked up at the exotic man dressed in desert robes and a turban. He was tall and slender with narrow hips and shoulders but had elegantly long legs, arms, and a neck that held his head high above everyone else. His obsidian skin contrasted greatly with the whites of his large eyes and the teeth in his generous grin which was accented by the whiff of a mustache and chin beard. The man grinned grandly as he gave a graceful bow and moved out of their way.

"*Gracias*...." Diego mumbled, sounding a little unnerved by the man as they passed. Claudette looked back at him as they climbed the gangplank. He was still standing on the dock in the crowd, watching them intently as they boarded.

"It's about time," the man with the pipe at the top of the gangplank said in Spanish. "We were about to cast off without you."

"My apologies," Diego responded in English. "This is my wife, Claudette. She doesn't speak Spanish or Portuguese."

"Ah, I am charmed!" the man said with a bow. He was a short, stocky man with a belly that protruded from his waistcoat. He had thick short-cut black hair and brown eyes. "I am Capitão João Ferreira. Welcome aboard *O Libertador*. Come quickly now. Zé will show you to your cabin. We must be off quickly."

He then turned and shouted orders in Portuguese which sent his men into a frenzy of action, untying the ship from the docks and hoisting sails. "I will send for you once we are away. Please, join me for supper."

"Thank you, amigo," Diego said, then turned to follow the man the captain called Zé into the dark corridor of the first level below deck. Claudette bristled at the heavy stench of unwashed bodies that grew stronger as they descended the stairs. She had noticed it on the docks but dismissed it as part of the rough society of seamen. It grew stronger once they boarded the ship and was even heavier below deck. Clearly, the sailors didn't seem so dirty but the smell was undeniable. Diego seemed not to notice or care.

Zé led them to a tiny cabin at the very forward end of the boat. It was a tiny space with a bunk just large enough for them to sleep tightly bundled together against an oak wall that curved inward with the bow of the ship. There wasn't enough room to fully stand, so dressing would have to be done in a crouch. A thin sliding wood panel separated them from the hall outside. Zé said something Claudette assumed was in Portuguese before leaving them in their dark little closet, to which Diego replied with something that sounded like an affirmative.

"What did he say?" Claudette asked as she sat on the bunk, clutching Carlito tightly to her chest, trying to adjust her eyes to the darkness.

"I don't know. Something about dinner," Diego said. "The Portuguese sound like they're talking with their mouths full of cotton. I can barely understand them."

She could feel the ship moving slowly. The water was now running outside the oak wall, creating a steady drone with the creaking of the ship. She felt the room rise and then come back down with a splash, causing her stomach to roil. "How long will we be here?" she asked softly. Carlito was beginning to fuss. "Shhhh..." she whispered to him, stroking the back of his head.

"A few weeks, a month at the most," Diego told her, reaching out to squeeze her shoulder. "They'll make a stop in the Caribbean before continuing to Brazil. We can easily find passage to Mexico from there." Claudette smiled softly at him, then looked around the tiny dark room in silence. "We don't have to spend all of our time down here," he told her. "There's fresh air on the deck, and you can look to the horizon. It'll settle your stomach."

She hoisted herself up with a sigh and set Carlito on the bed, then started arranging their things to make the most of their little home. "Your *oud?*" she said, realizing it was not among their things.

"I sold it," he said. "There's no room, and we need the money."

"Hmm," she replied with a bit of regret. She realized his sword and musket were gone too. She decided it was best not to ask, but she was somewhat relieved that he had given them up. She could see that he still had his pistol and dagger tucked discreetly in his trousers. Although the sight of the weapons was still disturbing, part of her took some comfort that he still had them.

They finished arranging their things, then sat side-by-side on the bed in silence peering into the darkness as the ship rose and crashed on the waves.

"Would you like to make love?" Diego spoke at last.

"Not with the baby awake," she replied.

"Of course," Diego mumbled.

"Ah, pa!" the child cooed in the darkness.

"Go to sleep, Carlito," Diego said.

A knock on the sliding panel startled them both. Zé said something quickly in Portuguese from outside. They heard him walking away afterward.

"What was that about?" Claudette asked, holding her hand to her breast, recovering from the scare.

"I think it's time for supper," Diego said.

"You brought your child?!" *Capitão* Ferreira blurted as they entered his quarters. The other officers sat around the table near him, holding glasses of wine.

"I'm sorry, I don't have a maid to leave him with," Claudette said, reeling with embarrassment.

"Perhaps we can fetch one from below," Ferreira quipped darkly, bringing a round of grim chuckles from his men.

Claudette blinked at him in confusion, then spoke. "I'm sorry, I'll take him back to our cabin. Diego, you stay."

"Nonsense!" Ferreira said. "We would gladly suffer a child for the presence of a beautiful woman at our table! Come, sit! We need to practice our English anyway. We might need it if we can't avoid any...um... *Imperial entanglements.*"

"Imperial entanglements?" Claudette repeated, taking her seat.

"The British don't like our kind of business now that they're out of it," Ferreira said. "Come, have a glass of wine."

"What business?" Claudette asked, accepting a glass.

Ferreira looked to Diego, who shook his head silently, then returned his eyes to Claudette. "Farming equipment...but such talk of business isn't for women, and frankly, it's boring. Let us talk of other things."

The wine, roasted lamb, stewed beans, and bread along with cheerful banter, soon made her forget her curiosity over the captain's cryptic jokes. "Enjoy the fresh food while you can, darling," he told her. "It'll be salt pork and pickled vegetables soon enough."

They finished with roasted walnuts, sweet port wine, and grapes. Carlito slept soundly on the floor, snuggled in a blanket. Claudette sat back in her chair and enjoyed the sleepy warm cloud of alcohol and a full belly.

"You'll have a hard time getting past the blockade," Ferreira told Diego, as he cracked open another walnut and picked the pieces off the table to eat, "now that the Americans have declared war on Mexico."

"All the more reasons to get home, my friend," Diego said. "I must defend my country and drive the heretics out."

"Bah! Little chance of that," Ferreira said. "Your country can't even govern itself, let alone stand up against the might of the United States. Once they get in, you'll never get rid of them. You should have taken their money instead."

"Mexico will not be sold piece by piece to the filthy bearded heathens," Diego said. "I've seen Americans. They are a filthy, starving, backward people. There's no way they can pose a threat to Mexico."

"No, my friend," Ferreira chuckled lightly, shaking his head, "what you have seen are the pioneers who've crawled over the mountains into Alta California after surviving the long trek across the continent. Their cities and factories in the northeast rival any in the world in grandeur and modernity. Their vast plantations in the south supply the world with cotton. Their might, wealth, and drive to rule the New World will simply overwhelm you and all those who oppose them. Best to do business with them than fight. You'll always be ruled by somebody, you might as well make money while you can."

"I will die first," Diego said grimly.

"Alright," Claudette hoisted herself from her chair, "I've had enough of such talk. I'm going to bed."

"I'm coming too, my love," Diego said, getting up from his chair and scooping Carlito from the floor.

"Smart man," Ferreira said. "With such a woman, why go fight when you can stay in bed?"

"Honor," Diego said flatly.

Ferreira laughed. "Honor...?" he chuckled. "I tell you, my friend, your country kicked out your best chance against the Americans."

Diego turned back and raised an eyebrow.

"While your countrymen panic and fight among themselves," Ferreira continued, "Santa Anna tends to his gardens in Cuba, living in exile. He's fought the Spanish, the French, and the Americans. He knows how to win. Mexico needs a strong leader right now, not a squabbling republic."

"Perhaps I can smuggle him in with me," Diego smiled.

"Good luck with that," Ferreira laughed as the couple made their way through the door.

Claudette floated down the corridor to their tiny cabin, smiling softly with her eyes nearly shut. The ship lifted and crashed in the water, causing her to lose her balance. Diego caught her arm with one hand while holding the baby in the other. She laughed as she clung to the wall to pull herself up. "I think I've had too much wine."

"The port was very strong, my love. Come, let's get in bed." He pulled her back up to her feet. She let him guide her to their cabin. He laid the boy down and helped her out of her dress. She snuggled up into his arms and smiled, feeling the rocking of the boat and hearing the water run past the outside of the wall.

There were bodies everywhere. The city was in ruins. She was looking for him. "Diego!" she called out. The only response was the wind and the groans from the dead. Were they dead? She couldn't tell. They were still, but their dead eyes followed her as she moved through the streets, searching.

"Diego!" She saw him, standing in the middle of the road. He was smiling and beckoning her. She ran to him. He kept getting farther away. Now he was covered in blood with his sword in his hand. He was waving to her. Was it goodbye? He was gone. She stopped, fell to her knees, and began to weep. She wasn't alone. The dead were moaning and weeping with her.

She snapped her eyes open. Beams of light spilled through the tiny spaces between the wood planks above them. Relief rushed through her. They were still in their tiny cabin. Diego was breathing softly in his sleep, his arm was still around her. Carlito was sitting up, mumbling happily to himself in his infantile language as he played with his little wooden horse on wheels. She smiled, looking at the boy, not wanting to interrupt him from this moment. The moaning and weeping were still there.

Claudette sat up with a jolt. "Ah, ma!" Carlito called out, stretching his hand to her.

"Shhhhhh…quiet, my child," she told him in French. She strained her ears, listening for the source.

"What is it…?" Diego said softly in English, sitting up and rubbing his eyes.

"Where is that coming from…?" she said quietly. There were words, too. Strange words of an unfamiliar language. She lay back down, listening intently. She stared into the darkness which pooled around the floor. She could make out the planks of wood, the spaces in between, and the darkness below. And then she saw them: eyes, human eyes, looking up from the darkness.

"Huh!" she gasped, "They're people down there!" She scrambled to the floor, pressing her face to the ground, trying to peer through the cracks. There were shadows of bodies and eyes, dozen of eyes. She leaped to her feet and threw open the sliding wood panel.

"My love…" Diego called out to her, trying to catch hold of her cotton shift as she bolted out of the cabin. He could hear the Portuguese sailors respond to the woman in her nightgown dashing down the corridor.

"Out of my way!" she shouted as she shoved them aside and then thrust herself down the stairway into the darkness below. "Huh?!" she gasped. There were hundreds of them, chained together, lying on the floor. Their naked black bodies barely reflected the small wisps of light that found their way through the planks above. The stench of unwashed bodies, vomit, urine, and excrement was suffocating. She brought her hands to her mouth and fought back the impulse to throw up. She was surrounded by eyes blinking at her in the darkness. She could hear crying, moaning, and someone pleading in a language she couldn't understand.

"I'm so sorry…" she said in French, as she stumbled among them, "I don't understand…" She stifled a sob. The staircase darkened behind her. She spun around. Diego was descending the steps. Carlito was fussing in his arms, squirming in agitation. He set the boy down. "You knew!" she accused him. Diego just looked at her in silence. The sickening realization poured into her. "*Mon Dieu*, you helped bring them here, across the desert! You're a monster!"

"I'm a monster who would do anything for his family. Come," he beckoned, "this is no place for you or the boy."

"This is no place for anybody!" she yelled. "My God, we have to help them!"

"My love, we cannot interfere with the cargo…"

"The cargo?! These are people, Diego!" Just then, she could hear Carlito cooing in delight. Another voice was singing softly. "Huh, my boy!" she gasped in French. They both turned to see. Carlito had crawled into the arms of one of the women chained to the floor. She was now comforting him, singing to him in her native language. Claudette turned her eyes back to Diego, not bothering to wipe the tears running down her face.

He let out a sigh and dropped his shoulders, "You are right. What do you want to do?"

Claudette went to work immediately. Diego carried buckets of water to her as she cleaned and tended to as many of them as she could. She found some of them were already dead in their chains. Diego went up top to alert the sailors. They came down to remove the bodies. Diego helped carry them topside, where they were unceremoniously tossed into the sea.

"That woman is making a fool of you," Ferreira told him.

Diego merely shrugged, "She has a tender heart."

"Hmmm, well, I suppose I can't complain. She's doing the work no one else wants to do. I should give her a cut of the profits!" he laughed.

"I don't think she'd accept," Diego said.

"Ba! You Mexicans have no sense of humor!" Ferreira slapped him on the back.

Claudette spent her days down below, tending to the people, feeding and washing them. The women chained to the floor watched over Carlito in turn, freeing her up to do her work. Diego helped as much as he could bear, carrying buckets up and down the steps, which the sailors found amusing and great cause for teasing. He still took his meals with them and supper from time to time in the captain's chambers where he apologized for her absence and, for what they deemed to be, strange behavior.

"You really should come to supper with me," he told her. "They're beginning to wonder about you."

"Let them. How can I take any comfort on this ship when there are people suffering?" she answered. Diego merely shrugged, knowing it was useless to argue.

It was mid-morning. They had just finished distributing the gruel to the prisoners. Claudette was about to start cleaning the excrement and vomit from the night before when they started hearing the commotion above. "I'll go see what it is," Diego said.

"Of course," she said with a smirk, knowing he'd find any excuse to get out of the dark dingy hull.

Diego climbed up topside. The sailors were all gathered at the stern, pointing out into the distance. A tower of black smoke was on the horizon. He shielded his eyes with his hand and squinted at the ominous cloud.

"We suspected that we were being followed ever since we left Tangiers," Ferreira told him as he handed over his spyglass. "Now our fears are confirmed." Diego peered through the telescope to see a ship steaming its way through the water. He could make out the Union Jack flapping in the wind.

"Good!" Claudette said, having emerged from below to see what the fuss was about for herself. "Let them find us." She then waved her arms in big arching motions. "Over here!" she shouted.

"You fool of a woman!" Ferreira growled. "They'll hang you with the rest of us. The British consider slavers the same as pirates."

"My life for the freedom of hundreds is a fair bargain," she said defiantly.

Ferreira started to reply, but Diego put his hand on his shoulder and gave him a look of warning. Ferreira thought better of it. Instead, he turned his focus to Diego. "You need to learn how to control your woman," he said, then shrugged off Diego's hand and began barking orders in Portuguese.

The men scrambled, hoisting and tightening their sails, trying to make the most of the wind. The steamship kept coming, getting nearer and nearer as the day went on. Claudette came up from her work below frequently to check on its progress. The men watched in silence as the ship got closer. The afternoon heat began to build, making her drowsy. She thought about slipping back into their cabin for a brief nap. Perhaps Diego could watch over Carlito while she slept.

An explosion rocked her from these thoughts. She screamed as smoke and flames shot out of the approaching ship. The ball whistled over their heads and splashed into the water ahead of them. "They're shooting at us!" she exclaimed.

"It's a warning. They're signaling us to stop," Ferreira said flatly. "They'll blow us to pieces if we don't." He then began giving orders. His men started loosening the sails and taking them down.

"What are you doing?" Diego asked.

"We can't outrun a steamship. We must hope for mercy," he said grimly. Diego turned his eyes back to the approaching ship and watched as it neared.

"Black James!" one of the men shouted from the rigging, pointing at it.

"Black James, Black James!" other men started yelling.

Claudette could hear the panic in their voices. She was surprised to hear the English name coming out of the Portuguese sailors' mouths.

"Black James…?" she mumbled in confusion.

"Here are your English saviors, woman," Ferreira said bitterly, shoving the spyglass into her hands. "Take a look at your impending death."

She blinked at him in shock, then looked through the glass. She could see the ship coming. The forward deck was covered with black men, most of them shirtless and in loincloths. Their muscles glistened with sweat. They held knives, machetes, short sabers, and pistols. They were chanting and beating their chests, howling out some war cry. "*Mon Dieu!*" she gasped, lowering the spyglass.

With her naked eye, she could now see the Union Jack coming down. A black flag with a skull and crossbones rose in its place. "Is this some kind of a joke? Pirates?! That flag is something out of a cheap romance novel!"

"It's no joke, woman. Black James is known for his theatrics, but that flag, in all seriousness, means the death of all of us," Ferreira told her, then started barking out orders. The men immediately began to raise the sails again in a panicked fury.

Chapter Twenty-Four: Black James

"Open up the arms locker and start distributing weapons to the men," Ferreira said flatly in Portuguese. He held the keys out limply in his hand, not taking his eyes off the approaching ship full of half-naked pirates chanting and prancing on the deck with their blades glistening in the sun. Zé took the keys while not taking his eyes off the ship either. "And hurry," Ferreira added.

Zé snapped out of his trance, turned on his heel, and called out to two of the men to follow him. The three disappeared into the hull. The rest of the men stood dumbfounded, watching as the ship full of dancing howling black marauders got nearer and nearer. The pirates began to take notice of their audience and started taunting them, hurling insults in multiple languages while pumping their weapons into the air.

Claudette could have sworn she heard English words among the insults. "My God, Diego," she said, gripping his arm tightly, "are we in danger too?"

"I don't know," he said flatly, his eyes fixed on the ever-nearing ship. "I don't know how they'll tell us apart from the crew, or if they'll even care."

Some of the pirates were now yelling at the others, and soon most were backing up to make room as three of them stepped forward with ropes and grappling hooks which they began to twirl in the air.

"Diego, I'm scared!" she dug her nails into his arm.

"Get the baby below and hide," he turned to her. Tears were running down her face.

WACHUNK! WACHUNK!

She screamed as the grappling hooks came over the guardrail and dug into the wood. "Go!" Diego yelled, shoving her back. She stumbled and then wrapped her arms tightly around Carlito as she caught her balance. Carlito stared wide-eyed at the unfolding scene. She turned to run.

BAM!

The steamship turned at the last moment as it hit their boat, causing everyone to lose their balance. Zé and his men tumbled to the ground as they emerged from the hull, sending muskets and cutlasses scattering across the decks. The steamship ground alongside their boat. The sickening grinding sound competed with the panicked shouts of the men who struggled to find footing as the ship shuddered from the impact.

The pirates reeled in the ropes attached to the grabbling hooks and made them fast, locking the ships together, then they started spilling over the gunwale.

Diego pulled out his pistol and shot the first grinning face that came over the rail. The man's face exploded into a mist of blood as he flew back into the water with a splash.

The sailors scrambled to pick up the weapons from the floor. The pirates were upon them immediately, hacking them to pieces with their blades.

"Defend the ship, brave amigos!" Ferreira shouted, then turned and ran down the steps into the hull.

"Follow him!" Diego said, pushing Claudette towards the stairs and shoving his pistol into his trousers. They plunged down the steps. They could hear the screams and the wet sounds of blades hacking into soft flesh behind them. Ferreira sprinted down the corridor to his cabin. They chased after him. They could hear the footfalls of more people coming down the stairs. Ferreira opened the door to his cabin, slid inside, and slammed it shut. He was setting the bolt as they ran into the door.

"Open up, you fucking coward!" Diego shouted, pounding on the door with his fist. There was no answer. He spun around, pulling out his pistol and dagger, then stepped out in front of his wife and child, covering them with his body from the corridor filled with blood-splattered, half-naked pirates. Their dark skin dissolved into the gloom of the hallway, but their eyes and grinning teeth were everywhere.

A quiet fell over the hall as they loomed, ready to pounce on the tiny family. The light at the top of the stairs suddenly blotted out. An enormous form was descending the steps. The pirates rose from their crouches and made room for this dark form as it made its way through the crowd.

"Huh!" Claudette gasped in terror as the man emerged in front of his men. He towered over the rest of them. His black skin rippled with muscles that were covered in tattoos and whip scars. An archaic tricorne hat sat on top of a wild forest of dreadlocks. His beard spilled out in braids over his enormous chest. The ends of the braids smoldered with wisps of smoke that smelled of incense. Despite her terror, Claudette couldn't help but feel there was something oddly familiar about this man's appearance.

The enormous pirate eyed them for a moment, then spoke in English with a booming voice that betrayed a Caribbean accent. "You are willing to die for this woman and child?" he said.

"No," Diego said, glaring deeply into the big man's eyes. "I am willing to kill you…" he then afforded himself a quick glance at the other men crowding the corridor around him. "…and maybe a few of your men too," he said grimly, returning his eyes to their leader.

The hulking pirate glared back at him. His scar-covered muscles twitched and rippled with tension as dozens of eyes around him watched with great anticipation. Claudette could hear the waves lapping against the hull and the creaking timber as the two ships rocked together with the sea.

Suddenly, there was a laugh; a deep full-belly laugh that bellowed through the dark corridor. Soon, the rest of the pirates joined in. The big man recovered and called out to one of his men, "O-ka-né, take them aboard the *Dessalines*. They are under my protection. Let no man harm them or I will feed him to the sharks. Is that clear?"

Another tall man emerged from the crowd. This one was slender and moved with ethereal grace. Claudette's eyes widened with recognition, realizing he was the same man they had bumped into on the dock. Okané caught her look and smiled with a wink. "Of course, Captain," he said.

The pirate captain returned his eyes to Diego, "Are you going to lower your weapons, or do we really have to fight?"

Diego lifted his pistol, aimed it at him, and pulled the trigger.

CLICK!

A collective gasp rolled through the hall. Diego straightened himself out of his crouch, then tossed his pistol to the floor with a shrug. "It was empty anyway," he said.

After a tense moment of silence, the captain burst into another laugh. The rest of the men joined in. "I like this man!" he said, laying his enormous hand on Diego's shoulder. Diego nearly buckled under the weight. "Give them a shot of rum when they are aboard. I think they need it now."

Okané smiled and beckoned them forward. "Come!" he said. Claudette followed Diego through the crowd of pirates, clinging to the baby who was reaching out and touching the dark faces as they passed with childish curiosity. Behind them, they could hear the men hacking through Ferreira's door, then the screams of the Portuguese captain that turned into blood-drenched gurgles. Then the sound of blades hacking into him drowned out his screams completely. Claudette closed her eyes and shuddered in horror.

The scene on the deck was worse. The pirates had left no man alive. They were now tossing body parts overboard. The water boiled and churned as a host of some terrible creatures fought for and devoured the bloody morsels the moment they hit the water. The deck itself was covered in blood which stained her shoes and the bottom of her dress and made the walk slippery and treacherous.

Okané led them onto the steamship. It had two masts for sails, one forward and one aft. In the center were two enormous paddle wheels on either side of its hull. Black smoke trickled out of the two smokestacks that protruded from the front and rear of the pilothouse. Much to Claudette's relief, the smell of burning coal began to overpower the iron smell of fresh blood from the other ship.

They followed the tall African into the hull, then to the rear of the ship. There, he opened the door to the captain's chamber and beckoned them inside. Sunlight rolled through the large rear window and bounced off the white-painted oak interior. There was a bunk next to it that Claudette could not believe was able to contain the enormous man who slept there.

Okané bade them to sit at a table set in the center of the room. He placed two mugs before them, uncorked a bottle, and poured some of the amber liquid into each one. The scent of vanilla and clove wafted through the air and tickled Claudette's nose.

"The captain will be with you shortly," he told them, then left the room.

They sat there, staring at the window, not really focusing on anything as the ship creaked and rocked with the waves. At last, Diego picked up his mug and took a drink. "Ah," he let out with a smack of his lips.

Claudette raised the mug to her nose and sniffed. The strong scent of alcohol was balanced with the sweet smell of spices. She took a sip and immediately shuddered as the liquid burned its way down her throat. She coughed, placing her hand on her chest, shook her head, then took another drink. She could feel the rum warming her stomach. That warmth began to spread through her body.

She sighed, slumped back into her chair, and gazed at the room around her. The walls were covered with shelves stuffed with books. Books that didn't fit on the shelves were stacked around the room. There was a globe on a wooden stand and a telescope on a tripod standing on the floor. The table in front of her was covered in maps, charts, and compasses. Among these things were small model boats and toy soldiers set up in tiny battles all over the table.

She sat up in her chair and picked up one of the lead figurines. It was painted meticulously to resemble a grenadier of Napoleon's Imperial Guard, complete with a bearskin hat, bushy mustache, blue coat, and white cross belts. The little figure even had a tiny musket tipped with a bayonet which he held at the ready. *Why would such a brute of a man have toys like these?* she wondered.

She let out a yelp as the door opened. She quickly set the figurine down, not wanting to be caught with it in her hand.

The big man had to duck to enter the room, which suddenly seemed a lot smaller with him in it. Claudette and Diego both sank into their chairs as he loomed over them. Quietly looking them over, he spoke at last, "Okané says you were with the caravan that brought the slaves to the port."

"I was," Diego said flatly.

"I'm told you shot and killed one of my men in the attack," the pirate captain continued.

"I did," Diego replied.

"Hmm," the big man pondered, stroking the braids in his beard which were still smoldering at the ends. "For this, I would have you hacked to pieces and fed to the sharks."

Claudette let out a gasp that caught his attention. He smiled mischievously, then returned his eyes to Diego. "We have a school of them that follow us because we feed them often…if you know what I mean," he chuckled darkly. Diego just sat silently, blinking at the large man towering over him. "Every once in a while, we take one and eat it," he continued. "I think it's a fair trade," he said, looking off as he pondered, stroking his beard.

He leveled his big brown eyes on Claudette, causing her to sink farther into her chair. "And you," he said, a smile returning to his face, "you are the one the slaves are calling the 'White Angel, no?'" Claudette blinked at him in silence. "What is your name?"

"I am…Claudette…" she stammered, "Claudette Moreau de la Vega. This is my husband, Diego de la Vega, and our child Carlos Moreau de la Vega."

She flinched as the big man took off his tricorne and tossed it aside, unleashing a mass of dreadlocks that looked like black tentacles of some horrible sea monster. He took her hand, bowed deeply, and kissed it.

"It is a pleasure to meet you, Claudette, the White Angel," he said as he rose. "I am the Dread Pirate Black James, Slayer of the Slavers, Scourge of the Sea, at your service."

Claudette blinked at him for a minute, taking in the image of the shirtless pirate with the smoldering beard before her. It was then that the resemblance struck her, "Black James…? Like infamous Blackbeard, Edward Teach?"

James's eyes bulged with excitement as a smile exploded across his face. "Yes! Yes, that is the one!" he said gleefully, pointing his finger at her with each word. "Look! Look…wait one moment!" he said excitedly, then dashed to his shelf and pulled out a book which he plopped before her and quickly thumbed through the pages until he arrived at an illustration of the famous pirate, complete with a smoldering beard.

"You see?!" he said, tapping the image with his big finger, then patting his chest with his other hand as he posed.

"I…uh… saw it right away," she told him, "I just couldn't put my finger on it."

"Thank you," he said joyfully. "I've read everything about him. I try to tell my men his stories, but they don't know who he was."

"That's…um…surprising," she said. "Edward Teach was a famous man," she told him.

"I know!" James was quick to agree. "I try to carry on his legacy. Here, let me get you some more rum!" he said, uncorking the bottle and pouring them each another round. He poured himself one and drank it down with one gulp as he sat in one of the chairs.

"Tell me, why were you on the slave ship? Where are you going?"

"We ran away from France," she told him, "to be together. We are trying to return to my husband's homeland…Mexico, to live together as a family."

"Ah, ga!" Carlito interrupted, reaching out to touch the man's braids.

James turned his eyes to the boy and took him from her before she could even think about protesting. Carlito cooed with delight as he took one of the braids and stuck it in his mouth. James let out a chuckle. "This is your son?" he said, bouncing the boy in his arms.

"Yes," Claudette said, still stunned to see her baby in the arms of a giant pirate.

"I see why you would kill for him," James said, turning his eyes back to Diego. "…and for the White Angel," he finished, nodding toward Claudette. "I would kill for my children too…" he said softly. A tear rolled down his face.

"Your children…?" Claudette said, reaching out to touch the big man's arm.

James turned his eyes to her. The deep sorrow in them caused her to put her other hand on her heart as if his pain had struck her there.

"Their mother passed away giving birth to my boy," he said with a sniffle. "She was my angel…" He took another pull from his rum, then replenished his and their cups. "I have a little girl and a baby boy. They are slaves in a place called *Ten-a-sée*, deep in the continent. I could not free them. So I free the ones I can."

Claudette squeezed his arm, "I'm so sorry…"

James smiled and wiped his tear away, "Let us talk of other things, White Angel. I will spare your husband's life." He then turned to Diego, "But you must take Abebe's place on this ship until I replace him, killer man."

Diego nodded, "That is fair."

"What will you do with the slaves?" Claudette asked.

"I will recruit the very strongest for my crew," he told her, leaning back in his chair. "The rest will we unload at Haiti where they can be free. No white man and his whip dare step on that island. I will sell the captured ship there, too."

"What about us?" Claudette asked nervously.

James thought for a moment. "The American slavers have blockaded your country," he said to Diego, then looked to Claudette. "I cannot go there," he said, shaking his head. "But I can take you as far as Cuba. There are many Mexicans there living in exile, even their last president. If there is one man who would know how to get past the blockade and fight the Americans it is *el Presidente* and *General* Antonio López de Santa Anna."

Part III: The New World

El Presidente and *General* Antonio López de Santa Anna sat at his desk in Havana. He was reading the dispatches from the American envoys once again. He had read them countless times as if he would somehow find clues to his own intentions written in their words. He shrugged and tossed them on his desk, which was already littered with piles of other letters that needed responses. Were the Americans the fools he hoped they'd be or were they playing him the fool?

A knock came to the door. "Your Serene Highness…?" a meek voice came from outside.

"What is it? I'm very busy," Santa Anna said with a sigh, having accomplished nothing in the hours he spent rereading letters and newspaper articles that morning.

The door opened slightly. A servant stuck his head through. "There's a man here to see you."

"A man? Does this man have a name? Or are you merely taking in any vagabond off the street who wants an autograph from the Napoleon of the West?" the general said, raising an eyebrow.

"He says he is Don Diego de la Vega from the Pueblo of Los Angeles in Alta California," the man said.

"I know where Los Angeles is, you imbecile!" he admonished, then paused as the name struck him. He sat upright in his chair. "Don Diego de la Vega?! Here in Havana?!"

"That is the name he gave me, Your Serene Highness," the man said with a slight bow. The general blinked at him for a moment, then looked off as he pondered. "Hmmm…" he mused, rubbing his chain. "Give me a moment to prepare before you bring him up."

"Yes, your Excellency," the servant said as he withdrew and closed the door.

"Don Diego de la Vega!" Santa Anna gasped. He hoisted himself from his chair and grabbed his crutch. Wearing nothing more than a shirt, he hobbled over to his bed where his pants and false leg, which was still in its riding boot, were lying on the floor.

He plopped down and quickly donned his pants, then shimmied up the left pant leg so he could strap on his prosthetic. With a grunt, he pulled the belts tight. It was better to endure the pain than the embarrassment of his leg coming loose.

Once he got the other boot on, he hobbled over to the mirror. There he threw on his military jacket and began fastening the buttons. He took a look at himself. *Should I shave?* He smirked at his image. No, it was better not to seem too prepared. He looked better as a handsome rugged soldier than an overly polished peacock, he thought.

He stopped buttoning and let the top flap of his jacket hang open to expose some of his white shirt, olive skin, and manly chest hair. He plopped back into his chair and threw his boots up on the desk. "Ignacio!" he called out through the door, "you may go and fetch him now."

"Yes, Your Serene Highness," his servant said.

Santa Anna smiled in satisfaction as he listened to the man make his way down the stairs. He gave his boots and sleeves one last inspection as two sets of footsteps came up the stairs. *Too cavalier,* he thought suddenly, jolting out of his chair. He quickly hobbled to the window and placed his false foot on the sill, then looked outside, putting on the best pensive expression he could muster.

A light knock came to the door.

"Yes?" Santa Anna called out.

"Don Diego de la Vega, Your Serene Highness."

"Send him in, please."

The general stared out the window, waiting to hear the footsteps enter the room and the door shut behind them.

"Ah, *el muy señor* Don Diego de la Vega," he said, smiling grandly as he turned to his guest, "it is a great honor to finally meet you." His smile fell away as he looked upon the young man dressed in ragged black clothes standing before him. He blinked in silence for a moment.

"What is it, Your Serene Highness?" the young man prodded.

"I imagined you being older..." Santa Anna said, "being a hero of Mexican independence and all..."

"Oh, you must mean my grandfather, señor," Diego offered.

"Ah, yes! Of course!" Santa Anna said, recovering his smile. "How is the old *Fox?*"

"He's dead, Your Serene Highness."

"Oh...I'm sorry to hear that..." Santa Anna said, collecting himself. "Still, it is a great honor to meet the grandson of the great hero of the north. Come sit down." He directed him with his hand towards a chair, then walked carefully to his, trying hard not to show any discomfort. He sat with a plop and threw his boots back on his desk. "So, what brings you to Havana?"

"I'm trying to get back home with my wife and child," Diego told him, leaning forward in his chair. "I heard you may return to fight the Americans. I want to fight them too. I'm here to offer my sword."

"Fight the Americans?" the general asked incredulously. "Young man, the American president has asked me to broker a peace with those fools in Mexico City running the government now." He then sighed and looked up at the ceiling. "I swear, I'm gone for a little more than a year and the country falls apart." He returned his eyes to the young man before him. The disappointment in Diego's eyes made him nearly cringe with shame. "The Americans are allowing me to pass through the blockade so I can talk to some sense into whoever is in charge these days," he said, tossing his hand to the side as if it was a matter of small importance.

"I see," Diego said flatly.

Santa Anna looked him over for a moment, then dropped his boots back to the floor. He leaned forward. "You offer your sword, eh? For the defense of Mexico?"

"And my life, señor," Diego replied, the fire returning to his eyes.

"Let's not get too dramatic here," the general chuckled. "Do you have any military experience?" he asked, raising his eyebrows.

"I fought the French in Morocco in Emir Abd al-Qādir's cavalry, Your Serene Highness. I sent several of them to their maker with my sword," Diego told him, straightening himself in his chair.

"*Dios mio*, you are a dramatic one!" He laughed, "I would expect nothing less from the grandson of the *Fox*! Here, have a drink with me. I would toast any man who's killed Frenchmen like me." He poured rum into a couple of crystal tumblers and offered one to Diego. "It's not our mezcal, but it'll do. ¡*Salud!*"

"*Salud,*" Diego raised his glass and followed the general's example by tossing it down with one gulp.

"Ah," Santa Anna sighed as he poured another round. "You know, the French bastards took my leg at the Battle of Veracruz," he said, now taking a sip.

"You are a great hero of Mexico, señor," Diego sipped his drink as well. "I hear your leg was buried with full military honors."

"Bah!" the general waved the comment away with disgust, "My ungrateful countrymen dug it up and dragged it through the streets yelling 'down with the cripple!'"

Diego blinked at him for a moment in surprise, then took another drink, "Is this why you won't fight for them now?"

The general paused, scrutinizing the young man sitting before him. "Show me this sword with which you dispatched so many Frenchmen."

"I sold it in Tangiers to help pay for our passage," Diego told him.

Santa Anna looked him over for a moment and then broke into a laugh. "Bah! That won't do at all!" he said. Then he took out a sheet of paper and dipped his pen into an ink well. "I will take you and your family with me to Mexico. But first, you will take this to my tailor and have him make you a uniform of a sub-lieutenant of cavalry. You'll need a sword worthy of your bloodline as well. Be sure to take this to the armorer and purchase a suitable weapon."

Diego looked over the letter of credit once the general handed it to him. "This is awfully generous, Your Serene Highness."

"Eh…the Americans are paying me well to bring peace," Santa Anna said, tossing his hand to the side dismissively.

"Then why am I buying a uniform and sword?"

"No more questions until we cross the American blockade," the general smiled slyly.

"Well, what do you think?" Diego asked.

Claudette had heard his boots come up the stairs to their little room above a cafe in Havana. She turned from the window to see. As much as she didn't want to admit, he looked resplendent in his cavalry uniform.

The green waist-cut jacket had two rows of brass buttons that flared out into a 'V' accenting his narrow waist and broad shoulders. The shoulders were adorned with straps that bore the rank of sub-lieutenant. A stiff, upright collar circled around the back of his neck and opened at his throat. He wore a red sash at the waist and blue pantaloons that buttoned up along the sides of his legs. He left the bottom buttons unfastened to make room for his black leather boots. A straight sword with a brass crossguard, which curled upward on one side and curved downward on the other, creating a knuckle guard that attached to the pommel, hung loosely at his side. His pistol and dagger were tucked into his sash.

"You'll make a beautiful corpse on the battlefield," she said, putting her hands on her hips.

Diego grinned mischievously. "Come, help me get out of this," he said, unbuttoning his jacket, "I'm burning up!"

She smiled and helped him undo the buttons. She knew the little boy in him was exhilarated to be donning the uniform of his country. Especially since it was provided to him by the great *cauldillo* himself, General Antonio López de Santa Anna, the hero of Veracruz.

Still, the thought of Diego once again throwing himself into battle filled her with dread. He said that Santa Anna's only purpose in returning from exile was to broker a peace deal on behalf of the Americans. They were paying him handsomely to do so. They were also allowing him through the blockade, which was their ticket home. But there seemed to be some sly undertone when they spoke of the journey to come as if there was some inside joke about his true purpose that she was not privy to. A purpose that required a uniform and a sword for Diego.

She had worried that Black James would also throw him into battle by holding him to his obligation of taking the place of the pirate Diego had killed. She still shuddered at the memory of Diego calmly drawing his pistol and shooting the man as he came over the rail.

But James was eager to unload the liberated slaves and sell the captured ship. So instead of attacking other ships, Diego spent his days aboard the Jean-Jacque Dessalines, helping with the chores of running the ship. It didn't take long for some of the pirates to test him. They quickly learned that Diego was a classically trained swordsman. Soon he was sparring with them and even teaching fencing lessons.

Claudette continued her work of tending to the now-freed prisoners. It amazed her how quickly sunlight, fresh air, and good food revived their health and spirits. "I've never seen such a smiling people!" she told Diego as they relayed how they spent their day to each other that evening.

The Africans loved to chant and dance. They made drums out of anything they could find. She cringed with fear as they snatched Carlito off the deck and twirled him around, passing him from person to person. Carlito giggled madly at the attention, cooing and reaching out to touch the black faces with fascination.

Still, some of the Africans were just too sick to recover from the abuse and the dingy conditions they had endured in the lower decks of the *O Libertador*. They succumbed to their sickness, much to the wails and tears of their companions. James had them buried at sea with a ceremony that seemed to combine some familiar rites of Catholicism mixed heavily with African magic and mysticism. Even the ever-giggling Carlito was struck silent with awe as an African holy man chanted and danced to the beat of somber drums.

It was a bittersweet moment when the liberated slaves disembarked at Port-au-Prince in Haiti. They lined up so that each could kiss and thank the *White Angel* personally and say goodbye to little baby Carlito. The woman who had held and cared for him that first day, took Carlito into her arms one last time and spoke sweetly to him in her native language. Claudette learned that her name was Adaego and that she had been separated from her own child when her village was raided by a rival tribe. Adaego had cared for Carlito like he was her own. Now she was telling him goodbye, and even though the language was strange, the child seemed to understand he was losing something. He cried and reached for her after she gave him back to his mother and kissed him one more time on the head. She turned, smiled, and waved to him once more before walking away forever.

Several of the pirates took brides among the freed slaves and retired to the island. They were replaced with volunteers from the newly freed slaves who fancied a life of adventure at sea over the prospect of working for wages on the sugar plantations.

The biggest surprise came from Black James himself. He tossed a small bag of coins in front of Diego who was sitting at the table. It was the last evening they would dine together.

Diego flinched as the bag landed in front of him with a jingle and a thump. "What is this?" he asked, recovering himself.

"Your share of the prize money, Killer Man."

"Prize money? But I fought against you."

"You did what a man must," James said with a smile and a shrug, "and since then, you have been useful enough."

Diego blinked at the bag, then looked back at him. "I can't accept this. I helped bring the slaves through the desert and put them on the ship."

James smiled warmly, seeing the shame in his eyes. "I know. The money is mostly for the services of the *White Angel*," he said with a chuckle. "The men have voted. You will take your share. Do not disappoint them."

Diego picked up the bag and handed it to Claudette, never taking his eyes off the big man. "Thank you, my friend," he said, offering his hand.

James took his hand and shook it. "Never let me catch you transporting slaves again."

"You won't," Diego said. A single tear rolled down his face.

"I believe you," James said with a laugh. "You're a better man than you think, Killer Man. Come, let's not be so dramatic," he said, pouring them rum. "Tomorrow we'll be in Havana and say goodbye. Tonight let us drink and eat like pirates!"

Diego refused to touch the bag of coins ever since. Instead, he had Claudette manage the money as they paid for their room and bought the food and things they needed during their time in Cuba. It didn't take long to find the famous Mexican exile. She was surprised at how quickly he got into the general's good graces and secured their passage to Mexico.

"He knew of my grandfather's fight against the corrupt dons and the *peninsulares*."

"Your grandfather must have been a great man," she told him.

"You wouldn't know it by talking to my father," Diego said, shaking his head. "He wanted me to be an educated businessman like himself, but the sword is mightier than the pen in my family."

"Well, maybe there's hope for you yet," she said with a smirk. "I think I'll rather like your father."

"Pffft…" Diego scoffed, tossing his hand aside dismissively, "I'm sure you two will get along just fine then."

Within a few weeks, it was time to make the crossing to Veracruz. They packed their things, paid their bills, and waited for the general and his entourage at the docks. Claudette couldn't help but be nervous about meeting the famous man. That only increased as the train of carriages arrived carrying the general, his family, and their baggage.

Diego waited for the man to climb down from his carriage and help the young lady and gentleman with him before approaching.

"Your Serene Highness, this is my wife, Claudette de la Vega," he told him in English. "She speaks French and English, but unfortunately not Spanish."

"Ah, we should amend that if she's going to be a Mexican!" he said as he turned to greet them. He was a handsome man in his fifties with olive skin like Diego. He had short-cut, thick black hair with streaks of grey and soft brown eyes. "My goodness, what a beautiful woman!" His eyes crinkled with playful kindness. "Now I know why you've kept her from my sight, Don Diego. I'd hide her away too!" Claudette blushed as the general took her hand. "Je suis charmé," he told her with a sly wink as he kissed it.

"*Merci. Parlez-vous français?*"

"*Assez pour me causer des ennuis.*"

Diego cleared his throat, breaking up their banter. "This must be your son," Diego said, gesturing to the teenage boy.

"Yes. Introduce yourself, Manuel. Practice your English."

"I am Manuel," the youth said, enunciating each syllable carefully. "My father says your grandfather was a great swordsman. A hero of the north."

"So they tell me," Diego said, shaking his hand.

"I suspect Diego here is quite handy with a sword as well. Perhaps he could give you some fencing tips on our journey."

"I would like that very much," the young man said eagerly.

"Diego," the general turned to him, "I see you purchased a straight blade. Is not the curve of a saber more suitable for a cavalryman?"

"The point is more deadly than the blade, Your Serene Highness."

"Interesting…" Santa Anna said, looking him over. "Perhaps you'd do well among my lancers."

"It would be an honor, señor."

"…Um…you must be his daughter," Claudette offered her hand to the teenage girl, hoping to move the conversation away from war and fighting. The young lady stared at her in confusion. The three men went silent.

Santa Anna stiffened and cleared his throat, "She is my wife."

Claudette could feel the warm blood rushing to her face. Knowing that she was blushing made her face burn even more. She felt her legs grow unsteady and weak. Diego put his hand on the small of her back to steady her. She blinked away the dizziness, determined not to faint in front of the famous man.

Santa Anna regarded her for a minute. His eyes softened and the smile returned to his face. "My wife, Dolores, does not speak English yet. Perhaps you could help her with her studies."

"Of course," Claudette said with a short bow, grateful for the reprieve.

He turned to his wife and said something in Spanish. The girl performed a curtesy and spoke with the measured cadence of well-practiced words, "Pleased to meet you."

"Come, we must not keep the ship waiting," Santa Anna beckoned. Claudette walked cautiously along the quay. She was still feeling lightheaded from embarrassment. The steamship loomed ahead. Its British flags filled her with dread. It was strange to be boarding a ship of the ancient enemy of her country. The world seemed such a strange web of ever-changing friends and enemies.

She was careful, holding on to the guidelines as she made her way up the gangplank, grateful that Diego was carrying the baby now that Santa Anna's servants had taken their luggage.

"Welcome aboard, General," the captain called to them. He was waiting at the top of the gangplank with several others there to greet the famous passenger and his entourage. That's when she heard a very familiar voice next to him.

"Well, it appears they'll let just about anybody aboard these ships these days," the voice said with a slight French accent.

"Huh!" Claudette gasped as she looked up to see Pierre's big blue eyes grinning at her. The world started spinning, and everything went black.

She could hear voices, although, at first, she could not make out the words.

"I'm sorry, my wife isn't accustomed to the tropical climate."

That was Diego. She was safe.

"Your wife?!"

That was Pierre. She was in danger.

"You two know each other?" She could hear Santa Anna's voice in the mist. Someone was fanning her.

"We are old schoolmates from our days in Barcelona," Pierre was explaining.

This is really happening!

She opened her eyes. Her head was resting on Dolores's lap. The girl was fanning her. A look of relief washed over the young lady's face as she saw Claudette come to.

"*Gracias,*" Claudette said to her softly. Dolores smiled back. "I'm sorry," Claudette said, now in English to everyone as she sat up, "I'm not yet accustomed to the humidity. How long was I out?"

"Just a few seconds, my dear," the captain said. "We'll get you to your cabin quickly." He then motioned to two of his men, "See her and her family to their room immediately." He then turned to her, " I hope you recover in time to dine with us, young lady."

"Yes, of course," she smiled softly, trying to act as normal as possible.

Pierre stood before her as she was helped to her feet. "Nice to see you again, too," he said with a smile.

"My God, what is he doing here on this ship?!" she hissed under her breath once they were safely ensconced in their cabin.

"I don't know, but I don't think he's a threat," Diego said with a shrug. She just looked at him as if expecting more. "...at least not openly," he added.

"Diego, what's happening?"

He sighed and shook his head, "It's a war. It's hard to know who are friends and who are enemies."

"I don't think he's our friend," she said shaking her head.

"He's got good reasons not to be."

Pierre was nothing less than pleasant and charming at the captain's table. If he had any remaining animosity for them, no one seemed to be aware. Even Diego seemed to be at ease with his old friend as they retold the story of fighting off hooligans together on the streets of Barcelona.

To Claudette, it seemed she was the only one with any memory of terrible things that had passed between them, she and perhaps Pierre, who gave her sly looks, winks, and seemingly innocent remarks like, "Oh, the fickle ways of women…" which seemed to be a reference to their past.

More frustrating, there seemed to be no clue as to why he was aboard and why he was on such familiar terms with the captain and General Santa Anna. Diego was dismissive as they whispered about it in their berth. "I stole his woman," he said with a shrug. "It is well to be on good terms with him again."

"Diego," she gasped, "he tried to kill you! He tried to make you a murderer. He had me locked in an asylum where I was beaten like an animal. How can you say it's well to be on good terms with him?"

"Hmm…" he pondered in the darkness, "I don't know, it's crazy…."

"Ugg!" She elbowed him, "You drive me crazy!"

He laughed, then wrapped his arm around her, "…and you, my sweet love, drive me crazy…" he said, drawing her into him and inhaling her scent through his nose.

"The baby…" she scoffed at his advances.

"…is mercifully asleep and Pierre is alone in his bunk not far from us, probably wondering right now what this would be like," he said, cupping her breast with one hand and grasping the flesh of her inner thigh with the other.

"You are a devil," she gasped as she turned to him.

"Yes, but I am your devil," he said, kissing her. "Let us play among the flames…"

As improper as it seemed, it was also deliciously enticing to be making love not far from the man who had almost forced her into an unwanted marriage. She bit her lip, trying to stifle her moans, yet deep down, she hoped that Pierre, alone in his bunk, could hear; that every moan, creak, and grunt hit him like the strike from the paddle that she had endured because of him.

She turned to her side once they finished and snuggled deep into he lover. Diego wrapped his arm around her and held her tight. He was already breathing softly. She closed her eyes and smiled, listening to the hum of the steam engine, the turning of the paddles, and the water rushing past the hull. For this one moment, she was at peace, and everything was fine in the world.

WHAAP!

"Ayee!" Manuel hissed in pain as he clutched his right arm.

"Keep your elbow tucked in," Diego told him. "It should be in line completely behind the guard of your sword."

"*Si, señor,*" the youth said, shaking off the sting from Diego whacking his elbow with the flat of his blade.

"English," Diego reminded him.

"Yes, sir," Manuel said dutifully.

"Once again, *en guarde!*" The two sank into their stances and began the exercise anew, advancing and retreating, thrusting and parrying. They had found some space on the deck for a fencing lesson and then stripped down to their shirtsleeves and waistcoats. Santa Anna had told him not to go easy on the boy. Diego made sure the fear of pain kept him in good form. A few idle crew members gathered to watch the lesson.

"Shouldn't he be learning the saber, Diego?" Pierre's voice broke through the clanging of blades, causing Diego to instinctively turn to the new threat with his sword in hand. Pierre smirked at the startled look. "After all, a gentleman would typically fight from horseback in a war, although you probably wouldn't know that."

Diego smirked at the subtle insult and shrugged it off. "The blade will hurt a man, but the point will kill him, regardless if he's on foot or in the saddle."

"Hmm…interesting point," Pierre shrugged as he walked over to Manuel. "May I?" he asked, pointing to the young man's straight sword with a raised eyebrow.

"Of course, sir," the young man said, handing it over. Pierre hefted it a few times, testing the weight.

"It's been so long since I've had a bout," he said, looking at the blade, then turning to Diego. "Would you indulge me?"

"Of course," Diego said guardedly. Their small audience became silent. He could see someone in his periphery taking out a notepad and pencil. Several others crowded around, hurrying to register their bets before the match.

Pierre glanced over at the collection of gamblers, then turned his eyes to Diego with a smile. "Looks like we're the main event today," he said as he removed his jacket and set it aside.

"Let's put on a good show, then," Diego said darkly, then sank into his stance.

Pierre stepped forward and tapped his blade to Diego's. Diego stood still, holding his ground as the Frenchman moved in and out with fast footwork, testing the distance and Diego's reflexes with quick thrusts.

"Well...?" Pierre said with a huff, slightly winded from his exertion, "...are you going to fight, or do I have to do all the work?"

"You are doing a fine job of beating yourself. I didn't want to interrupt." That got a laugh from some of the sailors. Pierre rolled his eyes with a slight scoff.

"Well played," he said with a shrug. He sank back into his stance and then circled his opponent, locking eyes with him as they turned.

With a sudden shout, he drove forward, thrusting, then circling around Diego's blade and thrusting again, trying to find a way past his defense.

Diego moved back under the barrage of attacks, blocking and also looking for an opening for a counterthrust. The blades clanged and rattled as the two moved across the deck. The intensity increased with each second. Diego began to wonder if they were truly having a gentleman's match or if he was fighting for his life.

"Huh?! Diego!" Claudette's voice cut through the din. He mistakenly turned his eye away to spot her among the crowd. Pierre was quick to take advantage, lunging in fully. Diego barely avoided the blow, leaping to the side and blocking the blade narrowly from piercing his chest. Realizing it would have been a killing blow, his eyes turned back to Pierre's. There was anger in those blue eyes as the man panted through his snarl. Diego blinked at him with startled bewilderment.

"Ship ahoy! Eleven o'clock starboard!" a shout came from above.

Many of the crowd turned and rushed to the bow. Diego, once again, looked off to see where the others were running, then cringed once he realized he had just made the same mistake. Pierre was quick to make him pay. He lurched forward, swinging his blade around. Diego dropped his arm and leaned back, hoping to evade the cut. Pierre's tip just caught his upper arm, tearing his sleeve and scraping the skin.

"Ayee…" Diego hissed in pain as he clutched his arm. He could feel the warm blood seeping through his fingers.

Pierre stood upright. A smile replaced his snarl as he dabbed his forehead with a handkerchief. "Hmm…I still find hurting a man immensely more satisfying than outright killing him. I mean, you might as well enjoy the journey," he said, then cleaned the blood off the blade with his handkerchief and handed it back to Manuel. "There's your lesson for today, boy. Never take your eyes off the prize."

"It's American!" one of the sailors shouted. A flash of fear spread across Pierre's face before he quickly regained his dismissive smugness. "Well, I suppose I should freshen up for our guests," he said, picking up his jacket and walking towards his cabin.

"My God, Diego! Are you hurt?!" Claudette ran to him.

"It's just a scratch," Diego said dismissively, clutching the wound.

"What were you doing sparring with him like that? He wants to kill you!" she hissed under her breath.

"Maybe this blood will satisfy him," Diego looked down at his bloody hand covering the wound.

Claudette shook her head, looking into his eyes pleadingly, "He's the type of man that can never be satisfied."

"What happened here?" Santa Anna's voice took their attention.

"Nothing, Your Serene Highness," Diego turned him, "just a fencing accident. It's a scratch."

"Well, clean it up quickly and get dressed, Don Diego. We are to receive our American friends soon."

"Yes, Your Serene Highness."

"…and Diego," the general stopped them, "civilian clothes, not a uniform. We're all friends here. Remember."

"Yes, sir."

She could feel him brace himself each time she brought the needle through his skin. It was funny to her that even in the privacy of their cabin, he was determined not to show any pain. She was gentle nonetheless. She had learned in the tents of Abd al-Qādir's *smala* that it was more mercifully to be quick with the needle when stitching a wound.

She wrapped it with a cloth and helped him into a fresh shirt. She couldn't help but wonder why the general insisted he not wear his uniform in front of the Americans. Once again, why did he have to have a uniform in the first place? She caught the quick flash of steel as he tucked his pistol and dagger into his sash and out of sight.

"Do you really need those?" she sighed.

"We are surrounded by enemies," he told her with dark conviction, "and the worse of them are about to board our ship."

They joined the crowd on deck and watched in silence as the American gunship approached. A quiet dread hung over them as it neared. Its flag with stripes and twenty-eight stars fluttered grandly in the wind. Were they really the bearded monsters Diego had described? She imagined them being like the English, but wild and feral, uneducated and quick to violence. Surely, this rising nation in the west had to have some semblance of civilized people to have come as far as they have, but the nervousness she saw in the faces around her, especially in Diego's, Santa Anna's, and Pierre's made her worry. She clutched Diego's arm as they watched. She was now somewhat relieved that he was armed.

The ship lowered its sails and then lowered a longboat into the water. Men in blue uniforms boarded it and began to row toward them. The ones wearing the white shirts with open collars did the rowing as the men in blue jackets stood tall and imposing. None of them had beards, she remarked. In fact, they all looked immaculate and clean-shaven, not quite the Huns she was expecting. She looked to the others around her as they watched them approach. Pierre was doing his best to look aloof, but she could see the muscles in his neck tensing and twitching.

"Welcome aboard," the captain greeted the first man to climb the rope ladder onto the deck.

"Thank you, sir," the American officer smiled and shook his hand. She was stunned to see that he was handsome, affable, and quick with a smile as the two captains introduced themselves and their retinues. What stood out the most was the way he spoke. *Is that English?* she wondered at first. He was hard to follow. He spoke quickly with softened vowels and overpronounced 'r's which sounded strange to her French ears.

"And this is our illustrious passenger, General Antonio Lopez de Santa Anna," the British captain said at last.

"Ah, the man of the hour," the American smiled grandly, taking the general's hand. "It's a pleasure to meet you, sir."

"The pleasure is mine, sir." Santa Anna gave him a short bow. "May the friendship between our countries live forever."

"Hear, hear, my friend," the American shook his hand. "Everything seems to be in order. My orders are to make sure the general passes through the blockade unmolested. I just need to inspect the cargo and then we can escort you through."

Only the soft breeze could be heard in the moment of silence that ensued. Smiles became strained and then fell away. Claudette could feel Diego tensing beside her. Pierre's face had gone white as the muscles in his neck and cheeks rippled in agitation. After a pause, the British captain spoke. "I'm sorry, my friend, but you'll do nothing of the sort."

"I beg your pardon...?" the American replied, his own smile dropping away.

"This is Her Majesty's ship on a diplomatic mission. We will not be subject to an American inspection." The silence continued as the two men regarded each other. The American let out a nervous chuckle.

"Sir, I can hardly allow you to pass our blockade without inspecting your cargo," he said, straightening himself. "Now, if you'll step aside, we'll be quick with our work." He stepped forward, extending his arm out to move his British counterpart out of his way. The men behind him straightened themselves and began to follow with grim-set faces. The back of his open hand came to rest on the British captain's chest.

The Englishman stood still with hands folded behind his back. He looked down at the American's hand on his chest with a frown.

Diego and Pierre instinctively moved to the entrance of the hull and blocked it with their bodies. The British captain looked back up and nodded to his men. They scrambled to join the two guarding the entrance. Others came to stand at his side.

The Englishman turned his eyes to the American captain once more, "Need I remind you that our countries were recently at the brink of war over the Oregon territory? Do you really want to be the one that caused the incident that threw us all into the abyss?" The two captains stared at each other for a moment as every man braced himself for action. Claudette found herself holding her breath.

The Englishman continued, "Sir, I would advise you to carefully consider your next actions. The very first, I suggest, should be removing your hand from my person."

The American looked down at his hand with a frown, then promptly removed it. "Of course, my apologies, sir," he mumbled.

"Apology accepted," the Englishman quickly replied.

The American cleared his throat and scanned the collection of faces who were watching him intently. "My orders are to allow the general to pass through the blockade unmolested," he spoke out loud to the crowd, "and that's just what we'll do, Captain," he finished, turning to his British counterpart. "We will escort you in."

"Thank you, sir. You are too kind," the British captain replied, his smile returning to his face. Claudette could feel the tension washing away from the crowd with the breeze. With great relief, she watched the Americans climb down the ladder and return to their ship.

"Well, that could have been messy," the British captain said mildly.

They followed their American escort. Soon, they could see the other gunships looming across the horizon. They passed through the line with an eerie sense of dread. Each ship seemed to bristle with endless potential for destruction. Claudette looked down at the wooded planks under her feet and suddenly felt as if they stood on nothing more than a delicate bundle of sticks, ready for the torch.

"Land ho!" a man shouted from above.

She moved with the rest to the bow to watch the shore appear on the horizon. Their escort signaled and turned off to rejoin the blockade. The Mexico she had heard so much of, that her lover longed for with nostalgic zeal, lay open before them. She could see the church towers and palm trees rising above the imposing stone seawall. Mountains sat fat and towering behind the city in the summer haze.

She felt a deep rhythmic pulse emanating from the shore. It became clearer as they neared until she could make out the "umps" and "pahs" of a tuba. Soon, the sounds of trumpets, violins, and guitars began to emerge on top of this beat with a bright and festive melody.

Throngs of people cheered as their ship eased into port. The men wore straw hats with enormous brims that she could only guess were used to block the relentless sunlight that splashed over everything. The women wore beautiful dresses in explosive colors with veils and scarves to protect their heads. The smell of grilled meats, maize, and smoked peppers swirled around her, teasing her empty stomach.

She sensed the party of onlookers shifting behind her. She looked to see that they were making way for the general. He looked resplendent in his uniform. He smiled and winked at her as she curtsied and moved out of the way. The crowd below went wild as he came into their view, smiling and waving at them.

"What a transformation!" she heard him say to no one in particular. "They were throwing rocks at me when I left."

Diego, now in his uniform as well, led a security detail down the gangplank. They moved the crowd back and set up a dais on the wharf. She carried Carlito down with the next wave of passengers, dignitaries, and the general's family. She had never seen so many happy and excited people before. *This is what it must have been like in the time of the Emperor,* she thought, recalling the stories she had heard about Napoleon, far before her country had turned into the cynical nation she grew up in under the *July Monarchy* of Louis Philippe.

The cheering exploded into a high pitch as Santa Anna mounted the gangplank. Diego and his men fought to keep the crowd from surging forward to touch the man who was now descending from above to stand among them. Women tossed flowers into the air creating a blizzard of colorful petals.

The general smiled grandly and waved as he stepped onto the dais. A tear rolled down his cheek as he clasped his hands together and then touched them to his heart. He looked to the heavens as if to humbly thank his maker for this outpouring of love. It wasn't until the crowd stilled that he brought his eyes back to them. They grew silent in great anticipation of what he would say.

"My fellow children of Mexico," he said, scanning the faces of the crowd, "the Americans have sent me here to broker a deal that will favor their expansionist ambitions in our north." Groans and jeers seeped out of some in the crowd. Their neighbors quickly hushed them. The general just smiled, nodding his head, then shook it.

"The United States are fools if they think I could betray my mother country!" The crowd exploded into cheers once more. "I would rather be burned alive and my ashes scattered into oblivion before I would do such a thing!" he said, thrusting his finger into the air. The crowd roared in ecstasy at his words. The general smiled, then turned and signaled to Pierre who was standing at the top of the gangplank. Pierre turned and signaled to someone unseen behind him. Soon, men were carrying long wooden crates off the ship and stacking them behind the dais. Two brought a crate and set it before the general. They then began to pry open the lid.

"Your cowardly interim President Paredes has abandoned you. But I am here now, my children, and together," he paused, reached down into the crate, pulled out a musket, and held it high above his head, "we will fight and we will drive the imperial Americans from our land!"

Claudette gasped at the sight of the weapon. She couldn't understand the speech, but the message was clear. She then looked at the countless number of crates being stacked behind them. She shot an accusatory look at Diego who only managed a shrug before looking away to the crowd. She then looked to the top of the gangplank. Pierre was already looking at her when she spotted him. His arms were folded. He held a satisfied grin on his face.

"Where is my Californian?" The general called out. Diego turned to him with an alarmed expression that seemed to ask, *me?* "Come, my son," he beckoned with a smile. Diego climbed the dais and stood next to the general. "Here is the grandson of the great

Don Diego de la Vega, the famous *Fox* of the north who fought the corrupt and cruel *peninsulares* during our struggle for independence from Spain. I'm sending him north to recruit our brothers in Alta California. Mexico must stand as one to fight the heathen invaders! Will you stand and fight with us?!"

The crowd exploded in cheers. The band started up again. Thousands of flowers were thrown into the air. In the flurry of petals, she could see Diego, beaming with excitement under a mask of humble stoicism as he shook hands and bowed politely to well-wishers.

Chapter Twenty-Seven: Fathers and Sons

Getting away from Pierre and his constant leering smiles couldn't come soon enough for Claudette, even though Diego seemed eager to welcome this strange friendliness.

"I wronged him," he said with a shrug once they were alone. "I'm happy to see he's willing to forgive and forget."

"Have you forgotten the wrongs he's done to us? To me?!" she gasped at him.

"Maybe we should learn to forgive too. It's what God commands. It's better to have him as a friend than an enemy."

"Ugh!" Claudette scoffed. "Trust me, Pierre's no friend. And he has forgiven or forgotten nothing!"

To her great relief, she and Diego set out almost immediately for his home far to the north in Alta California.

"Are you sure you don't need an escort, at least to the Port of Acapulco?" Santa Anna offered with questionable sincerity. "The mountains are full of bandits and rebels, you know."

"An escort would only slow us down and make us targets," Diego responded, politely reading the general's reluctance to spare any men. The Americans were already pushing in from Texas in the northeast, handing the Mexican forces humiliating defeats at Palo Alto and Resaca de la Palma.

"I need men, Don Diego," the general told him, placing his hand on Diego's shoulder. "Bring me the brave *Californios* who would rally to your grandfather's noble name to face the *Yanqui* invaders who defile our county."

"California will fight, Your Serene Highness," Diego told him, mounting his horse and turning towards the mountains to the west. "The Anglo-heretics will die on our swords," he said, turning once more to the general before giving his horse a kick and sending it on its way.

Claudette urged her mule alongside him. Carlito was swaddled in a blanket slung around her shoulder. "What did he say to you," she asked, having not understood the Spanish conversation.

"He said for us to have a nice trip."

It took three weeks to trek through the mountains and the tropical rainforests of the interior. It was an arduous, and at times, terrifying journey on which they avoided the main road as much as possible. But she took comfort in Diego's confidence. The boy who grew up on long cattle drives through such terrain and the man who rode for weeks on patrol in the northern deserts of Africa seemed to come alive before her eyes. Diego could find food and water from just about anywhere to supplement their supplies. He could build fires to make coffee and flatbread from the corn meal they had brought to go with their smoked meats. He did this only in the early morning to avoid detection from would-be bandits.

He could also hear others in the jungle, far before she did. They moved quickly off the trail and hid their animals. Claudette watched in terror as armed men rode by, unaware of the small family watching from the bushes. She held her hand over the baby's mouth, praying he wouldn't begin to fuss.

At last, they descended from the mountains into the port town of Acapulco. There they found passage on a schooner bound for *El Pueblo de Nuestra Señora, la Reina de los Ángeles.* Claudette was quite happy to finally get out of the dangers of the jungle and into the slight sense of civilization that the ship provided. But Diego grew quieter and more detached the farther north they sailed.

"What is it, my love?" she asked when she found him at the bow after she had put Carlito to bed. He was staring off into the twilight. She wrapped her arms around him, feeling his tense muscles melting into her embrace.

"My father doesn't know we're coming," he said softly. "I haven't written him since we left France. I…" he paused for a moment to collect himself, "…I haven't had the courage." She felt his shoulders slump under the weight of his shame.

"Oh, my love, I'm sure your father will be proud of the man you've become! Just wait until he sees little Carlito! He looks just like you! How could he not be proud?"

Diego turned to her. The regret and sorrow in his eyes were startling. "You don't know my father," he said with fear creeping into his voice, "…and Carlito and I look nothing like him. He only sees his own father in me: A man he never wanted me to be, a man who left my grandmother a widow and my father an orphan."

"I will stand beside you, Diego," she said, cupping the back of his neck and looking into his eyes. "We will face him together." He smiled shyly, then looked down for a moment before turning once more to watch the stars begin to pop out of the firmament above the amber waters. Claudette squeezed him once again, then rested her head on his shoulder.

His wariness grew as they neared the Pueblo of Los Angeles. He stood, silently staring at the American warship moored outside the harbor. "Ah, pa!" Carlito blurted, as he reached out to the ship.

"Shhh…" Claudette bounced him gently. He began to squirm, trying to wiggle out of her arms as he reached. "You silly boy! Are you going to swim to it?" she cooed. Carlito let out a giggle and began pulling on the wisps of her black hair and putting them in his mouth. "And now you're going to eat me?"

Diego finally let out a chuckle. It was the first time she saw him smile since they started their journey. "¡Ven aquí, mi hijo!" He took the boy and held him high before bringing him down and nuzzling his neck with loud kisses. Carlito broke into a peal of laughter. Diego put him on his hip and then turned to watch the American ship loom ahead.

"Do you think we are in any danger?" Claudette asked, looking out to the ship as well.

"I don't know," he said, not taking his eyes away from it.

Claudette found herself holding her breath as they passed by. The cannons protruding from the gunports looked as though they could destroy their ship in one volley and then level the small village with the next.

A squad of American marines was waiting at the dock. They wore light blue uniforms with white cross belts and short-brimmed caps that rose about an inch and a half before flaring out into wide flat circles above their heads. They boarded the ship, read the manifest, and inspected the cargo. One of them approached Diego with his hand out. "Your papers," he said gruffly.

"I have none," Diego told him, matching the marine's tone with his own haughty disdain. "I am Diego de la Vega, son of Ramon de la Vega of the De la Vega Hacienda. This is my wife and child."

"You gotta have papers to get off this boat, *Pedro*," the man replied, straightening himself for a confrontation.

"I am a Mexican citizen, disembarking in my home port with my family," Diego's voice grew dark and menacing. "Do not stand in my way."

"Or what?" the man said drawing nearer. "This ain't Mexico no more, *hombre...*"

Claudette's eyes widened with fear as she watched the two men stare each other down. "Diego..." she uttered softly.

"Jones! Stand down," an American sergeant hollered at him. "His father is an ally. It's alright."

The marine took a step back and bowed theatrically. "Welcome to the United States, Señor," he said with no lack of irony.

"California will always be Mexico," Diego said as he brushed past.

"Hmmmph!" the marine replied before being silenced by the sharp eye of his sergeant.

Defiant as Diego was, she was grateful that he at least agreed to hide his weapons in their luggage. She was also relieved that the Americans allowed them to disembark without further inspection or harassment.

"Your father must be a great man for them to show him such deference," she said quietly, as they loaded the carriage that would carry them to the De la Vega Hacienda.

"He is no such thing if he's allied with these heathen invaders," Diego replied bitterly. He helped her up into the open-air seats. He then handed her the baby and climbed in next to her.

The driver gave the horses a slap of the reins, putting them into motion. Claudette kept quiet, knowing not to probe anymore while he wrestled with his demons. She wrapped her hands around his arm and leaned her head on his shoulder as they rolled through the small village of sunbaked adobe buildings.

"Where are all the people?" she asked. The streets were almost empty save for a few uniformed Americans, who eyed them suspiciously as they passed.

"Hiding from these animals for sure," Diego said, eyeing them back with intense hatred.

The carriage rattled through town and then started climbing the hills beyond. The air was hot and dry like she remembered from North Africa and unlike the damp sticky air of Veracruz. The hills were covered in brown scrub brush, green cactus, and short trees. As they crossed over the first summit, she could see hundreds of cattle meandering in the fields, tended by men on horseback wearing the same wide-brimmed straw hats she had seen in Veracruz. Many of them carried pistols on their hips and used long whips to keep the beasts herded together. Carlito cooed in awe and reached out toward the large longhorn beasts.

On the next ridge stood the high white walls of an estate house. She could feel Diego tensing at the sight. The walls dwarfed a lone servant kneeling before them. He was dressed in simple white linens with a large straw hat. He seemed too busy trimming the rose bushes that adorned the walls to notice the approaching carriage. At last, the man turned to wipe the sweat from his brow. It was then that he finally noticed the approaching visitors. He quickly got to his feet, removed his hat, and bowed his head in a submissive show of respect, revealing his white hair and sun-kissed skin.

"*Abuelito!*" Diego gasped, then sucked in a sob as he leaped over the edge of the carriage.

"Diego!" Claudette reached out to him, startled by his sudden burst of emotion. But he was already running toward the old man before she could stop him. Diego threw his arms around the man, lifting him off the ground and rocking him back and forth before collecting himself and gently setting him down. The old man chuckled in a silent laugh, beaming in delight at Diego.

Diego began to speak to him. Claudette strained to listen as the carriage stopped and the driver came around to open the door and lower the step. Whatever it was, it wasn't Spanish. It was guttural and unworldly, like nothing she had heard before. The old man nodded and smiled grandly. He mumbled softly, completely unintelligible sounds but he also moved his hands in ways that Diego seemed to understand and then reply to in the strange language.

"My love, this is Bernardo! He rode with my grandfather in his fight against the Spanish *Penisulares* even before my father was born."

"Pleased to meet you, sir," Claudette managed, still exasperated by the sudden strange encounter. Diego turned to him and spoke in the strange language once more, seemingly introducing her and Carlito to the old man. Bernardo smiled and nodded, mumbling unintelligibly as he did. "What is that language you're speaking?" she asked, turning to Diego.

"Oh, it's not a language," Diego shrugged, "it's just how the peasants speak."

The temptation to correct this flawed logic flashed through her mind but she shrugged it off. "Does he not speak Spanish?"

"Well, he doesn't speak anything," Diego said matter-of-factly. "Spanish priests cut out his tongue for speaking heresy," Diego said, then said something in the native language as he gave the old man a slap on the back. Both of them laughed. Diego turned back to her, "Bernardo just won't give up the old ways!"

"*Mon Dieu*, that's awful!" she gasped.

"Oh, my grandfather made them pay for their cruelty, I assure you!" He then said something else to the old man that caused another laugh. Claudette caught a glimpse of the meaty scarred stub in the man's mouth as he chuckled. She swallowed hard, then forced a smile, making an effort to politely laugh with them.

"Trust me, Bernardo understands much more than he lets on," Diego told her. "He pretends he can't hear either, but he hears everything!" The old man drew his attention with a tap on the shoulder, then relayed some kind of message with his hands. Diego laughed, then translated, "He says not so much anymore in his old age."

"Hmmm…" Claudette mused, realizing that the old man had understood him perfectly in English. She smiled at him now, not out of nervous politeness, but in acknowledgment of the old man's cleverness. Bernardo's eyes seemed to read the understanding. He smiled back knowingly, giving her a wink. He then gave Diego a series of hand signals, then simply waved Claudette to follow him into the house. Before she could register what was happening, Bernardo scooped up Carlito and carried him into the courtyard. The boy looked into the old man's face with awe, feeling the dark wrinkles with his hand.

Behind the high white walls was a courtyard with a glossy tile floor painted with intricate patterns of blue, white, yellow, and red. A fountain sat in the middle with hundreds of exotic desert plants and blossoms sitting in pots set all around. The house was large and square with a red tile roof and white stucco walls. Bernardo opened the two grand oak doors revealing the foyer inside. It had a red terracotta floor with bear skin rugs, a high ceiling, and a sweeping staircase with wrought iron handrails. Dark oak furniture with iron trimming contrasted with the amber stucco walls.

Claudette looked up at the paintings in awed silence. There were portraits of stately men and beautiful women dressed in classic Spanish fashion. Her eyes came to a painting of two beautiful women sitting side-by-side, holding each other's hand. Although, one of the women didn't quite seem right. Claudette narrowed her eyes as she examined the painting closer. The face of one of the women looked just like Diego, but paler, and was wearing men's breeches and jacket. They were light pink and satin with a white lacy shirt and a gold-colored waistcoat and cravat.

"Who is...?" she began to ask just as Diego noticed her looking and spoke up.

"Those are my grandparents. My grandfather was a very handsome man!" Diego said with pride.

"I'll say..." she said, now seeing that the person in pink was indeed a man.

Next to that portrait was a painting of another beautiful woman. She was a dark-skinned native dressed in traditional clothing. Her raven black hair was adorned with feathers, and her neckpiece was a riot of colorful beads. Her eyes were dark and penetrating. Claudette took a step back, bringing her hand up to her chest, feeling the woman's eyes reaching into her soul from beyond.

"Who is this?" she asked softly.

"That is my mother...God rest her soul," Diego said with reverence.

Claudette nearly leaped out of her skin when Bernardo reentered the room. He brought a tray with wooden mugs and a stone pitcher from which he poured them each a cup of wine. Claudette watched his face closely, then with a gasp, turned back to the painting of the beautiful native woman. She turned back to see Bernardo, now standing before her, smiling as he offered a mug of wine. She looked at him as she took it. "*Merci*," she said softly, looking into his eyes and then once again, at the painting. When she looked back at him once more, he was smiling knowingly. He took a quick glance at the painting as well, then returned his eyes to her and winked.

He then turned to Diego and pantomimed something as he mumbled incoherently. Diego acknowledged in the native language as the old man left the room. "He says my father will be joining us shortly," Diego said. He seemed to go pale after saying this. She went to him and hugged him, kissing his cheek.

"It'll be fine…" she whispered.

A door suddenly opened, startling her. She turned to see a paunchy middle-aged man with soft brown hair and round spectacles burst into the room. She felt Diego stiffen as the man approached. Before could she could process what was happening, the man slapped him hard across the face, causing her to let out a yelp. Carlito began to cry. Diego snapped his reddened face back to his father. His jaw was twitching with restraint.

"*¡Has deshonrado y avergonzado a esta familia por la última vez! ¡Vas a volver a España inmediatamente para responder de tus crímenes!*" his father spat.

Diego stood silent for a moment, wiped his face with his sleeve, then reached down and picked up his son. "It's okay, Little Bug," he smiled at the boy, crinkling his eyes with soft kindness. Carlito looked at him with tear-swollen eyes, sniffling. Diego took out a handkerchief and dabbed the tears and snot from the child's face. "Here," he handed him to Claudette, who took him with stunned silence, "take care of your mother, please."

He then turned back to his father, who drew a long breath through his nose and exhaled, calming himself down a notch. "This is my wife, Claudette Moreau de la Vega, and our son, Carlos Moreau de la Vega. She does not speak Spanish, only French, and English. Claudette, this is my father, Don Ramon de la Vega."

His father took a cursory glance at the young French woman and her baby, only to find her dark scornful eyes glaring back at him too much to bear. He let out a slight scoff as he returned his eyes to his son. "Well, at least I got my money's worth for your English lessons."

"Glad you approve," Diego said.

"Do not get cheeky with me, boy," Señor de la Vega was quick to regain some of his anger. "The Spanish crown demands your immediate arrest and return for robbing the church and attempting to murder a friar."

"Had I attempted to murder him, he'd be dead, Father," Diego said, anger now creeping into his own voice.

"You attacked a holy man, by the saints!" his father shouted.

"He insulted my mother...your dead wife!" Diego shouted back, stealing a glance at Bernardo before returning his eyes to his father. "Was I to do nothing?!"

Señor de la Vega laughed bitterly, "The world is not some low-life tavern where you have to constantly defend your schoolyard sense of honor with violence, boy. Now you will consider yourself under arrest until we arrange for your return to Spain to answer for your crimes."

"I will not! This is not Spain anymore, Father. Or did my grandfather, who fought them off, not tell you? I'm not going back to Spain. I'm staying here to fight the Americans like my grandfather would have...like he would have expected of you."

"Your grandfather was an overly romantic fool who threw away his life for personal glory, not thinking once about the family he left behind," Señor de la Vega said bitterly

"You're just mad because I grew to be a man like him!" Diego said, pointing to the painting. Claudette followed his finger back to the man dressed in pink and gazed at him in bewildered confusion. "...and not some soft-handed clerk like you!"

Señor de la Vega laughed. "Your grandfather was an effeminate popinjay who only felt comfortable acting like a man when he was prancing around at night behind the safety of a mask!"

"That is not true."

"Go ahead...ask any still alive who knew him! No, you're nothing like him. You're not some dandy, overcompensating for a lack of manliness with a sword. You're a child, dreaming of a romantic past that never was and fighting for a future that'll never be."

"At least I'm willing to fight for my dreams and a rightful future of Mexico instead of hiding behind a desk making deals with these Anglo-devils."

"The Americans are the future of California, my boy. Even your dead grandfather couldn't change that if he were here. If you must fight, you would do better fighting with them."

"I will die first,"

His father looked at him for a moment. His mask of arrogance and anger fell away. It was replaced with regret and sadness. "I know...and this is how I failed you. Go to your death then. Bother me no more."

"Gladly," Diego said turning on his heel. Claudette looked once more at Señor de la Vega before turning to follow her husband.

"You can leave the boy here," his father said softly.

"Like hell," Diego replied.

Claudette could hear Bernardo mumbling something incomprehensible behind her as they made their way to the door. Señor de la Vega was replying in Spanish. His angry tone was gone. He now spoke to the mute man in what seemed to be an apologetic, even respectful tone, apparently agreeing with whatever the old man was conveying in his novel way.

She had to jog to catch up with Diego, whose anger had him storming off in long strides as he walked through the iron-reinforced oak gates of the hacienda. She followed behind him, careful not to disturb the silence of his dark agitated mood. She yelped when he suddenly stopped and turned. "*¡Tranquilo!*" he smiled, putting up a hand. "Here," he reached out, "I'll take the boy."

"Where are we going?" she asked, catching her breath.

"There's someone I must visit," he told her. "It's not too far."

He led her through a winding dusty trail lined with scrub brush, cactus, and desert trees. They descended into a narrow valley, then began to climb another hill. She could make out a small chapel nestled on the rocky summit. Diego crossed himself, looking up at the cross on the steeple as they walked around the small white building. Behind lay two gravestones enclosed by a small iron fence. The gate creaked as he undid the latch and swung it open. He pulled the tall weeds away and dusted off the stones to reveal the names carved into the marble: Diego and Lolita de la Vega.

He fell to his knees. Claudette rushed to him, worried he was unwell or needed comforting. He was praying. She knelt next to him and prayed too. He sat afterward, staring at the graves. She put her arm around him and held him tight. Once again, not wanting to disturb his silence.

"Your grandfather talked like a sissy boy," a voice spoke in Spanish from behind, startling them from their reverie. Diego spun around, leaping to his feet. Claudette stood, swooping up the baby with one hand and clutching Diego's arm with the other.

There, stood a haggard old man in dusty well-worn clothes and a wide-brimmed hat. Despite the apparent years worn into his face, he still struck an impressive figure. He was tall and barrel-chested with a heavy white mustache covering most of his mouth.

"Sergeant Gonzales!" Diego gasped, calling the old man by a title the man had obviously retired from years ago.

The old man looked off to the side with a frown and shrugged. "...he acted like a sissy-boy too," he said with some sort of wisdom and acceptance that perhaps his old age was now allowing. He turned his eyes back to Diego. They were full of fiery passion, "...but he fought like a lion, whether he wore the mask of a bandit or the uniform of a soldier."

Diego and Claudette blinked silently as the old man mused in reverent memory. "He was my enemy...my rival...he was the only man to ever best me with a sword," Gonzales said, looking at the grave. "But most of all," he said, returning his eyes to the couple, "he was my friend...It was an honor to fight alongside him," the old man said, wiping a tear from his eye with his sleeve.

"My grandfather was a great man," Diego said, not knowing how else to respond. Then asked, "How did you know I was here?"

Gonzales shrugged, "Los Angeles is a small village. The news of your arrival and your English-speaking wife traveled fast." He looked back at the graves, "I knew you'd come here, eventually. I come here often myself..." The old man stared at the graves for a moment with a sad reverent smile. He then turned his eyes back to Diego. "They say you've come home to raise a company of men to fight the Gringos. Is that true?"

"Yes, for the defense of Mexico," Diego said darkly.

The old man removed his hat and clutched it in his hands. "It would be an honor to serve a De la Vega once more if you would have an old man who both hated and loved your grandfather. I humbly submit to your command if you would have me, señor."

"This is dangerous business, old man," Diego said, "you'll most certainly die."

"Pft," Sergeant Gonzales spat, his old bravado returning. "I have nothing left to live for but to die an honorable death. And to have the honor of riding with the *Fox* once again."

"The honor would be mine to have you then," Diego said, extending his hand.

"Ha! By the saints, you remind me so much of him!" Gonzales laughed, taking his hand and pulling Diego into a bear hug.

Bernardo was waiting for them at the foot of the hill where Sergeant Gonzales had tied his horse. He had brought a wagon laden with supplies and their bags, as well as some horses. "Bernardo, you old Indian devil!" Sergeant Gonzales bellowed as he threw his arms around the much smaller man. "It's turning out to be just like old times, eh?!"

Bernardo explained, in his novel way, that Señor de la Vega "didn't know" anything about the supplies or horses, but of course, he knew.

"He can rest assured that I will not involve him in what I do next. That is unless he decides to join us," Diego told him as Bernardo was preparing to return to the hacienda. The old man smiled and rolled his eyes as if to say that would never happen.

Sergeant Gonzales turned out to be a boon to their recruitment efforts. He seemed to know every ruffian and bandit from the hillsides to the valley. Soon, rough men on horseback were arriving at their camp daily armed with knives, pistols, and old muskets. Others came with only the will to fight.

Claudette found these men to be terrifying. She wondered how someone as young as Diego could hold them under any authority or discipline. Yet they seem to be in awe of his noble name, the legend of his grandfather, and Diego's own dark and taciturn demeanor.

Sergeant Gonzales took care of the rest. He was big, loud, and comfortable with giving orders to men. Claudette found him to be somewhat of a bully, yet ferociously loyal to Diego. She could see him look at her husband with an eerie reverence as if he were looking at the ghost of his long-lost friend, returned from the grave for one more adventure. Diego needed only to tell the big man his wishes, and Gonzales would whip the other men into compliance.

Their small force was woefully under-armed. Weapons and ammunition were scarce. The Americans had confiscated most of the guns and arrested any man caught carrying one. But the men were crafty and well accustomed to life on the frontier. With the woodworking and blacksmithing skills they had grown up with working on the ranches, they went to work manufacturing steel-tipped lances.

"You're going to fight the Americans with these?!" Claudette said, looking at the archaic weapon that Diego was so proudly trying to show her. "You really are Don Quixote!"

"The Americans only have shipborne Marines with no horses. They can only hope to get off a volley of musketry before we ride them down. We'll reach beyond their bayonets and sabers with these," he said, gripping the weapon and shaking it for emphasis.

It all seemed foolish and unlikely until she saw them drill. The men locked in tight with each other, nearly hip to hip on their horses. Then surged forward at a full gallop creating a thundering wall of bristling steel as they dashed across the field.

She could see that Diego was completely in his element. He was a natural teacher, sharing the lessons he had learned in North Africa about guerrilla cavalry tactics with his fellow *Californios*. She recalled her own lessons from the desert as well as she joined the other wives. It was like being back in Al-Qādir's *smala* again, but this time, the women spoke Spanish, which was a lot easier to pick up with her French ears than Arabic. She found herself understanding more and more as she pitched in with tending to the children and making food like the flatbread they called *tortilla*. It too was much like the bread she made in Africa, but made from cornmeal instead of barley.

Cornmeal, beans, and other supplies came by the cartload from the surrounding haciendas. "The Dons sure like to kiss the Gringos' asses in public," Sergeant Gonzales explained, "but they hate them as much as we do in private." He then barked at the men to unload the carts.

Bernardo visited often as well, bringing supplies and news from the village. The small band of fighters sat around the fire in the evening and watched the old man act out the latest. To Claudette, it was like watching a mystical Aztec warrior performing an ancient dance. But Diego could read the intricate details Bernardo conveyed with his hands. He shared them with the rest. "He says that the Americans have split their forces. They sent about twenty of them to garrison San Diego."

Diego paused his translation for a moment. Claudette saw something flash across his face. Was it confusion…? she wondered. Or perhaps fear?

"*¿Quién?*" he asked the old man for clarification, unconsciously defaulting to Spanish instead of the native language they shared. The old man signaled with his hands again while trying to form the sounds with his mouth.

Diego cleared his throat, "He says Cérbulo Varela attacked the barracks with a handful of men. They were driven off by the Americans but came back with more men and are now demanding that the Gringos surrender."

"Ah, that Cérbulo is wilder than a drunk rooster!" Sergeant Gonzales said. "And tougher than a rabid wolf!"

"We should go at once!" one of the men blurted. The rest joined in, shouting their enthusiastic agreement.

Diego sat quietly, staring into the fire. Claudette began to feel uneasy with his silence as the men began to quiet and turn to their young leader. The uncomfortable silence weighed heavily on her as Diego seemed not to notice the rough and tumble men looking to him, waiting for leadership. The urge to reach out and nudge him was overwhelming. She was about to say his name.

"We ride at dawn," Diego said suddenly, looking up from the fire, which flickered in his large green eyes. The men exploded in cheers. Diego looked back to the fire as the men celebrated with boasts and stories about the wild Cérbulo. Claudette looked at him with concern. Diego just stared. She put her arm around him and rested her head on his shoulder. He only smiled when the earthen jug of *mezcal* came around, nodding a thanks before taking a pull.

She waited until they returned to their tent to ask, "This Cérbulo is someone you know?"

"Yes," he said, laying on his side away from her.

After waiting for more, she prodded him again, "Is he a friend?"

"No."

"An enemy?"

Diego sighed and turned onto his back. "We fought several times as children," he said, shrugging as he stared at the tent ceiling.

"I see…" she said softly.

He let the silence rest for a moment before speaking again, "He won every single time."

Diego and Carlito were already up when she woke. Diego was sitting cross-legged in front of the small fire outside their tent. He was shaving with a small mirror and a tin cup full of hot water. He was shirtless but in his blue pantaloons. It was the first time she had seen him put on his uniform since they disembarked in Veracruz. His cavalry boots sat next to him. They looked as though he had recently polished them. Carlito was pawing at them, then pulled one into his mouth and bit down.

"*Non, non!*" she chided, picking up the boy. Carlito groaned in protest as he tried to reach back for the boot. "Here!" she said, picking up his wooden horse, which he promptly put in his mouth instead. Diego looked up and smiled.

"Special occasion?" she asked, setting the boy back down.

"I want the Americans to know who they're dealing with," he said with a wink.

"I'm sure they'll be very impressed," she told him with some irony. She wondered if it were truly the Americans he was trying to impress.

He stood up, kissed her, then put on his shirt and sash. "I'm an officer in the Mexican Army, not a mere bandit."

"Of course."

Diego just smiled in response. He tucked his pistol and dagger into his sash, hung his sword at his side, then put on his jacket and hat. He kissed her and the baby once more, then walked off to his men, his sword bouncing against his hip.

The laughs and boasts of the men went silent as he approached. The uniform had an immediate effect on them. Diego bound into the saddle and settled his horse's agitation with the reins and a light pat on the neck. He put on his riding gloves. Sergeant Gonzales handed him his lance and said, "Now we're a real army!" The men let out a cheer.

Diego nudged his horse up to where Claudette was standing. "We'll send for you and the other wives once it's safe," he told her.

"Be careful, Diego," she said.

He smiled, then looked to his boy, "I'll do what I can." He gave his horse a light kick, putting the beast in motion. Sergeant Gonzales put his pinky and index finger into his mouth and let out an ear-piercing whistle. The men fell in behind, their lances pointing toward the morning sky as they rode off to fight.

The once deserted streets were now filled with people cheering and shouting "*¡Viva México!*" at the sight of the young man wearing their nation's uniform and his men riding into the village.

"They sneaked out of the government house," an old man said, pointing at the now-abandoned building. "They're up on Fort Hill."

"They won't last long up there!" a woman piped in. "There's no water!"

Diego nodded in acknowledgment, then prodded his horse on as he led his troops through town. A crowd had gathered around the base of the hill. Many were armed. Most weren't and were merely there to watch and enjoy the festive atmosphere. There were street vendors cooking tortillas and selling them with grilled meats. Bands played and people danced happily as armed men watched the barricades on top of the hill for any movements from the Americans.

A cheer broke out at the sight of Diego and his men approaching.

"The Mexican government has not abandoned us!" someone shouted.

The music suddenly stopped. A path opened in the crowd and from it came a young man, tall and wiry, with a pistol and fighting knife hanging loosely on his hip. Diego grimaced, preparing himself for battle, a battle he would have to fight in front of all these people and his own men. Cérbulo Verula's eyes burned with intensity as he approached. Diego's horse fidgeted with apprehension as he came closer. "*Tranquilo...*" Diego murmured to the beast as he patted it on the neck with a gloved hand, trying to calm himself as well.

Cérbulo stopped and looked up. He was now a full-grown version of the boy that had beaten him up so many times in his youth. He was tall and lean and still had that wild unpredictable look in his eye that Diego feared so much from his childhood.

"We are happy you are here, Lieutenant..." Cérbulo stopped himself mid-sentence. He was now scrutinizing the face of the man in uniform before him. His eyes suddenly went wide with recognition, "…Diego de la Vega!" Diego swallowed hard, bracing for the humiliating fight with his old nemesis. Cérbulo's stern face broke into a grin. He turned to the crowd. "The De la Vegas are with us!" A cheer broke out. The music began to play again.

"Diego, you are a man now! Look at you!" Cérbulo let out.

"They fed me well in Spain," Diego shrugged, not knowing how else to respond.

"Come," Cérbulo beaconed, "let me introduce you to General Florés. He's in charge now. He'll be happy to see that Mexico has sent help."

Diego handed his reins to Sergeant Gonzales and climbed down from his horse. Cérbulo immediately threw his arms around him. "I'm so happy to see you!" He exclaimed. "Come!"

Diego looked back up at Sergeant Gonzales, "Wait here. I'll be back."

Gonzales smiled with pride, "Yes, Lieutenant."

Cérbulo led him through the crowd. Many turned to see the dashing young officer in their country's uniform. They ooh-ed and ah-ed. Some even reached out to touch the fine material of his green jacket.

General José María Florés looked up from his writing desk as they approached. It was set up under a canopy in front of his tent. He was a short, stocky man with a receding line of black hair and a thick mustache.

"General Florés," Cérbulo blurted, "this Don Diego de la Vega, returned from Spain. His family have been ranchers here for generations. I worked on their ranch as a child. He's a good man."

"Hmm, sub-lieutenant I see…" Florés said, looking at Diego's uniform. "Mexico sent you?" he asked.

"This is Mexico, General" Diego stiffened.

"Yeah, yeah…" Florés smirked dismissively with a wave of his hand. "Who sent you and why?"

"General Santa Anna sent me. I'm to raise a regiment of lancers."

"Santa Anna?! I thought we got rid of him." Florés said, gaining a few chuckles from the men around him.

"I returned with him from Cuba. He's coordinating the defense of Mexico now."

"Now I know we're in trouble," Florés said, rolling his eyes. The chuckles turned into a full round of laughs. "You're recruiting lancers? How many you got?"

"About thirty so far, señor," Diego said.

Florés looked to his men around him, then back to Diego. "Hardly enough to take back to Mexico, eh?"

"It's a work in progress, señor."

"Well, congratulations," Florés said. "You and your men are part of the Army of Alta California under my command until further notice...unless you've got somewhere else you've got to be...?"

"We're here to fight, General, and to drive the Gringo-heathens from our homeland," Diego said with dark passion.

Florés raised an eyebrow and looked to his other men then back to Diego. "Well, I'm sure you're in the right place then. Captain Cérbulo!" He turned to the other young man. "Find a place for Sub-Lieutenant de la Vega and his men, and make sure they get food and fodder for their horses. We'll need them ready for the fight to come."

The fight never came. Claudette and the rest of the wives arrived in time to see the surrender. After a day of holding out on Fort Hill and hoping for reinforcements, the Americans ran out of food and water. US Marine Brevet Captain Archibald H. Gillespie took General Florés's generous terms and marched his men out of the fort and toward a waiting merchant ship in the bay. They were allowed to keep their muskets, pistols, knives, and sabers.

Diego and his men escorted them through town using their lances to protect them from the crowd that had come to throw insults and rotten vegetables at the marines who once had held them under strict martial law. With great relief, he watched the last of the Americans board the Vandalia. The sailors pulled in the gangplank, untied the ship, and pushed off. The crowd cheered as the merchant vessel began to slowly move away from the dock. The marines stared back from the deck in sullen silence, their short visors shadowing their eyes.

Diego let out a breath as Florés and his aides pulled their horses up around him.

"They're gone, General," Diego told him.

"Yes, for now," Florés said, watching the ship move through the bay, "but they'll be back with more."

"We should have killed them while we had our chance," Cérbulo said, spitting on the ground.

Diego kept silent but found himself agreeing with his old enemy.

"Patience, my friend," Florés said with a slight smile that was obscured by his mustache yet still twinkled in his eyes. "We'll have the opportunity to kill a lot of them."

Chapter Twenty-Nine: The Old Woman's Gun

"It's here," the old lady said, pointing to the rough patch of dirt in her yard. "...and don't you hooligans go stepping on my tomato plants!" She whipped her finger back around to point at Diego and his men.

"Of course not, señora," Diego assured her. "We thank you for your service to Mexico."

"Hmph!" she answered with a shrug. Diego nodded to Sergeant Gonzales.

"Alright, boys," Gonzales told the men, "start digging, and don't step on the tomatoes!"

They went at it with pickaxes and shovels. At last, a loud clang rang out from a pickaxe striking hard metal.

"It's here!" a man shouted. The others dropped their tools and began clearing the dirt away from the long brass tube buried in the ground.

"Does it still work?" Diego asked.

"They fired it the Sunday just before the Gringos came," Gonzales said. "I nearly jumped out of bed! The old lady and her daughters buried it once the Americans started taking our guns."

"Hmm..." Diego mused as the men hoisted the brass cannon out of the ground and onto a cart.

"Damn it..." US Navy Captain William Mervine cursed under his breath, looking down at the dead child in the arms of his sailors.

"It was an accident, sir. The boys are nervous. They're seeing phantom Mexicans everywhere," one of his men offered. It was a bad omen. They had just put to shore 350 sailors, marines, and Bear Flag volunteers for the assault on Los Angeles, and already the cabin boy was dead from an accidental shooting before they even began to march.

"Take him back to the ship and keep him out of sight of the others," Mervine said.

This was all the fault of that damned fool of marine, he thought. The newly promoted Captain Gillespie, in Mervine's opinion, should never have been left in charge of such an important post. Gillespie's orders were simply to maintain order and keep the peace with the newly conquered citizens. Instead, the over-zealous martinet provoked the mob into an armed revolt. Now, a child was dead, and this was only the beginning of the long march back to Los Angeles where more of his men would most likely die in the coming battle.

"My men are ready to march, sir." Gillespie approached him with a salute, then gave a quizzical look at the dead boy being carried away.

"Very well, Captain, your men may take the vanguard," Mervine returned the salute.

"Aye, Aye, Captain!" Gillespie shouted, then turned to start barking orders at his men. Mervine grimaced at his loudness. *This is why the man is forty-three years old and only now a brevet captain of marines,* Mervine thought, watching Gillespie march off. *He's nothing more than a sergeant in officer's clothing.* Still, he was happy for the man's enthusiasm.

Captain Mervine commanded the USS Savannah, a frigate sent to relieve Gillespie and his men. Instead, they intercepted a merchant ship that was carrying them away. He found Gillespie and his men aboard, stewing in embarrassment, eager to avenge their humiliating defeat. Now they were the spear-point of this collection of marines, sailors, and Bear Flag volunteers armed with muskets, cutlasses, boarding pikes, and belaying pins. They had to leave their cannons behind because they had no horses to pull them.

The men trudged northward in the hot California sun, flinching at everything that moved during the first hour until eventually succumbing to the drudgery and boredom of the long march. Captain Mervine watched the surrounding ridges move in closer and closer. The valley was getting narrower as they progressed.

"There!" someone shouted. This time Mervine saw him: a man on horseback high on the ridge top. He wore a blue and green uniform and carried a lance. The marines drew their muskets to their shoulders, but the man withdrew, fading from view.

"I could send a detachment after him, sir," Gillespie was quick to offer.

"No, no, let them watch. He's just a scout. No need to waste any time. They know we're coming," Mervine dismissed him with a wave of his hand. Still, the sight of the uniform was disturbing. Was this uprising something more than local rabble?

The American procession continued on. Mervine began to wonder whether he should have had them carry more water and rations. They certainly needed better shoes. His sea-faring men weren't accustomed to long marches.

CRACK!

"Get down!" someone shouted. A crackle of musketry snapped him from his thoughts. Tiny dust clouds popped up around him. Mervine flinched, involuntarily clenching his eyes shut.

"Shoulder arms!" Mervine's eyes popped open at the sound of Gillespie's voice. "Fire!" A ripple of musket fire crackled across the line of marines. "Fix bayonets!"

"Wait…!" Mervine stammered, coming out of his crouch.

"Charge!" Gillespie shouted.

"No, you damn fool!" Mervine tried to shout above the din. It was too late. Gillespie was running and stumbling up the slope with his cutlass in hand. His men were charging with him with their bayonets held forward. "Damn it!" Captain Mervine shouted, ripping his bicorne off his head and throwing it to the ground.

Captain Gillespie's lungs were on fire as he reached the top of the ridge. The second volley from the Mexicans never came. He was sure they were waiting for them on the other side of the crest. His men filed in around him, panting heavily, frantically scanning the brush for the enemy as well. They were nowhere to be seen.

"Reload!" he shouted, narrowing his eyes, willing them to see the enemy who he was sure was somewhere right in front of him. The muskets clattered as men quickly rammed another round down their muzzles. The ramrods made a sharp zinging sound as metal slid against metal.

"Shoulder arms!" he yelled, still frantically searching the ridge top for the enemy, who he insisted must be there. The muskets rattled as the men drew them back to their shoulders, then silence. He could hear the light breeze and his men still trying to catch their breath. Still, there was nothing else.

"Backward step, march!" he called. The men slowly backed their way toward the downward slope, still searching for the phantom Mexicans.

"We should kill them while we have the chance!" Cérbulo hissed under his breath. They were lying on their stomachs underneath the prickly desert brush.

"¡Tranquilo!" Colonel José Carillo whispered back. "Not here, my friend. We want them to keep coming."

Cérbulo let out a derisive snort. Diego could feel the tension rolling off the men lying around him. The small detachment of Americans was so close. But if they fired now, they'd soon be fighting all of them. Carrillo was right. It was better to be patient and to draw them into the trap they had waiting for them instead of killing a few now. He turned his eyes back to watch the marines slip out of sight as they backed their way down from the crest.

"You damn fool!" Mervine let Gillespie have it upon his return. "You're going to get your men killed before we even get to Los Angeles!"

"Sir, we were under fire. I was engaging the enemy," Gillespie stammered, embarrassed to be dressed down in front of his men.

"Captain Gillespie, you are wasting ammunition and we cannot spare the caps!" Mervine scolded. "Do not act without my orders again! Do you understand?!"

Gillespie stared at him, seething with pent-up rage.

"Do you understand, Captain?!"

"Sir, yes, sir!" Gillespie shouted, drawing himself to attention.

"Good," Mervine said in a softer tone, allowing some of his own fury to seep out of him. "Now if you would, sir, please return to your position at the vanguard and let us make haste to our objective, which is Los Angeles, and not some random Mexican bandits taking potshots at us."

"Sir, yes, sir!" Gillespie shouted, then spun on his heel and stormed off.

Captain Mervine let out a sigh watching the marine walk away with his overtly military stride, "...that man..."

The march dragged on, only to be interrupted by occasional potshots taken by the unseen enemy. Each time the men would flinch or throw themselves to the ground, causing them to become more and more unnerved as the day dragged on.

After six grueling hours of marching in the California sun, they made it to an abandoned ranch and set up camp. From there, they could see Mexican horsemen watching them from afar. Without horses of their own, there was no use confronting them.

"They'll just disperse before we even get close enough for a volley," Mervine told his fellow officers. "Don't worry. We'll have our chance to fight them once we get to Los Angeles. Tell the men to rest well. We march at first light."

No one rested well. The Mexicans harassed them with gunfire and wolf calls all through the night. The frayed and frazzled men were then woken by the rumbling of wild horses stampeding through the camp, kicking up dust, and blotting out the early morning light.

"My God! They're everywhere!" a man cried in distress.

"Hold your tongue and get ready to march!" a sergeant chided.

The American column was moving once again. Men choked and gagged on the dust, covering their mouths with handkerchiefs or with the collar of their shirts. Some were sipping the last of their water in desperate hope of washing the dirt from their mouths. Captain Gillespie pushed his men on as the path narrowed. The dust was beginning to settle, allowing them to see farther ahead.

"What in the world...?" a sergeant muttered. From the brush that lined the path ahead, a cart rolled out, seeming of its own volition. "Halt!" he called, putting up his hand. The rest of the column came to a stop.

"What is it?" Captain Gillespie asked, making his way to the front.

"Up there, sir. That's a cart moving on its own onto the path," the sergeant pointed.

Gillespie squinted and shielded his eyes as the sun was beginning to break through the dust. He watched the cart move into the center of the trail. He could hear the squeak of pulleys somewhere out of sight. He then made out the ropes that were being used to move the cart into position. It was then that the sunlight broke through and glinted on the brass cylinder that was strapped on top of the cart.

"Fuck! Get down!"

BOOM!

Fire and smoke shot out of the cannon as the men dropped to the ground. He felt the air being sucked away as the four-pound ball bounded off the ground and whizzed past them. Then came a crackle of musketry from the ridgetop on their flank.

"Ayeeee!" One of his men screeched in agony as a musket ball found him.

"Shoulder, arms!" Gillespie shouted as he saw the cart bearing the cannon being dragged back into the bushes. "Fire!" The marines fired their own volley. But with no visible enemy, the balls splattered against the dirt and rocks, kicking up dust.

Another rattle of musketry rained down on them. More men cried out in fear and pain. "Reload!" Gillespie barked, scanning the heights, cursing the enemy who wouldn't reveal himself for a proper fight. The sound of the squeaking pulleys and the creaking cart snapped his attention back forward.

"Get down!"

BOOM!

This time the ball bowled down two of his men as they desperately tried to ram the next round into their muskets.

"Fall back, you damn fools!" He could hear Captain Mervine shouting himself hoarse, trying to maintain order in the chaos. Gillespie grimaced at the thought of retreating in the face of the Mexicans. Another rattle of musketry rained down on them. Thankfully, the Mexicans were wild with their shots as they popped up, fired, then hid.

"Pick up the injured and fall back!" Gillespie shouted as the cannon fired again, causing men to dive out of the way of the bounding ball. "No one gets left behind!" His men flinched and ducked the musketry raining down from above as they snatched up their wounded, some of which were screaming in agony. Others were silent and unconscious as they were slumped over the shoulders of their comrades who carried them away.

Captain Mervine ordered a retreat. With no artillery and no horses, his men were sitting ducks to the Mexican cannons and cavalry.

"Keep your eyes on the ridges and shoot any damn Mexican that shows his face!" Gillespie ordered his marines.

The Mexican horsemen followed the Americans all the way back to San Pedro Bay, harassing them every step of the way. They fired from above, then fell back before the Americans could find targets. Colonel Carrillo finally stopped them once the US naval ship was in sight. "Her guns will tear us apart," he told his men. So they stood on the hilltop and cheered. They waved a US flag they had captured in the chaos of the retreat to taunt the Americans who were rowing their launches back to the ship.

Diego and his men stayed to watch over the US vessel for the next few days. They watched as a detachment rowed to a small island in the bay and buried their dead. Then, much to their relief, the American frigate pulled anchor and sailed away.

The celebration was still going on as Diego and his men rode into the Pueblo of Los Angeles. It had started with the victory at Dominguez Ranch, or what people were now calling "the Battle of the Old Woman's Gun." Now the fresh news of the American ship sailing away brought a new round of cheers from the crowd. Trumpets, guitars, and fiddles played in the plaza as women danced in their bright, colorful dresses. Wine, mezcal, and aguardiente flowed freely as the smells of fresh corn tortilla and grilled meats drifted through the evening air.

Diego eased himself out of the saddle after the long ride back from San Pedro Bay. He was overtaken immediately by the arms of his wife as he turned. "My love!" Claudette gasped, kissing him and squeezing him tight. Diego chuckled at the surprise and frantic attention.

"Where's the boy?" he asked.

"Asleep and being cared for by the abuelas with the other children. Come, let me get you a cup of wine and some food. It's delicious!" She tugged him along to follow her.

"Wait!" he stopped. She turned back to see what was the matter. He looked at her in her pretty white cotton dress. Her thick black shoulder-length hair was held back on one side with a flower tucked behind her ear. The torches and lanterns flickered against her white skin and dark eyes, making her seem to glow in the twilight.

"What is it?" she asked, concern growing on her face.

"I love you," he said simply. She smiled then stepped closer, wrapped him in her arms, and kissed him.

"I know," she whispered. "I love you too. Now let's eat!"

General Florés climbed onto a table as the band finished a tune. The crowd began to cheer even before he could speak. He smiled grandly, urging them to quiet with his hands until there was room to talk. "Friends, neighbors, *Californios*...we have chased away the cruel invaders from our homes through the sheer force of our will!" The crowd erupted in cheers. "But they will be back..." A collective groan rippled through the audience. "...and in larger numbers. Tonight we celebrate, but tomorrow we plan and prepare. We will be ready, my friends! California will be free of Anglo rule!" The crowd burst into cheers once more as the band began to play.

Florés waved to the crowd and shook hands with the well-wishers who came to congratulate him on the victory.

True to his word, he got started the next day. He called for an assembly of the remaining politicians and landowners who hadn't fled to Central Mexico at the arrival of the Americans. They convened at the Pueblo of Los Angeles and promptly elected Florés as governor and military commander of California. Florés then started reorganizing his army. He sent a force north to watch for any movements from the American stronghold at Monterey. He sent another force south under the command of General Andrés Pico to watch the American concentration at San Diego.

Chapter Thirty: The Fall of California

"One shot and then the lance, boys," General Andrés Pico told his *Galgos* or "Greyhounds," as he liked to call his swift-mounted lancers. They had gathered at the deserted native village of San Pascual to prepare for battle.

"Make sure your carbines and pistols are dry and loaded," Diego said, turning to his own men. It had rained hard that night, soaking the men as they tried to cover their powder with their bodies. Now they were groaning at the result as they checked their firearms.

"It's okay, boys," Sergeant Gonzales told them, "the Gringos have wet powder too, but they don't have lances!" That got a grim chuckle from the men.

Diego narrowed his eyes and tried to peer through the fog-covered valley at the American force gathering on the other side. The reports were true. There were a lot more of them than they had expected.

Pico and his men had been following a small detachment of Americans riding east out of San Diego. This party was led by none other than the despised Captain Gillespie, whose cruel reign over Los Angeles had started the uprising. Now the *Californios* were hoping for some payback.

At first, General Pico believed Gillespie was merely leading a foraging party. But scouting reports were coming in saying that a larger American force was marching in from the east. That force, along with Gillespie and his men, were now drawing up into battle lines across from them.

"They're coming," someone said, snapping everyone's attention to the valley floor.

Diego furrowed his brow at the seemingly strange tactic. A small lead detachment of Americans had spurred their horses into a gallop, but they were still three-quarters of a mile away from the village and had quickly outpaced the rest of their forces. The rest of the Americans seemed to be caught off guard by this as well. They were now scrambling to fill in the huge gap in their line.

"Ha! They're making it easy for us," Pico chuckled, stroking his pronounced mustache. He then pulled his carbine from his saddle holster and shouted, "Shoulder arms!" The order was repeated by officers and sergeants along the line. Pico looked back at the small detachment of charging Americans, shrugged his shoulders, and shouted, "Fire!"

Not all their pistols and carbines fired due to the wet powder, but enough did to have a devastating effect on the ill-timed charge. The officer leading it took a musket ball straight to the forehead and flew off his galloping mount. Horses and men tumbled to the ground around him.

Pico watched as the rest of the American force stumbled through the wreckage of the first wave. He saw an opportunity. "Fall back, men! Fall back!" he shouted.

"They're retreating!" an American officer shouted. "After them!" The American dragoons thundered into the village and then had to slow their mounts to navigate around the huts, boulders, and brush. When they emerged onto the field on the other side, they found the *Californios* had reformed into a battle line.

"Fire!" Pico shouted.

The Americans screamed in outrage as several dropped from the withering musket fire. They tried to shoot back with their pistols and carbines, but the damp powder kept many from discharging. They then pulled their sabers and charged.

"Lances ready!" Pico shouted. The *Californios* leveled their spears. Pico unsheathed his saber and held it high in the air, "*¡Viva California! ¡Abajo los Americanos!*" he shouted, swiftly slicing his saber forward. The entire Mexican line lurched forward as one and thundered toward the galloping Americans. The leader of the American charge singled out General Pico and rode toward him with his saber held high. He slashed down at Pico's head. A loud clang of metal rang out as the Mexican general blocked the blow. Then two lancers at his side drove their spears into the American officer, throwing him off of his horse. He landed on his back with a thud. Winded, he was just able to look up once more before another lancer rode by and ran him through with his spear.

"For God's sake, men, come up!" Another American officer beckoned his men into the fight as he emerged onto the field. More and more came spilling into the fray, trying to fire their pistols and charging with their sabers.

Diego deflected a saber blow from a charging man, then redirected the point of his lance to allow the man to impale himself through the sheer force of his own galloping horse. The lance snapped in half as it punched through the man's chest, throwing him to the ground. Diego pulled out his pistol and shot a second man charging him from another direction. He watched as the riderless horse ran past, slowed to a stop, lowered its head, and began eating grass while his rider lay dying in the dust.

Diego looked back up. Men were fighting all around. A Californian yanked an American off his horse with a lasso. Sergeant Gonzales rode up quickly and ran the man through with his lance just after he hit the ground. Captain Gillespie emerged onto the battlefield with a collection of marines. He was barking orders as they rolled out two mountain howitzers and started unlimbering them.

"Sergeant Gonzales!" Diego shouted as he pulled out his straight saber with a metallic zing. He pointed it at the new threat, "To me!"

Gonzales beckoned four others nearby to ride with him to Diego's side. Together they launched themselves at the American gunners who scattered at the sight of the charging horsemen.

"Rally! Rally! Face them!" Gillespie shouted at his men. He turned around just in time to take a lance to the chest, knocking him down, and pinning him to the ground. The marine screamed in rage as he yanked the spear from his body. He scrambled to his feet, fumbling with his flint and steel, trying desperately to light the linstock needed to fire the cannon. Diego and his men turned their horses to make a second pass. Gillespie managed to light the linstock just as Sergeant Gonzales's lance hit him in the mouth, breaking a tooth, and knocking him to the ground once more.

"Hurry!" Diego shouted, jumping off his horse and beckoning the others to join him.

"No..." Gillespie gasped, spitting out pieces of his broken tooth as he propped himself up to watch. The Mexicans secured one of his howitzers using their lassos and began to haul it away with their horses.

Another American crew showed up and began unlimbering their bronze four-pound cannon next to Gillespie's remaining howitzer. Gillespie slowly dragged himself to his feet, wheezing for air. He picked up his burning linstock and stumbled over to the new crew. "Here," he gasped, handing it to one of the men. "It's already lit," he said, then collapsed.

The leader of the new crew looked down at him in bewilderment, then handed the burning linstock to one of his men. "Load grapeshot and fire both guns at will!" he shouted. "And get him to the rear!" he said, pointing to the unconscious marine.

The sudden explosion of cannon fire startled nearly everyone on the field, who, up until that point, had been locked in desperate hand-to-hand fighting after expending what could be fired with damp gunpowder. The hastily fired first volley of artillery flew high, but General Pico wasn't going to wait for the Americans to adjust their aim. "Fall back, my Greyhounds! We're not going to fight cannons with lances!" he shouted.

The Mexican horsemen broke off their individual fights and quickly dashed out of range before another volley of canister and grapeshot could be fired. The battered and bruised Americans watched in frustration as the *Californios* rode off with one of their cannons as a trophy.

A month later, that trophy, an American-made 12-pound mountain howitzer, sat on a ridge overlooking a shallow point in the San Gabriel River, just about ten miles south of Los Angeles. Alongside it was a hodgepodge of captured guns and old Spanish relics. They sat poised to keep the gathering American force from crossing the river. With homemade powder and a scarcity of the mix-matched rounds for each gun, training had been kept to a minimum.

General Florés and his *Californios* stood around their guns and lined the high ridges, watching the enemy below. They were as mix-matched as the artillery pieces. Among them were wealthy landowners of pure Spanish blood, mestizos, pure-blooded natives, blacks, and every possible combination in between. Some were loyal to Mexico. Others dreamed of an independent California. Missing were the *Californios* who welcomed the Anglo invaders. Some of which could be seen below, taking their places among the US forces.

General Pico had followed up his thrashing of the Americans at San Pascual by surrounding them on a hill the next day. Pico and his men had laid siege for days until a larger US force came and rescued the trapped Americans. Outmanned and outgunned, the Californios had to watch in frustration as the reinforced Americans escaped their hilltop tomb and crawled back into the fortifications at San Diego. Now the Americans were on the move to take back Los Angeles. The Californios had come to stop them.

"Here they come!" Sergeant Gonzales called out, pointing to the surge of movement below. The Americans formed themselves into a hollow square, protecting their flanks from cavalry attacks with four walls of men armed with bayonets like a hedge of sharp steel that no horse would charge. In the center were their supply wagons, cannons, and officers on horseback directing the movement. The giant square began to move into the water.

"*¡Fuego!*"

BOOM!

The Mexican guns kicked violently, pelting the water with solid shot and canister. A few of the Americans dropped into the knee-deep water. But most of the Mexican volley went wild or fell short of the target due to poorly made powder and untrained gunners.

"Quickly!" one of the American officers urged his gun crews. He reached from his saddle and grabbed a tow rope, adding his horse's power to the men trying to stop a gun from sinking into the ground beneath the water.

"Quicksand be damned! Come on, boys!" he shouted.

Through sheer force of will, they shoved their cannons forward, scrambling for the other side as the Mexicans frantically reloaded their guns. Skirmishers from both sides began to exchange musket shots as the Americans unlimbered their guns. The Mexican guns fired wildly again, failing to hit their targets while the calm and well-trained Americans set their aim and elevation.

"Fire!"

BOOM!

The two American 9-pounders roared to life with jets of smoke and fire. One of the shots smashed into a gun carriage, causing it to explode into a cloud of sawdust and splinters which pelted the men nearby. The Americans quickly reloaded as the Mexican gunners floundered in panicked disarray.

"Fire!"

The American guns opened up again, this time destroying the remaining Mexican artillery and injuring several of the crew members.

"New Orleans!" men shouted as they began to scramble up the hill with their bayonets, now that the Mexican guns had been silenced.

"*¿Qué es New Orleans?*" Sergeant Gonzales mused from his saddle as he stroked his chin. He was among General Pico's lancers, standing ready on the flank. They watched as some of the Americans tumbled to the ground from a volley of Mexican musketry from above.

"*Quién sabe...*" General Pico shrugged as he pulled his saber, "*¡Vámanos, amigos!*" he said, then shouted. "*¡Viva California!*"

"*¡Viva California!*" his men shouted as they couched their lances and spurred their horses into a thundering wave of spearheads and horseflesh.

"Shit!" an American officer shouted. "Form square!" The Americans quickly reformed, creating a wall of bristling bayonets. The Mexican horses instinctively veered away as their riders emptied their pistols and carbines into the mass of men.

BOOM!

The cannons fired once more, sending the Mexican horsemen scurrying away. With the cavalry threat gone, the Americans pushed forward, scrambling up the hill, waiting for the next volley of musketry to pour into them.

It never came.

They reached the top, only to find the wreckage of the Mexican guns and two dead bodies left behind. The Americans camped there that night, wearily watching the campfires of the Californians twinkling on the hilltops ahead. They pushed on to Los Angeles the next day. The Mexicans returned with fresh cannons they had brought from the village. But they were no match against the

American guns and their well-trained artillerymen. The Mexican horsemen threw themselves at the invaders again and again. But the Americans held their square each time, repelling them with well-disciplined volley-fire.

After watching too many of his men fall from their saddles, General Florés called off the attacks. They collected their wounded and fled to the hills. There they watched in frustration as the American flag rose once more over the Pueblo of Los Angeles. All they could do now was wait as a delegation of officers went under a white flag of truce to negotiate terms with the American occupiers.

The wives and families joined the camp now that a ceasefire was safely in effect. Claudette rested her head on Diego's shoulder. She held his hand as they sat quietly, watching the sunset over the village he called home. She knew that no words could soothe his outrage and frustration. All she could do was simply love him as he sulked in silence: bruised, bandaged, and bloodied. His horse had been shot out from under him. They had to pull a piece of grapeshot from his thigh with nothing more than mezcal to ease the pain and clean the wound.

Now he sat while everything crumbled around them, his despair numbing the physical pain. Their tiny force dwindled over the days that followed. Men succumbed to the feeling of hopelessness in resisting the seemingly constant flow of this well-supplied juggernaut from the east. Each morning there were fewer and fewer men until only the most devoted, or too injured to flee, remained.

"Here they come!" one of the men shouted.

Cérbulo jumped to his feet. He spat on the ground and crossed his arms as Generals Florés and Pico rode up with their staffs. Claudette helped Diego to his feet and hobble over to where the remaining men were gathering to hear the results of the negotiations. General Florés took off his wide-brimmed hat and waved it at the gathering crowd. He waited for them to quiet before replacing it on his head.

"You have fought bravely, my friends," he told them, scanning the crowd, making eye contact with as many as he could. "You know it, I know it, even the Gringos know it." A dark chuckle spread among them. "But there're too many of them, and more are coming with more supplies and more weapons." A collective groan swelled from the crowd. "They come like an unstoppable river as our numbers fall, our supplies and weapons become scarce, and our homemade powder fails us. Our politicians in Mexico City can offer no help. I see no point in spending any more of our lives when our own country can't support us. The Americans offer a choice. If you surrender and swear not to take up arms again against the United States, you may go home with a full pardon. You'll have an opportunity to become American citizens with full rights once hostilities are over and a treaty is finalized."

This caused a mix of groans and chatter among the crowd. Florés put his hands up to indicate there was more. "Those of us who are bound to our loyalty to Mexico will be allowed to leave Alta California. The choice is yours but make it quick. I am ceding command to General Pico. He will be in charge of the formal surrender. I am returning to my home state of Sonora. Any of you who wish to leave with me is welcome."

Diego stood silently as the two generals shook hands and parted ways. People were chatting all around. Claudette looked up at him, trying to read his thoughts. "We can still be very happy here, Diego. Does it matter who's in control?"

He looked down at her, blinking as if he couldn't quite understand her words.

"Diego!" Cérbulo's voice cut through the din of chatter. Diego turned as his one-time enemy approached. "It was an honor to fight alongside you after all these years," Cérbulo told him.

"The honor was mine, my friend," Diego said, looking up at the man as he took his hand.

Cérbulo shook his hand firmly, smiling. Then the smile faded as his look became more quizzical. "What is it…?" he asked.

Diego paused, looked to the ground, then back up at his old nemesis. "I always thought you hated me."

Cérbulo's smile slowly returned. "I did. I hated you a lot," he said. When Diego said nothing, he continued. "I hated you for being mestizo like me, but you lived like a prince because your white father was rich while I was nothing more than a farmhand. Yet you worked the herd with us…like you were one of us. It was almost like…you were taking away the only thing I had over you."

"What was that?" Diego asked.

"That I was tough," Cérbulo said.

"I remember from our fights that you were tougher," Diego told him.

Cérbulo scoffed with a laugh, "I was bigger and a few years older than you, for sure. But you kept getting up and coming back for more, no matter how hard I tried to beat you down. You never told on me to your father. I don't know if I…could have done the same." Cérbulo paused for a moment, looking at the ground. He then looked back at Diego. "Join us," he said at last.

"Join you?"

"A few of us have decided we're not going to flee or surrender," Cérbulo told him. "We're taking to the hills. We'll attack the Gringos when and where we can and enjoy as much of their loot as we can carry."

Diego smiled slyly. He looked to his wife, who was struggling to follow their conversation in Spanish. He then returned his eyes to Cérbulo. "I would love to," he said, "but I have sworn an oath to General Santa Anna and to Mexico. I promised to bring him men to fight for our country, and I will. Come with us. We will push them out of Central Mexico, then liberate California."

Cérbulo laughed, "I'm a Californio first, my friend. I will fight them here."

Claudette watched as the two finished their conversation with handshakes and hugs. The tall Californio took her hand, bowed, and spoke a farewell in the language she was only beginning to understand. What she could understand was that a decision had been made: a decision that would carry them to the dark fate she had been warned about time and time again. She had put away her cards and crystal ball months ago, unable to look into the abyss without the sickening empty feeling of dread pouring into her stomach and reaching into her heart.

The clop of hooves and the creaking of a wagon broke her from her thoughts. The sight of the smiling old native driving the cart swept her icy melancholy away.

"Abuelito!" Diego called out to him. "What are you doing here?"

The old man mumbled tongueless words as he signaled with his hands.

"You're going to Central Mexico with us?" Diego said out loud in English for Claudette's benefit. "What about your work on my father's ranch?"

The old man mouthed words and signaled again. He and Diego chuckled warmly. Diego turned to Claudette.

"He says he retired," Diego told her. She couldn't help but giggle. It was hard to remain unhappy in Bernardo's presence.

The caravan was prepared to leave at dusk. General Florés thought it was best to leave under the cover of night in case the Americans changed their minds or insisted they give up their weapons. Every man agreed that even if the Americans were going to allow them to pass freely, they'd be utterly helpless without their arms against the marauding natives who viewed anyone outside their specific tribe as an invader and a fair target.

Claudette sat in the back of Bernardo's wagon with her husband and child. Diego's wound was still too raw for him to ride. She snuggled into him and watched the flickering lights of Los Angeles slowly pull away. She looked to her husband. He was staring at the village below. She could sense the turmoil roiling inside him.

"What is it?" she asked at last.

"I shall never see my home again," he said softly.

She wanted to tell him he was wrong, to allay his fears but she knew he was right. Instead, she rested her head on his shoulder and held him tight as the wagon creaked its way down the dusty trail.

Chapter Thirty-One: *Los San Patricios*

August 1847: Mexico City

"Is he still out there?" General, and now once again, President Antonio Lopez de Santa Anna asked his aide.

"Yes, Your Serene Highness. Shall I tell him to go away?"

The president sighed. "No, I'll see him," he said, throwing his cavalry boots onto his desk and leaning back in his chair. "Give me a few minutes, then send him in."

His desk was covered with unread dispatches, letters, and requests for men and supplies he did not have or could spare. His office at the Palacio Nacional had been a non-stop carousel of petitioners, stealing his time for their petty infighting and personal ambitions, time he desperately needed to plan the defense of the city and his country from the barbarians at the gate; time he spent mostly staring at the wall, lost under the immense weight of soul-crushing apathy.

He belonged in the field, leading men, not sitting here under a mountain of paperwork and a line of petitioners. He was a fighter, a leader of men, not some lowborn clerk. It had been his sheer force of will that had inspired men, good men, patriots to his banner. He had to mortgage his own properties and spend a fortune to arm, clothe, and feed this army.

They had driven north, smashing into Zachary Taylor's Army of Occupation at La Angostura, capturing flags, cannons, and prisoners. They were on the verge of victory when devastating news reached their camp: an insurrection had broken out in the capital. He had to release his prisoners and beat a hasty retreat back to Mexico City to quell the rebellion. Of course, the riots ended the moment his army marched into the city. He had to install a new government and offer amnesty to the insurrectionists for the sake of national unity in the face of the true enemy.

With the capital pacified, he was preparing to return north and finish Taylor's army for good when the next devastating news hit: The Americans had landed a second force on the central coast and took the all-important port of Veracruz. The path to the capital lay open.

He had mustered his forces and rushed out to stop them. They dug in at Cerro Gordo, a massive hill that dominated a narrow passage along the National Highway that the Americans would have to take to get to the capital. But as a detachment of Americans attacked his front, a second column found a way around the Mexican flank and surprised them from the rear. His men broke in complete panic. His personal camp was overrun so quickly that he had no time to strap on his prosthetic before escaping.

"They took my fucking leg!" Santa Anna hissed under his breath, clenching his fist as he looked at the spare prosthetic he was now wearing. It was hidden in a cavalry boot, propped up on the desk.

They had retreated to Puebla, but the cowards there were already planning to surrender the city. So in complete disgust, he pulled his tattered forces back to Mexico City to defend the capital. Even there, the ungrateful citizens jeered at them as they rode in. "You have only come to compromise us!" the rabble shouted.

The humiliation was more than he could bear. The incompetence of his officers, the cowardice of his men, and the utter lack of support from the citizens enraged him. It seemed he was the only one who cared about the nation's honor...except for that fool who had been waiting outside of his office for the last three days to see him.

"Sub-Lieutenant de la Vega, Your Serene Highness," his aide said, opening the door. Santa Anna sighed and waved him in. The young man marched to his desk, doing his best to hide a limp. The uniform that Santa Anna had bought him almost a year ago was now well-worn and blood-stained, but otherwise clean and pressed. His well-worn boots were brightly polished as well. His straight saber bounced against his hip and his spurs clinked as he walked across the marble floor. He came to a swift halt before the desk, snapped his heels together, and straightened his body to attention.

"Sub-Lieutenant de la Vega, señor, reporting for duty!" he shouted.

"Yes, yes, I know who you are, you fool. My damned aide already announced you. At ease," the president said. "Why are you here taking up my time?"

"I've…uh…returned from California, señor. I await further orders."

"It took you long enough. What have you been doing all this time?"

"I fought with Generals Pico and Florés against the invaders, señor," Diego offered.

"Yes, and you lost, months ago."

"We escorted General Florés to his home in Sonoma, señor. I had been wounded in the leg during battle, then my wife got sick with tropical fever. We had to convalesce before we could travel again."

"Wounded in the leg, huh…?" Santa Anna raised an eyebrow. He then slammed his feet on the ground and pounded the desk with his fist. Diego flinched. "I fucking lost my leg in the service of my country!" He looked down at his spare prosthetic before looking back up. "Twice, God damn it! What are you willing to give?!"

Diego looked to the floor for a moment, then back at Santa Anna, "My life, señor."

The president nearly winced at the shame and pain in Diego's eyes before refocusing his anger. "Don't be so damn dramatic," the president sighed. "You were supposed to bring me men from California. Where are they?"

"We lost many in battle, señor. Many decided to stay in California after the loss. Several decided to stay in Sonoma …"

"I didn't ask you for excuses," Santa Anna interrupted. "I asked you how many men did you bring me?"

Diego looked down at his feet, "Two, señor."

"Two…?"

"Yes, señor," Diego said, looking back up. "They're waiting outside," he pointed to the window.

"Hmm…" Santa Anna hoisted himself from his chair, walked over to the window, and looked down. A large old man was waving his hat at him. A much smaller old native sat on a wagon. With them were Diego's wife and child. "You brought me two old men, a woman, and a baby….If I were the Americans, I would turn around and run away while I still could."

"I'm sorry, señor," Diego said softly, dropping his eyes to the floor.

"No, I'm sorry," Santa Anna said. Diego looked up with new hope, only to be cut down further. "I'm sorry I sent a boy to do a man's job. Here…" he said abruptly, as he hobbled back to his desk and plopped back down in his chair. He began scribbling orders. "You belong with the rest of the boys. My son says you're a decent teacher. The military academy needs a fencing master." He finished writing and then handed him the order. "You are to report to the military academy at Chapultepec Castle. Since you can't handle being a hero yourself, maybe you can train the heroes of tomorrow."

Claudette gasped at the heat as she fanned herself and clung to her parasol. Even after losing so much weight from her bought with fever, the sultry Mexican summer was too much to bear. She looked in the back of the cart where Carlito cooed and pushed his wooden horse back and forth, seemingly unaffected by the heat in his little straw hat. She was grateful that at least he wasn't fussing for the moment. It had been a dreadful three days waiting to learn Diego's next assignment. He had been so impatient to report to Santa Anna and to return to duty. But the president didn't seem all that interested in seeing him. "He's a very busy man," Diego had assured her, after the first day of waiting.

"Of course," Claudette agreed, but she couldn't help but feel, more and more, that coming to Mexico City was a mistake.

"There he is!" Sergeant Gonzales erupted, then took off his hat and started waving it madly at the window above. She shaded her eyes as she looked up at the president peering down at them. Something about his face didn't seem too inviting.

She sighed softly as Gonzales, once again, broke into a long rant in Spanish that she could barely understand, but felt compelled to nod and mutter "uh-huh" to not seem rude.

"Well, if my eyes don't deceive me," a familiar voice speaking in French turned her hot blood to ice, "I do believe Mexico City just got prettier!"

"Pierre!" she gasped. She turned to see the tall handsome man grinning as he approached. His big blue eyes sparkled with delight as he grinned with his odd upside-down smile. His long blond hair was tucked underneath a straw hat. She had to admit, he looked dashing in his white linen suit.

"*Mon Dieu*, you look emaciated!" he said, bowing to kiss her hand. "Can your husband not afford to feed you?"

She let out an embarrassed laugh. She wasn't quite sure how to respond to the slight. "I caught tropical fever in Sonoma after we fled California."

"Ah, the coast is dangerous this time of year for the pure-bred European," he said, then turned as Carlito was cooing at him. The little boy was offering his wooden horse to the stranger for inspection. Pierre laughed and patted his head. "I see your mixed-breed son carries enough native blood to keep him safe. It'll serve him well working the sugar plantations when he's older."

Claudette opened her mouth to reply but was stunned into silence as she tried to process the meaning of what seemed to be a sweetly spoken insult. She could sense Sergeant Gonzales and Bernardo drawing nearer out of protective instinct, even though she doubted they understood the French words being spoken.

"Ah, there's our dashing hero now!" Pierre said suddenly, turning away from them and toward the palace. She could see Diego walking out with his eyes on the ground. The look on his face told her that the meeting hadn't gone well. His face went pale as he looked and saw Pierre standing next to her.

"Be kind to him…" Claudette said softly, tugging his sleeve.

"Of course, madam," Pierre replied. "It wounds me that you'd think I'd be otherwise." He then turned his attention back to Diego, "*¡Hola, viejo amigo!*"

"*Hola, amigo*," Diego said, accepting the handshake. He introduced Bernardo and Sergeant Gonzales. The two men nodded to the Frenchman as he shook their hands.

"Ah, pa!" Carlito let out, reaching for his father. Diego picked him up and propped him on his hip.

"My, my," Pierre said, now in English for Claudette's benefit, "he sure looks like you! No doubt who the father is here!"

"Why would there be?" Diego grimaced, straightening himself.

"Of course, my friend," Pierre smiled. "I meant no slight. Please excuse me if I spoke carelessly. I only meant to say that your son favors you in all the best ways. Please accept my apology."

Claudette squeezed Diego's arm, causing him to deflate some of his tension.

"Of course," Diego said at last.

"Say, why don't you accompany me? I have a shipment of Brown Besses I'm about to deliver to a regiment of men who should be well acquainted with them. I could use the company."

"I have orders to report to Chapultepec," Diego demurred.

"What are you to do there?" Pierre raised an eyebrow. Claudette turned to see her husband's response as well. Diego paused for a moment, then sighed. "I'm the new fencing master at the academy."

A slight sneer curled into Pierre's upside-down smile. "The kids can wait. Nothing's happening at the old castle right now except for nap time. The Americans are still licking their wounds and waiting for reinforcements at Puebla. We've got time. Come, I could use your help, especially since you have a cart and you both speak English." Diego raised an eyebrow at this last bit. He and Claudette looked to each other quizzically, then back to Pierre as he continued, "Come on, let's have some fun before the war flares up again."

Diego turned to Claudette, who could only offer a shrug. He turned back to Pierre. "Alright, lead the way," he said.

"Excellent! Wait here while I fetch my horse. I'll be right back!" he said, then turned to walk toward the stables.

Sergeant Gonzales came and put his arm around Diego's shoulder. "Something tells me he's not your friend," the big man said in Spanish as they watched Pierre walk away.

The first thing Claudette noticed when they rolled into the camp of the *Legión Extranjera de San Patricio* was the sheer number of Europeans. She hadn't seen so many in one place since they left France seemingly a lifetime ago. There were several men of African descent mixed in with them as well. The men drilled and marched around their collection of cannons. At the center of their camp flew a green flag with a silver cross, a golden harp, shamrocks, and the words *"Erin Go Bragh."* On the other side was a picture of Saint Patrick and the words *"Libertad por la Republica Mexicana."*

She could detect several languages spoken among the men as their cart came to a halt: French, German, Polish, Italian, Gaelic, but mostly English. But it was an English with a musical lilt that made it difficult to understand yet pleasant to the ear.

"There ye' are, ye' bloody Frog bastard! Where are me fuckin' guns?!" Claudette was startled by the large blue-eyed man with heavy sideburns approaching their party. He wore sky-blue trousers, a red sash, a dark blue jacket, and a black leather shako adorned with a red pompom.

"John, you Irish rascal!" Pierre leaped from his horse and hugged the big man. "Let me introduce my friends," he said, guiding him over to the others. "Major Riley, this Mrs. Claudette Moreau de la Vega."

Riley removed his hat and took a deep bow to kiss her hand. "My deepest apologies, madame, if I had known I was in the presence of such a beautiful lady, I would have watched my filthy mouth," he said, looking up from his kiss with a twinkle in his eyes.

"Oh, please," Claudette said, blushing as she fanned herself with her other hand, "I've been living among soldiers for some time now. I'm quite used to it."

"Is this the one ye' said broke ya' heart?" He looked to Pierre with a wink. Pierre's eyes went wide with shock. A nervous chuckle was all he could muster in response. "I can rightly see why!" Riley continued, returning his eyes to Claudette, who had gone completely red with embarrassment. "And ye' must be the rogue who'd done it now, aren't ye,' lad?" Riley turned to Diego, mercifully taking his attention off her.

"Sub-Lieutenant Diego de la Vega, sir!" Diego came to attention and saluted.

"At ease, lad," he said, offering his hand. "What a fine cut of man ye' are! I'd run away with ye' too if I were a wily lass. Glad to have ye' here with us in the fight, m'boy! My stars above, aren't ye' a bull of a man!" he said, now turning to Sergeant Gonzales. The old soldier snapped to attention.

"Señor!" Gonzales barked

"Sergeant Gonzales doesn't speak English, I'm afraid," Claudette told him.

"Aye, well, *bienvenidos amigo*," Riley said, offering the old man his hand.

Gonzales took it and tried his best English, "How do you do?"

"This is Bernardo, sir" Diego pointed to the old man on the driver's bench. "He understands some English, but he does not speak."

"Glad to meet ye', good sir," Riley bowed. Bernardo smiled and uttered unintelligibly as he signaled with his hands.

"Good heavens above! What happened to his tongue?!" Riley recoiled.

"It was cut out in his youth, sir, by Spanish missionaries," Diego told him.

"Is there no end to man's cruelty?!" Riley gasped. Bernardo smiled and shrugged, then replied with hand signals.

"He says to not worry," Diego translated, "he and my grandfather paid them back in full."

"Aye, rightfully so. Good to have ye' with us, sir." Riley patted the old man on the back.

"Ah, ga ba!" Carlito called out, pressing his wooden horse into the man's side.

"Well, if it isn't the US Cavalry attacking m'flanks now!" Riley chuckled, picking up the child. Carlito squealed in delight as Riley hoisted him in the air before handing him back to his mother. "Well, shall we get to the business of handin' out the guns, then?" Riley turned back to Pierre. "I got a whole new batch of men, courtesy of the Yankees. They be itchin' to get some payback soon, I suppose."

The legion was called to order, then company by company, they lined up to receive their new weapons. Claudette sat next to Pierre at a table brought out by the men. She kept the ledger, writing down the names and companies of the men, then recorded that they received a musket and a bayonet. Diego and Sergeant Gonzales busied themselves opening the crates and handing out the weapons while Bernardo kept Carlito occupied.

"Private Liam Shelly, 1st Company, Saint Patrick's, ma'am," a young man said shyly, as he came to the table. Claudette looked up from her ledger and smiled warmly at him causing his freckled face to turn even redder. She was returning her attention to writing when his brass US belt buckle caught her eye. She gasped and looked back up at him. "Um…thank you," the young man said nervously, then shuffled off to receive his weapons. She looked back along the line. Several of the men were wearing light blue American uniforms.

Bewildered, she looked around to see if anyone else was noticing the number of enemy soldiers seemingly amongst them. No one seemed to care.

The men re-formed into ranks with their new muskets proudly placed on their shoulders. A priest came and gave mass in Latin. Claudette followed the rest in kneeling, rising, and responding to the prompts. She felt Diego's hand softly take hers. She turned and smiled at him. He winked, causing her to giggle shyly before returning her attention to the sermon. The priest gave the homily in English in which he emphasized the sanctity of defending this Catholic nation from an invading army of heretics. She could hear rumblings of agreement from the men as they listened. They then lined up to take the communal bread and wine and to have their muskets blessed with a dash of holy water.

The priest gave a final prayer in English. Then the master sergeant released the men for the day. They gathered in clusters and chatted excitedly about their new guns. "Never thought I'd be carrying the ol' Brown Bess again!" one of the men said admiring his musket.

"Aye, I almost wonder if we've been tricked back into Her Majesty's army!" his mate added, causing a round of laughs.

"I'd rather serve the Devil himself than the damn English!" another piped in.

"Or the bloody Yankees for that matter!" said another.

"We'll be shootin' the bastards soon enough. I've already made a list of who I'm shootin' first," said the first man, gaining a round of laughter.

A general sense of celebration broke out as Mexican women arrived with carts full of food. Major Riley insisted that Pierre and his party stay for supper, promising them rooms for the night in the house he had commandeered for his headquarters. "Ye' can get back to ye' dour existences in the mornin.' There'll still be plenty-a war to being havin' then."

Guitars and fiddles began to play as the women lit lanterns and torches that flickered and glowed in the early twilight. Fireflies began to flutter about adding their own illumination to the show. A soft evening breeze swept away the afternoon heat.

With Carlito safely under Bernardo's care, Claudette and Diego sat down with their cups of wine and terracotta plates full of beans and roasted pork. The food was spiced with cilantro and chili pepper. They scooped it up with freshly made tortilla as they watched the Mexican town folk dance. The women spun around, twirling their colorful skirts, throwing them from side to side with the rhythm.

Earthen jugs of mezcal were passed around as they finished their meals. The instruments passed around too until Diego, not being able to help himself, happily accepted a guitar and joined the ensemble. Claudette, feeling the effects of the food and wine, closed her eyes and let out a satisfied sigh. The moment of serenity passed quickly as she sensed a new presence sitting down next to her.

"It's not a bad life here, is it?" the familiar voice said in French.

"No, it's not," Claudette said, opening her eyes. She watched her husband speaking with the other musicians. "We are very happy here."

"Hmm..." Pierre said. He watched as well as Diego and his new friends decided on the next tune and then began to play. "Do you love him?"

"With all my heart," she said, shaking her head as if any other reply would simply be untrue. Pierre was silent for a moment, then spoke.

"Perhaps I do too..." he said wistfully. She turned to him and raised an eyebrow. "...probably as much as I hate him," he continued with a shrug and his charming upside-down smile. She elbowed him softly.

"You're a beast!" she laughed, then caught herself. She couldn't let his charm wear away the anger and the memory of the terrible suffering he had caused her.

Pierre sat silently, sensing the turmoil inside her. "You're right," he said plainly without humor. "I want to apologize for what I did to you." She stared off at the dancers, not really focusing on anything, fighting to hold back her tears. She could feel his eyes on her. "Love will make you do crazy things..."

"Love?!" she said, turning and boring her dark eyes into him, causing him to flinch. "What do you know about love?" She swiftly turned her eyes back to her husband and the other musicians, knowing that if she held Pierre's gaze any longer she would dissolve into tears.

"I've much to learn, it is true," Pierre said, at last, looking off to the musicians as well. He watched for a moment then spoke again. "If anything ever happened to him, would you ever consider me?"

Claudette scoffed, shaking her head slowly, daring not to look at him for fear of crying.

"How can you ask me such a thing?" she said softly.

The music stopped. A group of soldiers walked up to the musicians. "For cryin' out loud, boys, give us somethin' we can dance to!" one of them said. The Mexican musicians shrugged, most of them not understanding the English. "Somethin' like this, lads!" the man said. He pulled out a tin whistle and started playing a jaunty tune with a rollicking beat. The melody was both dark and happy at the same time. One of the other Irishmen gestured, asking if he could borrow a fiddle. The Mexican fiddler shrugged and handed it to him. Soon the fiddle was joining the melody. Another man started marking the beat with a hand drum.

"Allow me to join ye,' lads," another man approached with a strange instrument tucked under his arm. It was a set of pipes into which he pumped air from a bladder with his arm. The instrument gave off an eerie constant drone as he played individual notes with his fingers. It sounded like a chorus of sheep singing in the green fields of Ireland. Diego listened intently, nodding his head with the rhythm. It was a one-two beat, but each beat had a triplet feel. He dashed his fingernails across the strings, fingering the odd chord changes with the music.

"There ye' go, lad!" one of the men slapped his shoulder. "That's it!"

Men removed their jackets and danced in their shirtsleeves with their hands clasped behind their backs. They kicked high with their feet never seeming to fully touch the ground. Other men grabbed their Mexican sweethearts or any girl standing alone. The couples lined up in groups of four and started dancing together in intricate and complex patterns. Some broke into laughter as they bumbled their way through the dance moves.

"Ah, it's a *céilí*!" Pierre said, dropping his previously serious tone.

"A what?" Claudette turned to him.

"A *céilí*, an Irish country dance. Come!" he said, getting to his feet and offering his hand. "Let's forget all this drama for a moment and have some fun while we still can." Claudette frowned, looked around, then sighed and took his hand. He dragged her into the line of dancers in which she was immediately swept up and twirled around as they interchanged with other couples. Suddenly all the worry seemed to slip away as she laughed and spun, her skirts opening like a blossom in the sun. The Mexican girls smiled at seeing her join in. The Irishmen winked at her, then blushed when she smiled back. She caught a glance of Diego who was watching her intently. She blew him a kiss which caused all the darkness to disappear and give way to the boyish grin she loved so much. He looked back to his fellow musicians and threw himself into his rhythmic strumming with new fiery passion.

At last, the first set of jigs ended just as Claudette passed Pierre off to yet another pretty Mexican girl. "Whew!" she let out breathlessly, fanning herself. "You must excuse me. I'm still recovering my strength from the fever!" With that, she withdrew, leaving Pierre with a disappointed look on his face. He made a move to follow, but his new partner tugged on him with a smile, bidding him to stay and dance with her. She dragged him back into the mix as the music started up again with a new set of reels.

Claudette slumped back down in her spot, grateful to have ridden herself of Pierre for the moment. She picked up her cup and frowned as she looked into its empty bottom.

"Never fear, lass," the big Irishman plopped down next to her. He removed the cork from a bottle with his teeth and filled her cup, then his own.

"Thank you," she said, taking a sip.

"Aye, just takin' m'opportunity to talk to a pretty lady, now that you're alone," Riley said with a chuckle. Claudette's eyes went wide with fear as she looked at the big imposing man. Riley let out a laugh. "Take it easy, lass. I'm not flirtin' with ye,' I'm just being Irish."

Claudette laughed and blushed slightly, "My apologies, I didn't mean to…"

"Oh, it's fine. But I can see why the boys be fightin' over ye,' I do."

They watched the dancers for a moment until Claudette could no longer contain her curiosity. "Those men…in the American uniforms…"

"Aye, yes. Fresh from the Yankee side, they are. We'll get 'em properly dressed in the mornin.'"

"They're deserters?!" she asked, eyeing the men with new scrutiny.

"Aye, the whole lot of them," Riley answered, taking a sip.

"Aren't you concerned about their loyalty? Can you trust such men?" she wondered incredulously.

"Sure! I'm twice a deserter m'self. Far be it from me for judgin' another man such as I," he said with a shrug.

Claudette looked at him with new eyes, "I'm sorry. I didn't mean to speak out of turn."

"Ay, no offense taken, darlin.' It's a fair question," he winked at her then refilled their glasses. Embarrassed, Claudette turned back to watch the dancers. At last, Riley broke the awkward pause between them. "I joined the British Army because I was hungry. I did well too for an Irishman despised by the English. They made me sergeant and all. They sent me to Canada, far from home. I suppose I got lonely and tired of being cold. I crossed over to Michigan and started a life there workin' for another Irishman. Got little love from him either. I suppose I got cold and lonely there too. Michigan is a cold and lonely place, lass. God save the poor souls doomed to a life there."

"I joined the Yankee Army at Fort Mackinaw, lookin' for a way out. I was happy to come to sunny Mexico, I was, lass. Made m'way to sergeant again too, I did. But the Americans are worse than the damn English when it comes to hatin' an Irishman. Even the bastards that can trace their grandpappies to the old country hate the new man fresh off the boat. They be puttin' the lash to them for th' most minor offenses, they do. But worse than that, lass, they be hatin' the old religion, the one true faith, forcin' us to participate in their damned heretical sermons and bannin' us from attendin' mass, they do."

Riley let out a sigh and watched the dancers for a moment, then continued. "The Mexicans offered us the freedom to practice our shared faith. They promised us all land, too, once we get th' war sorted out. For th' first time, I feel like I'm fightin' for a country that doesn't hate me, and maybe…that's a country worth dyin' for…"

Those last words sent a shiver down her spine as she watched her husband play music with these men who were willing to die for this country that he loved so much. She wondered if he was so willing to die too. A group of Poles and Germans came and took over the instruments. Diego handed off his guitar and walked back to her as the new musicians started up a heavy polka beat. This brought a new cheer from the crowd as many of the Mexicans rushed to the dance floor to join in.

"Well played, sir," John Riley said, getting up while clapping his hands. "I've been guardin' ye' lady for ye' while ye' were gone. A fine lass she is."

"You have my thanks, friend," Diego said taking the seat Riley was offering.

"And ye' shall have some of m'wine too, lad," Riley said, filling Diego's cup.

"Stay and have another drink with us," Diego offered.

"Why, I'd be charmed to, lad," Riley said, then looked over his shoulder. A rider was approaching the camp, and from the look on the man's face, it seemed to be urgent. "It seems I have some business to attend," Riley said, then excused himself and strode off to meet the messenger. Diego watched intently as the horseman saluted Riley, spoke to him briefly, handed him a piece of paper, then rode away. Riley read it over as he walked up to the band. The musicians instinctively finished their tune, allowing the major the opportunity to speak.

"Boys," his big voice filled the air, causing everyone to quiet, "the Americans are on the move. A column has moved out of Puebla and is swingin' around to approach us from the south." This caused a murmur among the crowd. "I recommend ye' be gettin' some sleep now, lads, because we be movin' out in th' mornin' to meet them." A cheer broke out among the men eager for action and perhaps some payback from their one-time commanders.

Claudette looked at Diego. He was silently watching the men talk excitedly and clap each other on the back. She knew he was disappointed that he wasn't going with them. She also knew not to talk about it or to let him know she was relieved he wasn't.

She didn't realize how tipsy she was until she got to her feet when an orderly came to show them to their room. She could see Pierre beckoning a young Mexican girl to come with him as the orderly approached him as well. She couldn't help but feel some satisfaction as the girl begged off, pulling her arm away with a smile and a shake of her head. The look of embarrassment and defeat was even better when he turned and realized that they had been watching his failed attempt at wooing the girl to his bed. Still, it was awkward walking with him to the house. She was relieved once the orderly deposited him in his room and closed the door.

The orderly then presented them their room next door, bidding them goodnight as he closed the door behind him. Diego started taking off his uniform. She watched for a moment, thinking how dashing he looked in his cavalryman's jacket, and how lovely his olive skin contrasted with the white shirt beneath. He pulled the shirt off and then plopped onto the bed with a sigh. She sat down and wrapped her arms around him, then kissed him softly on his bare shoulder. She could feel his tension softening with her touch. "What is it?" she asked at last.

He let out a breath, then spoke as he looked up to the ceiling. "I saw you dancing with him…"

"I didn't know how to say no, my darling, I swear, I…"

He chuckled lightly, waving his hand as if to fan away her fears. "It's alright, my love," he said then turned to her and smiled. The candlelight sparkled in his big green eyes. There was a deep warmth and kindness in them as well as soft echoes of pain. He took her hand and squeezed it. "It's alright," he said again, nodding his head. He looked away again as if looking into her dark inquisitive eyes was too much to bear.

"Diego…?"

"If something were to happen to me…you could go to him. I'd be happy to know you and the boy were safe."

"Diego," she said firmly, squeezing his arm, "nothing is going to happen to you. You're going to teach. We're going to have a life…"

He turned back to her. The intensity in his eyes was enough to stop her mid-sentence. "You've seen it. You know it's coming. I can feel it in you," he told her.

"Diego, you're drunk. This is foolish talk," she pleaded.

"It's why you stopped looking at your crystal ball. It's why you don't read your cards anymore," he continued.

"Gypsy parlor games, all of it!" she said emphatically, boring her dark eyes into him. The hardness in his eyes broke. He smiled softly, as if he knew she was lying and felt sorry for her, felt sorry for all the pain they both knew she would have to endure. She tightened her jaw, fighting back the tears that were now threatening to overtake her.

She lurched forward and kissed him, then scrambled onto his lap and started grinding into him as she smothered him in more kisses. "Shut up and make love to me now," she gasped. Diego widened his eyes, then he looked at the thin wall that separated them from Pierre's room. She followed his eyes, then turned back to him with a devious smile. "Oh, I want him to hear. May his loneliness be complete!" she said, pulling off her dress.

They threw themselves into each other, frantically making love with desperate abandon as if they had a thirst they could not quench. At last, they lay in each other's arms, their sweat soaking into the bottom sheet, the rest of the bedding discarded on the floor. Claudette could feel their combined heat radiating off them and mixing into the humid tropical air.

She woke to the sound of him snoring. The candle had burned itself down to a stub. She got up to blow it out. Diego mumbled something and reached for her, then turned and went silent. She waited for a moment until she could tell by his breathing that he was asleep again. The night air had become cool. She covered him with the discarded blankets and then moved to the dresser to blow out the flame. Her bag sat on the floor. She felt something calling her from deep inside it. She looked back at her husband. He was still asleep.

She dug into the bag and pulled out her crystal ball. She closed her eyes and breathed slowly, clearing her mind, then peered into it, allowing her senses to spread out into the great void. She could see the reflection of the candle flickering inside the glass sphere. She peered deeply into it. The further she reached, the farther the flame seemed. It became more and more unreachable until it fluttered and died out.

The room seemed colder. A chill ran through her. She quickly put the ball away as if it were suddenly too painful to touch. She crawled under the blankets and snuggled up next to his warm body. His arm came around her and held her tight. She closed her eyes and reveled in his warmth, trying hard not to wake him with her weeping.

She woke to the sounds of horns, drums, and marching men. Diego was gone. The room was already filled with sunlight. She wondered how long she had been sleeping. She threw on her dress and slipped out of the room. She found him on the veranda in his shirtsleeves and pantaloons. He was standing there watching the troops march by, on their way to face the Americans. She wrapped her arm around him and rested her head on his shoulder. She knew he was frustrated he wasn't marching with them. She was grateful he wasn't.

Chapter Thirty-Three: The Truce

"Silence!" Sergeant Gonzales barked, "...and stand straight!"

The teenage boys flinched at the big old man's booming voice, then quickly came to attention. Gonzales walked along their ranks, prodding them with his switch to stick out their chests, suck in their guts, and hold their chins high.

They were all sons of wealthy and powerful men, many of whom made up the officer corps that was defending the country at this very moment. The students had been listening all day to the far-off cannons. There was definitely a fight going on somewhere south of them; a fight frustratingly out of view even from the heights of Chapultepec Castle which loomed from its hilltop over the western and southwestern approaches to the city. Once past this imposing fortress, an invading army would have to navigate one of the two narrow causeways that cut through the marshy fields to get to the gated walls of the city.

Chapultepec was meant to be a summer palace for the Viceroy from Spain. Now it was the home of the *Heroico Colegio Militar*, a military academy where Mexico's heroes of tomorrow were trained and educated. But for Diego, it was where his failures had left him as a babysitter of children instead of fighting for his country. To make matters worse, he wasn't much older than the children he was now teaching.

"Aren't you a little old to be enrolling?" a clerk had asked him, looking up over his reading glasses when Diego first reported for duty. He had to explain, much to his embarrassment, that he was not a student, but rather the new fencing master. He had to explain this a lot in the days that followed as fellow instructors challenged him for walking the halls without a pass. Even the students weren't quite sure what his role was.

"Men, before you master the sword, you must master your feet," Diego explained to his cadets. They blinked back at him in confusion. They were now lined up before him in what was a ballroom but was now used as a gym.

"Like so," he said, dropping into the en garde position. He then advanced and retreated, demonstrating the proper footwork. He broke the class into pairs for them to practice. He, Sergeant Gonzales, and Bernardo walked among pairs to coach them and correct their form.

One of the boys rose from his stance and walked to a window. He stared out with a blank look on his face.

"What are you looking at?!" Gonzales yelled.

The boy looked at him for a moment and then back to the window. "They're coming back…" he said, pointing with his finger.

"Who?!" Gonzales bellowed. He strode to the window with the switch in his hand, ready to give the insolent boy a whack. He lowered it slowly as he peered out the window.

The others rose from their stances and walked to the windows as well. Some stepped outside and stood on the walls to get a better view. Diego realized he had lost control of the class. He shrugged and stepped outside to join them on the wall. Students from all over the academy and their teachers were now joining the crowd. They spoke in low murmurs as they looked down at the spectacle.

Thousands of soldiers were crossing the valley below. There were no formations, no order; just mobs of men. Some were running. Many were missing their hats and muskets. Their uniforms were torn and dusty. Some were helping others walk. Others were outright carrying men on their shoulders. Wounded men lay on carts pulled by donkeys. Other carts were laden with the dead stacked like logs.

"This does not look good…" Sergeant Gonzales mumbled from behind. Diego turned to look at him, then at the boys in his class who had found their way outside.

"Back inside the gymnasium, everyone!" Diego shouted with a new sense of anger and authority. The boys flinched, blinked, then turned and ran back inside. Sergeant Gonzales turned to him and smiled. He patted Diego on the shoulder before following the boys. Now, other teachers were beginning to order their students back into the classrooms as well.

Diego's students were all standing at attention when he re-entered. He walked along the ranks, eyeing each boy intently. "Your time as children is over," he told them. "Your country may very well need you far sooner than you expect. When it does…you must be ready to fight! You must be ready to die for your flag!" he said, pointing to the green, white, and red flag bearing the eagle with a serpent in its claws, a symbol of their ancient Aztec roots. He scanned their faces. They beheld their banner with stoic determination. Tears of pride rolled down some of their faces. "Will you be ready!?" he shouted

"Yes, sir!" the boys shouted back in unison.

"Good! Twenty laps around the gym! Follow me!" He led them in the run. Sergeant Gonzales jogged up alongside him. "You don't need to run, old friend," Diego told him.

"I'm not dead yet," Gonzales laughed, slapping him on the back.

The news traveled quickly. General Valencia had ignored orders to hold at the village of San Ángel, which lay about seven miles south of the city. Instead, he moved his army farther south, past the village of Padierna, using the seemingly impassable lava fields of El Pedregal to protect his left flank. But the Americans surprised him by finding a path through the lava and enveloping his men with enfilading fire.

Santa Anna marched a force out to save him but was cut off. They fought a desperate retreat the next day. The Irishmen and their fellow comrades of the *San Patricios* made a gallant stand at the Churubusco River. This allowed the rest of the army to escape. But the Americans eventually overwhelmed the *Patricios*. They captured John Riley and about eighty of his men.

"*Mon Dieu*, what will happen to them?" Claudette gasped. Diego had been telling her the news as they lay in bed that evening.

"I don't know," he said, staring into the darkness. "They're not just prisoners of war, they're deserters…traitors, even."

"God, help them," she whispered, shuddering as she squeezed his hand. The idea of something cruel happening to those happy, smiling men filled her with dread.

The next day brought happier news. A truce had been declared.

The vicious two-day fight had left both sides badly bruised and depleted. Claudette hoped and prayed, like so many others, that this was the beginning of an ever-lasting peace. Suddenly, things didn't seem so dire. The quieting of the guns had brought back the gentle sounds of birds and the late-summer breeze rustling through the trees. A general calm lay upon the city and on the faces of the citizens as they negotiated the busy markets. Claudette bought flowers from an old lady's stand to liven up their room at the castle.

"Non, non!" she chided Carlito, who was trying to put a sunflower blossom in his mouth. She shifted him to her other hip to keep him from picking at the petals as she walked.

The cool breeze brought the promise of autumn. She closed her eyes and sighed, feeling its embrace. She decided she'd explore the academy's library today. Maybe there were some books in French, English, or perhaps she should try something in Spanish, the language of her new home. Perhaps, she'd find a novel written for young readers, like the students of the academy. She thought maybe she could learn by reading children's books to Carlito. The thought of a good book and a hot cup of coffee on a cool autumn morning filled her with delight. Perhaps now, she, Diego, and Carlito could truly begin their lives without the constant threat of death and doom hanging over them.

But Diego knew better.

Even though neither side was allowed to make any movements or fortify their positions, Santa Anna was making the most of this reprieve. Hidden from American eyes by the city walls, work crews fortified the defenses while commanders replenished and reorganized their troops. Diego was eager to pitch in any way he could. He volunteered himself and a crew of equally eager cadets for everything from building defenses to sentry duty, all in the hope of having some kind of role in the fight to come.

"Remember, men," he told his students during their fencing lessons, "you must be ready to fight and die for your country." The boys took this with grim determination. "You must defend your flag!"

Ironically, the first thing he and his cadets were called to defend were the Americans.

The US forces were overextended and cut off from their supply chain out of Veracruz. As a condition of the truce, Santa Anna allowed them to buy supplies in the city. But an angry mob turned them away at the gates, hurling rocks and insults from the walls at the bewildered American quartermasters and wagoneers. The president quickly sent apologies and promised he'd provide protection when they returned. The Americans came back the next day, once again, with a train of about a hundred empty wagons pulled by mule teams.

Diego scanned the walls one more time, making sure they were clear of civilians. Only military personnel would be allowed up there this time. He turned and looked at his men. They were really just boys, scared boys in shakos, trying to look brave with their British muskets and bayonets. He wondered if he looked the same. Behind them, a murderous crowd was gathering.

"Let the Americans die of starvation!" someone shouted.

"…and the traitor, Santa Anna!" came another.

"…and you cowards that defend them!" a third shouted.

"Courage, men," Diego looked to his boys, "remember your duty." Some of the cadets nodded and mumbled assent. Some were visibly shaking, clutching their muskets for assurance.

Diego turned to Sergeant Gonzales and nodded. The big man winked at him, then turned toward the sentries and bellowed, "Open the gates!"

The big wooden doors creaked and moaned as the sentries dragged them open. The angry shouts from the crowd grew until the overlapping words became indiscernible as the crowd surged forward.

"Hold them back!" Diego shouted. His boys pushed back with their muskets and bayonets, creating an opening in the mob for the Americans and their carts. Diego turned back to the gates.

A young officer led the column of carts through the portal. With him were a handful of other young officers, followed by carts driven by sergeants and some privates to help with loading. None of them were armed. The lead man sat high on his horse. He was clean-shaven with thick brown hair tucked under his cap. He had bright blue eyes that scanned the hostile scene before him. He smiled softly as his eyes found Diego's. He leaped from his saddle with the grace of a well-trained horseman. Then led his horse by the reins. Diego was surprised to see he wasn't nearly as tall as he had seemed once he was on the ground. The man approached him with an extended open hand.

"You must be our escort," he said. "I am Lieutenant Ulysses Grant, quartermaster for the 4th US Infantry, but my friends call me Sam."

Diego looked at the man's hand for a moment and then back into his eyes, "I am not your friend, Lieutenant. The quicker we do this, the better I can protect you. I suggest you get back on your horse and follow me."

A flicker of hurt surprise flashed in the man's eyes. He retracted his hand awkwardly, then placed it on his hip before dropping it all together as if he were not quite sure what to do with it. "Alright then," he said, stiffening up, "we will follow your lead, Lieutenant." He turned and bounded back into the saddle, once again with the ease of someone well accustomed to riding horses. With a grimace, he gave Diego a nod, then turned and beckoned his wagon train to move forward.

The crowd surged forward as well, ramping up their insults. Diego's cadets created a wedge, using their muskets and bayonets to create a path.

"Here are your damned supplies, you sons of whores!" someone shouted.

Stones and rotten fruit began to fly through the air, pelting the Americans as they tried to shield themselves with their arms. Diego and his cadets cringed and ducked as they pushed forward, plowing a path through the mob. Hands reached up and grabbed at the American officer leading the column. He swatted at them, but this only infuriated the crowd more. Diego turned just in time to see him snatched from his horse and swallowed by the crowd.

"¡Mierda!" he hissed before plunging into the mob, batting people away with the flat of his sword. The man's horse reared in panic, causing some to leap out of the way. Diego reached into the pile of people, feeling the punches as he worked to pry hands off the crouching American. He began hammering people with the hilt of his sword until they finally broke away.

"Arrgh!" he roared at the crowd with his sword in his hand, bearing his teeth as he stood over the man lying on the ground, daring the next person to come forward and die. Some of his cadets shuffled in quickly and created a ring of bayonets to hold them off. There was only a brief moment of stunned silence before the men in the crowd started yelling again and prodding the others to surge forward with them to overtake Diego's grossly outnumbered force protecting the downed American.

A sudden shriek of fear rippled through the mob as people began to look up from their prey to the new approaching threat. Diego heard the whinnying of horses and the clatter of hooves. People started screaming and running as mounted lancers came crashing into the crowd. Diego moved out of the way as the American lifted himself off the ground and began dusting himself off. "Are you hurt?" Diego asked him.

"Just my pride, I suppose," the man said with a soft smile as he picked up his cap and slapped it against his thigh to dust it off before placing it back on his head. Diego did not smile back.

"Sam!" one of the other American officers shouted as they ran to him. "Are you alright?!"

"Yes, yes," the officer said, pointing to Diego, "thanks to this man here." The small group of American officers looked at Diego with stunned awe. The one called Sam then turned to him. His voice took an earnest tone. "Thank you," he said. "I believe you've saved my life."

"Do not thank me, Gringo," Diego said, staring deep into the man's blue eyes. "The next time you see me, I'll be coming to take it."

The man regarded him for a moment as his smile faded. "I shall remember your face well, then."

Chapter Thirty-Four: Punishment

The truce did not last long. The peace talks fell apart over where the new borders would be drawn between the United States and Mexico. Frustrated, US General Winfield Scott could no longer politely pretend not to notice that Santa Anna had been overtly violating the terms of the truce by fortifying his position, all while stalling for time. The Americans attacked the very next day.

This time, the cadets had a grand view of the fight from the heights of the castle walls. The Americans attacked *el Molino del Rey*, or the "King's Mill," which lay just about a thousand yards southwest of Chapultepec Castle. It was an industrial compound of long, low-sitting stone buildings which included a mill, a slaughterhouse, and an old foundry that once had been used to make cannons. Santa Anna did nothing to stop the Americans from believing it still did. His spies told him this was where they would attack. He made sure there would be a significant force waiting to greet them.

Juan Escutia flinched at the deafening explosion as he approached the academy. He remained crouched for a moment until he was certain he was still alive. The castle was still there when he opened his eyes. It loomed over him like a monster, ready to swallow him whole. He stood slowly and then glanced back at the path he had taken from the city. He could turn around and go home right now. It would only take him about a week to get there. His father would be ashamed and probably give him a good beating, but his mother would understand. She would protect him…his sweet mother.

He felt his throat tightening at the thought of her. He sucked in a sob and quickly wiped the tears away with his sleeve before anyone caught him crying. That would only make this nightmare even worse.

"*¿Hola?*" his voice echoed through the halls. He blinked in awe at the high ornate ceilings, the checkered tiled floors, and the large stained glass windows. It was like he was in a strange dream where he was alone in this abandoned palace, surrounded by sheer opulence unlike he had ever seen.

Finally, in the silence, he could hear it: distant cannons, crackling muskets, and people murmuring. The sounds got louder as he moved through the halls until he could see people coming in and out of the large doors that led to the rear terrace. There were hundreds of people outside. Many were students in uniform. Nobody seemed to notice him. They were all fixated on what was happening in the valley below.

The roar of cannons was now deafening. An enormous plume of black smoke rose into the sky like some giant monster set to swallow the world. Sulfuric smoke and hot ash wisped through the crowd. White flakes were settling in people's hair and on their shoulders like some kind of demonic snow.

He moved through the crowded grounds, past the fountains, to the balustrade. He peered down into the hellish scene below. Thousands of soldiers swarmed around a collection of buildings in the distance like angry ants. There were constant flashes of musket fire and sharp jets of flames spitting out of the big guns. Men were clubbing, hacking, and stabbing at each other in chaotic masses of roiling violence. Piles of lifeless bodies lay everywhere. In the center, a building burned with ferocious intensity. The black smoke blotted out the sun creating a huge shadow over the scene. It was lit instead by the inferno below that licked the sky with flames, creating what seemed to be the twilight of humanity itself.

Diego saw the boy stepping cautiously through the crowd. The young man wore civilian clothes and a wide-eyed frightened look on his face as if he expected to be set upon by a thousand enemies at any moment. The boy made it to the balustrade and looked down. His face went immediately pale. Diego made his way to him. The boy flinched as Diego set his hand on his shoulder. The young man looked embarrassed as he spun around.

"Are you new?" Diego asked him, smiling to settle the boy's nerves.

"Yes, sir" Juan stammered. "I have my admission papers right here," he added, then frantically began searching his pockets.

"*¡Tranquilo!*" Diego soothed. "We have plenty of time for that. I'm sure everything is in order." The boy cracked a shy smile for the first time. His eyes were puffy and crusted with a few flakes of dried tears. Diego smiled warmly at him. "Come, today may be the best lesson you learn during your entire time here. Look at those men below." Juan turned back to the valley. Streams of men were falling back from the buildings where the battle raged. Many were wounded, carried in carts, or helped along by others. One heavily bandaged man carried the national flag, using the staff to help him hobble along.

"You see that man? He did not let our flag fall to the enemy. He took those wounds to save her honor. Those men you see laying dead on the ground gave their lives so that Mexico may live and fight another day. They are heroes of the nation, son. You must not be afraid to die for your country." The boy turned back to him. His puffy eyes were now full of wonderment. Diego smiled and squeezed his shoulder. "Every man dies, but few of us get the honor to die in glory for our country."

The Americans took *el Molino del Rey* but paid dearly for it. Over a hundred men were dead and hundreds more were wounded. Their reward was a couple of old gun molds found in the old foundry that hadn't been used in years. Then a powder magazine exploded in one of the buildings, killing and wounding even more men: men the isolated American army could hardly afford to lose.

For the Mexicans, there was much to celebrate in what technically was a defeat. They had lost the collection of old stone buildings that they had been using as an outpost, but they had fought hard and bloodied the seemingly unstoppable Americans.

The celebrations didn't last long. The Americans were on the doorstep. It was clear they would try to enter the city through the gates of San Cosme and Belén. Chapultepec Castle was the only thing standing in their way. It guarded the two narrow causeways that led to the gates. The causeways were the only path through the marshy wetlands that surrounded the city walls.

More and more troops poured into the castle and prepared for battle in the days that followed. The cadets drilled endlessly, practicing on the big guns of the castle and with their muskets and sabers. Fear and excitement mixed on their faces. "Have courage, men," Diego told his wide-eyed boys. "We will hold them here. We will protect our nation's honor with our lives."

Claudette was not so excited about the battle to come. She had been volunteering in the hospital set up in the grand corridor of the castle. There she witnessed the ugly result of war. Hundreds of men lay wounded and dying on the floor. Piles of severed limbs grew outside the windows as surgeons tossed them away. The hall echoed with screams, moans, and sobs. She sat and held the hand of a dying man, listening to him call for his mother. "*Tranquilo, hijo,*" she said, using her burgeoning Spanish. "*Estoy aqui.*"

He looked at her with a sudden lucidity that startled her. "*Llévame a casa, ángel,*" he said. A soft serenity spread over his face. She smiled at him, holding his gaze until she realized she was looking into dead eyes. She looked at the ceiling and let out a breath. Then wiped away a tear before looking back at the man and closing his eyes with her hand.

The putrid smell of blood, vomit, and urine was overwhelming, making her dizzy. She shook off the threat of fainting and got to her feet. She had to get some fresh air. She pulled off her blood-crusted apron as she made her way past the wounded and dying men calling out for help.

Outside she could see people gathering along the balustrade, watching something below the castle walls with great interest. Diego was there with his boys. They were all quiet, fixated on whatever it was they were watching. She smiled at the sight of him. Perhaps a moment with her love could wash away all the ugliness she had been forced to see this day.

"What are you looking at?" she asked as she neared them. Diego turned to her with a look that scared her. He shook his head as if to warn her not to look. "What is it?" she asked, now with frightened curiosity as she pushed through the crowd of boys.

The distant sounds of slaps and screams came to her ears as she peered over the wall. Off in the distance, she could see the Americans had tied more than a dozen barebacked men to posts. A man was beating one of them with a whip. There were more of these men, wearing their San Patricio uniforms, standing on carts under a gallows with nooses tied around their necks. They were being made to witness the floggings before their deaths. The man with the whip backed away as another man approached the victim with a red-hot cattle brand. He pressed it into the poor man's face before Claudette had the chance to look away. The scream, though distant, was sickening.

"*Mon Dieu!*" she gasped, quickly drawing her hands to her mouth in horror. She sucked in a sob. "Does their barbarity know no bounds?!" she cried, tears blurring her eyes.

"My love..." Diego reached for her arm.

"Let go of me!" she screeched, tearing her arm away. The others began to turn to watch the scene unfolding behind them. "This is a world full of ugly fucking monsters!" she screamed as she turned and stumbled away.

"Claudette…!" Diego called after her, holding out his hand. She shoved her way through the crowd that was making their way to the balustrade to watch the spectacle. Diego dropped his arm as she disappeared into the crowd. He knew he should go and comfort her. But he could not be a coward in this moment. He could not turn away from the horror, not in front of his boys. He would watch for the sake of those men being tortured and killed before them. These men had sacrificed themselves for his country. They had fought for the true cross against the heathen invaders. He would not turn his back on them now. Diego turned back to watch the next man take his flogging. He flinched at the sight but dared not look away.

Claudette shoved her way through the crowd with unmasked disgust at the eager faces anticipating the show. She was careless of their shouts of indignation as she pushed them aside. She was racing away from the sound. She did not want to hear more of any of it. She didn't want to hear the lash, the screaming, or the reaction of the crowd. She wanted silence, darkness, and to be away from everyone and everything that filled this disgusting, cruel world.

She shuffled down the steps into a supply cellar. She could hear the gasps and shouts from the crowd. "Damn them!" she sobbed. She threw herself to the earthen floor and sobbed until she was heaving, gasping for breath. She could see their faces in her mind, those smiling Irish faces, the clever way they spoke, the way they danced to their music, the way they knelt with her and prayed. She could see those faces now, stoic and stern as they marched to the scaffold. She could see those faces, suddenly covered with black hoods, never to be seen alive again.

She screamed and pulled at her hair, retching what little she had in her stomach onto the floor.

She didn't know how long she lay there. She wasn't sure if she had fainted or slept. She didn't know if she would ever have the strength to pull herself off the floor again. She heard a door creak. Someone was coming down the stairs. A candle began flickering shapes onto the walls.

"My love!" Diego gasped, dropping to his knees and scooping her into his arms.

"Let's leave," she said softly. Then clutching his shirt and balling it in her fist, she spoke more forcefully. "Let's leave now, walk away from all this. I don't care about countries, honor, or duty. We can run away and live as poor farmers. We can live…together…raise Carlito in a world full of love. He deserves to have a father, Diego, not a martyr…please…!" she began to cry. "Live with me!"

"I can't live as a coward," he said softly. "If I must die, I must die like a man."

"Like a man?!" she said, suddenly furious. "Did they die like men!?" she shouted, gesturing to the outside world upstairs. "Like men, dangling from a rope with their heads covered so we don't have to see their tongues sticking out and their eyes bulging as they soil themselves?!"

"My darling, please…" Diego shook his head, fighting his own sense of impending loss, "you are asking me to do something I just can't do."

Claudette pushed herself out of his arms and stood. "You are asking me to do the same," she said, dusting off her hands as she walked away, leaving Diego to sit on the ground soaked with her tears.

Chapter Thirty-Five: Friendship

Claudette heard him enter the room. She was lying in bed, curled up on her side, facing the wall. She did not stir. She could feel her heart racing. It seemed so loud. Surely he could hear it too. He had to know she wasn't sleeping. Diego sighed. She slowly opened her eyes. His silhouette flickered against the wall from the single candle he had brought into the room and set upon the dresser behind him. She could tell that he was stepping lightly, trying not to wake her. Still, his boots clanked on the floor. His saber rattled as he unfastened the belt and propped it against the wall.

She had been dreading this moment, this awkwardness that had wedged itself between them. She had been furious, practicing in her mind all day what she'd say when he came crawling back. Then she was mad when he didn't. Sure, he'd have real reasons to come home late. He would tell her about the preparations they were making for the attack to come. But they would both know he had been avoiding her.

Then she had gotten sad. *Have I wasted the last of our time?* she caught herself thinking as she put Carlito to bed. The ugly hollowness had crept into her stomach again, making her want to fall to the ground and cry; cry for the loss that was coming.

No, she had shaken off the feeling of dread. She would be reasonable when he returned. They would talk sensibly. She would make sure he knew she loved him and only cared for his and Carlito's safety and happiness.

She started feeling the anger again as she got ready for bed. Was he staying away on purpose? Would he come home at all? She never did fall asleep, and now he was here. All the things she wanted to say, all the things she should say, were trapped inside this bubble of silence.

He plopped down next to her, took off his boots, then began to shimmy off his trousers. She could reach out now and touch him. He got up just before the urge overtook her. He blew out the candle and crawled into bed. She knew his eyes were open. She knew he was staring into the darkness.

"I'm taking Carlito to the city," she said, at last, her own voice sounding alien to her, "...to a nursery so he'll be safe during the battle."

Diego was silent. She was about to ask him if he had heard her when he spoke. "You should stay there too," he said at last.

She let out her breath. His answer crushed her. Was he so quick to be rid of her? She chided herself for being foolish. Of course, he was thinking of her safety.

"I belong in the hospital," she finally managed. "I have duties too, you know." Her tone sounded more bitter than she had intended. She regretted it immediately.

"I understand," he said softly.

Of course, he understood, she thought bitterly. Duty was everything to him. He held it higher than love and family. She felt the anger and bitterness pour into her again. She tried to push it away, which only made the tears come once again. She began to sob quietly. She felt his hand on her hip. A wave of relief washed over her with his touch. This only made her cry more. He wrapped his arms around her. She felt herself melting into him. If only this moment could last forever, she thought, if only tomorrow would never come.

She woke with a fright. The room was cold and dark. She reached out and found him sleeping nearby, radiating warmth. She snuggled up next to him, warming herself with the heat that poured off his body. She felt him unconsciously conforming his body to hers. She smiled softly and drifted back to sleep.

He was gone when she woke again. It was dark, but there was a little bit of grey light permeating the room. It allowed her to make out the shape of the dresser, the small writing desk, and the frame of the door to the adjoining room. There she could see a dim flicker between the bottom of the door and the ground. She drew herself out of bed and stepped quietly across the floor.

She gently pushed the door open. Amber light washed over her as she peered inside. Diego was there. She could not deny that he looked absolutely dashing in his uniform and boots. His sword dangled cavalierly at his side. He was holding a candle and looking into Carlito's crib. She wrapped her arms around him and rested her head on his shoulder.

"Why don't you pick him up?" she whispered.

"I don't want to wake him. He's too clever. He'll know I came to say goodbye."

"For now," she corrected him.

"Of course, for now," Diego kissed her head and gave her a squeeze. They were quiet for a moment as they looked at the sleeping child. So much like an angel, he seemed, unsullied by the horrors of the world around him. Claudette had to fight the urge to sweep him up into her arms and smother him with kisses. "He's very handsome," Diego said at last.

"Like his father," Claudette added. Diego let out a humorous scoff. "He's kind and caring like his father too. Like the person his father really is," she added.

Diego chuckled, then spoke, "Perhaps I'll get another chance to be that person: a kind, caring, poor farmer, raising my son properly."

"Ooh, I like that person!" Claudette said, giving him a squeeze.

"Well, maybe not the poor part."

They both chuckled, then quickly quieted themselves as the boy stirred and then settled again in his sleep. A bugle began to sound off in the distance. Diego sighed. "I must go."

"I know. Duty calls," Claudette said, once again regretting the bitterness that seeped into her voice. Diego reached out and lightly squeezed one of her fingers.

"I love you," he said.

"I know," she said, looking at the ground. She couldn't bear to look up into his big green eyes. She knew she'd fall apart at one glance. She could hear his boots clank as he walked away down the hallway. "I love you too…" she mumbled, then regretted not saying it sooner. She wanted to run after him and shout it, but she was frozen where she stood, unable to do anything but stare at the ground.

"Why the hell aren't your pants fastened?!"

Diego smiled as he heard Sergeant Gonzales yelling at an unfortunate student. The cadets were hurrying into their places for morning formation. "What ungodly thing have you been doing to yourself all night?!"

The other students giggled before Gonzales's quick eye snapped them back into silence

"I'm sorry, Sergeant," the poor child gasped as he fumbled to fix his uniform.

"You will be sorry, boy, if I catch you with your whistle out!" Gonzales gave just enough of a flick of his switch toward the boy's crotch to make him reflexively double over. The rest of the boys burst into laughter.

"Silence!" Gonzales shouted, then spied Diego approaching. "Class, attention!" Gonzales and the boys snapped into straight and rigid postures. Even Bernardo straightened himself, still unable to drop his smile.

"At ease, men," Diego said. "Dress your line smartly now, boys. Let's look our best." Gonzales and Bernardo moved up and down the ranks, making sure the boys were evenly spaced in straight lines as Diego took his place in front of the class. They were one of the many classes formed up like platoons on the parade ground of the castle, waiting for the morning announcements before starting the day.

Diego watched the boys stretch their arms out to space themselves from the cadet on the right. A giggle rippled through them as Gonzales forcefully moved one of them into the correct spot. These were the students with whom Diego started and ended each day. After morning formation, they'd normally go on to other teachers to study various topics while he taught fencing to the parade of students that cycled through his gymnasium. But today would be all about preparing for the attack to come.

Suddenly, his students no longer looked like men to him. It was as if the morning breeze blew away the illusion only to reveal the real faces of children standing before him, children preparing to face battle-hardened soldiers just outside the walls.

"Academy, attention!" the school's sergeant major shouted. Diego spun around and snapped to attention, as did all the classes in unison. He was relieved to take his eyes off his boys. The sight of their youthfulness was suddenly too much to bear.

The school's commandant approached the center of the formation with his riding crop tucked smartly under his arm. He stepped onto the dais and spun around to face the students in a well-practiced maneuver. He then nodded to the sergeant major to call them to parade rest.

"Men," the commandant addressed them, "you have been doing your country and your parents proud. Every one of you should take pride in your efforts in the face of the enemy. Your country needed you and you have heeded the call." He paused to look at the young faces which were beaming with pride with a hint of terror. He smiled warmly at them before continuing, "But you are needed elsewhere now. Once released from formation, you will go to your rooms and pack your things. In one hour's time, you'll be ready to march back to the city where you'll be reassigned to the Citadel. There you'll await further orders. Teachers and staff will remain here and assist with the defense of the castle."

A few groans leaked out of the ranks. They were quickly silenced by the sergeants. Diego smiled softly as the relief washed over him. The boys were being moved away from the castle into the safety of the city walls. They would not be here when the Americans attacked.

Claudette took advantage of the large procession marching out of the castle. Knowing that she was the fencing master's wife, the boys were very protective of her. They charmed her with their chivalric sense of duty as they fussed over her and Carlito. They found her a spot on a supply cart where she and her child could ride comfortably to the city. She smiled and thanked the young gentlemen, causing some of them to blush madly at the pretty French woman paying them attention.

She was surprised at the hundreds of adult soldiers marching with them as they made their way along the mile-and-a-half causeway that cut a path through the marshes and flood plains outside of the city walls. *Why are they leaving?* she wondered. Perhaps the Americans were planning to attack somewhere else, she gathered. This idea gave her a warm sense of hope as the sun finally peeked out of the horizon and dazzled the water with golden ribbons of light. Perhaps all this dread she had been feeling was nothing more than silliness.

"Ah, ga!" Carlito let out with excitement. He was pointing at a dragonfly that had perched on the edge of the cart. The sunlight sparkled on its transparent wings.

"Ah, yes," she told him in French. "The angels are watching over us!"

She closed her eyes and drew a deep draught of the morning air. She'd get a cup of coffee as soon as they got to the city. It would be the first thing she'd do, she decided. The thought of it filled her with warm happiness.

She opened her eyes again and immediately began to feel the dread seep back into her stomach. The high city walls were looming ahead. They were approaching the Belén Gate, a fortified entrance into the city at the end of the causeway. Soldiers and laborers were busy digging trenches and building earthworks outside the large oak doors and the small fortress built into the wall. It certainly seemed like they were expecting a fight here, a fight they seemed sure would take place after the fall of Chapultepec Castle. Claudette felt a shiver run through her. It was as if this place held a painful memory of something that was yet to happen.

"*Bon jour, mon ami!*" the familiar voice broke her from her trance.

"Pierre! What are you doing here?" she asked in French, surprised to find some comfort in his presence. Pierre beamed his upside-down smile as he approached the cart and helped her down. He was in rolled-up shirtsleeves and a waistcoat. His long blonde hair was tied back with a few golden wisps that had broken free and lay delicately over his handsome face.

"Customer service, my dear! The president wants cannons protecting every entrance and I just happened to have a few for sale. Voila!" he exclaimed, gesturing to the guns being rolled into their placements, "A 12-pounder and two 8s to protect the good Mexican citizens from the dreadful Yankee Imperialists!"

"You should be ashamed," she said, somewhat playfully, "making profit from war!"

"If not me, then who, mademoiselle?" he smiled slyly. "Besides, I believe in the Mexican cause. I'm merely covering my expenses."

"I'm sure you are…" she said, playfully narrowing her eyes at him.

"Ah, pa!" Carlito reached out and whacked Pierre's arm with his wooden horse.

"Ah! I should be so offended, monsieur!" Pierre laughed as he scooped the child up into his arms. Carlito giggled in delight. "If you were not so adorable, I would demand satisfaction!" Claudette let out a laugh at the joke but couldn't help but wonder if there was any real resentment toward the child that looked so much like his romantic rival. Pierre handed him back to her. "So now we know my nefarious reasons for being here, what about you? What brings you so far from the protection of your dashing hero in his castle to the presence of us mere mortals in the city?"

Claudette laughed and rolled her eyes. "I'm looking for a nursery to watch over Carlito until the danger has passed. I don't want him in the castle when the Americans attack."

"Ah, noble effort, although the president seems to believe the attack will come elsewhere."

"I don't want to leave it to chance."

"Of course," Pierre agreed. "I happen to know of one, exclusive for the children of generals and dignitaries, not the riffraff of the street. I can get you in, but it'll cost you…"

Claudette's eyes widened with apprehension. "What is your price, then?"

"You must take coffee with me afterward."

"Ah, you know me too well," she laughed.

"I know that you are French like me, and we share the same delight in simple pleasures."

Carlito howled in despair as Claudette tried to hand him off to one of the ladies at the nursery. "I'll be back soon, my love, when all is safe," she tried to soothe him but found herself fighting to contain her own tears. It wasn't until he became distracted by a little girl who was trying to push her doll onto him that he stopped crying. The lady set him down, and he quickly crawled off to join her and the rest of the children. "He's only here for a minute and he's already got a girlfriend!" Claudette scoffed.

"He's going to be quite popular!" Pierre added with a laugh.

They sat at a sidewalk cafe afterward and enjoyed rich, dark coffee mixed with scalded milk. Between them sat a plate of small cakes sweetened with cinnamon and honey. Pierre asked her about her work in the hospital. He commended her for her bravery and selflessness in the face of such horrors.

"I merely sell the weapons. I haven't the courage to witness the results," he said with self-effacing humor that she couldn't help but find charming. He told her about his business of buying weapons and smuggling them into Mexico. "Europe's armies have been shrinking and modernizing since Napoleon's wars," he told her, "leaving plenty of surplus arms looking for a home."

"There must be a better way to make a living than dealing in death," she chided.

"I'm merely helping patriotic people liberate their country, my dear," he smiled at her.

"Hmph...!" was her response, knowing it was worthless to continue the argument.

Pierre insisted on escorting her through town as she picked up a few things from the market. "You can't be too careful in any city," he told her, "but especially one under siege!"

She wanted to be annoyed by his presence, but truthfully, she found his familiar company comforting. Still, she took great pleasure in letting him know that she was picking up some things to surprise her husband that evening.

"He's been under so much pressure with preparing the castle and for the assault."

"I can only imagine," Pierre was gentlemanly enough to try to seem sympathetic.

He insisted on hiring an open-air carriage to carry her across the mile-and-a-half causeway that connected the city to the castle. "You don't have to ride all the way with me," she told him as they passed the Belén Gates.

"There's a war on, my dear. I'd hardly call myself a gentleman if I let you go alone. But truthfully," he smiled somewhat nervously, "I've had such a good time seeing you, I don't want it to end."

"You are too kind," she said, then blushed and looked away to the flooded plain along the road.

"Claudette..." he said, then paused to gather his nerve. She slowly turned her eyes to him. "Do you think we could have worked if...if things had played out differently between us?"

"Oh, Pierre," she said kindly, shaking her head, "you mustn't ask me such things."

"I know, it's just that…I know I made a lot of mistakes and perhaps…I didn't realize that…I loved you until it was much too late."

"Pierre, please…"

"I love you still."

She turned her eyes back to the swamps. The sunlight glistened on the water between the reeds. An awkward silence settled between them as the carriage rattled along the causeway. He spoke again at last.

"Ah, we are almost there. I'm sorry. I misspoke. Please don't allow my impertinence to ruin our chance at friendship," he said, the confidence returning to his voice. She finally dared to look at him again. He smiled in relief, "I just want you to know, I'd be here for you if something should happen to him."

She sighed as she gathered her things. "Nothing is going to happen to my husband," she told him and quickly got out, denying him the chance to exit first and help her down the step.

The driver lifted the reins to urge the mules back into motion. "Wait!" Pierre told him in Spanish, then sat back in his seat and watched her walk away with her packages. Her thick black hair bounced against her delicate shoulders as her white linen skirt swished back and forth with her step. He felt himself becoming aroused, then felt the old rage come seeping back in. He bit down on his knuckle. How could one person cause him so much torment?

A collection of cadets walked past the carriage, stealing his attention. *I thought they had all left already*, he thought. "Boy!" he called to one of them in Spanish. The young man stopped and turned to him with trepidation.

"Yes?"

"Do you know the fencing master Sub-Lieutenant Don Diego de la Vega?"

"Yes, we are going to him now," the young man said.

"Good! I'd like you to carry a message for me," Pierre said, flashing a coin to pay for the trouble.

The young man shrugged and stepped forward. Pierre took out his notepad and began to write.

Chapter Thirty-Six: The Commencement of Hostilities

Diego stood with one boot propped on the parapet. He leaned forward, feeling the stretch in his leg as he watched the Americans in the valley below. Their endless campfires flickered like stars in the early twilight. He found the neatly ordered rows of tents strangely satisfying. Here was perfect order in this chaotic world, he thought.

He put his foot down and turned at the sound of approaching steps. There were dozens of cadets standing before him. "What are you doing here?" he asked, scanning their youthful faces. "You're supposed to be at the Citadel in the city."

"We volunteered to stay," one of the boys stepped forward.

"The commandant tried to stop us, but we insisted," another said. "He finally said we could stay but had to report to you for orders."

Diego raised an eyebrow, "Why me?"

Another boy stepped forward. "Because it was you who told us we must be ready to fight," he said, then pointed to the flag waving above the castle, "that we must be ready to die for our country."

Diego felt a rush of vertigo as he looked up at the flag. He looked back at their young faces. All of them were watching him with pride and reverence, waiting for him to say something profound. Nausea crept into his stomach. Gone were the faces of the men he once saw. All he could see now was Carlito's baby face repeated on every boy in uniform before him. He suddenly realized this was something he'd never want for his own son. How could he ask this of other men's children?

What have I done?!

"Please do not deny us our manhood," one of the boys said as if reading his thoughts. "We love our country as much as you do. We deserve to be here too."

Diego cleared his throat and regained his composure, realizing they were reading his face too well. "Of course you do," he told them. He nearly flinched at the relief that spread on their faces. "I'll have sentry assignments for you shortly. We will reconvene here in fifteen minutes. Dismissed!"

The boys came to attention and saluted. Once he returned the salute, they dashed off to the barracks with the glee of school children set loose on the playground. Diego groaned, watching them go. One remained.

"Cadet Escutia," Diego called him, recognizing the newcomer who had been so frightened during the battle at *el Molino del Rey*, just days before.

"A man told me to give this to you, señor," he said, fumbling nervously through his uniform jacket until he produced a folded piece of paper.

"Thank you," Diego said, raising a wary eyebrow at the note. "You may go, Juan, but be back with the others soon!"

"*¡Sí, señor!*" Juan said with a salute. Diego returned it and then watched him run off with the rest. He couldn't help but smile at the young man who only a few days earlier had been fighting back tears at the sight of battle.

He frowned again as he looked back down at the letter. He unfolded it, noticing the elegant handwriting. He was surprised to see it was in English.

9 September 1847

Diego,

You owe me a debt and we are running out of time. It would be unjust, ungentlemanly, and cowardly of you to die a hero to your country without redressing your sins with me first. You betrayed my trust and abused my kindness. I demand satisfaction. I'll be at the base of the west-facing wall before dawn. Come alone with your sword. No seconds required.

If you ever had any love for me as a friend, you will pay me this debt now.

Pierre Godfrey

Diego sighed, folded the letter, and stuffed it in his pocket. He took one more look at the perfectly ordered American camp as the darkness began seeping in all around. Time was running out indeed.

Claudette chided herself for being nervous. She knew even the smallest gesture would be appreciated, but for reasons she didn't quite want to think through, she wanted tonight to be special. Even though they seemed to have patched things up that morning, she worried the rift between them had been allowed to grow in their time apart since.

She felt guilty for spending the day with Pierre. She struggled over whether she should tell Diego. She had done nothing wrong, even though she couldn't stop feeling like she did. No, she would tell him later. She wanted nothing to ruin this evening.

Is he staying away? she wondered. The very thought brought back the sickening dread in her stomach where it grew and threatened to reach into her heart and break it. She felt the tears coming. *God, no, not now*, she prayed, fighting them back. She didn't want to look like she had been crying when he got home.

"Huh!" she gasped. She could hear his boots coming down the hall. She knew the sound of his step by heart. She scanned the small writing desk she had set up as a table. *Damn it, I should have opened the wine to let it breathe*, she thought. She made to get up, then plopped back down on the bed, suddenly not sure what to do with her hands or how she should be sitting.

Diego steeled himself as he entered the corridor that led to their room. Things were already bad enough with the world outside without the argument between him and his wife. Worse yet, he was beginning to see that she was right. She had always been right. He wanted to tell her so. He wanted to tell her that he wanted the life she wanted too: a life together with Carlito, far away from all the ugliness of war. *Perhaps this is what it really means to become a man*, he scoffed, thinking about his previous boyish yearning for adventure and glory.

But telling her that now would just make matters worse. He still couldn't turn away from his duties: his duty to his boys, to the army, to his country, and to Pierre. *Should I tell her?* He shook his head no. She'd never understand. He checked one last time to make sure that Pierre's letter was tucked deep inside his jacket as he approached the door. He felt bad for holding secrets from her but was certain that she must not know about the appointment he had with his old friend in the morning.

He paused for a moment, drew in a deep breath, and opened the door. The amber candlelight washed over him. The smell of roasted chicken and baked bread suddenly reminded him that he hadn't eaten in hours. But all thoughts of food vanished at the sight of her.

"I'm so glad you're home," she smiled, "have you eaten yet?"

The sight of her struck him silent. It was as if in all this chaos, he had forgotten just how beautiful she was. She was sitting on the bed. Her thin white nightgown barely concealed her lithe body. Her thick black hair fell softly on her shoulders. Her red lips contrasted with her light skin. Her dark eyes glistened in the candlelight. He found himself becoming aroused and embarrassed.

"I...uh...had something for lunch," he told her.

Her smile grew. She could see the effect she was having on him. "Come," she lifted herself from the bed and walked toward him, "I picked up half a roasted chicken and some real bread from town today."

Diego closed the door behind him and swept her into his arms. She smelled of rose water and clean linen. He kissed her, trying not to crush her tiny body with his passion. She gently pushed him back. "We need to open the wine and let it breathe before we eat."

"Of course, my love."

"Plus, it is better to make love on an empty stomach, is it not?" she said slyly, allowing his arousal to press up against the soft curve of her stomach.

His eyes went wide with embarrassment. Then the mischievous boyish smile she loved so much came to his lips, pushing away the dark apprehension he had walked in with. "I believe so," he told her.

He uncorked the bottle using his gun worm, a small tool in he kept in his pistol cleaning kit. It had two iron swivels at the end used to pull debris from the barrel. She marveled at how deftly he used it to open the bottle.

"You've done this before," she said at the sound of the pop.

"You learn to use what you have on long cattle drives," he winked.

"Come, let me help you wash," she said, helping him out of his jacket, boots, pants, and shirt. It still stunned her to see the marks and scars that he had not only acquired from his "Catholic education," as he liked to joke, but from all the battles he had fought in Africa and California.

"Wait a moment," she said after leading him to the wash bowl on the dresser. She grabbed her nightgown with both hands and pulled it off over her head. He gasped at the sight of her standing naked in the candlelight. The curve of her hips framed the tiny dark patch of hair between her thighs. Her small teacup breasts seemed almost too delicate to touch. She smiled at his reaction. "What? I don't want to get my nightgown wet."

"Perfectly reasonable," he told her with a smirk, then his expression grew serious. "It's just that…this reminds me of our first night together. How beautiful I thought you were. How I couldn't believe I was with you."

"Oh, you're sweet!" she said as she soaked the rag, wrung it, and began to wash him.

"Except it's different now," he nodded with new conviction.

"How so?" she raised an eyebrow. She wasn't sure she wanted to know.

"With everything we've been through…with what we've shared…you are somehow more beautiful to me now than I remembered from back then." She felt her heart flutter and the threat of tears. "And the fool that I was that night could never have comprehended the love I that feel for you today."

"Oh, shut up before you make me cry!" she gasped, throwing herself into his arms and devouring him with kisses. He backed her into the bed and laid her down gently. She wrapped her legs around him greedily, squeezing and drawing him into her with impatient anticipation. She could feel his firmness sliding against the wetness that cooled once outside of her in the evening air like morning dew on the grass. She groaned as he buried his face in her breasts, running her hands through his thick black hair as he kissed them. She reached down and guided him into the slippery warmth inside her, gasping at his heat that now filled her.

The lovemaking was frantic and desperate as if they expected to be torn apart at any moment by the world outside. At last, they lay panting in each other's arms, their sweat intermingling between their bodies. After a moment she broke the silence, "I must have a glass of wine!"

"Ha, me too!" he chuckled.

They sat at the little desk in their nightshirts, enjoying the savory chicken the soft, moist bread, and the dry red wine, which balanced out the saltiness of the meal. The flavors were somehow richer and more satisfying after lovemaking. Claudette told him about the trip to the nursery, leaving out the part about Pierre, of course.

Diego laughed at the story of how Carlito's tears only ended once he was distracted by a pretty little girl. "Ha! Just like me! I was the same way!" She laughed too, but couldn't help but wonder how many pretty little girls had distracted Diego before he had come into her life.

They finished their meal with dark chocolate and the last of the wine. The room had become cooler as the night progressed, so they blew out the candle and got under the covers. They whispered and giggled like children, secretly staying up past their bedtime. They finally fell asleep, snuggled next to each other for warmth.

At some point, in the middle of the night, they both became aware of the other's wakefulness. They reached for each other in the darkness, then began to kiss, which turned into making love once more. Except this time, the passion from before was replaced with a bittersweetness. As if they knew they were stealing back this moment from fate. As if it were a moment they were not supposed to have.

Sometime after, Diego could tell that she had drifted off again from the soft sound of her breathing. It seemed to him that he never slept again, although he recalled walking through a small grove of trees as a light drizzle fell on him and the leaves. He couldn't remember why he was there or what he was doing, only that he was content.

He was awake now, staring into the darkness. It was time. He slowly peeled himself away from her, put on his uniform, and hung his sword at his side. He was careful not to wake her. He took one last look at her dark form, cuddled up in the bed by herself, before stepping into the hall and closing the door behind him.

The pre-dawn chill was invigorating as he walked across the grounds. The boys on sentry duty stiffened as he passed. He chuckled to himself. Clearly, they wanted to prove they weren't sleeping. Ironically, though he thought, he was the one with something to hide.

He passed through the small gate and took the path that wound down along the wall into the valley below.

"There's a man out there," a wide-eyed cadet guarding the base of the path told him, "just around the corner," he pointed with his finger. "Said he was waiting for you. I didn't know what to do."

"You did fine, Vincent," Diego smiled, putting his hand on the boy's shoulder. "Do not disturb us, no matter what you hear. Keep everyone away. If that man comes back alone, you are to let him pass. Do you understand me?"

The boy looked at him for a moment. Diego could see the comprehension of what was really happening settle in his eyes. "*Sí, señor*," the boy nodded.

"Good man," Diego squeezed his shoulder.

It occurred to him that he might want to draw his weapon and have his guard up before rounding the corner. But Pierre wasn't that kind of man. Diego shook his head. It seemed strange that he was almost happy to see his old friend and adversary this morning. He was surprised to find him sitting on a folding chair next to a small table near the wall. His horse was tied to a tree nearby.

"Ah, there you are!" Pierre said in English as he stood to greet him. "Come, sit and have some coffee, it's a little too early for mezcal." Diego lifted an eyebrow, surprised to have Pierre address him in English. "Come," Pierre prodded, "I intend to run you through with my sword, not poison you." Diego allowed a half smile as he took a seat at the small field table. Pierre poured him a cup from the kettle he had brought. "It may not be hot anymore, but warm enough, I hope. There's food too," he said, gesturing to the fresh warm bread, cheese, and honey.

"Thank you," Diego said with apprehension. The coffee was warm. It was mixed with scalded milk that eased his throat as it went down and settled his stomach. Pierre looked at him slyly. "What is it?" Diego asked, taking a piece of bread and drizzling it with honey.

"You never let on that you spoke English, you sneaky boy!"

"You shouldn't have assumed I didn't."

"Ah, good point," Pierre said, easing back into his chair. He took a sip of his coffee. "I was wrong about a lot of things. Pity…we could have done great things together." He paused for a moment, then gave Diego a side-eyed glance, "I would have found you a girl of your own, you know."

"I love her," Diego said plainly.

Pierre turned to him fully, eying him for a moment, "I suppose you do. The problem is: so do I and now one of us must die for it. Love is such a dangerous thing."

"I suppose it's too late to say I'm sorry," Diego said, staring off to the dark patch of trees that lay in the valley between them and the American camp. Grey light was beginning to seep into the darkness.

Pierre scoffed humorously, "…and send her back to me? Sure, I'll start re-inviting all my wedding guests now."

"That is not what I meant."

"Of course not, and there lies the problem. We can't undo what's been done, and I can't live with the result. I must kill you and claim your widow for my own…or die by your sword. Either way, I'll have my satisfaction, or my torment will be over."

Diego sat up as he let out a breath. "Shall we get on with it then? I have duties to attend."

"Duties that'll be sorely left undone," Pierre said with dark humor, lifting himself from his chair, and standing to his full height. Diego remarked that the tall Norman was an impressive man with sharp eyes and long legs and arms, which gave him a reach advantage in a duel.

They removed their jackets, slung them over their chairs, and proceeded to stretch in their shirtsleeves and waistcoats. Diego squatted a few times, bouncing slightly before extending his leg and grabbing the toe of his boot. He flipped his bangs to the side to catch a glance of his opponent who was now still and watching him intently.

Pierre had already removed his scabbard and leaned it against his chair. He stood tall, holding his sword loosely before him. Diego shrugged and stood upright. He pulled his sword out with a metallic zing, then unfastened the belt and set it with the scabbard on his chair. He faced Pierre, gave a nod, then sank into his stance. Pierre lifted his sword and sank into his.

Diego raised an eyebrow as he looked at his opponent's sword. Pierre caught the intrigued expression and laughed lightly, "Yes, yes, it's the very one you gave back to me on the dock at Marseilles. I thought it would be fitting to give it back to you now for good."

"Poetic for sure," Diego said, then stepped forward. They tapped the tips of their swords and began to move back and forth, testing each other's defenses and measuring the distances.

"Ha!" Pierre called out, circling his blade under his opponent's, then flicked it upward to open a space through which he quickly drove his point toward Diego's heart. Diego folded over, barely evading the point as he hopped to the side. He tamped Pierre's blade down with his own, then drove his point forward in a full lunge. Pierre cringed as he leaned back. Diego's blade barely touched his shoulder before Pierre was able to dash it to the side with his own blade.

Diego continued the attack, circling his blade back around and driving it home. Pierre parried it downward as they crashed into each other. Pierre shoved him back with his free arm, their swords too close to maneuver. Diego landed back on his back leg and crouched back into his stance like a cat. A mischievous grin spread across his face.

"You're enjoying this too much," Pierre scoffed humorously.

"It's like being back in school."

Pierre shrugged as he settled in his stance. "We did have some fun together…" he said nostalgically, then shouted suddenly with rage, using the brief friendly moment to launch a surprise attack.

Diego shuffled back quickly, parrying the frantic thrusts, then drove forward with his own. Pierre sprung forward, dropping his rear knee to the ground as he ducked his body under his opponent's blade, then brought his point up towards Diego's heart. The two froze in their positions.

"Damn you…" Pierre whispered. His own blade had stopped just at the surface of the cloth that covered Diego's heart. Diego's blade poked lightly into the bare skin of Pierre's neck. Both of their elbows were bent as they had pulled back at the last moment before impact.

BOOM! …KAPUSHHHHH!

They cringed, covering their heads with their arms as the wall above them exploded into a shower of broken rock and dust.

BOOM! …KAPUSHHHHH!

"*Merde!*" Pierre shouted as another part of the wall exploded into a ball of dust and flying shards. They look at each other in shock and horror. "The Americans…they're attacking!"

Diego looked at him wide-eyed, then recovered his senses. "Ride back to the city. The president must know!"

"*Oui!*" Pierre said. Several rounds smacked into the wall, causing both of them to cringe and duck again.

"I must get back to the castle… to my boys!" Diego said, standing up. Pierre could only manage a nod as more shells slammed into the wall. He turned to his horse and soon was galloping up the hill toward the causeway that would carry him to the city.

Chapter Thirty-Seven: The Feast of the Gods

The Americans pounded away all morning at Chapultepec, chipping away the wall and punching holes in the castle roof. President Santa Anna arrived near noon to see for himself after receiving numerous reports about an impending assault on the hilltop palace. He was greeted almost immediately by a shell that exploded nearby and showered him and his horse with dirt. He steadied his terrified mount, then brushed the dirt away from his uniform with mild annoyance as he scanned the grounds. Teams of engineers were running to and fro, making repairs where they could. Stretcher-bearers shuttled wounded men to the hospital set up in the grand corridor of the castle. Along the wall, gun crews returned fire. He watched as a shell came screaming in and struck one of the cannons, sending the crew members flying asunder.

He found General Nicolás Bravo sitting at a small field table in the middle of the parade ground. He was eating eggs and sopping up the runny yolks with tortilla as shells and solid shot struck the ground nearby. Santa Anna smirked at the sight. He nudged his horse forward. "Isn't this a dangerous place to have breakfast, General?"

Bravo, a few years older, a hero of the War of Independence, and a man who had been president several times himself looked up as he wiped his mouth with a napkin. He shrugged. "I'm just as likely to get killed anywhere else. I might as well make a good show for the boys."

"Hmph," Santa Anna considered for a moment and then agreed internally with a shrug of his own. "Perhaps your boys would have made a better show had you sent more down into the valley to threaten the American batteries."

"I barely have enough to defend the walls. I need reinforcements before the assault begins."

"This is nothing more than a feint," Santa Anna said dismissively. "I have every reason to believe the real attack will be at San Antonio Gate south of the city."

"If you say so," Bravo said, raising his eyebrows with comical incredulity.

Santa Anna grimaced at the older man's lack of faith in his president's military acumen. "If an attack should happen here, I'll send more troops at the critical moment. Until then, General, I suggest you send some guns and men into the valley to keep them off our walls if you're so worried." With that, he spurred his horse and rode off, leaving the general behind to his breakfast among the falling bombs.

Diego stood at the parapets watching the American batteries fire below. As a fighting man, it was frustrating to endure the bombardment with nothing to do other than check on his students, who were working the cannons or pulling sentry duty. He had entertained visiting his wife in the hospital. But unlike him, she was busy tending the wounded. He would just be in the way. Which would only worsen his sense of worthlessness.

He turned at the sound of feet marching and the creaking of cannon wheels behind him. Troops were marching by with two teams of horses pulling cannons. They were headed to the small gate that would take them down the path into the valley below. He spotted one of the soldiers wearing a cadet uniform and snatched him by the arm. "Where do you think you're going, Cadet de la Barrera?"

The young man looked startled at first. Then his expression turned to indignant annoyance. "I'm to command one of the guns, Sub-Lieutenant."

"The hell you are," Diego told him. "You're staying here, safe behind the walls."

The young man glared at him for a moment, then slowly softened his expression into a smile. "I received my commission, Diego." Diego flinched at the young man, who he had only seen as a boy before, now calling him by his first name with familiarity. De la Barrera continued, "I appreciate your concern, But you have to understand we're almost the same age. I've been student-teaching here for a year now. You know that. It's time."

Diego blinked at him for a moment, then let go of his arm. "Be careful, Juan."

"If my duty permits," De la Barrera smiled warmly, then turned to rejoin his battery.

It was time. Bernardo had seen it. He had given up fighting years ago when his best friend died in his arms. He was supposed to die with him, but fate had stolen that honor away from him. Instead, he was made to swear that he'd watch over his friend's son as if he were his own. For this, Bernardo put away his war club and dagger to live a peaceful life.

That son married Bernardo's daughter, and together they had given him a grandson that he watched become a man before his very eyes. That grandson was now the pinnacle of his pride.

But for Benardo, giving up the war club for a peaceful life had come with a cost. He was condemned to *Mictlan*, the underworld reserved for men who die of old age. It was far from the rising sun where warriors who died in battle or were ritually sacrificed, feasted and fought in glory alongside the war god *Huitzilopochtli* forever. Their blood fed and satisfied the gods who, in turn, allowed the world to continue. This warriors' paradise was where his best friend was now, a place from where Bernardo had been excluded.

But true friends never abandon each other, even across the divide that separates the living from the dead.

Bernardo's invitation came with the sunrise just after the bombardment had begun. The creature walked out of the light, only a shadow at first. Bernardo had to shield his eyes from the sun to see the fox approaching him. In its mouth was a dead snake which it dropped at the old man's feet and then scurried away. Bernardo picked up the serpent and immediately felt its power pushing away the pain in his knees and back, causing him to stand taller.

He spent the rest of the day with the snake draped around his neck as he gathered feathers and began making the ancient weapons.

Now he sat in the early morning darkness of the next day, breathing in the smoke from the smoldering herbs set before him. He hummed the ancient war song, mouthing the Nahuatl words as he slit open the snake and began to paint his face with blood.

The explosion woke Claudette with a jolt. A second one came, and soon she could hear the moans and whimpers of the injured men around her. She sat up and blinked her eyes in the darkness, trying to remember where she was. She saw the dim grey outlines of windows above. Some of the windows were broken. Orderlies came in now and started lighting lamps revealing the hundreds of wounded men around her. Now she remembered.

She had worked all day in the make-shift hospital set in the grand corridor of the castle as the American bombs shook the ground. People screamed and flinched as shells smacked into the walls or crashed into the roof. She had lost track of time until, at some point, the bombs had stopped and the windows darkened. She worked by lamplight into the evening until at some point, she must have laid down in exhaustion and fallen into a deep sleep.

Now the bombing had begun anew, marking the beginning of a new day. She hoisted herself off the floor and made her way to the privy. She wondered if Carlito could hear the bombs from the safety of the nursery in the city. Was he scared, confused, and wondering where she was? The thought was heartbreaking, though she was happy she had gotten him away in time.

Her thoughts turned to Diego. She wondered if she'd see him among the wounded or worse. She shuddered at the thought, then became angry. He had not gotten away in time, nor would he ever try. She knew he'd be the last to protect himself in the face of the enemy. "Obstinate man..." she mumbled in French, then splashed her face with water. She looked at herself in the mirror by the dim light spilling into the room. The dark circles around her eyes and her wild hair made her look like a witch, she thought. "Pfft..." she scoffed at these silly thoughts. She tied her hair back and then filled an ewer full of water.

She walked back out into the grand corridor. Already men were crying out from thirst. She dipped her ladle into the ewer and began to work.

Diego stood at the parapets watching the sun rise over the American camp as the bombardment continued. He could see the tiny soldiers forming up and then marching into position. Clearly, they were planning an assault.

Then movement on one of the nearby hilltops caught his eye. The Americans had been building a long scaffold there. Now a procession of donkey carts arrived, which the soldiers arranged underneath the scaffold. Twenty-nine prisoners in their *San Patricio* uniforms climbed onto them, two for each cart. Their hands were tied behind their backs as soldiers strung the nooses around their necks. No hoods were offered. Instead, the men stood on the carts facing the castle so they could witness the battle.

"They must be awfully confident there's going to be a show today," Sergeant Gonzales said, pointing at the spectacle. Diego turned to see the big old man had joined him on the parapet. He turned back to watch the condemned men. There was one noose left unoccupied. The breeze caused it to bump softly against the condemned man standing next to it.

The soldiers stacked a few crates under the empty noose. Then they brought a man out on a stretcher. "¡Por los Santos....!" Diego gasped as they lifted the man from the stretcher and propped him up on the crates. It was clear that he had recently lost both legs.

"You got to hand it to the Gringos," Gonzales laughed, "they sure are mean sons-of-bitches!"

Diego shook his head at the sight in silence. That's when he noticed it: silence. "They stopped firing..." he said, turning to his sergeant. Gonzales furrowed his brow as he pondered the meaning. His eyes widened at the distant sound of bugles.

"Look! They're advancing!" he pointed as the sound of snare drums added to the martial music. Diego turned to look but instinctively ducked at the sound of the renewed cannonade. Grapeshot and canister rattled against the wall, killing some of the unsuspecting spectators nearby. He and Gonzales crawled back up and peered over the parapets at the scene below.

The Americans were raking the castle walls with anti-personnel rounds and blasting shells into the swampy cypress woods below that lay between them and the forward Mexican batteries. Then their troops began spilling into the woods as Mexican skirmishers came running out the back toward the safety of their earthworks. A cloud of smoke came billowing out of the trees behind them.

Diego watched as De la Barrera's battery fired shell after shell into the Yankee-infested woods. A round of canister punched a hole into the first wave of Americans to emerge. "Get out of there..." Diego grimaced as he watched the young man and his crew work their gun.

De la Barrera's gun got off one more round, knocking down several enemy soldiers as they swarmed in. Diego watched the young man pull his sword and stand to face them as the rest of his crew fled. Within seconds, he was overwhelmed, never to be seen alive again.

Cadet Vincent Suárez shuddered as he watched the Americans overrun the forward defenses from his sentry post at the foot of the trail that led up the hill to the castle. "Quickly!" he shouted, beckoning with his hand as the fleeing Mexican soldiers shuffled past him. A surge of enemy soldiers was behind them, closing the distance.

"Halt!" he yelled uselessly at the charging masses. He brought his musket up and fired into the hoard, then dropped it down to reload without even looking to see if the first shot had hit anyone. He snapped on his bayonet for good measure, then brought it to his shoulder. They were upon him now. He shot one. The man's angry face exploded into a mist of blood. Suárez then lowered the weapon and shoved the bayonet into another man's stomach.

Someone punched him in the face. Then there was searing pain as multiple blades punched through him. Another man kicked him in the stomach, doubling him over. He fell to the ground, wheezing for breath as he watched hundreds of black shoes and blue pants run past him until everything went black.

"They're climbing the walls!" a soldier turned and shrieked just as a musket ball struck him in the head. He dropped to the ground like a pile of rags.

"Fall back!" an officer shouted. They had been firing down from the parapets at the American advance, but the enemy had closed the distance and now the Mexican cannons were unable to tilt down far enough to hit them. The American cannoneers and sharpshooters, however, made peering over the wall instantly deadly. A shudder of horror ran through the defenders as the tops of over fifty ladders appeared on the wall.

"They're coming! Someone should ride to President Santa Anna!" Diego heard an aide plead with General Bravo. "We need reinforcements!"

Bravo shook his head sadly, "He's already sent what he was willing to spare. Anymore would never get here in time."

"Fall in line and load your weapons!" sergeants yelled, getting every man and cadet into position to give the Americans a volley as they came over the wall. Diego looked down the line and grimaced at the sight of cadets among the ranks. The first of the round peaked caps began to appear over the tops of the parapets.

"Hold your fire!" the sergeants were shouting. Diego could see the musket barrels shaking along the line as men tried to steel themselves at the sight of the enemy. He spotted the new cadet Juan Escutia nearby, shuddering, barely able to hold his musket still. He should not be here.

Now the Americans were pouring over the top and reaching down to help the next man up. General Bravo swung his sword down in a grand sweeping motion. "Fire!" came the command. The Mexican line exploded with jets of flames and smoke. The screams and shouts of the Americans broke through the smokey haze as several of them fell back over the wall to their deaths.

"Reload! Fix bayonets!" came the command. Diego dropped his carbine and started ramming home another round. Then, out of the corner of his eye, he saw a reed-thin javelin fly past him, cutting through the smoke and impaling itself into one of the enemy soldiers rising over the parapet. The man looked in horror and surprise at the spear which had punched through him. He clutched at it as he fell back, screaming, onto the men climbing the ladder below him.

Then came the eagle.

"*Abuelito...*" Diego gasped at the sight. Bernardo dashed past him, launching another javelin from his *atlatl*, a paddle-like weapon used to throw javelins like a sling. He wore a loincloth, a headdress made of eagle feathers, and a snake skin wrapped around his neck. Feathers adorned his arms and legs. There was something ghostly different about him in the flash that Diego saw him go by. He seemed younger and strong. His muscles twitched as he dropped his atlatl and took up his war club with both hands. It was a brutal weapon with jagged pieces of razor-sharp obsidian embedded into its sides.

The faces of the Americans coming over the wall blanched in terror as this strange creature leaped into the air with its war club drawn completely back over its head. For an instant that seemed like an eternity, the creature soared through the air as if taking flight, only to fall upon the mob of soldiers cowering at the top of the ladders and in various stages of coming over the wall.

Bernardo buried the obsidian-laden club into one of the men's head, squashing it like a melon. He then drew his dagger from behind his back and began stabbing men as they all plummeted together to the depths below.

"*Abuelito…*" Diego gasped again, this time sucking in a sob.

"Present arms!" came the order. Diego wiped away the tear and raised his carbine. "Fire!" The Mexicans unleashed a devastating volley, but still, the enemy came. They were now pouring in on all sides. Diego could see the castle was lost. Men were beginning to throw down their arms and run. Juan Escutia looked to him with fear in his eyes, pleading to be told what to do.

"Go get the flag!" Diego told him, pointing to the tower behind them from which it flew. "We must not let them capture it!" Relief flashed across the boy's face before he ran off. He would not be part of the melee that was about to ensue.

"Fall back!" someone called

There were few left to heed the order. Many had begun to run already. The Americans were now over the wall in numbers and enraged by the bloody cost they spent taking it. They attacked with musket fire, bayonets, and swords as the Mexicans retreated, fighting their way backward. Diego dropped his carbine and was now fighting off bayonet thrust with his sword.

"The flag! Get him!" he heard someone yell in English. The men he was fighting looked away, now distracted by the new spectacle. Juan Escutia had emerged from the tower with the flag in his hands. He was now cut off from the rest of the Mexican defenders.

"Get him!" someone shouted. Suddenly the mob of soldiers shifted away toward their new goal, every man wanting to be the one who captured the flag. Juan's eyes went wide with terror. He turned and ran toward the northeast corner of the castle grounds. The Americans gave chase.

"No!" Diego shouted. He lurched into the crowd, pushing, punching, stabbing, and slashing his way to the front. Now the arms of several men were restraining him, holding his arms, legs, and head as he fought. He dropped his sword as he struggled against them. Juan climbed up on the parapet and looked down at the two-hundred-foot drop below. He looked back at the crowd of angry men reaching for him. He saw Diego struggling to get to him, then looked back over the precipice. As arms reached out to grab him.

"Everyone, just fucking stop!" came another voice in English.

The crowd grew calm as two American lieutenants shouldered their way through. They were both dark-haired and dark-eyed men. Diego could feel the men holding him loosen their grip. "It's alright, son," one of the lieutenants said, holding out his gloved hand to the boy. "Nobody is going to hurt you. Please, come down." Juan's mouth trembled as he looked at the man with tear-blurred eyes.

"*Esta bien, Juan. Baja,*" Diego said, trying to smile to assure the boy that everything was going to be fine. Juan looked at him for a moment. He shook his head as his face crinkled up again into a mask of tears. He turned and stepped off the ledge, taking the flag with him.

"No!" Diego shouted, lurching forward, breaking the grip of the men who held him. He could hear the sickening thud as he reached the parapet and looked down. Juan's body lay broken on the rocks below. The flag fluttered with the breeze beneath him like broken wings.

A deathly silence fell over the men. At last, a hand fell on Diego's shoulder. He turned to see the dark eyes of one of the American lieutenants looking at him with sorrow. "Here," the man said, pressing the handle of Diego's sword to him. "Take your sword and go. The fighting's done here."

Diego looked at the man and then to the other lieutenant, who nodded at him in return. He took his sword and sheathed it. The American soldiers moved to the side, creating a path for him through the crowd as he walked away.

Twenty-nine men stood and shifted uncomfortably on the scaffold on top of Mixcoac Hill. The thirtieth man sat legless, propped up on a stack of crates as he feverishly slipped in and out of consciousness. Their necks, wrists, and ankles were sore from the ropes that had held them in place for hours as the battle played out before them. A collective groan came from their dry and chapped lips as the Mexican flag began to lower on the distant tower.

"Be of good cheer, lads!" one of them called out. "We'll soon be dining with Saint Patrick himself."

"They bloody well better have decent beer up there," another called out, causing a chuckle among the condemned men.

The American colonel in charge of the execution scoffed and shook his head. "Everything's gotta be a fucking joke with these damned micks," he mumbled.

"Three cheers for the Mexican flag boys!" another called.

"Huzzah! Huzzah! Huzzah!" the men answered.

Silence prevailed once again as the condemned men, their American executioners, and Mexican muleteers waited for the American flag to rise. "The daft bastards forgot to bring their damn flag, it seems," one of the condemned said, causing howls of laughter again.

Colonel Harney shifted uncomfortably in his saddle. He had already whacked one of them in the mouth with the flat of his saber for being cheeky. How much more of this did he have to endure? What the hell was the holdup? He grinned when at last, the stars and stripes began to rise. He pulled out his saber and held it high. The snare drums began to roll.

"Well, lads," one of the condemned men said, "it's been an honor to fight with ye.'"

"Aye!"

"And ye' too," they called out to each other.

"God save Ireland!" one shouted in defiance and the rest cheered.

Colonel Harney dropped his sword with a swoosh. The mule drivers cracked their whips, causing the animals to move forward. The men struggled to stay on the carts for as long as they could, but were soon swinging and struggling for breath. The crates fell away from the legless man who did little more than just swing back and forth like a sandbag suspended from a theater rope.

The American soldiers watched as the condemned men flailed and gasped for air. Some even lost control of the bladders and bowels, until all of them were still, idly bumping into each other as their ropes slowly came to rest.

At last, a sergeant approached the colonel with a salute. "Sir, execution complete! Shall I cut them down?"

Harney looked at the swinging corpses with a disgusted sneer. "No," he said, returning his eyes to the sergeant. "I was ordered to hang thirty men. I have no orders to unhang them." With that, he gave them one more look, spat on the ground, and rode away.

Chapter Thirty-Eight: The Gates of Belén

Claudette wasn't quite sure when the bombardment had stopped. She had spent most of the morning trying to ignore the earthshaking explosions and the falling plaster as solid shot and shells smashed into the castle. She did her best to appear calm for the sake of the patients as many of the others flinched and screamed in terror with each explosion. Instead, she held a smile and assured them that everything was alright, even as she held the hands of mutilated men and watched over them as they died.

There was no end to the work. Wounds needed to be cleaned, bandages changed, patients fed, and given water. Those who had passed away needed to be removed to make room for those who could be saved. At some point, she realized that the bombs had stopped. *Thank God! Perhaps they'll allow us a chance to get caught up before they start killing us again*, she thought bitterly.

There seemed to be fewer volunteers now, doctors and nurses too. Where they were going, she wasn't sure. Many of the familiar faces she had seen and smiled at in a moment of shared exasperation were simply gone, leaving her and just a few others to attend to the overwhelming number of wounded men.

All wasn't quiet now. The explosions were gone. She stopped in the middle of the room and stood silent. "Huh!" she gasped at the sound. There was screaming and musket volleys outside, not far at all. She looked around the grand corridor and realized she was the only one left standing in a sea of wounded and dying men lying on the floor.

She screeched in terror at the sound of the door. She whipped around to find Diego barreling into the room. His face was white as if he had seen some unspeakable horror. "We must go now!" he said breathlessly. His eyes were wide with frayed apprehension.

"The patients...I...can't leave..."

He snatched her hand. "There's no time! They won't hurt them," he told her, dragging her through the corridor.

Diego turned his face from her, hoping she couldn't see the doubt he felt about the Americans not hurting the injured after he had witnessed them put a noose around a legless man.

They joined the rest of the soldiers, staff, and volunteers fleeing the castle along the Belén causeway. She kept looking back, expecting to see a wave of American soldiers crashing upon them from behind. She imagined that at any moment a shower of musket balls and cannonballs would scythe them down like late summer wheat. She could see the Americans swarming the castle like ants on a fallen piece of food. Their flag was already flying from the tower.

The mile-and-a-half trip to the city wall went quickly. There, a chaotic scene awaited them. Panicked civilians begged and shoved their way into the city. Officers and sergeants frantically placed men into position, sometimes shoving them into the trenches.

General Andrés Terrés strode out to the approaching mob of refugees from the castle. "Where are the rest of you?!" he said, the stress creaking in his voice. The soldiers from the castle looked among themselves. One of them shrugged, "Dead or captured, General."

"My God! Where's General Bravo?!" his eyes were now bulging with fright.

Once again, the soldiers looked among themselves for the answer. "Um...not with us!" Sergeant Gonzales said at last.

Terrés blinked at the big man, trying to process the turn of events.

"They're coming! They're coming!" someone shouted.

All eyes turned down the causeway. Through the shimmering hot air rising from the road they could make out the blurry image of blue-clad soldiers marching from the castle. In this brief moment of silence, they could hear the distant rattle of snare drums.

"Good God, do they ever stop?!" Claudette gasped at the sight.

The sound of horse hooves came from behind.

"The president is here!" someone shouted.

General Terrés let out a sigh in relief. He turned and trotted toward President Santa Anna and his entourage who were dismounting and approaching the defenses set out in front of the gate. Claudette spotted Pierre among them. Gone was the easy confidence that he usually wore with accustomed casualness. He looked pale and frightened. *Things must be going poorly*, she thought as his eyes met hers. She quickly looked away, embarrassed that he caught her gaze.

President Santa Anna's face was a mask of fury as he hobbled on his false leg toward his general. "Your Serene Highness," Terrés addressed him with panic in his voice, "I don't have enough men to hold the gate. We need to withdraw or be reinforced…"

Santa Anna interrupted him with a slap across the face with his riding crop. Everyone around cringed at the sound. "You fucking coward! You call yourself a general?!" Terrés could do no more than look at the ground and hold his quickly swelling face. "You're a disgrace and traitor!" Santa Anna screamed as he tore Terrés's epaulets from his shoulders. "Get out of my sight before I have you shot!"

"And you!" he said, looking up at the crowd of soldiers who had just arrived. "You're all still alive while the American devils occupy our castle?!" Diego felt the president's eyes bore right into him. "How dare you call yourselves men?!"

Santa Anna now turned and shared his glare with every man around him. "Listen here! If you call yourselves men…Mexicans… patriots…you will hold this point at the expense of your lives. Our army will live to fight another day, but the sake of our nation demands your sacrifice now. You will hold the enemy here to the last man so that the rest of the army can escape. Do you understand?!"

"Yes, sir." a few said.

"Do you understand?!" Santa Anna shouted.

"Yes, sir!" the men shouted back.

"Good, make your country proud," he said, then turned and hobbled back to his horse.

Pierre remained. He stood, blinking blankly at Claudette and Diego. Diego spoke at last, "Take her with you. Watch over her."

"Of course," Pierre mumbled, then turned his eyes to Claudette, "Come…"

"Take this. Protect yourself," Diego told her, handing her his pistol.

Claudette turned her eyes from Pierre to Diego as she took hold of the weapon. It felt heavy in her hand.

"Wait a minute…" she stammered, then found courage. "No, Diego. You're coming with us. All of this is pointless. Don't be a fool."

Diego smiled softly, shaking his head, "The sons of other men died today because I told them to. I told them to do things I would not ask of my own son. I told them they had to die for their flag... their country. Who am I now to turn away from my duty while their fathers bury them?"

"Diego, no...please," her face began to contort with tears and sorrow. Diego smiled softly, tears of compassion welling in his eyes.

"You know, my love, this was always meant to be," he said. "You had seen it."

"I'll die with you!" she shouted, wrapping her arms around him and sobbing. Diego held her close, stroking her hair as she shuddered, then finally broke away, holding her by her arms. He looked deep into her eyes with a smile filled with soft compassion.

"No, my love," he shook his head. "You must not die here with me today. You must live for our son. You know it to be true."

She looked up at him. Her vision blurred with tears, "Oh, Diego...I will never love another!"

"Don't be so dramatic, Little Claudia," he said with a smile. She let out a laugh, then broke into shuddering sobs as he held her tight once more.

"Come," Pierre said lightly in French as he put his hand on her shoulder, trying to peel her away, "we must go while we can."

Diego pulled back to look at her face one last time. He smiled and kissed her forehead. "Go. Maybe you'll find me with your crystal ball."

"...I'll search for you until the day I die," she said.

Pierre pulled her away. "Come, we must go now," he said, now in English as well, as he pulled her away.

"I love you," she said, reaching her hand out to him. Diego reached out to touch her retreating fingers, just missing them by a few inches as Pierre dragged her away.

"I know," he said softly. She could hear the metallic zing of his sword coming out of its sheath as she stumbled away, dragged along by Pierre as they hurried through the gates with the fleeing crowd.

"Here, Caballeros, we make our stand!" she could hear Diego roar to his men in Spanish, the language now crystal clear to her. "Here, we will bleed out the last drop of our blood for the pride of our country and the defense of our families! Here, we will make them pay a bitter price for victory!" She could hear the men cheer uproariously to these words.

"Why do you have to be so damn dramatic..?" she sobbed, clutching her free hand to her heart as they moved farther away.

Diego felt the big hand on his shoulder. He turned to Sergeant Gonzales who was beaming at him with bitter pride. "I want to thank you," the big man told him.

"What for?"

Gonzales sighed, then looked down the road at the approaching Americans before returning his eyes to Diego. "It was my destiny to die fighting alongside the *Fox*. All these years, I thought I had been denied that honor, but you came back for me. I never should have doubted you. You have always been my friend."

Diego smiled at him and squeezed his arm, "Then let us die well together, my friend."

Chapter Thirty-Nine: "So Far from God"

Claudette stumbled along as Pierre dragged her through the crowd. She kept looking back at the gate as the last of the refugees made it through and the big wooden doors were shut and latched. Another sob broke from her at the sense of finality of the closing gate. The sound of musket and cannon fire was starting anew. She flinched at an explosion that threw dirt and debris up over the wall.

"Fuck! Where is my horse?!" Pierre yelled in French. She turned back to him as he frantically looked around the crowd for his mount. "Someone stole my fucking horse!" he shouted. She blinked at him, overwhelmed with grief, fear, and confusion. "Come on!" he said, tugging her arm. "They couldn't have gone far. We need to find my fucking horse."

"Wait!" Claudette dug her heels into the ground. He turned to her with impatient annoyance. "I have to get my child."

"There's no time," Pierre grimaced, trying to control his rage. "We have to get far away from here, or we'll be captured or dead."

She shook her head in confused horror, "Pierre...he's my child..."

"Let's make one thing clear," he said, stepping closer and sticking a finger from his free hand in her face while clutching her wrist tightly with the other. "I'm willing to take care of you," he hissed, "even give you a second chance after the humiliation and ruin you've cost me. But I will not raise another man's half-breed bastard. Do you understand me?!"

"You're a monster..." she gasped.

"A monster who's going to save your life. Now let's go!" He tugged her arm and began to turn.

"Let go of me!" she shouted, trying to pull her arm free.

"Claudette, I am a gentleman," he gritted through his teeth, yanking her to him, "but by God, if you make me, I will slap some sense in you if you don't come now,"

"I will fucking shoot you!" she screamed, pulling out her pistol and cocking it. People were beginning to slow down and stop to watch the drama play out before them. Pierre's eyebrows went high with surprise. Now aware that there was an audience, he let go and raised his hands with a smile.

"Alright, let's not get crazy now…" he said in Spanish for the sake of the people around them.

She immediately took the opportunity to turn and dart into the crowd.

"Damn it!" he shouted as she disappeared into the thick of them. He looked back toward where he thought the horse thief might have gone, deeper into the city. The battle outside the gates was growing louder. "Damn it…"

There were very few people left on the cobbled street where the nursery was. Those she did see scurrying past were going the other way, trying to find sanctuary deeper in the city. She could hear the battle raging outside of the wall.

The door to the nursery was locked. "No!" she gasped, then started pounding on the door with the butt of her pistol. "Let me in! My son's in there!" she shouted in Spanish. She took a step back, took the gun in both hands, recocked it, and pointed it at the lock. She was bracing herself to pull the trigger when the door cracked open. She recognized the eyes of the woman she had met there before, peering out in terror at her.

"Oh, thank God!" Claudette gasped, shoving the door open and brushing the woman aside. She could hear multiple children crying in the parlor as she strode down the hall.

"I'm here all alone," the woman said, following her. Her voice was trembling with fright. "All the others are gone…You're the only parent who's come by…"

Claudette burst into the room. The children flinched and began to cry with more intensity at the sight of the raging wild woman with a gun in her hand. Carlito sat on the floor with his back to her. He turned to look with his big green eyes, wide with fear and crusted with dried tears. "*Oh, mon bébé!*" she gasped. She uncocked the pistol, tucked it into her skirt, and swept him off the ground into her arms.

"What should I do?!" the woman asked as Claudette made for the door.

Claudette looked at her for a moment. Guilt and pity rushed through her as she pondered what to do or say. "Stay with the children. The Americans will not hurt you."

"Alright," the woman said, looking to be on the verge of tears. Claudette couldn't bear to look at her anymore. She stormed out, leaving the woman to her burden.

Guilt and shame burned through her as she hurried down the empty street. *Should I have stayed? Helped her? Defended the children?* She squeezed Carlito, thankful to have him in her arms.

"Hey, lady!" The words shouted in English filled her with dread, stopping her in her tracks. She looked up to see an enemy soldier on horseback with a saber in his hand.

"Mon, Dieu!" she gasped, then turned to run.

"Hey! Stop!" the man shouted. She could hear the hooves clopping on the cobblestones behind her. She pivoted quickly down an alley. Still, she could feel the horseman bearing down on her. She turned another corner. The streets were completely empty as all the people had fled into the center of the city.

She found a door that had been hastily left open. The horseman came bursting out of the alley. She darted inside, quickly latching the door behind her. She heard the hooves clatter to a stop just outside the door as she ran upstairs. There was pounding on the door now, as the man was ramming it with his shoulder. "Open up!" he shouted.

She screeched as she heard him break open the door. She dashed into one of the rooms and locked the door behind her. She could hear his heavy boots charging up the stairs. She fell to the ground, shuddering as she clung to her child. The man charged down the hall and now was working the knob, trying to open the locked door.

She pushed Carlito to the side and pulled out her gun as the man started throwing his shoulder into the door. She pulled back the hammer as the door burst open and the man came stumbling in.

BAM!

The sound was deafening. She could barely hear the muted sound of the man falling to the floor in the cloud of smoke. Carlito was crying. She tossed the gun to the side and snatched him up, shushing him as they rocked. The man sat up and leaned against the wall. He looked down at the blood which was now flowing freely from his chest. He looked back at her in disappointment, "Gee, ma'am, I wasn't going to hurt you none…"

Claudette glared at him, waiting for him to move, to do something, whatever he was going to do. The man just looked at her. After a while, she realized he was dead. The tears came now. She held her baby and cried until she could cry no more. They had to get out of there.

She pried the sword from the man's hand and checked his pockets. There was American money, a watch, and a folded letter. She took it all and left the man sitting there with his disappointed look frozen on his face for eternity.

Out in the street, she could hear that the battle had abated. Now there was only the occasional musket crack. *The Americans must be in the city now*, she decided. She wove her way through the empty streets. Carlito rested on her hip as she held him with one arm. She carried the saber with the other. Relief washed over her as she came upon a river of people, flowing down the street, looking for safety. She joined them, holding her child tight as she moved with the crowd.

"Claudette!" she heard the voice call her name. She quickly looked down in panic. "Claudette!" Pierre called again. She chanced a look. He was on a horse, scanning the crowd, calling her name in all directions. She looked down again, hiding her face and her child as she walked past.

She could still hear him calling for her as she allowed the flow of refugees to sweep her far away until his voice was lost in the distance.

A letter finally came, but not from France. Instead, it was from a place somewhere deep inside the United States, even though it had a French name. *"Detroit..."* Claudette said, looking at the envelope as she walked away from the postmaster.

She had been writing home for months, hoping her parents had enough forgiveness in their hearts to help her and her child.

Life had been hard but bearable since the fall of Mexico City. She and Carlito had been living in refugee camps set up by the Americans for widows, orphans, and other destitute people displaced by the war. It was strange that the people she had once feared were now supporting her and her child. They were also a source of information about the outcome of the war, but no help in finding the remains of her husband.

"Lady, we don't even know where half of our own troops are buried, let alone the Mexicans," was the answer she got from her endless inquiries.

She and Carlito had been moved around several times. They were settled now in the port town of Veracruz on the Gulf of Mexico, close to the American supply chain that fed them. But the Americans were planning to withdraw altogether, and she had to find a home for Carlito and herself. She had been checking daily to see if there were any replies to the countless letters she sent home. She was on the verge of writing Diego's father in Los Angles when the letter from Detroit came.

March 3, 1848

Claudette,

I am your father's cousin. Your family has asked me to arrange passage for you and the child to come here to Michigan. Enclosed is a letter of credit to pay for your passage. You are to come directly to Detroit. Do not return to France. You are not welcome there. We will discuss your future when you arrive. Write to inform me of your progress and when I should expect you.

Zacharie Moreau.

She read the letter over and over during the course of their travels, trying to discern the meaning of the few words it offered and its tone.

She also read the letter she had taken from the American soldier on that ugly day in Mexico City. It was a letter he had written to his wife, Sarah, but had yet to send it. "David Smith…" she said softly, reading his signature.

In the letter, he wrote about how much he adored the Mexican children he encountered in Pueblo and his compassion for their widowed mothers. He wrote about wanting to help them, just as he hoped someone would look out for her and their children if he should fall in battle.

The letter broke her heart, rendering her to tears every time she read it, yet she insisted on torturing herself with it time and time again. She wanted to write to Sarah herself, to explain what happened and her regret. Claudette had been denied the knowledge of her husband's death. Didn't this woman, this mother, deserve to know the fate of hers?

After crumpling up and tossing away dozens of attempts, she succumbed to her cowardice and posted the man's letter anonymously without her addendum once her steamer arrived in New Orleans. She hoped that would be the end of the man's disappointed face haunting her dreams. But she knew it would never be.

It was a long journey of riverboats, coaches, and trains to get to Detroit. It took weeks. She found that the Americans were not the bloodthirsty barbarians she had imagined. The women were very kind and compassionate toward the young widow and her toddler. The men were gallant and gentlemanly, although she had to emphasize many times that she was still mourning her husband to ward off their romantic advances.

The rain drizzled down the window as the Kalamazoo-Detroit liner pulled into the station with a billow of steam. Carlito was asleep on her lap, clinging to his wooden horse as he drooled. She could feel her heart beat faster as she got up and collected her bag with the sword strapped to it, wrapped in a blanket. The gnawing nervousness crept back into her stomach at thought of meeting this distant relative who had been so terse in his correspondence. She wondered if he'd even be there at the platform and what she would do if he wasn't.

Carlito began to stir as she stepped off the train. It didn't take long to find the man. He was standing among the crowd watching her intently with cold eyes.

"You are Monsieur Moreau?" she asked.

"Mr. Moreau," he corrected her. "Where are the rest of your bags?"

"This is it," she told him, indicating with her head the bag she had slung over her shoulder.

"I see," he said, taking it from her. "Follow me."

"*¿Dónde estamos, Mamá?*" Carlito muttered, still sleepy from his nap.

"*Nous sommes presque à la maison, mon amour,*" she whispered back to him.

Mr. Moreau stopped and turned to her, "I suggest if he's going to be an American, he should speak English."

"Of course, sir," she said. "Carlito speaks it just as well, and French too."

"English is all he needs. And he should have a proper English name, like Carl."

"Of course."

"An English surname too, so people won't know he's a Mexican bastard."

Claudette swallowed the rage rising from her gut. She wanted to tell him that her son was no bastard, but their survival depended on the kindness of this man.

"He can be Carl Moreau, then," she said.

"You have forfeited the right to that name," Mr. Moreau said as he opened the carriage door for her. "You'll have to come up with something else."

She thought about the letter written by the man she had killed and how he said he wanted to help the children and their widowed mothers. "Smith," she said with conviction, "he'll be Carl Smith."

"That'll do," Mr. Moreau said, settling into the seat across from her. She heard the slap of the reins and then the carriage began to roll. "Your parents have paid for us to watch over you. There's no place for you at our estate in the country, but you'll be comfortable in the townhouse we keep here in the city. You and the child will have everything you need: food, money, and a servant. We'll even pay for the child's education. However, there are some conditions."

Claudette sat quietly, waiting for him to continue.

"You may never return to France. You are never welcome at our home. You will raise the boy as an American. He should know nothing of his father. Any violation of these terms and you'll be cut off. Do you understand me?"

"Yes."

"If you should marry, you'll become the ward of your husband, but I doubt any respectable man will want to take on a Mexican bastard."

"Diego and I were married before God," she said at last, not able to contain her anger anymore.

Mr. Moreau smiled slowly, "You don't say…?"

The rain fell steadily outside their new home, dampening the sounds of the city. Claudette sat silently in the gloom, listening to it fall. She could hear the tiny wheels of Carl's pull horse rolling on the wood floor upstairs. The walls were bare. *I should hang some pictures*, she thought. She had already mounted the saber she had taken from the dead soldier above the mantel: a dark reminder of what it took to get here. "David Smith," she said the man's name again, seeing his dying eyes once more in her memory. She wondered if his wife was crying for his loss somewhere at this very moment.

She shook the thought from her head. "Why do I torture myself so?" she said softly. She turned her eyes away from the weapon and looked back at the bare walls. She decided she'd put something happy there, something to make her feel better about herself.

"Diego…" she said softly.

She had no picture of him, no painting, nothing but her memory of his pretty boyish face. It was already fading. She sat up straight, closed her eyes, and concentrated, trying to conjure his face. She resolved to do this every day so she'd never forget. But it was fading. She was losing him all over again.

The nausea and dread seeped back into her, causing her to collapse her head into her hands and weep again. She could hear his soft footsteps. She felt his little hand touching her knee.

"Don't cry, Mama," his little voice said meekly.

She pulled her head from her hands and looked into Carl's big green eyes. They were full of heartbreaking sympathy. His thick black locks curled inward and lightly touched his chubby olive cheeks. Here was her picture of Diego, alive in this little boy.

"Oh, my sweet child!" she gasped, wrapping him in her arms and squeezing him tight, "Don't ever leave me."

The End

Carl and Claudette's story continues in: Rampage on the River: The Battle of Island No. 10 which is the first book of the 2nd Michigan Cavalry Chronicles trilogy set in the American Civil War.

...And coming soon: The Prussian Prince (Which is the current working title), the exciting continuation of this story, and the 2nd Michigan Cavalry Chronicles trilogy.

Historical Note

If you did not already know, Alexandre Dumas is one of my favorite authors of all time. I have modeled myself after him. If you've read my novel *The Perils of Perryville* you might recall Claudette mentioning him to her son toward the end. I wanted to make sure I paid that line off in this book. Dumas would have been forty-two in 1844. He was on the eve of releasing *The Three Musketeers* and writing *The Count of Monte Cristo*. He was also in the process of buying an estate outside of Paris and building a large luxurious home, which would be known as le Château de Monte-Cristo.

If you detected *Run DMC* in his dialog, you are correct. They are one of my favorite bands. I thought the little homage would be a fun inside joke for my fellow Gen X-ers. And yes, those are the lyrics to "Thank You" by Dido that Claudette says to Diego after they spend the day together on the Moroccan beach.

Dumas was the grandson of an enslaved African woman in Haiti and her French nobleman lover. Dumas's father came to France as a young man and attended a military academy. General Thomas-Alexandre Dumas was the highest-ranking officer of sub-Saharan African descent in Europe ever at his time. He commanded Napoleon's cavalry during the Egyptian campaign.

Alexandre Dumas was known to be quite a talker and a ladies' man, even during his marriage to Ida Ferrier. One playwright said he was:

"...the most generous, large-hearted being in the world. He also was the most delightfully amusing and egotistical creature on the face of the earth. His tongue was like a windmill, once set in motion, you never knew when he would stop, especially if the theme was himself."

Even though my depiction of Dumas traveling to *le Château d'If* for research is fictional, he did make several trips there in his life before and after he wrote *The Count of Monte Cristo*. Dumas went again years after publishing it. Just like in this novel, he had to hire a boat. A second boat captain paid the first captain for the right to take him. When Dumas tried to pay for his fare the man said:

"No, Monsieur Dumas, you don't pay. You're our breadwinner with your Monte Cristo novel. We really should give you a pension for all the fares you provide for us from those who want to go to le Chateau d'If!"

Le Chateau d'If ceased to be a prison by the end of the nineteenth century. It has been a tourist attraction ever since. For a small fee, you can take a ferry there and walk the grounds. They sell copies of Dumas's The Count of Monte Cristo in several languages at the gift shop. Maybe someday they'll sell this book there too. I can only dream.

If you guessed that Pierre and Diego drank absinthe before the serenade scene, you are correct. It's made from wormwood and is known to be hallucinogenic, especially if you drink a lot of it. It's been banned in several countries although several of those bans have been lifted since. I had quite a bit of it when I lived in Torres Vedras, Portugal. My description of its effects is from my own experience.

Some of you opera fans may have recognized that Pierre was singing the aria *"Quanto è bella, quanto è cara"* from Gaetano Donizetti's comedic opera *L'elisir d'amore* or The Elixir of Love which premiered in 1832. It soon became one of the most performed operas of its time. At last check, it ranks thirteenth on Operabase's list of the most performed operas today. It's a nice song and a good sample for those unfamiliar with opera. I recommend searching YouTube for a rendition of it if you're curious. Here is the translation of the lyrics:

Quanto è bella, quanto è cara!
Più la vedo, e più mi piace...
ma in quel cor non son capace
lieve affetto ad inspirar.
Essa legge, studia, impara...
non vi ha cosa ad essa ignota...
Io son sempre un idiota,
io non so che sospirar.
Chi la mente mi rischiara?
Chi m'insegna a farmi amar?

Translation:
How beautiful she is, how dear she is
The more I see her, the more I like her
But in that heart, I'm not capable
Little dearness to inspire
That one reads, studies, learns
I don't see that she ignores anything
I'm always an idiot
I don't know but to sigh
Who will clear my mind?
Who will teach me to make myself beloved?

Was *L'elisir d'amore* performed in Marseille in the spring of 1844 as I depicted? I don't know. I haven't found any evidence that it wasn't, so I went with it. Please forgive me if you find evidence that says otherwise.

The Pastry War, also called the First Franco-Mexican War or the First French Intervention in Mexico, was literally fought over pastries, or at least partially. A French bakery was looted among several French businesses during one of the many riots and upheavals that occurred in Mexico in 1832. The French government demanded reparations. So did the British. Both nations sent a fleet to blockade Mexican ports in 1838. The British brokered a peace deal, but the French attacked. It was at the Battle of Veracruz that Santa Anna lost his leg. Eventually, the Mexican government agreed to pay the reparations and promised to protect French citizens in Mexico. Ultimately, they did neither, which led to the French invasion of 1861. It's for the Mexican defense of Puebla during this Second Franco-Mexican War that we celebrate *Cinco de Mayo*.

Yes, that bone-handled pig hair brush is an early toothbrush that had been around for millennia. Ironically, the modern form of three rows of bristles was invented in England in 1844, the same year of the scene in which Pierre is preparing himself for his visitor from the gendarme. The animal hair bristles were eventually replaced with nylon starting in 1938. By the way, the first electric toothbrush also came out in 1938.

Judas Ben Duran was a real person. He was fluent in multiple languages and acted as a translator for Abd al-Qādir. He was also a go-between for the Algerian resistance leader and the French. I'm not sure if he would have been with Al-Qādir during his time in Morocco, but I've found no evidence that he wasn't.

Abd al-Qādir was a fascinating man. You'll find his name also spelled Abdelkader and various other translations of the Arabic script into Roman letters. I am happy to have discovered him in my research and to be able to share a little of him with you.

He was raised to be a cleric, but the French invasion of his homeland required him to become a warrior, and a warrior he was. Regardless of his prowess on the battlefield, he was known for his great compassion and sense of honor, especially with French prisoners, even while the French were conducting a scorched-earth, total war campaign on the Algerian resistance. He became a folk hero among the French public and foreign observers as they recoiled at French atrocities committed during the war.

He surrendered in 1847 under the promise that he could live in exile. The French reneged on that promise and threw him in prison. He was finally freed after much public protest and petitioning from French military veterans who had once been his prisoners.

He settled in Damascus. In 1860, an anti-Christian riot broke out in which over 3,000 Christians were slaughtered in the street. Abd al-Qādir mounted forty of his warriors and went out to gather as many as he could. He brought them to his home and protected them from the mob. One of the Christians he saved wrote:

"We were in consternation, all of us quite convinced that our last hour had arrived... In that expectation of death, in those indescribable moments of anguish, heaven, however, sent us a savior! Abd el-Kader appeared, surrounded by his Algerians, around forty of them. He was on horseback and without arms: his handsome figure calm and imposing made a strange contrast with the noise and disorder that reigned everywhere." - Le Siècle newspaper, 2 August 1869

For that incredible show of bravery, heroism, and humanity, Abd al-Qādir received accolades from nations around the world: including the *Medal of the Legion of Honor* from France, his one-time enemy. American President Abe Lincoln sent him an engraved pair of pistols, which are on display in a museum in Algeria today. The Kansas town of Elkader is named in his honor.

The raid on the French supply train I described in Chapter Twenty is completely my invention. There is little recorded about the emir's clandestine movements and guerrilla tactics during his time in Morocco. Although many sources say he carried out plenty of such raids during this time. Was he outside of Tangiers during the French bombardment? I don't know. But he was hoping for the Moroccan Sultan's support, so there's a good chance that he would have been there with his small force, waiting to help fend off a French landing while the Sultan's main forces were in the east and about to fight the Battle of Isley. We know that Ab al-Qādir was not at that battle.

The Massacre of El Ouffia, which Judas Ben Duran describes in Chapter Twenty-One, happened in 1832. By the way, if you detected a Star Wars reference there, good job! It was totally intended. I got the title of Chapter Twenty-One from the 1984 Charles Bronson film, *The Evil That Men Do*, which is based on a 1978 novel by the same name. It's a good film. I highly recommend it.

I wanted to use the more contemporary *Dahra Cave Massacre* as an example of French atrocities, but that wouldn't happen until a year after this point in my narrative. Basically, French troops chased a tribe of about five to seven hundred people into a cave, then set fires at the entrance to smoke them out. When the fires were done, the French found that everyone inside had died from asphyxiation; the men, women, children, and the elderly. The French commander who had ordered the fires, Achille de Saint-Arnaud, once wrote:

"I shall leave not a single tree standing in their orchards, not a head on the shoulders of these wretched Arabs... I shall burn everything, kill everyone."

I point these things out, not to pick on the French, but to illustrate that no nation or people are truly innocent or are always in the right, including my own.

The Terror that Claudette refers to is, of course, the infamous darkest days of the French Revolution when thousands of people were sent to the guillotine, often for dubious and trumped-up charges.

Don Carlos María Isidro Benito de Borbón, for whom baby Carlito is named in this book, was a claimant to the Spanish throne during the mid-nineteenth century. The Spanish throne was occupied by Isabella II at that time. This spurred a series of armed conflicts called the Carlist Wars that persisted all the way into the 1870s. The truth is, I had to come up with a reason for Carl's name after he starred in my first three books as the main character. I thought this would be a great historical reference. It also fits Diego's character as being somewhat of a staunch Catholic reactionary.

It's believed by most historians that Santa Anna was paid a large bribe by the Polk administration to return to Mexico and broker a peace deal that would favor the Americans. Santa Anna would later say:

"The United States was deceived in believing that I would be capable of betraying my mother country. Before such a thing could happen, I would rather be burnt on a pyre and that my ashes were spread in such a way that not one atom was left."

I used part of that quote in the speech I had him give at Veracruz. It's believed that he used the money Polk had given him to raise an army. It's well-known that many of the Mexican troops carried surplus British muskets that had been used in the Napoleonic Wars. I merely connected the dots in my narrative as to how they could have gotten there.

Of course, Diego, Claudette, Carlito, and Pierre are fictional characters and were not on the British ship that brought Santa Anna back to Mexico. There is no evidence that the ship was smuggling guns either. However, I thought it would be a clever way to do so since the US and British had recently been close to war over the Oregon Territory. Forcing a British ship to submit to an American inspection would certainly have been provocative.

Cérbulo Varela, General José María Florés, General Andrés Pico, Naval Captain William Mervine, and Marine Brevet Captain Archibald H. Gillespie were all real people. So was the old lady who had the cannon buried in her yard, Clara Cota de Reyes. They all played their parts in the Conquest of California much as I described.

Gillespie commanded the garrison at Los Angeles. He and his marines confiscated weapons, imposed strict curfews, and even banned meetings of two or more people. They arrested anyone who dared to complain. This finally provoked local militia captain Cérbulo Verela to lead an uprising.

The only description I have of Cérbulo was that he was "a wild and unmanageable young fellow, though not a bad man at heart." I like the idea of him being a one-time bully to Diego as a kid, but becoming a friend as an adult. I knew guys like that.

As the uprising grew, they elected professional soldier Captain José María Florés to be their acting general. He then became the acting governor of California and led the fight against the American invasion. He retired to the Mexican state of Sonora after the fall of California. He died in 1866. He was only forty-eight years old.

The American bungling of the Battle of San Pascual was due to miscommunication and perhaps too much zeal. Typically, in a mid-nineteenth-century cavalry charge, you would start at a trot and then go into a full gallop for the last forty paces. This is to keep a tight formation to reserve your horses' energy and to ensure you are at peak speed when you crash into the enemy.

US General Stephen Watts Kearny ordered his dragoons to trot. Captain Abraham R. Johnston misheard this and ordered his advance guard into a full gallop when they were still three-quarters of a mile away. It's reported that Kearny said, "Oh, heavens! I did not mean that!" as Johnston and his men dashed away from the main column. The battle of San Pascual was the biggest and bloodiest for the Americans in the Californian theater.

Brevet Marine Captain Archibald H. Gillespie survived his horrific wounds, including a punctured lung and a broken tooth. He fought again at the Battle of Rio San Gabriel, just a month later. He rose to the rank of Major before retiring from the Marine Corps in 1854. He died in 1873 in San Francisco at the age of sixty.

The Battle of Río San Gabriel was fought on January 8, 1847. It was the thirty-second anniversary of the Battle of New Orleans. This was why the Americans were shouting "New Orleans" as a battle cry.

John Riley was a real man. His origins and death are shrouded in mystery, but all accounts have him as being tall and muscular with blue eyes and brown hair. I went with the consensus that he was born in Ireland, where he joined the British Army. He deserted in Canada and fled to Michigan. There he enlisted in the American Army and was shipped to Mexico, where he deserted and joined the Mexican Army. There he rose to the rank of major. Because Riley deserted before the declaration of war, he was spared the hangman's noose. Instead, he was flogged and branded as a deserter. The Mexican government gained his release and the other surviving *Patricios* in the peace negotiations. Riley returned to service in the Mexican army. He left the army in 1850 for medical reasons and died shortly after. The cause of his death remains unknown. Riley and his fellow *Patricios* are considered heroes in Mexico and Ireland today.

The instrument I described in Chapter Thirty-Two is called uilleann pipes. They are an Irish form of bagpipes. They are quieter and have a sweeter sound than the Scottish Highland pipes you hear at military events and funerals. Uilleann pipes are still played today in traditional Irish music along with tin whistles, fiddles, banjos, and other instruments. The traditional Irish hand drum is called a *bodhrán*. It's typically an animal skin stretched over a round wooden frame. The player holds it by the wooded cross support inside the drum with one hand and strikes the skin with a wooden beater with the other. You can find examples of both these instruments on YouTube. If you're lucky, there might even be an Irish bar in your town that hosts Irish folk music sessions. I highly recommend checking it out.

The punishment of the *San Patricios* was meted out on three separate days at three different locations. Fourteen were whipped and branded, and sixteen were hanged on September 10, 1847, at the village of San Ángel, which lies six miles from the castle walls of Chapultepec. This is the event I describe Claudette witnessing in my narrative. She probably would not have been able to see this, even from those heights. The Americans did hang thirty more in plain view of the castle walls during the Battle of Chapultepec to ensure that both armies could see it. They wanted the condemned men to witness the American flag rise over the castle before their deaths. I combined these events so that Claudette would witness this before the battle.

The legless man was Francis O'Conner. He was gravely wounded at the Battle of Churubusco and had to have both legs removed. Even though the surgeon said he would soon die on his own, Colonel William Selby Harney insisted that he be hanged with the rest of them, stating: "Bring the damned son of a bitch out! My order was to hang thirty and by God, I'll do it!"

A truce was called after the Battle of Churubusco. The Americans were to be allowed to enter the city to buy supplies, but a mob turned them away the first time they tried. A riot broke out when they came back the next day. It was put down by mounted Mexican lancers. Lieutenant Ulysses S. Grant was a quartermaster for the 4th US Infantry at the time. He mentions the riot in his memoirs, although he doesn't specifically say he was there when it happened. But he didn't say he wasn't either. He was a quartermaster, so there's a chance he was. I saw this as a great opportunity to connect this event to a scene I have with him in *The Perils of Perryville*. I won't spoil that scene here if you haven't read it yet, but I hope you do.

The Americans attacked e*l Molino del Rey* at dawn on September 8, 1847. The battle lasted two hours. The powder magazine stored in one of the buildings exploded just before noon, killing and injuring several American soldiers. This probably happened well after the Mexicans had withdrawn. I suggested that the explosion happened as the Mexicans were withdrawing in my narrative, which was possibly not the case.

Juan Escutia did arrive at the academy the same day as the Battle of Molino del Rey. Much about him is a mystery. His admission papers were lost during the battle, but it's believed he came from the city of Tepic in the state of Nayarit. He was one of the fifty or so boys who insisted on staying to defend the castle after most of them had been sent to the city for their safety. It's believed that he leaped to his death with the flag to keep it out of enemy hands.

Escutia is estimated to have been somewhere between fifteen and nineteen. He and five other boys are known as *Los Niños Héroes* for sacrificing their lives at the Battle of Chapultepec. Among them were Juan de la Barrera and Vicente Suárez, both of whom are depicted in this book. There was also Fernando Montes de Oca; Francisco Márquez, whose body was found near Escutia's; and Agustín Melgar. Melgar found himself separated from the others on the north side of the castle. It is said he shot and killed at least one attacker before being mortally wounded. After which, he hid behind a mattress and bled to death.

They are national heroes. You can visit several monuments dedicated to them in Mexico City. US President Harry Truman did so in 1947. He laid a wreath at their cenotaph and held a moment of silence. When asked why, he said, "Brave men don't belong to any one country. I respect bravery wherever I see it."

I agree, Mr. President.

US Marines participated in the storming of Chapultepec Castle. The red stripe on their dress trousers commemorates the men who died there. The line, "From the Halls of Montezuma," in the "Marines' Hymn" is a reference to that battle.

Montezuma, or Moctezuma II, was the last great ruler of the Aztec Empire. The Spanish built Chapultepec Castle more than two centuries after his death. However, the hill was considered a holy place by the Aztecs. It was once the site of a temple where they practiced human sacrifice to appease their gods. Catholic missionaries replaced the temple with a chapel in 1554. Construction of Chapultepec Castle on the same site started in the 1780s and finished in 1864. You can visit it today. It is a UNESCO World Heritage Site. The word Chapultepec means "hill of the grasshopper" in *Nahuatl*, the language of the Aztecs.

President Santa Anna slapped General Terrés with his riding crop and tore off his epaulets after the general had abandoned his post at the gates of Belén and allowed the Americans to get a foothold in the city. Santa Anna attempted to win back the gates but was ultimately repelled. He escaped with his army that night. He fought again at the Siege of Pueblo and the Battle of Huamantla but could not overcome the American invaders. Santa Anna went back into exile, this time to Jamaica. He returned to the presidency one more time from 1853 to 1855. During that time, he sold territory to the US that is now part of Arizona and New Mexico. This created the border that lies between the US and Mexico today.

Santa Anna would go into exile one more time before finally returning and dying in Mexico City in 1876 at the age of eighty-two. He was buried with full military honors.

The title of Chapter Thirty-Nine is from a quote attributed to Mexican President and, for all intents and purposes, dictator Porfirio Díaz. He ruled Mexico from 1884 to 1911. Díaz lamented American meddling in Mexican affairs by allegedly saying, "Poor Mexico, so far from God, so close to the US…"

I should point out that *So Far From God* is also the title of John S. D. Eisenhower's non-fiction book about the Mexican-American War, which I relied on heavily in writing this novel. I highly recommend it if you are interested in learning more.

I hope you've enjoyed our time together as much as I have. Maybe I was even able to tell you about some real people and events that you didn't know. If you liked this and want more, I pick up baby Carlito's, or Carl's, story in my *2nd Michigan Cavalry Chronicles* trilogy, which takes place in the American Civil War. Claudette is in it too! The first book is called *Rampage on the River: The Battle for Island No. 10*.

Have you read those already? No worries, I'm planning on writing a sequel to the trilogy next. It'll pick up Carl's story after the Battle of Nashville and take him on a grand adventure in Europe as empires clash and set a path that will eventually lead to WWI! It's going to be a lot of fun!

I plan to write novels like these until I die, which I hope is a long time from now. So stay with me! I've got more to come! Like or follow me on social media. I'm on all the big ones.

Sources

Merry, Robert W. (2010) *A Country of Vast Designs: James K. Polk, the Mexican War and the Conquest of the American Continent*. New York, NY: Simon & Schuster

Eisenhower, John S. D. (1989) *So far from God: the U.S. war with Mexico, 1846-1848*. New York, NY: Random House

Fowler, Will (2007) *Santa Anna of Mexico*. Lincoln, NE: University of Nebraska Press

Twain, Mark (1869) *The Innocents Abroad*. Hartford, CT: American Publishing Company

Howe, Daniel Walker (2009) *What Hath God Wrought: The Transformation of America, 1815-1848*. New York, NY: Oxford University Publishing

Kiser, John W. (2008) *Commander of the Faithful: The Life and Times of Emir Abd el-Kader* (1808-1883). Rhinebeck, NY: Monkfish Book Publishing Company

Churchill, Charles Henry (1867) *The Life of Abdel Kader, Ex-sultan of the Arabs of Algeria; Written from His Own Dictation, and Comp. from Other Authentic Sources*. Harvard University, MA: Chapman and Hall

Santa Anna, Antonio Lopez de (1967, written 1874) *The Eagle: The Autobiography of Santa Anna*, Austin, TX: The Pemberton Press

Walker, Dale L. (1999) *Bear Flag Rising*. New York, NY: Forge

Neufeld Santel, Gabriele M. (1991) *Marines in the Mexican War*. Washington, D.C. History and Museums Division Headquarters, U.S. Marine Corps

Miller, Robert Ryan (1989) *Shamrock and Sword: The Saint Patrick's Battalion in the U.S.-Mexican War*. Norman, OK: University of Oklahoma Press

Grant, Ulysses S. (1885) *Personal Memoirs of U. S. Grant*. New York, NY: Charles L. Webster & Company

Smith, Justin H. (1919) *The War With Mexico, Volume II* (of 2). New York, NY: The Macmillan Company

Podcasts
Revolutions Podcast, by Mike Duncan
Age of Victoria Podcast, by Chris Fernandez-Packham
The Civil War Podcast, by Rich and Tracy Youngdahl
History of California Podcast, by Jordan Mattox
History That Doesn't Suck, by Professor Greg Jackson

Inspirations
The Richard Sharpe Series, by Bernard Cornwell
The Curse of Capistrano, by Johnston McCulley,
Gone for Soldiers, by Jeff Shaara
The Conte de Monte Cristo, by Alexandre Dumas
Treasure Island, by Robert Louis Stevenson
Don Quixote, by Miguel de Cervantes
Captain Alatriste, by Arturo Perez-Reverte
Country of the Bad Wolfes, James Carlos Blake
Modeste Mignon, Honoré de Balzac
Crónica de una muerte anunciada, Gabriel García Márquez
"*One Man's Hero*," A film by Lance Hool

Sound Track
"Viente Años," The Buena Vista Social Club
"It's Tricky," Run DMC
"Quanto è bella, quanto è cara," from Gaetano Donizetti's *L'elisir d'amore* or *The Elixir of Love*
"Half Believing," The Black Angels
"Overture," from Gaetano Donizetti's *L'elisir d'amore* or *The Elixir of Love*

"Finale," from Gaetano Donizetti's L'elisir d'amore or The Elixir of Love

"As Time Goes By," by Herman Hupfeld, performed in Casablanca

"The Ballad of Dwight Frye," Alice Cooper

"Ten Years Gone," Led Zeppelin

"Thank You," Dido

Traditional Algerian Oud Music

"Jarabe Tapatío" or "The Mexican Hat Dance," Traditional

"No One Gets Left Behind," Five Finger Death Punch

"Knocking on Heaven's Door" by Bob Dylan, as performed by Eric Clapton

I've created a playlist of these tunes on YouTube. Send me a message through social media and I'll send you the link!

Works by Cody C. Engdahl

Novels:
The 2nd Michigan Cavalry Chronicles Trilogy
- Rampage on the River: The Battle for Island No. 10 (Book I)
- The Perils of Perryville (Book II)
- Blood for Blood at Nashville (Book III)

Mexico, My Love

Nonfiction:
The American Civil War WAS About Slavery: A Quick Handbook of Quotes to Reference When Debating Those Who Would Argue Otherwise

How to Write, Publish, and Market Your Novel

Made in the USA
Columbia, SC
27 November 2022

71900314R00217